DARK
DAWN
OVER
STEEP
HOUSE

THE GOWER ST DETECTIVE
BOOK 5

DARK DAWN OVER STEEP HOUSE

M.R.C. KASASIAN

PEGASUS CRIME
NEW YORK LONDON

Dᴀʀᴋ Dᴀᴡɴ Oᴠᴇʀ Sᴛᴇᴇᴘ Hᴏᴜꜱᴇ

Pegasus Books Ltd
148 West 37th Street, 13th Floor
New York, NY 10018

First Pegasus Books hardcover edition December 2017

ISBN: 978-1-68177-564-7

10 9 8 7 6 5 4 3 2 1

Printed in the United States of America
Distributed by W. W. Norton & Company, Inc.

FOR

Andrew who found me
Ed who rescued me
Laura who took me in
Maddy who nurtures me
And
Tiggy who provides the love.

Introduction

I WAS APPROACHED BY a man from the London County Council yesterday. They want to put a blue plaque on the front of 125 Gower Street, commemorating Sidney Grice's many years and countless triumphs here. I can only imagine how my guardian would have revelled in such glorification, especially as his detested rival Sherlock Holmes, being fictional, will never qualify for one.

I told the official that I understood such luxuries have been suspended for the duration and he agreed, but they were anxious to consult me on the wording while they still could. I asked where they were going but it was obvious from his embarrassment that I was the one not expected to be around for very much longer. I showed him the door.

I am an old woman now and, whilst I flatter myself that my memories have not faded, they are increasingly all I have got. So many people have gone – Sidney Grice, Inspector Pound and Molly – almost all my friends and those I loved.

For the best part of an hour, after the man left, I felt very sorry for myself. But a stiff gin soon bucked me up, and the fact that my doctor has strictly forbidden tobacco made the cigarette I smoked with it all the more pleasurable.

The official had made me feel redundant – I who had assisted in bringing so many wicked people to justice and single-handedly captured the awful Shadow Man of Shanklin, as the press had so fatuously dubbed her. But I would not be consigned to the scrapheap so easily. I can still put my memories to good use, as I hope will be evinced in this account.

I am coming to accept now that I cannot live long enough to recount all of my guardian's and my investigations. Some of these are quite well known already and do not need further repetition. I doubt that there are many people not familiar with every detail of *The Mountain of Fear* and thousands have seen the stage production of *The Mystery of the Breathing Horse*.

I catch my reflection in the mantle mirror. Could this slightly sozzled old lady really have been the young woman who battled with malevolence made flesh in that harrowing summer of 1884?

M.M., 19 February 1944
125 Gower Street

1

The Silver Locket

February, 1884

THERE WAS A message engraved in the locket.

To my darling Siddy with all my heart.

The glass was cracked, but I did not need to read the flowing *Connie* to know that the picture was of my mother. And – not for the first time – I wondered that I did not look like either of my parents.

'Give that back.'

I hardly heard the words but, when I looked up, I saw the curl at the corner of his mouth that I had seen in our twin reflections. 'Dear God in heaven,' I cried. 'Are you my father?'

'Where did you get that locket?'

'It fell on the steps when you were stabbed.'

'You had no right to keep it.'

'I forgot about it with everything else going on.' I clipped the locket shut. 'And you had no right to keep it from me.'

This was the closest that I had ever seen my guardian to panic. He lunged over the table, catching it with his knee and scattering our afternoon tea.

'What?' I closed my fist around the locket. 'Will you prise it from my fingers like a clue from a corpse?' I pulled back just in case. 'Why did you take me in?' I struggled to control my voice. 'By your own admission you are not a kind man.'

'You are my goddaughter.'

'You do not even believe in God and why would my mother be sending you love tokens?'

Sidney Grice sank back into his chair. He closed his eyes. 'I am not your father,' he said quietly. 'Your father was your father.'

I had never known Sidney Grice to tell a lie and I could not believe that he was doing so now. 'What are you hiding from me?' I looked at him.

My guardian's right eyelid was losing its tone and he had trouble closing it properly. His glass eye stared blindly back at me. 'No more than I am hiding from myself,' he answered carefully.

His plate lay in the ashes, broken from when he had dropped it, all those long minutes ago when I thought perhaps I knew him.

2

Death among the Dead

THERE ARE SO MANY threads in the tangled skein of events that I scarce know where to start. Some threads were spun whilst I was away but others stretch even further back to before I came to London, and the longest to before Sidney Grice became a personal detective.

And so I shall begin with what became known as *The Case of the General Surgeon*, for that is where the threads began to weave together.

In the early evening of Saturday 2 July 1881 – the same day that President James A. Garfield was shot in Washington DC – Mr David Anthony Lamb, a retired surgeon, was visiting his family plot in Brompton Cemetery. He had had the reputation of being a kind man – devoting two days a week to tending those unable to pay for medical treatment – with a sympathetic manner and great skill. He had been unable, however, to save his wife and six children during an epidemic of typhoid and, in the end, he was unable to save himself.

Two other mourners, twelve-year-old brothers at their mother's grave, some fifty yards away, heard what they took to be the sobs of a bereaved man and chose not to intrude. It was only when they heard thumping and sounds of a scuffle that they became concerned.

A man's voice was raised above the cries, repeating hoarsely

Lies, they were lies, with something unintelligible in between. There was a final crash and the sounds of running. Both boys glimpsed the back of a man's dark coat as he rushed away, becoming lost from sight between the towering monuments and behind a mock Greek temple.

Anthony Lamb had been attacked with a marble funerary vase. His face had been pulverized. And, when he managed to turn away, the blows had fractured his skull so severely that his brains exuded from his bald pate.

Inspector Quigley was asked to advise on the investigation a fortnight later, but could give no real assistance. There had been unseasonably heavy rain for several days after the murder and the first police on the scene, then hordes of sensation seekers, had trampled all around the area. To frustrate him further, the cemetery board had decreed that the site be tidied as soon as possible. Quigley had instructed that the vase be sent to his office at Marylebone but, due to a misunderstanding, it had been thoroughly cleaned before it reached him. He was also frustrated by his application to have the body exhumed being successfully opposed by John Box's sister and last remaining relative. The boys, having repeatedly embellished their story for the benefit of their friends, no longer knew exactly what they had seen or heard. And a man reported covered in blood, running away down nearby Hortensia Road, turned out to be the victim of a violent robbery.

For a while there were calls for extra watchmen in the graveyard but, as the trail grew cold, memories faded. There is never a shortage of fresh horrors to thrill the public in London.

Quigley dropped the case and promptly forgot about it.

Sidney Grice was not called upon to investigate the murder but, ever the assiduous archivist, he filed all his newspaper clippings of the case in his study at 125 Gower Street under L for *Lamb*, B for *Brompton* and cross-indexed under twelve other categories, including S for *Still to be Solved*.

6

3

The Hockaday Legacy

O N THE NIGHT of Monday 4 February 1884, whilst British officers were being slaughtered in far-away Soudan, Geraldine Hockaday was raped. Geraldine was the daughter of Sir Granville, a high-ranking official in the War Office, and the case was hushed up as much to protect his own reputation as hers. For not only was the offence itself a stain on the family reputation, but it had taken place in a notorious location, an alleyway behind the Waldringham Hotel in the East End of London, where she had gone with friends in search of adventure.

Sir Granville intended to marry his daughter off to a respectable but impoverished gentleman from Braintree, who – for a generous dowry and the prospect of a parliamentary seat – was prepared to overlook the fact that she had been despoiled. Geraldine, however, had lost nothing of her independent spirit and neither her father's threats nor her mother's pleas could persuade her to enter into the marriage or stop her from reporting the matter to the police.

The police had no difficulty in finding a suspect. Two night watchmen and a member of the public had come across and overpowered a man who was half-carrying and half-dragging Geraldine down the alley. But Granville Hockaday was more than a match for his daughter when it came to being stubborn and she had reckoned without his ruthlessness. He made it clear that if Geraldine tried to testify in court against her attacker, as her father he could have her certified as a moral delinquent and put into an asylum. The case was dropped.

And so the detained man, His Illustrious Highness, Prince Ulrich Albrecht Sigismund Schlangezahn, second cousin to the German Kaiser and one of the wealthiest landowners in Prussia, was released without charge. And Geraldine Hockaday's attacker was free to prowl the streets of London and strike again without fear of the consequences of his actions – that is, until Geraldine's brother, Peter, back from fighting Egyptian rebels at Kassassin and outraged at his younger sister's treatment, took her to share his lodgings in Gosling Lane and sought the help of London's most famous and expensive personal detective, Mr Sidney Grice.

With his help, Geraldine identified the man who had lured her down the alley, a mean and petty criminal with multiple aliases but known throughout the area of Limehouse as Johnny 'the Walrus' Wallace.

4

The Girl on the Bridge

SIDNEY GRICE WAS humming contentedly as he arranged several rows of clear glass wide-mouthed corked bottles on his desk.

'What is it today?' I asked and he crooked his left eyebrow.

'What is what?' he enquired amiably enough.

'Your experiment.'

'It is what it was yesterday and the day before,' he replied and went back to humming again, under the impression that he had satisfied my curiosity.

'Yes, but what is it?'

I wended my way over the scattered newspapers and between the piles of books, some opened face down on the oak-planked floor, many bookmarked with scraps of paper, pencils, twigs, parts of a rabbit's skeleton – whatever came to hand. A braid of black hair had been inserted into Mr Edward Wilson's *A Brief History of Doorstep Whitening in Preston*. That marker came from a victim of Frances Forrester, the Featherstone Flayer.

'I am making a comparison of the rates of dissolution of human tissues in various concentrations of Oil of Vitriol, Aqua Fortis and Acidum Salis.'

'Sulphuric, nitric and hydrochloric acids,' I translated for the benefit of Spirit, my cat, but mainly to prove to Mr G that he had not baffled me – yet.

Spirit was stretched over the back of my armchair, watching the proceedings with interest. Perhaps she thought the bottles contained snacks, but even Mr G would never think of feeding her with these specimens – nineteen of them bobbing about in various stages of corrosion, as my godfather stirred the liquids with a long, clear glass rod.

'Where on earth did you get all those?'

I had seen Mr G's extensive collections of fingers and bones and various other body parts – he was especially proud of his pickled hand of Charlotte Corday, the one with which she had stabbed Jean-Paul Marat during the French Revolution. But I had not known that he had amassed so many human ears.

'Oh, I came across a notice for them in *The Anatomist's Monthly*,' he said airily. 'They came with all the internal organs of a noble bachelor but I have given those to my mother.'

He struck a pair of eight-inch tweezers like a tuning fork against the side of a bottle, listening intently to something only he could hear.

'But why would she want them?'

'Exactly what she asked me.' He held a bottle up to the light. 'This is the nineteenth time since we met that I have reflected that you bear more similarity to my mother than your own.' He shook the bottle. 'I am often struck by how complex is the construction of our auditory organs and how negligently most people use them.'

He fished out an almost intact ear and placed it to drain on a sheet of blotting paper, where it fizzed lazily. And I gave my attention to a copy of the *Daily Telegraph* which had so far escaped Mr G's habitual ripping out of anything that interested him and shredding of the many articles that aroused his righteous anger.

There were the usual advertisements on the front page – Mr Clapper, a barrister-at-law who had not slept for sixteen months until he tried Du Barry's Food to decongest his brain;

a Great Firework Display at Crystal Palace, one shilling, to include a re-creation of the great device of the bombardment of Dover; a woman who learned to play the pianoforte in three days having never attempted such a feat previously. I cast a quick eye over a report about a delegation from the Berlin Conference visiting London to decide how to divide Africa between the European powers.

And then an article entitled *Tragedy on Westminster Bridge*:

An unhappy and sordid event which is becoming all too common in our modern age occurred on Westminster Bridge in the early hours of Sunday morning.

We are reliably informed that Father Roger Seaton, a curate at nearby St Mathew's Roman Catholic Church, was taking his habitual constitutional bicycle ride along Westminster Bridge when he spotted the figure of a woman standing precariously upon the parapet on the downstream side of the bridge.

When Fr Seaton stopped to ask if the stranger needed any assistance, she wailed, 'I am beyond any earthly help now.'

Fr Seaton dragged his Rover safety bicycle on to the pavement and hurried towards the woman. She was young, not much more than a girl, he noticed in the dawn light, and he was of the opinion that she might have been handsome had her features not shown the signs of violent acts upon her person, not least of which was a laceration on her brow. He implored the unfortunate lady to take care and not to do anything rash, but his pleas were futile.

It was too late, the stranger insisted. She gave him to believe that she had been outraged against her will and spent the night running through the streets of London in blind terror of being abused similarly again.

Fr Seaton cautiously approached the young lady, trying to reassure her that another's sins would not be heaped upon her on the Day of Judgement.

'I shall find out soon enough,' she vowed as her would-be saviour drew close to the barrier between them and, at that point, the wronged girl let out a piteous cry and plummeted from her precarious perch.

Fr Seaton expressed his hope that the young woman had slipped as she edged away, for suicide, he explained to our correspondent, is a mortal sin in the eyes of the Roman Catholic Church, condemning the offender to eternal damnation. On questioning, however, he was forced to admit he thought it more likely that she had jumped.

As the inhabitants of and visitors to our great capital city cannot help but be aware, there had been heavy unseasonable rainfall for three days before the tragedy and the River Thames was swollen. A lighterman and his mate heard a cry and saw the troubled girl enter the water near their barge but despite their efforts to rescue her with their boat hooks, the torrents swept her quickly beyond their reach and she was lost from sight and must be presumed to have succumbed to the rushing waters.

The identity of the girl remains a mystery, though Fr Seaton has given a detailed description of her to the Thames River Police. It is believed that she had long dark hair, was aged between sixteen and twenty years and wore an expensive dark blue dress but no hat.

It would appear that she was yet another victim of the violent, licentious and lewd behaviour which bedevils our society and makes the streets unsafe for any lady of good standing to travel unaccompanied without fear of violence upon her person.

We cannot help but question what the Metropolitan authorities are doing to ameliorate the situation.

'How sad,' I commented.

'Indeed,' Sidney Grice agreed. 'It makes one ponder why most people are given two ears to begin with. Oh, that.' He glanced at what I was reading. 'If you would care to use one of the eyes which fate has thus far permitted you to retain, it refers to events on the morning of the third of this month.'

'Why is it still out then?'

He placed the ear in the left-hand dish of his scales. 'There is an announcement on page five, at the top of column two, which I thought might be of interest to you.' He balanced scales with a series of weights decreasing in size until they were pentangles of foil. 'I have encircled it in a noose of my secret formula Startling Sapphire Ink.'

I leafed through the *Telegraph* until I found it. '*Hints for a Lady on keeping her coiffure fresh and hygienic*,' I read out indignantly.

'Unless of course you do not wish to do so.'

Sidney Grice hummed again as he replaced the ear in a bottle labelled *Vitriol, seven per cent solution.*

The Wages of Sin

I HAD HEARD TALK of Hagop Hanratty. He ran an empire. Its boundaries were mainly, but not exclusively, within the East End of London, from the Limehouse Basin along the Thames through the docklands to Pennyfields, where it existed in an orderly alliance with neighbouring Chinatown.

Born of an Armenian mother, Alidz née Sarafian, Hagop never knew his father, Joseph, who was killed in a brawl in Crumlin Road Prison, halfway through an eighteen-year sentence for extortion.

With his father's viciousness and mother's business acumen, Hanratty built up a string of businesses, starting with a jellied-eel stall and terrorizing other costermongers until he had a near monopoly of that highly lucrative trade, expanding into the supply of other foods and alcohol, buying and building his own premises. By the time I arrived in the city, Hanratty owned – by Sidney Grice's reckoning – a sizeable portion of the Whitechapel area. His activities were multifarious and nefarious for Hagop did not care what he was involved in so long as it was profitable.

Hanratty was no uncouth thug, however. He had a reputation for being a man of cultured tastes and great charm. His three gin palaces glittered, his music hall – The Hallows – attracted the most famous acts in England, and his theatres put on a range of plays and spectacles to rival anything produced in the more opulent West End. The Waldringham Hotel was one of

Hanratty's pet projects. Whilst its reputation was risqué, its seeming immunity from the unwanted attentions of the police and criminals alike made it an attractive proposition to those wishing to feel secure in their escapades. He began to attract the fashionable, wealthy and powerful to his entertainments, catering for a wide variety of tastes, not all of them legal.

Most importantly, Hanratty kept an iron grip on his empire. The only crimes committed were at his behest and it was his boast that a woman could walk unaccompanied down any of 'his' streets at any hour of the day or night without fear of molestation. He did not take kindly, therefore, to being proved wrong. So, when Johnny 'the Walrus' was brought to trial – contrary to Sidney Grice's advice – for complicity in the attack on Geraldine Hockaday, and released to general dismay, Hanratty let it be known that Wallace was no longer under his protection and he would not be overly concerned if his former minion were to be quietly and quickly removed.

6

The Empty House

Friday 1 August 1884

THE WINDOWS WERE boarded over and the house had obviously been empty for a long time. Dust had made heavy curtains of the cobwebs draped across the hallway and none of them had been disturbed before Sidney Grice sliced our way through with his cane.

I made to follow but he stopped with one foot on the step and his other on the threshold, and put out his arm. 'You promised to wait outside.'

A grey mouse scuttled along the gully by my feet. 'I *have* waited,' I reminded him, 'while you picked the lock.'

'I shall not allow you to risk your safety.'

'But you are risking yours,' I pointed out, 'and your life is worth much more than mine.'

It was rare that an appeal to my guardian's vanity failed and I could see that he was swayed by that argument.

'Nevertheless—' He tipped the brim of his soft felt hat.

'Besides which, you cannot mean to leave me outside here without a chaperone.' I waved my furled parasol to indicate the dilapidated filth-strewn street. It was deserted and we both knew that I had been unaccompanied in far worse places than this. Mr G clicked his tongue.

'Very well,' he decided as the mouse doubled back and

scrambled on to the roadside by my feet. 'But you will stay close by and do *exactly* as I say.'

The mouse rose on its hind legs like a puppy begging titbits.

'Probably and possibly,' I responded to the two instructions.

I found a few stale breadcrumbs in my cloak pocket – left over from feeding the pigeons – and sprinkled them on the ground. The mouse wandered away.

Sidney Grice went inside and I followed into an unfurnished, narrow, uncarpeted hallway, running alongside the wooden stairs and straight to a frosted glass-panelled door that stood a few inches ajar. The dust lay thick and gritty and there was a strong musty smell. The walls bulged with lathes breaking through the thin damp plasterwork and the ceiling sagged in the middle, bursting like a lanced boil.

'Somebody has come in the back way.' I pointed to the faint cleated marks on the floor, coming towards us before going off and away to mount the stairs.

'Those are very like our man's footprints.'

'How can you tell?' They seemed unremarkable to me.

'See how they are twisted and are blurred at the edges by a slight hobbling shuffle? He is preternaturally vain about his undersized feet and squeezes them into the tightest boots possible,' Sidney Grice murmured. 'At least he appears to be alone.'

I closed the front door and there was only a pale glimmer through the boarded windows to light our way.

'Do you have your revolver?' I asked.

He tapped his satchel. 'I shall not get it out unless I have to. A man who sees a firearm pointing at him is more likely to use his own.'

I bobbed to retie my bootlace and he paused.

'The back door is still open. I can feel the breeze.' The whole hall felt draughty to me but I had come to accept that my guardian's senses were more finely attuned than mine. 'Listen.'

We stood noiselessly. 'I can hear nothing.'

'When do you ever?' Mr G did not wait for a reply. 'There is a hansom waiting in the alley. Whoever came wants to leave in a hurry and is willing to pay for the privilege. It is not difficult to hail a cab on the main thoroughfare.'

'Shall we go up?'

He nodded. 'Keep behind me and to the side. The boards are less likely to creak.'

The treads were still quite solid.

'I am surprised they have not been torn out for firewood,' I whispered.

'The locals would not dare. They know who owns this street,' Sidney Grice responded. 'Stop chattering.'

We climbed to the top and here the footprints scattered. Their creator must have been up and down the corridor. Some went to our left and through an open doorway, the rest to a half-closed door of the next room to the right and a shut one at the end.

'The open one?' I suggested and we edged towards it.

We stopped and Mr G pointed. There was a faint shadow on the wall, the silhouette of a seated man.

'Not a good idea to take him by surprise.' Mr G cleared his throat. 'Lord,' he boomed, 'I would welcome a cup of tea.'

'So would I,' I yelled as we approached. 'Let us seek a kettle in here.'

I knew he was in there, but I still jumped when I saw the man who sat facing the doorway and pointing a pistol straight at us.

'Good afternoon, Johnny.' I struggled to keep my voice steady.

The room was bare and unlit except for a pallid slopped rectangle where a board had been torn from a grimy window. Dusk was already falling.

Johnny 'the Walrus' Wallace uncoiled to rise a full five or six inches over us, and spreading almost as much to either side. His trousers were crumpled and he had been a few days in need of a shave.

'You two.' He was breathing heavily. His eyes, watery and red-threaded, were darkly underscored and congested. 'I fought it might be someone 'ere to kill me.'

He pitched to his right, rising on to his left toe to peer past us into the passageway.

'Oh, we may one day,' my guardian assured him cheerfully, 'but by judicial means.'

Johnny Wallace cackled and dropped back on to his heels. 'Leave it awt.' He leaned against the wall, distemper powdering the shoulder of his patched, grey cloth coat and black, low, curve-brimmed hat. 'You ain't got a ragman's scratch to 'old against me.'

The Walrus was not an attractive man. His skin was lifeless and pocked. His nose was twisted and snubby. His upper teeth were so splayed that he could never pull his lips together and there were red streaks from saliva leaking into the creases that ran down from the corners of his mouth.

Sidney Grice took one step forward. 'I am very sorry, Wallace —'

'I shall consult my s'licita over this.' Johnny wagged the barrel reprovingly. 'You can't not keep 'arrassin'—'

'That you have drawn such a conclusion,' my guardian continued smoothly. And Johnny Wallace paused and scratched his armpit, but 'Eh?' was all he could manage.

'Because I intend to harass you into the dock of the Old Bailey,' Mr G explained.

Johnny the Walrus slurped. 'Look – that girl, she wasn't not nuffink to do wiv me.'

'Miss Hockaday recognized you,' I reminded him, 'when we and her brother took her back to the Waldringham Hotel.'

Johnny Wallace did not flinch. 'I gave her directions,' he argued. 'I ain't never denied that. The Barnaby—'

'The what?' I interrupted.

'*Barnaby Rudge / Judge*,' Mr G translated.

'The geezer wiv a'norchard on 'is loaf.' Johnny rummaged through his poorly scythed marmalade thatch.

'I know what a judge is,' I said irritably, and I understood that *loaf of bread* meant *head*. But I could only guess what he meant by an *orchard*.

'Said there was no case to answer,' Wallace concluded smugly. 'Don't know what all the fuss was anyway. She was pro'lly lookin' to get it when she got it.'

'You disgusting toad.' I stepped forward unthinkingly and Johnny the Walrus turned the muzzle towards me.

'No funny business.'

'I shall not hurt you,' I breathed, wishing that I could, 'yet.'

'You?' Johnny Wallace put out his chest. 'Why, you ain't big enough to 'urt a —'

'Oh, for heaven's sake,' Sidney Grice burst out. '*Ain't? Ain't?* You are worse than my maid and she is very bad indeed. If you mean *are not,* just say it, man.'

'You *are not*,' Johnny Wallace corrected himself, "ardly big enough to—'

'No, no, no,' Mr G broke in again, pacing the floor and waving his stick like an irate schoolmaster. 'Either Miss Middleton *is not* big enough or she *is hardly* big enough to hurt whatever feeble creature you—' his cane whipped down and the gun flew to Johnny Wallace's tiny feet – 'were going to mention.'

Johnny Wallace bent but Sidney Grice flicked the revolver back over the floor towards me and I cautiously scooped it up. I do not like guns. The last time I had handled one, I almost killed a constable.

'I shall give you a receipt for it later,' I promised and popped it into my handbag, having very gingerly lowered the hammer first.

'Damn,' Johnny Wallace cursed. 'Damn, that frobs. Dammit.'

'Ladies,' my guardian reproved.

'Sorry.' Johnny Wallace rubbed his wrist. 'But I still don't not understand. Eeva she aren't 'ardly big enough or she are and I don't not fink she are.'

'You explain,' my guardian told me, but I had had enough of that game.

'Perhaps later.'

Johnny Wallace sucked his teeth while he considered the situation. 'If you was goin' to arrest me the place'd be crawlin' with bluebokkles long before now,' he decided. 'So what's your game?'

'We have another witness, Mr Walrus,' I told him for I knew that he hated being called that. 'A lady of excellent repute.'

'What was she doin' round the Waldy then?' Wallace sneered.

'Trying to save women from vermin like you,' I replied. 'This lady will swear in a court of law that she saw you follow Miss Hockaday down that alley before the gaslight was smashed and our client was attacked.'

'So?' Wallace shrugged. 'You can't try a man for the same crime twice.'

'That is true,' I agreed, 'but only if you are found not guilty. Your trial never went that far.'

My godfather seemed to have lost interest in us and was rooting about the room, though there was precious little to poke around.

'There weren't no lady.' Johnny pushed the tip of his tongue between front teeth. 'What lady?'

'Me.'

'You're makin' it up.'

'I most certainly am,' I agreed. 'But whose evidence is a court more likely to believe?'

'That ain't nice.' Johnny's voice took on a wheedling tone. 'Even if I did send her down the back way, it wasn't me what did 'er.'

'Then who did?' I demanded and Wallace coughed and his face twitched with fear.

'I'll take my chances in any court any day before I'd go against 'im.'

Mr G lowered his head and considered the statement. 'Very well,' he decided. 'If you will not tell us the attacker's name, at least give me that of your companion.'

Johnny Wallace scratched his groin and growled. 'Wha' companyun?' And, for the first time, Johnny Wallace seemed genuinely puzzled.

'In that case,' Mr G said quickly, 'I suggest you step smartly aside.'

Johnny Wallace laughed throatily. 'I don't not know what you're playing at.'

Sidney Grice leaped towards him and as he did so there was a snap like a twig breaking and I looked up to see a narrow metal pipe withdrawing though a hole in the ceiling and there were footsteps and the ceiling bowed, splintering into fissures.

Johnny Wallace doffed his hat. 'Funny,' he said wonderingly.

'Stand back,' my guardian commanded me.

I obeyed automatically, my eyes fixed on Johnny as he put a hand into his hat and poked a thumb through the crown.

'What has happened?' I watched the cracks speed overhead.

Sidney Grice ripped his satchel open and brought out his ivory-handled revolver. 'He has been shot.'

'Shot?' Johnny Wallace sniggered and tossed his hat aside. It flopped comfortably into a corner.

Mr G raised the revolver in both hands high above his head, pointing to where the ceiling was rupturing near the far wall. I put my fingers in my ears but the two detonations still made my head ring. A three-foot section of plaster disappeared, showering a fog of powder and splinters of wood all over us.

Sidney Grice was miraculously unsoiled. He lowered his gun and I hurried to Johnny Wallace. Johnny was patting his chest, not to clean the debris off his waistcoat but checking himself against my guardian's claim, oblivious to the dark pool appearing on his forehead. He blinked as it trickled over his eyes and, as he bent, I saw a cavity, the shape and size of a half-penny, just above his hairline. I ripped off my scarf, intending to stem the flow, but Johnny skilfully dodged past me. The blood was pumping now, bubbling like mud over a leaking water mains, and Johnny staggered sideways in a grotesque novelty dance, tricky little steps with crossed feet, one knee bending and then the other, limbo dancing with arms thrown out, then everything buckling as he went down. I tried to catch him, but Johnny was wrenched through my fingers by the heaviness of his fall.

The back of Johnny Wallace's head smacked on the bare boards and bounced twice.

'Blimmit,' he said.

I kneeled beside him and pressed my balled-up handkerchief uselessly over the cavity, the silk instantly saturated.

'You are – to all intents and purposes – a dead man,' Sidney Grice informed him chattily, leaning on his stick to contemplate the spectacle. 'So you had better hurry if there are any last-minute confessions you wish to make.'

Johnny drifted and I thought he had gone, but he rallied and made an effort to sit up. 'That woman—'

'Which woman?' Sidney Grice demanded

The wounded man's eyes were lost already but he sagged back and managed to raise a hand to beckon me. I put my ear to his mouth. Five words. I heard them sough and then a short faint cough, and then nothing.

I stood up and wiped my face but my hands were as bloody as my cheeks.

Sidney Grice dashed to the door.

'Look out of the window,' he rapped. And from the corridor he called, 'I shall look out of the front. Shout if you see him.'

I hurried to the window, grasped at one of the planks and heaved it, but it was solidly nailed into place. The gap was just about large enough to squeeze my nose and one eye through, and I was still unpinning my bonnet to do so when I heard two sets of crashes – one from the front room, where my godfather seemed to be having more success with the boarding, and a series from behind me and then above. The ceiling bowed and there was a loud cracking as it gave and a boot broke through.

'Gah!' somebody exclaimed, wrenching at his leg, snared in a tangle of lathes.

'Quickly,' I shouted and heard footsteps approach, then Sidney Grice burst in just as the boot pulled free.

He raised his revolver and I braced myself. But another bulge near the wall showed that the intruder was already over the adjacent room. Mr G was out in the corridor and through the next door, just in time to see another series of splits disappear into the neighbouring house.

'Either he gashed his leg or I got him.' Sidney Grice pointed to a dark stain above our heads. 'I shall have the hospitals and medical practices questioned. If he seeks help, there may be an honest doctor somewhere, though I have yet to meet him.'

We went back to Johnny.

'He said the *Empress of Cathay, ten thirty*,' I told my guardian.

'I doubt it.' He put his gun away.

'I heard him.'

Sidney Grice crouched and rifled through Johnny Wallace's pockets. 'As you wish.'

'Perhaps it is the name of a horse he had backed.'

Mr G tossed a rag aside. 'His watch has been broken.'

'Or a greyhound.'

My godfather whistled quietly, content in his work. 'But not recently.'

'Can we not get into the loft?' I asked, shocked by his inaction.

'We could.' My guardian stood up, brushing the dust from his knee. 'But, first, the killer might still be up there and will have had plenty of time to reload his – assuming it is a man – device. Would you care to be the first to introduce yourself into his line of fire?'

I admitted that I would not and Sidney Grice continued calmly, 'And, since my head is of much more use than yours, neither would I.' He fluttered his eyelashes. 'Second, as even you should know, the roof spaces of these terraces interconnect.' He peered out of the window. 'He could have climbed down into any of twenty-two houses to effect his escape.' He beat the plaster from his Ulster coat. 'What a nuisance.'

'Is that all you care about – the dust on your clothing?' I cried. 'A man is dead.'

My guardian blew sharply out between closed lips.

'And the world,' he swept his hand to indicate the whole of the humanity, for which he had very little regard, 'is a safer and better place without him.'

'Why was the shot so quiet?'

'It was an air gun,' he told me.

'An air gun?' I repeated incredulously. I remembered shooting crows with one in Parbold and even a direct hit did not always kill the bird immediately.

'A point four five two judging by the size of the wound.' Sidney Grice made a ring with his thumb and first finger to demonstrate the size. 'People think of air rifles almost as toys now, but I have seen a Bavarian wild boar brought down from five hundred yards with a Windbusche.' He ambled round the corpse. 'Whoever it was had the sense not to take the hansom and risk me seeing him gaining ingress.'

We went down to the kitchen where I pumped out a gush of brown water that stank so foully that I dared not use it.

'Do you ever think of the pity,' I beat the dust off my cloak but the cloud quickly settled down on me again, 'that these men must have been babies at their mothers' breasts once?'

Mr G winced at my coarseness but only said, 'Oh, March, of

course I do…' he handed me a cloth from his satchel, 'not.' He looked about him. 'There is a cab going to waste out there. Come, goddaughter. It is quite two hours and four minutes since we consumed a cup of tea.'

*

'Man wott I brung 'ere? Dark coat and muffler. Must 'ave bin boilin' in this 'eat. Collar up, big-brimmed titfer down,' was the best description we could get from our driver.

'What sort of accent did he have?' I enquired.

'Dunno.' He tightened the right rein to turn us into the thoroughfare. 'Passed me a note sayin' *Chase Street and wait.*'

'I am only surprised he can read.' Mr G made no attempt to lower his voice as he raised an impatient hand. 'Show me.'

But the cabbie snorted. 'Took it back orf me.'

'Did you see his hand?' Sidney Grice asked.

'Levva glove.' He edged us into a steady stream of traffic. 'What's this all abart?'

We passed a hearse, the undertaker sleeping in the back, his brushed-to-a-gleam top hat rising and falling on his chest.

'Did you not find his behaviour strange?' I asked.

He double-clicked his tongue at the mare. 'Get all sorts in this job.'

'Of course,' I realized out loud. '*Orchard pig/wig.*'

'Not none so strange as you two, though.' The driver closed his hatch.

*

I could smell the blood on me when we returned to Gower Street, and I would never get used to that.

'Regarding your threat to Wallace, I would not have permitted you to perjure yourself.' Mr G rapped on the door.

'I was bluffing,' I admitted and he permitted me to witness the figure of a smile.

'It can be convenient sometimes,' Sidney Grice conceded, 'to work with a liar.'

Molly opened the door and I followed my guardian in with some satisfaction. I already knew he regarded me as untruthful, but I had never known him before to acknowledge that we worked *together*.

7

The Letter

Dear George

I almost started this letter My Darling George for that is what you are and always shall be to me.

I have been miserable since you went away. I pretend to have headaches to excuse my moodiness but it is my heart that really hurts. You cannot pretend that you do not love me and, if you did, I should not believe you. I saw the anguish in your eyes when we last parted.

So what is keeping us apart? The geographical distance between us can be breached in a matter of hours. I could be in Ely and in your embrace the very day that I hear from you.

The gulf that separates us is my money and I can do little about that at present, but I made an offer before and I am making it again. When I am twenty-five and can take control of my late father's estate, I shall assign every penny that I have inherited to you. We can live on that or, if your pride is really so delicate, you can give the money to any worthy cause of your choosing and we shall manage on your income. What use is my money to me when it keeps me from the man I love, who I know loves me in return?

I have lived too long with memories and ghosts. I want to cast them aside and live for the living.

Oh, George

I screwed up the letter and rammed it in my mouth to stifle a sob. I was not weak and I would not give way to weakness.

Dear God, George, I prayed, how can you look at the sun and know that I am under it too? How can you be so cruel? I am being crushed like this letter, shredded like the dozens more that I have written and never sent.

If I thought that death would bring us together or end my suffering, I would take it without a second thought.

And it was only that night, after I had written in my journal, that I remembered the name of a new coffee house in Montague Place and realized that, infuriatingly, Sidney Grice had probably been right yet again, and that I *had* misheard Johnny Wallace's last words.

8

The Empress Cafe

'WHAT *EXACTLY* DO you hope to achieve by all these visits?' Sidney Grice demanded.

I clipped the chain around my neck. It was my lightest cloak, yet still too heavy for the oppressive summer heat. But I might as well have run naked down Oxford Street for the way my godfather would have reacted if I had set foot outside without one.

Molly was sitting on the floor, dusting the undersurface of the hall table where her employer had been furious to discover a flake of a suspect's dandruff that had gone missing six weeks ago.

'I do not know.' I picked my bonnet off the hall table and he shook his head. 'But if you only looked for clues where you expected to find them you would never find any.'

I put the bonnet back.

My guardian tossed his head to flick back his thick black hair. 'On the contrary, eighty-four and one quarter per centum of the clues I seek are exactly where I expect them to be. It is only the remaining fifteen and three-quarters per centum that make my job interesting.'

'I aintn't not never had a clue,' Molly said wistfully. 'Everybody says so – even people. Do they taste good?'

'Not usually.' I put on my other bonnet, and my guardian treated me to a that-will-have-to-do shrug.

Ignoring Molly, he continued, 'Of course, the real challenge lies in calculating what the clues mean.' He turned his back on me and twisted the handle of his periscope stick to view me through it.

'Dontn't not you know neither?' Molly lunged at a cobweb on the gas mantle and it floated out of reach unscathed.

'Ox-brained sloven,' Mr G growled irritably.

Molly grinned. 'Ox's is very clever, aintn't they, sir?'

'They are not famous for it.' I selected a parasol from the stand and Mr G edged back uneasily.

But Molly was undeterred by my information. 'And that's where London is – aintn't it not? In Sloven England.'

Sidney Grice clipped the ferrule back over the lens of his cane. 'I am talking about the deductive process,' he snapped.

'You are not the only one who can do that.' I opened the door, disappointed to find no cooling breeze. 'For instance, I can deduce that you have recently acquired a navy-blue cravat with paler blue polkas.'

My godfather cocked his head to one side and then the other like an intelligent terrier. 'How on earth can you know that?'

'By doing what you are always trying to persuade me to do – using my senses.' He followed my gaze and saw Spirit coming down the stairs, dragging a frayed length of silk as proudly as if she had caught a rat.

'That dratted animal.'

The sun blazed and, because there was no need for domestic fires, the sky was almost blue through the factory fumes hanging in the atmosphere.

'Ladies,' I reminded him, and stepped out into the filthy acridness that Londoners call *air*.

'I shall get rid of that creature once and for all,' he threatened, shutting the door firmly, and I might have believed him if I had not occasionally caught him playing with her.

It was not far to Montague Place and I liked to walk,

watching the children racing with the hoop of a barrel in the street, listening to the vendors peddling their wares – beef sandwiches, coloured bottles, linnets in willow-wicker cages – and little Betty, from whom I purchased a sprig of lavender, at her usual patch on the corner of Torrington Place.

The Empress Cafe was quite a large establishment and almost always busy. If truth be told, I was half-convinced that my guardian was right. I had no idea who or what I was looking for, but, if it was important enough for Johnny Wallace to use his dying breath, I thought I should at least try. Besides, I rather liked it there. The decor was cheerful and modern with green floral tiles and paintings of Paris on the walls. It was difficult to imagine that the City of Lights had been in the grips of starvation and terror scarcely more than a decade ago.

The manager may have been sullen but his employees were quick and amiable, and ladies who sat away from the windows were allowed to smoke. I was shown a table in the far corner, and ordered a pot of coffee before settling down to survey the other customers and try, as always, to work out what constituted suspicious behaviour. The unshaven man immersed in a broken-backed novel – he had been at the same table by the cake counter every day – was he waiting for Johnny? The woman in grey with a brown paper parcel – she was obviously ill at ease – was she going to deliver something? Mine was a fruitless task.

My coffee had just arrived when the doorbell clanked and two women came in – a petite, pale young lady struggling on crutches, with her companion, slightly taller, statuesque and heavily veiled, arms linked to support her. The companion was engaged in an animated conversation with the waitress and I saw that they were being turned away.

I hurried over. 'Is there a problem?'

The woman on crutches was clearly having considerable difficulty standing up. 'Apparently they are full,' she said hoarsely.

She was in her mid-twenties, I guessed, and her face was badly scratched and bruised.

Her friend's veil puzzled me. It was Lincoln green and I had never seen one so impenetrable except in black for deepest mourning.

'It is too bad,' emerged a light feminine voice from behind the gauze.

The waitress was pink. 'The manager says I mustn't push people on to tables that are already occupied. Customers don't care for it.'

'These ladies are my guests,' I said. 'If you can make it to the back there.'

'For a half-decent beverage I could make it on to the roof,' the woman with crutches avowed, and struggled between the chairs and parcels on the floor to flop exhausted but triumphant at my table. 'This is very good of you.' She propped her crutches against the wall.

'Two coffees and iced buns,' her companion ordered, and the waitress hurried away.

'March Middleton,' I introduced myself. 'March.'

The lady with the crutches held out her hand. She had masses of curly blonde hair, topped by a neat periwinkle-blue bonnet, and a sweet face, but, the more I looked at her, the more damage I saw. Her right cheekbone was indented and she had a healing split in her upper lip.

'Bocking,' she said in her croaky voice. 'Lucy Bocking.'

'I am pleased to meet you.' I turned to her companion.

'Might as well get it over with.' She lifted the veil up over her hat, and I am ashamed to confess that I shot my hand to my mouth. It was difficult to judge her age for her face was shrivelled, not by time, but partly eaten as if by acid. Her eyebrows and eyelashes were missing and part of her upper left eyelid. And her skin was yellowed by streaks of scar tissue between angry scarlet pools of tissue-paper skin. 'Freda Wilde.' She gazed straight at me, daring me not to look away. 'Friends call me Freddy.' Her right hand looked normal as it extended towards me and her grip was strong.

'How do you do, Freddy? Do you mind if I smoke?'

She smiled lopsidedly. 'I would mind more if you did not.' And she delved into her voluminous handbag.

'Have one of mine.' I held out my father's silver case. 'If you do not mind Turkish. I find they have more flavour.'

Freddy took one, but Lucy shook her head. 'Not for me – but please do not let me stop you.'

Freddy was already lighting hers and held out the Lucifer for me.

'Is there a greater pleasure than your first cigarette of the day?' I sucked deep into my lungs.

'None that I can think of,' Freddy agreed, 'but this is at least my sixth.'

The waitress returned with more cups and another pot, and she was taking them off her tray when she caught sight of Freddy and slopped coffee on the tablecloth. 'Oh, I'm so sorry. Shall I change the cloth?'

'Do not trouble.' Freddy waved her away and added, 'At least she did not scream.'

I did not know what to say to that. 'Have you never smoked?' I asked Lucy. 'Like Woking Crematorium,' she replied, 'but I find tobacco irritates my throat at present.'

'You have a cold?'

Lucy's white face coloured and something struggled its way across it – a mixture of hate and fear that fought its way into her mouth as she choked out the words.

'You think a cold did this?' She indicated her crutches and her broken cheek. 'A man did this.' She cried out as she touched her throat. 'Or a vile creature posing as one.'

9

The Terror of Ferns

'I F I HAD wanted to do house calls,' Sidney Grice grumbled as he stretched to step over a damp patch, 'I would have become a plumber.'

'I am not sure Lucy could get up our steps,' I told him.

'What then?' he enquired. 'Am I to have them removed and my house lowered?'

He buttoned his coat collar. 'And now it is raining.'

I had not brought my umbrella, as my guardian had what he described as *a rational fear* of anything that flapped. He gave me his arm and I skipped out of our cab on to the kerb.

'It is not too heavy.' I held out my hand, palm upwards.

'*All* rain is too heavy,' he decreed. 'If it were not, it would not fall from the clouds.'

'Perhaps it will clear the air.'

'London air is never clear, nor is it meant to be.'

I looked about me. Grosvenor Square was one of the most exclusive developments in Mayfair, one of the most expensive areas of London and, therefore, the world. It was built round a large gated garden and was unusual in that most of the houses were individually constructed rather than the more conventional uniform terraces. It was no less imposing for that, though, and the property we faced on the north side was a splendid four-storey Regency villa with high arched windows. Carved into the white stone facade, and highlighted in ebony to match the front door, was the name: Amber House.

Mr G tapped the steps with his cane. 'She managed to ascend these.'

'There are only two and we have six,' I pointed out. 'I should have thought you would have observed that.' And, before he could retaliate, I added, 'At least this gets you out of the house.'

'I do not wish to be *got* out of my house. If I did I should never have gone into it.' He forced the wide brim of his soft felt hat down over his eyes. 'I trust you have not familiarized these women with Miss Hockaday's case.'

'For once your trust in me is not misplaced.' I knew better than to discuss another client's business, especially in so sensitive a matter. 'Do you think the crimes are connected?'

Sidney Grice prodded the foot scraper with his toe. 'All crimes are connected,' he proclaimed unhelpfully, 'if only by the fact that they are crimes.'

I stepped back to look up, narrowly avoiding a collision with a passing cobbler's handcart.

'Make your shoe good as noo,' he bellowed in my ear as I skipped clear. 'Fix the 'oles in your soles.'

'Be quiet,' my guardian snapped.

'I ain't done the bit abart 'ow you nevah saw shinier levvah,' the bootmaker grumbled as he trudged by. His lips, I noticed, were stained brown, and I wondered if he sucked his blacking.

I craned my neck to admire the house's decorative capitals. 'It does not look like Miss Bocking will have any trouble paying your fees.'

Mr G slid a shrivelled worm out of the way with his cane. 'Clorrence Bocking, her father, was reputed to have been the one hundred and nineteenth richest man in England.'

I went up to the door. 'Where did his wealth come from?'

'From stealing the design of a safety pencil sharpener and patenting it whilst the true inventor, his younger sister, was recovering from an accident with her self-tightening corset.'

'There was a court case about that, was there not?' I racked my brains for something that a detective should be doing but came up with nothing.

'Indeed.' My guardian ran a gloved finger down a railing. 'But, since it was a civil action, I have no record of it. I shall peruse the details before the week has expired.'

The door was opened by a neat maid in a rigidly starched hat and gleaming white apron, with a welcoming 'Good afternoon'. She spoke to us pleasantly. 'Can I help you?'

'Mr Grice and assistant to see Miss Bocking.' Mr G thrust his card at her.

'Please come in. Miss Bocking is expecting you.' We stepped into a rectangular hall, the pale marbled floor inset with an apron of green squares and the pale cream walls with a faint bamboo pattern, brightening it even in the weak daylight that seeped through the windows to either side of the door. 'If you could wait here one moment,' she requested after taking our overcoats and hats.

'If we could wait here, what?' Sidney Grice resisted her attempts to relieve him of his cane.

And the maid bobbed in confusion. 'I am sure I don't know, sir.'

'I am partially mollified to learn that you are sure of something, if only your ignorance.' He shooed her off with the back of his hand. 'Go.'

The maid bobbed. 'Yes, sir.' And she scurried away.

We watched her go down the hall and turn right.

It was a pretty entrance, I thought, periwinkle wallpaper and a marble floor veined in a hint of pink, and the stairs had a cheerful rose runner.

Sidney Grice swallowed noisily.

'Assistant?' I turned on my guardian. 'I have a name.'

'So does your cat,' he replied, and I was about to respond that he actually used hers, when a voice came from inside the room.

'I will deal with this, thank you, Aellen.'

The maid came out and turned back up the hall, and Freddy appeared in a dark blue dress with darker blue trim, and walked straight towards us. Her movements were graceful and, with her slender figure, she could have been a striking woman were it not for her injuries. Her face was as scarred as I remembered and, without her hat, I saw that she had short, sparse, straw-yellow hair.

'It is good to see you, March.' She took my hand briefly. 'Good afternoon, Mr Grice. I have read so much about you.'

'How much is so much?' My guardian stood on tiptoe to peer over her shoulder.

'A great deal.' Freddy looked edgily behind herself but there was nobody there.

The famous detective showed no interest in furthering that conversation, but appeared to have taken an avid one in Freddy Wilde's bosom, bowing until his long thin nose seemed about to be buried in it. Freddy leaned back, uncomfortably, but his crooked finger came up and tapped something metallic.

'That is an unusual amulet.' He straightened and I glimpsed an ornamented silver cylinder inset with a few bright rubies hanging from her neck. 'What does it contain?'

'Perfume.'

'Then please do not allow the aroma to escape.' Sidney Grice clasped his hands in supplication. 'It may make the webs of my toes tingle and I have little appetite for that experience.'

'It was my mother's.' Freddy fingered the chain. 'From Turkey, I believe.'

'Persia,' he corrected her. 'Safavid dynasty from the Herat region. The filigree style is unmistakeable to the tutored eye.'

Freddy looked impressed. 'March told me that your powers are quite miraculous.'

Mr G examined himself in the ornately gold-framed mirror. 'My senses are extraordinarily acute.' He removed a minuscule smut of soot from his nose. 'And my intellect without parallel. But I leave miracles to the Bible, shabby conjurors, shabbier politicians and miracle workers.'

'Very well.' Freddy stepped forward into the weak rays coming through the fanlight. 'How did I get this face?'

My guardian surveyed her briefly and expressionlessly.

'It is the face with which you were born,' He drew out a red paisley handkerchief. 'That it was hideously disfigured by fire is obvious.'

Freddy winced at his choice of words and tipped her head back. 'Go on.'

Sidney Grice shone the lenses of his pince-nez but did not clip them on. 'Not quite so obvious to lesser beings, perhaps, are the twin facts that you were unconscious while the heat wreaked most of its havoc and that you must have been about twelve years old.'

Freddy looked at him suspiciously. 'You have prior knowledge.'

'I have not.' He straightened the cuffs of his coat. 'That you were unconscious is witnessed by the conditions of your hands, eyes and lips.'

Freddy touched her cheek. 'How so?'

Mr G licked a finger to arrange his eyebrows.

'When a conscious person is caught in a fire they do one or both of two things. They try to beat out the flames, burning the palms of their hands and/or they cover their faces, so that the back of their hands takes the brunt of the damage. The skin on your hands is as unblemished as that of your face must once have been. That your eyelids were closed is demonstrated by the degree of damage that they suffered whilst your eyeballs – bar a wisp of scarring in the left cornea – are relatively unscathed.'

Freddy's eyes glistened. 'Go on,' she said unsteadily.

'The epidermis was seared off most of your face, including

your lips, except for those areas on the lower.' I looked and saw
that he was right. Between the scars and raw areas were several
straight-edged patches of clear vermilion border and small areas
of undamaged skin for about an eighth of an inch below, the two
middle marks being almost rectangular.

'And so?'

'Your upper teeth are proclined some thirty to thirty-five
degrees from what is considered aesthetically pleasing by those
of a more trivial disposition than mine, and you have a tendency
to slip your lower lip behind them. They protected those covered
parts from the full effects of the fire. Teeth are remarkably resistant to heat, as witnessed by many a murderer's attempts to
incinerate his or her victim's corpse. If you had been awake
during the conflagration your mouth would not have been
relaxed. You would have been calling for help or screaming,
with your mouth wide open.'

'And my age?' Freddy asked quietly.

'The patch in the left corner is almost twice the width and
length of the right,' Mr G put his handkerchief away. 'The left
was clearly a permanent tooth and the right a deciduous. As a
rule the permanent dentition of girls develops before that of
boys, especially wealthy girls – which you undoubtedly were
from your unfeigned accent – and the permanent canines erupt
between the ages of eleven and thirteen. You were in a transition
stage – hence I estimated that you were approximately twelve
years old.'

Freddy touched her left jaw with the tips of her fingers. 'It
was my thirteenth Christmas and my parents had lit the candles
on the tree. They left them burning. I do not know why. My
mother and father were killed, along with Lucy's brother and
our two maids.' She swallowed. 'People tell me I was lucky.'

I took her hand. 'How cruel life is.'

Freddy wiped her eyes. 'Your ward did not exaggerate your
powers, Mr Grice.'

My guardian ran a hand through his thick black hair. 'Perhaps I can put them to profitable use now – if you have finished your amble down memory lane.' Freddy gasped and I rounded on him.

'You could teach life a trick or two when it comes to callousness.'

But Freddy stopped me. 'I am sorry to waste your time, Mr Grice.' She blew her nose and composed herself. 'Lucy must be wondering what we are up to. I have left her in the fernery.'

'What terrors are contained within that final word,' Mr G mumbled.

We passed through a nice duck-egg blue drawing room into a vast conservatory that had been transformed into a miniature jungle. I had rarely seen such a profusion of ferns: mossy plants grew out of a tree trunk, which stopped just short of the lofty glass roof; two of the walls were made of boulders, creating cliffs – some twenty feet or more high – from which projected and hung larger plants; and free-standing bushes grew from peat beds round the sides and in the middle of the room.

'Green.' Mr G recoiled.

'I see you are exercising your detective's skills already,' a voice said.

And we peered between the masses of vegetation to find Lucy Bocking, quite tiny and dressed in dusky pink, in a high-backed cane chair at the far end of the room, her feet on a wicker footstool.

'Mr Grice does not like the colour,' I told her, and parted some fronds to make my way down a limestone path towards her.

'I loathe it.' He followed reluctantly. 'It is evocative of meadows and pastoral poetry.' He shook her hand. 'Good afternoon, Miss Bocking.'

'Please call me Lucy.' Her hair was pinned back by an ivory

comb carved into an intricate latticework, but the front still fell into a fringe.

'No,' he said. 'I am known as a casual fellow, but I dislike familiarity with my clients.'

'So I cannot call you Sidney?' she teased.

She had a choker around her neck with a cream-coloured button at the front.

'Even my mother never called me that.'

'What did she call you then?'

'The same as she does now.' He raised a puzzled eyebrow. 'Grice.'

Lucy's mouth twitched. 'So what did she call her husband?'

'Why, Mr Grice, of course.'

He wiped his hand on a handkerchief monogrammed myste-riously with the initial Q, and I bent to kiss her cheek. 'How are you, Lucy?'

'I am well,' she assured me, though clearly she was not. Her voice was still hoarse. Her cuts were scabbing and the bruises fractionally fading, but her right eye was still almost closed and her arms trembled when she held them up to me.

Sidney Grice and I sat in two bamboo chairs facing her, he with his satchel on his lap.

'Given the unsavoury nature of your case, if I am to believe – as I do occasionally – what Miss Middleton has told me...' he toyed with the strap buckle, 'I shall be obliged to say things which you will find embarrassing and I deeply so.' Mr G wrapped the strap loosely around his wrist. 'So I shall commence with a medical enquiry.' Was it the light or had he gone a tint of pink? He pulled the strap tight. 'Does your right acetabular-femoral joint hurt very much?'

'My hip?' Lucy half-smiled at his circumspection and half-frowned in puzzlement. 'But how did you know?'

'Your foot is turned forty-eight degrees medially, and the only joint capable of rotating axially that far in that direction, without dislocation or fracture, is in your pelvis.' He pulled on the strap, taking his reluctant left hand for a walk. 'If it were your knee or ankle you would be in traction.'

'How do you know I was not born pigeon-toed?' she challenged, as he loosened his leash.

'Those bovine epidermal boots, though in keeping with modern stylistic fads, are not especially new. If you were in the habit of walking in such a manner, the soles would have been more unevenly abraded.'

'Bravo.' Lucy clapped like a little girl at a magic show. 'And, in answer to your question, yes it does. I can hardly walk on it.'

'Good.'

'I am glad you think so.'

Sidney Grice slipped his hand out of the noose. 'Are you literate, Miss Bocking?'

'What?' Lucy laughed uncertainly. 'Yes, of course.'

And he thrust a blank postcard at her with a stumpy black pencil.

'Then kindly write neatly – though not in block capitals for I am not in the mood to look at those today – the names of your solicitor, if you have one, accountant, if you have one, and doctor, of whom you must have at least one.'

Lucy took them from him. 'Why do you need those details at this stage?'

'I do not.' Mr G laughed mirthlessly. 'And I might never, but I have a sick fancy to see their names in your hand.'

Lucy took the items silently and began writing.

'Shall I ring for coffee?' Freddy asked from behind us.

'Tea,' he instructed.

'I am not a servant,' she muttered and tugged a rope just inside the sitting room.

'What exactly are you?' Sidney Grice challenged as she returned.

'A companion.' Freddy said quietly.

43

'Freddy is my best friend, almost my sister,' Lucy began, but Mr G silenced her with a raised hand.

'One cannot *almost* be a sister,' he corrected her. 'Sorority is an absolute relationship between females, which has been created either by mutual genetic parentage or the legal process of adoption. To put it simply enough for you to comprehend, either one is a sister or one is not.'

'Lucy means that we feel like sisters to each other,' Freddy sought to explain, but my guardian shushed her also.

'If I had required one I should have employed the services of a professional interpreter, but I am hopeful that Miss Bocking will manage to express her thoughts more articulately.' He turned back to Lucy. 'Have you finished writing?'

'Yes.'

'Then pass the result of your labours to me.'

'Have you ever heard of the word *please*?' Lucy held the card out and he rose to take them back.

'I have,' he assured her gravely, 'indeed. Pray resume your exordium.'

Lucy clicked her tongue. 'Miss Wilde and I lived next door to each other as children. My parents were her godparents and her parents were mine. We played together and after the accident—'

'I have told them all about that,' Freddy broke in.

'Not *all*,' Mr G interjected. 'Merely a synopsis.'

Lucy patted her arm. 'Freddy came to live with us and has remained ever since, and now there are just the two of us.' She laughed croakily. 'And what a fine pair we make, me crippled and—'

'Stop,' Freddy hissed. 'Your wounds will heal and one day you will walk as though nothing has happened.'

'One wound will never heal,' Lucy struggled to get up on her elbows and Freddy put an arm under her shoulders, 'until I am avenged of the animal who did this to me.'

'I take it you use the word *animal* metaphorically.' Mr G

hauled out his hunter by the chain. 'I am not, *exempli gratia*, expected to search for a tortoise.'

'Is that a joke?' Freddy seemed ready to pounce through the fronds of bracken drooping between them from a terracotta amphora.

'You may infer the answer from two pieces of evidence.' My guardian's face had a mysterious aura in the dappled light. 'First, my demeanour and, second, the brief extract from my memoirs which I shall relate immediately.' An umbra fell across his eyes. 'I was approached five over two thousand days ago by a woman of good repute, who gave a lurid and graphic account of being molested by an escaped an-a-con-da. Her credibility was somewhat tarnished, however, by her description of what it did with its hands.'

Notwithstanding – or perhaps because of – the grave way Mr G delivered this information, the three of us burst out laughing.

'Oh.' Lucy put her hands protectively over her midriff. 'I really should not do that with cracked ribs.' She shifted in pain. 'I mean a man, of course,' she croaked. 'He ruined me for life, Mr Grice, and I want my revenge.'

'Vengeance,' Sidney Grice ruminated. 'I am not much interested in facilitating that, but the capture and punishment of criminals is something to which I devote every waking and many a sleeping moment of my life.' His face shone with a zeal that is normally only seen in paintings of visionary saints. 'Thank heavens,' he cried. 'I hear the clatter of bone china on a Japanese oak tea trolley with brass wheels approaching this miserable lair.'

10

Gretna Green and Garibaldi

ADIFFERENT AND YOUNGER maid brought the trolley, negotiating her way nervously along the meandering paved pathway through the undergrowth into the clearing. She had an anaemic face with the big, soft and timid eyes of a doe.

'Miss Wilde will pour,' Lucy told her, and the maid chirruped nervously as she left. 'The other servants have been teasing Muriel that you have come to arrest her, Mr Grice.'

My guardian leaned over the pot, lifted the lid and sniffed. 'I have little doubt she will end in penury with or without my help.' He replaced the lid. 'Any maid who serves morning tea in or after the first quarter of the post-meridian is either morally degenerate or a simpleton or both.'

'I think we only stock one kind of tea,' Lucy told him, and his cheek ticked twice.

'The stuff of nightmares.' He pulled his coat around him.

'Would you care for a Garibaldi?' Freddy held out a plate of golden glazed wafers of pastry filled with currants, and I took one.

'I would prefer to be offered information.' Mr G rattled his fingerplates on the lid of his hunter watch but did not open it.

Lucy licked her lips nervously. 'Perhaps I should start at the beginning.'

My guardian unclipped his satchel. 'You will start where and when I instruct you to.' He brought out a black cloth-bound notebook.

'You are the rudest man I have ever met,' Lucy complained and he smiled thinly.

'More ill-mannered than the man you allege assaulted you?'

Lucy gasped. '*Allege?* How dare you?'

'Once we become comfortable in each other's presence, you will marvel at what I have the courage to say.' Sidney Grice shook his pencil as if driving the mercury down a medical thermometer. 'But let me ease you on to that halcyon path by informing you that I am obliged to consider the possibility that you may be a liar.'

Lucy battled to keep calm. 'I did not get these injuries falling downstairs.'

'Perhaps you paid somebody to assault you in order to implicate somebody else against whom you have a grudge or wish to blackmail.'

Again it was Freddy who flared in indignation. 'If you live to be a hundred, and I hope you do not, you will not find anyone more honest than Lucy.' She crossed her arms. 'Why, she was so religious as a girl that she went to a convent for a year and nearly became a nun before the fire.'

'Which?' Sidney Grice rolled the pen close to his ear like a connoisseur appreciating a good cigar.

'The one that destroyed Steep House, my parents' home.' Freddy gripped her own sleeves.

Mr G listened to his pencil intently.

'Why was it called Steep House?' I asked.

'It was named after Mr Shorrow Steep,' Freddy explained. 'He built our house and Lucy's parents'.'

'He built Miss Bocking's parents?' Sidney Grice threw up his left hand like a schoolboy asking to be excused. 'Surely you are being whimsical?'

'I cannot think of anyone with whom I would be less likely to share a jest.' Freddy touched her temple.

'I can,' he assured her, a folded knife appearing in his left hand.

'Freddy meant her parents' house,' I explained, not sure if I really had to. 'Were the two houses of a similar design?'

'Identical.' Freddy viewed Sidney Grice warily. 'Except that our house was rendered.'

'Rendered what?' He tensed his thumb and the blade shot open.

'With stucco.'

'And did you sleep near your parents?' He tossed the knife high into the air to crash through the greenery overhead.

Freddy shook her head. 'My parents preferred the opposite wing to mine.' She paused as the knife hung at its zenith before hurtling down. 'They liked to watch the sunrise.' Freddy cringed as Mr G closed his eyes and caught his missile by the blade. 'But I always thought Lucy and I had the best rooms,' she battled on. 'We could spy on people coming and going, and our side windows looked straight into each other's across the hedge. In fact we used to put our favourite dolls on our window ledges to watch over each other.' She looked sideways at her friend in embarrassment. 'All very childish, I know.'

'Very,' Mr G agreed heartily. 'If we might return to our monstrously neglected client and my unhappily misinterpreted question.' He clinked the tip of the blade against his false eye. 'My *which* – if you can cast your agile mind back through the miasmas of time – pertained not, as you so recklessly assumed, to which house, but to which convent?'

'St Philomena's,' Lucy answered sharply.

'I shall write and ask if they would like a charitable donation.' He ran the blade repeatedly under his chin in a shaving motion.

'I did not think you liked nuns.' I was puzzled, especially as he was not in the habit of giving to any charitable cause.

'I liked one nun very much.' He flicked the steel up his

hairless philtrum. 'So much so that I went to watch her being garrotted.' The knife disappeared as mysteriously as it had arrived. 'I only know one completely truthful person and I inhabit his body – for I have no choice in the matter. Pray continue with your dubious account.'

Lucy folded her arms. 'I do not think we are compatible, Mr Grice,' she said, and he surveyed her coldly.

'If you mean that we will never be friends or become romantically attached and elope to Gretna Green, then I am forced to agree.' My godfather extruded a tiny length of lead from his pencil and somehow made that action look almost as dangerous as his antics with the knife. 'But I see no reason why we cannot have a professional relationship. I am the finest personal detective in the empire and you are wealthy and clever – two excellent attributes for a client.'

'Why *clever*?' Lucy asked uncertainly.

'Because there are four hundred and nineteen men masquerading as independent detectives for hire, many of them fictional, all of them charlatans, and yet you chose to consult me,' he said, and she coughed in amusement.

'Very well, Mr Grice. Where shall we begin?'

'With a simple yet pregnant question. Why—' Sidney Grice pressed a finger into his chin, moulding the dimple that it already had—'have you not reported the assault to the police?'

Lucy flushed. 'Do you think I want another brute mauling me?'

'Not all of the officers are brutes,' I assured her, though there were a few I would not expect much sympathy from.

'I am talking about the police surgeon,' Lucy explained. 'I have heard talk—'

'Most women have heard very little else,' Sidney Grice interrupted.

'Lucy meant—' Freddy began, but he silenced her with an upheld hand.

'You may go now.' He flexed the ankle of his raised foot.

Freddy bristled. 'I am not a slavey for you to command,' she retorted, and he shrugged.

'You may go nonetheless.'

Freddy put down her cup. 'I shall not be spoken to in this way.'

'I am afraid he speaks to everybody like that,' I told her.

'Then he needs to learn some manners.'

'I have created my own manners.' Mr G threw back his head. 'And I am overweeningly proud of them. They are not agreeable, nor are they intended to be. There are things I need to discuss with Miss Bocking. Go away.'

Lucy glowered at Sidney Grice, but he surveyed her as if he were watching an unamusing play.

'It might be best,' she said at last. 'I will tell you all about it later, dear.'

'That would be foolish but, being female, you probably will,' Mr G forecast.

'I am sorry he did not put it more nicely,' I apologized.

'He could not have been more obnoxious,' Freddy fumed.

'I promise you he could.' I pushed something spikey out of my ear.

'Goodbye.' My guardian wiggled his fingers in farewell and Freddy jumped up and stormed out.

'That was not very nice of you,' Lucy complained as the spike crept back in.

'Quit the effeminately adorned drawing room,' he called playfully.

And Freddy stamped away and slammed the door.

'You did not have—' she tried, but he hushed her again and called more loudly. 'Go.'

And the door handle rattled and there was a crash so violent that an ornament fell to the floor.

I nibbled at a corner of my Garibaldi.

'I am sorry I evicted her now,' Mr G broke the silence, 'before she had the chance to pour me another tea.'

I refreshed our cups as he proceeded.

'Now, Miss Bocking.' My godfather rubbed his left temple with the heel of his left hand. 'Regale me with your account of that eventful night. Give equal weight to that which you judge to be significant or trivial, pedestrian or dramatic. Tell me only what your youthful senses told you and not what you imagined, and do not waste time crying. You may weep to your heart's despair when I have departed.' He bowed towards her. 'Tell me what you believe to be the truth, Miss Bocking, and I shall put almost all my efforts into resolving this matter once and for all.'

His fingers danced in all directions and, surreptitiously, I slipped the stalk down the side of my cushion.

11

The Hollow Shepherd

SIDNEY GRICE PALMED the spoon from his saucer as if trying to pilfer it.

'Freddy and I were bored,' Lucy began.

'Why?' he demanded, and Lucy shifted uncomfortably.

'The life of a modern girl in London out of season is tedious in the extreme. There are no balls, nothing new at the theatre, no dinner parties, no—'

'I know what *tedious* means.' Mr G chipped at his tea as if the meniscus were a thin sheet of ice. 'I have to converse with Miss Middleton daily and I once sat through an entire production of *Hamlet* without being allowed to interrupt it once. This tea, incidentally, is horrid. And so what remedy was proposed for this insipid languorousness and by whom?'

'Freddy had been to a few opium dens in the past. They sounded terrifically racy and she had never come to any harm in them – except once when she had her purse taken on the way home – and so we decided to give it a go.'

Mr G took his spoon by the tip of the handle between his thumb and fourth finger, and stirred his black tea with great attention.

'So it was Freddy's idea?' I clarified.

'Well, yes, I suppose it was.' Lucy stretched her arms as if about to dive off rocks into the sea. 'But I did not need persuading.'

'You went by cab?' I asked, trying to ignore my guardian's sigh at my use of another leading question.

He shook the spoon dry and hid it under the corner of a napkin.

'It was the coachman's night off,' Lucy confirmed, 'and besides we did not want the servants to know what we were up to. It sets such a bad example.'

'Who instructed the driver and what instructions was he given?' Sidney Grice fingered the jackal ring on his watch chain.

'I said *Limehouse, if you please,* but,' Lucy let her arms drop heavily into her lap, 'he did not please in the least until Freddy offered to double his fare, and then he seemed quite pleased after all.'

'How did you decide which opium house to go to?' I asked.

'Luck really.' Lucy pulled a wry face. 'Rotten luck as it turned out. The cabby was getting nervous – beggars were crowding round us and children were climbing on the back for free rides, people were shouting coarse remarks and somebody threw dung at his horse. We came to the top of an alley that looked quite well-lit with lanterns in some of the windows or over the lintels, so we told him to stop there. We got out, but nothing would persuade him to wait or come back for us.'

'From which side did you disembark?' my guardian asked.

'The left.' Lucy touched her broken cheekbone gingerly. 'Why do you ask?'

'Because it is immaterial.'

Lucy tilted her head to the right. 'I am confused.'

Mr G mirrored her action. 'People inventing stories do not expect to be cross-examined on irrelevancies.' He straightened his neck and she followed suit. 'It flusters them to be diverted from their rehearsed versions with details they are unlikely to have considered. In many cases their whole account will instantly unravel and even the best of actors tend to direct their eyes to the left whilst their brains sift through plausible responses.'

Mr G drew a squiggle. He and she blinked simultaneously.

'So you know I am telling the truth?' Lucy curled a tress around her finger but he did not.

'It is not an infallible test.' Sidney Grice tapped a line of dots down the page. 'But, in future, if you decide to create a fiction without notice in my presence, you will fix your eyes in an unnatural manner.' He joined the dots in a sweeping curve. 'Beside which there are seven other signs which I stalk.' He underlined the squiggle. 'Continue.'

'We made our way down the alley. A group of ragged children followed us but Freddy got rid of them by tossing a handful of coppers over their heads into the court where we had been dropped off. They all chased after them and we ducked through one of the lit doorways.'

'Who chose which one?' I asked and Lucy hesitated, nonplussed.

'We saw a name on the wall written in Chinese, and under it in English *The Golden Dragon*, and we just dashed in.'

'What was the place like?' I asked.

'Seedy,' Lucy said. 'Gloomily lit and frowsty. There was an outer room with a tall Chinaman sitting on a stool. Freddy took charge. She asked if they sold poppy dreams and he nodded and smiled. He was very polite and formal. She asked how much and we gave him a guinea each.'

'Oh, I would only have paid ten shillings,' I said. 'Clearly you look more prosperous than I.'

My guardian's lips worked silently.

'Or more stupid,' she said. 'A boy showed us through.'

'Describe,' Mr G commanded.

'The boy?'

'I am not interested in your grandmother's wart at present,' he rejoined and she stifled a giggle. 'It is no laughing matter,' he reproved and Lucy's face stiffened.

'I do not need you to tell me that, Mr Grice.' She licked her lips again. 'The boy was about ten years old, I would say, Chinese in his features, dress and accent.'

'What did he say?' I asked and she put her hands together.

'Velly good evening, madams. Pleasee come this way. Ahh, so you likee—'

'Oh dear,' Mr G butted in. 'I was unprepared to hold an audition for an amateur production of one of Miss Middleton's melodramas.' I thought this rather unfair, as I had written my plays when I was a child and he had come across the jottings during a search of my room. He clipped his pince-nez on the tip of his long thin nose to scrutinize her over the gold wire frame. 'Where did he take you?'

'Through a secret door,' she said, 'though not very secret. The wall was covered with bamboo screens and they just slid one aside. It led down some wooden steps into a cellar.'

'Lit how?' He circled a symbol four times.

'By oil lamps hanging from the ceiling.'

'Were you not scared?' I asked.

'Terrified,' she admitted, 'but I was dashed if I was going to show it.'

'What was the room like?' I asked.

'Save that for your memoirs,' Mr G snapped. 'Let us cut to the chase. Presumably – correct me if I am uncharacteristically wrong – it was decorated in lurid pictures of an indecent nature and had couches round the walls. How many?'

'Four.'

'Occupied?' He scribbled *dashed* and fenced it into an ellipse.

'Only one of them – by a man.'

'Describe.' He pointed at her with the blunt end of his Mordan mechanical pencil.

'It was too dark to see him really well – average height and solidly built.'

'Could you see what he was wearing?' I asked and my guardian indicated towards me proudly.

'See how well I am training her – a relevant question at last.'

Lucy shook her head in mild amusement. 'No, but he was well-dressed.'

'How could you tell?' I smoothed down my dress and wondered if Mr G's pernicketiness was contagious.

'I heard his boots creak,' Lucy explained. 'So they must have been new. Old leather does not make a noise like that.'

'*Wunderbar.*' Mr G clapped his hands together. 'What an excellent client you are evolving into.' His hands flew apart as if they repelled each other magnetically. 'With your exemplary perspicacity we have travelled one thirty-fourth of our journey towards the resolution of this matter.'

Lucy wrinkled her brow. 'Because I noticed that a man had new boots?'

'Precisely so.' Sidney Grice's hands seemed drawn by the same power towards his knees, but he resisted the force and left them hovering a few inches above his immaculately pressed lilac trousers. 'The Putney Pickle Purifier might never have been caught had he parted his hair less carefully.'

Lucy tossed me a bemused glance, but it was not a case with which I was familiar. Mr G permitted his hands to rest on his knees, gradually and one at a time.

I struggled to get back on track. 'Who showed you how to smoke opium?'

'Freddy.'

'How many pipes did you have?'

'I think I only had one. I was unused to it and the effects were very powerful, and the next thing I knew—' Lucy made a fist and crammed it between her teeth.

Sidney Grice shook his watch and put it to his ear. 'Time has not stopped. Why have you?'

Lucy fought back the tears.

I rounded on him. 'Can you not see how painful this is for her?'

'Of course I can,' he said. 'And I have reconsidered my position.' He slipped his watch away. 'I shall have a Garibaldi after all.' Sidney Grice reached over and helped himself. 'I hope I shall not regret it.' He bit a crescent out of one of the long sides and chewed meditatively. 'I am happy to say that my hopes were dashed.'

'Happy?' I echoed automatically.

'It will be a sad day that my hopes are satisfied by an adhesive confection.'

'Why are you rambling about Garibaldis when Miss Bocking is on the verge of nervous collapse?' I demanded.

Lucy took her hand from her mouth and said, 'It is all right, March. He has brought me back from that brink.'

Mr G put the part-eaten biscuit on an empty plate with such care it might have been a unique piece of exquisite porcelain. 'I have already remarked that our client is that rarest of creatures – an intelligent woman.' He pushed the lead back into his pencil. 'I shall return tomorrow, Miss Bocking, at nineteen minutes to eleven in the morning since you have no tea fit to brew after that hour.'

Mr G snapped his notebook shut and put it into his satchel. Lucy opened her mouth and closed it before gasping, 'But we have not finished.'

'What on earth gave you that idea?' He sprang to his feet. 'You have become attached to a botanical specimen, Miss Middleton.'

I rose and saw that the broken stem had caught by one of its hooked leaves to the side of my dress.

'We *can* see ourselves out.' He pressed the bell button. 'But we shall not.'

I looked at Lucy, shocked and desolate in her chair.

'I am sorry about this.' I detached the stalk and placed it guiltily on the table. 'But we *will* bring the man who hurt you to justice.'

'Just catch him.' Lucy looked up at me, a new fire in her eyes. 'You can leave the justice to me.'

Lucy's head dropped and she did not react as I touched her arm in farewell and, when I looked out, my guardian was creeping across the drawing room round a hollow shepherd that lay in three segments and a hundred shards. He put a finger to his lips and signalled at me to stand back, wrenched the china handle round and threw open the door.

'By Jupiter,' he cried as it crashed against the display cabinet, upsetting a powder-blue shepherdess on to her back, 'has that woman no shame?' He exuded indignation. 'She is not even eavesdropping.'

'No need to frow 'em 'cause I'm 'ere to sew 'em,' the cobbler chanted from across the road as the maid showed us out of Amber House.

He had hung a sign with a picture of a shoe on the railings and pushed his cart into the bushes overhanging the railings.

'A poet laureate in waiting.' Sidney Grice opined, knocking against the sign so it fell, bent, to the ground. He sniffed, then stepped delicately over an earwig before brushing it carefully aside. 'I am so very sorry,' he apologized to it.

12

The Great Flood

I DID NOT speak to my guardian until after I had unbent the sign as best I could, rehung it and given the owner a shilling. 'What on earth was that all about?' I asked as calmly as I could.

An unoccupied hansom went by, but Sidney Grice made no attempt to hail it. 'Did you not understand any of it?' He set off in the opposite direction to home. 'At your suggestion Miss Bocking contacted me by letter to request that I attend her house to—'

'I am not a complete idiot,' I cut in.

'Work in progress.' He unscrewed the handle of his cane.

'I am talking about the way you marched out of that poor woman's house before she even had a chance to tell you what had happened to her.'

'First, I hardly marched,' he protested. 'If you can strain your memory all the way back to six and one third minutes ago, I actually crept from that frighteningly herbaceous vitreous construction through that revoltingly tasteful sitting room.'

'That is not the point.'

'Second, Miss Bocking did not give the impression of being poor – though she might be – and if you have information to that effect, perhaps you would like to divulge it. I do not have poor clients.' He reinserted the handle upside down.

'I meant poor in the sense of unfortunate.'

'A strange interpretation,' my godfather mused, 'since the poor are not unfortunate.' He clipped on his pince-nez to look at a dial in his modified stick. 'They are lazy. Just as I thought.'

'What?'

'According to my new barometer, Grosvenor Square is one foot lower than marked on the 1879 Ordinance Survey map. We are sinking into the sea, March.' His tone implied that he thought I might have something to do with it.

'Thank heavens I invested in the Trafalgar Square Gondola Company,' I quipped to a blank stare.

Mr G reassembled his cane. 'I think we have waited long enough.'

'For what?'

'Look and listen.'

I did both. 'What?' I repeated when I became bored, which happened very quickly.

'This is my city,' he declaimed. 'London in all its grandeur and its filth, this heaving heap of magnificent squalid stinking avarice that rules the world's oceans and vast swathes of its unsatisfactory continents. Countless millions are in thrall to us, March, and what do you see?'

I surveyed the bustling traffic and watched a pigeon land on top of a policeman's helmet. 'Nothing unusual.'

'Excellent.' Sidney Grice clapped his gloved hands together. 'I shall forge a detective yet from the shabby material with which you present me. And what do you make of your observation?'

The policeman shooed the pigeon away.

'Nothing,' I said, and he frowned.

'You should always make something of everything, but, forgive me, I am overtaxing your feminine brain.' He twirled round. 'Look about you, March. We are not even being followed. Do you not find that rather strange?'

I stepped to the kerb and hailed a cab. 'But to the best of my knowledge we have never been followed.'

The hansom pulled alongside.

'Precisely.' Mr G leaped aboard and held open the flap for me. 'And what could be more normal than that? Yet it is in the ordinary that the most extraordinary events are to be discovered. That is Grice's sixth law and therefore immutable.' He raised his voice. '125 Gower Street, driver.'

'Drop me off at Gosling Lane,' I called.

Our driver was bareheaded and wore no coat or neckerchief, and I envied him that, and the breeze that he must be enjoying on his lofty perch.

'Goslink?' He tossed his hands. 'That's not on my way.'

'It is now,' I asserted and he yanked his horse's head to the left.

'Miss Hockaday?' Sidney Grice enquired.

'Yes,' I replied, and he edged away from the rim of my new blue bonnet, which was brushing embarrassingly against that of his old soft felt hat.

13

Turkish Cigarettes on Gosling Lane

GOSLING LANE DID not live up to the rustic promise of its name. With not a goose to be seen, it was a short narrow thoroughfare north of Oxford Street and occupied by thin houses, many converted into sweatshops producing cheap shirts to be sold in the nearby bazaars. And I had hardly set foot on the befouled pavement before Sidney Grice tipped his head back. 'Drive on.'

I was glad that he did not think the man sharpening a carving knife on the kerbstone presented a threat, but I could not help remembering how George Pound was stabbed once, and I was relieved when the door opened a crack.

'Oh, it's you,' Mrs Freval said and I resisted retorting, as Mr G might have, that I was already aware of that.

I could sympathize with Mrs Freval's annoyance for none of her tenants ever responded to visitors. She lived on the ground floor alone but for a balding mongrel called Turndap because, she once told me, he just *turndap* on her doorstep.

'I am sorry to disturb you.'

Turndap poked his speckled nose through the gap, sniffing eagerly, and I rummaged for thruppence in my purse.

'I ain't a bleedin' doorman.' She pulled back affronted.

I leaned over to scratch behind the dog's ear and his back leg paddled the air. 'A present for Turndap.'

Turndap drooled blissfully on to my hem.

''E could do wiv a noo cap,' Mrs Freval conceded. 'The uvva dogs larf attis old one.'

A black dot landed on the back of my hand but then, I was relieved to see, jumped straight back to rejoin its friends in the greasy coconut-matting that served Turndap as fur. I dropped the coin into an outstretched apron. Mrs Freval never touched money, being convinced that the wren on a farthing had given her *glangula feeva* twenty years ago. And Turndap slumped mournfully as I mounted the stairs.

Geraldine Hockaday and her brother Peter lived in the three-roomed attic of number 8. By local standards this was luxurious. The four lower floors were divided into single rooms, some of which housed entire families, and one old woman appeared to have set up home on the lower landing. She was sprawled out, slurping from a jam jar and dribbling some taupe coagulum down herself. I stepped carefully over her rag-bound feet.

Geraldine was knitting when I went to see her, a tiny pink sock suspended from her needles like a cocoon. She loved to make baby clothes and lay them between sheets of tissue paper in a pine chest at the foot of her bed.

We blew kisses in greeting, her lips puckering like a child trying to whistle.

The small sitting room was simply furnished with a plain wooden dining table on one side and two sagging armchairs facing a bricked-up fireplace on the other. Alongside the only possible source of heating permanently blocked, the floor gave little comfort, with draughts rising between the bare boards. I dreaded to think how cold that apartment would be in the winter.

'I am well,' she responded to my enquiry and she looked healthy enough, though pale from being housebound. But Geraldine's bush-baby eyes flicked about, looking everywhere for the attack she constantly anticipated.

'How did it go?' she asked the moment I sat opposite her.

I drew a breath for I knew that Geraldine had high hopes that something would come of our meeting with Johnny Wallace.

'I am sorry to say that our witness was murdered before he could tell us anything.'

Geraldine had a pointy pink nose and a pointy chin to match. She was a slight girl. I have often been described as *scrawny*, but being near her made me feel huge and ungainly.

'But how?' She mouthed the words in shock before she uttered them and I wished I could have sat beside her and taken her hand, but she disliked being touched by anybody. I had seen her inarticulate with terror when Peter had accidentally bumped into her once.

'He was shot but his killer got away.' I wished I could have told her something else, but I could not break a confidence by mentioning Lucy.

Geraldine went back to her knitting while she digested the news. 'I cannot pretend to feel sorry for Mr Wallace,' she decided, a whiteness floating to the surface of her cheeks, 'for it was he who directed me down that alley.' She shuddered as if being plunged through broken ice on a pond. 'And blocked my escape, but he was the only one who knew.'

'We have not given up,' I vowed, but Geraldine did not seem to be listening. 'Mr Grice will think of something,' I tried, all too aware of how hollow my assurance sounded.

The discs grew until her face was alabaster but still there was no response.

'He always does,' I said helplessly.

'I learned a new stitch yesterday,' she announced, and the needles whirled and clicked in a series of complicated manoeuvres, tucking her wool through and around itself. 'See?'

She held her handiwork up for inspection.

'Lovely,' I said, though one stitch looked much like another to me.

Geraldine put her knitting in her lap with the exaggerated care of somebody who is not really aware of what they are doing. 'Peter pawned his inheritance to pay Mr Grice's fees – everything he had and ever expects to have.'

I watched the ball of wool fall off her knee and down her dress.

'I know and I am sorry.' The ball rolled over the floor to come to rest at my feet. 'If you would like us to give up this case I will get Mr Grice to reimburse you.'

I knew that Sidney Grice would not consider paying her back. In his mind the case was still open and he did not like admitting defeat. But I was quite willing to refund his charges. It was difficult to pretend that we had achieved anything.

'Is that what you want?' Geraldine jumped as if I had sprung at her. 'To desert me?'

'No. I want to catch the man who did this to you.'

Her nose crinkled like an inquisitive mouse. 'This?' she repeated uncertainly, as if I meant the room.

Geraldine picked up her needles and the sock fell off one of them.

'I hope it does not unravel.' I stooped to retrieve the ball.

'It is all unravelled,' she said simply.

14

Of Mice and Moustaches

MOLLY WAS ON her knees, scrubbing the hall floor, but she struggled to her feet, hauling herself up with a soapy hand on my sleeve when I went to see if she was all right. She had been moaning so loudly that I could hear her from my bedroom at the back of the house on the second floor.

'Oh, miss.' Her eyes were even more darkly under-bagged than usual. 'I cantn't not be all right, can I?' She noticed the suds on my dress and gave them a quick rub with her raw wet hand. 'Oh, what a night. I had a terrorable dream.' She dropped her brush in the bucket, splattering my hem with dirty water, and folded her arms in preparation for her narration. 'I was sitting in Mr G's armchair with my feet up by the fire and him feeding me hot butter muffings, and you fetching me a big pot of tea and trying to curtsy like a proper lady's maid, when I felted a scritch and heard restling noises on my head and, when I put my hand up, I undiscoverered a huge teensy mouse making its nest in my hairs and, when I pulled it out by the tail, it bit me.'

She held out her hand to show me two neat puncture marks on her right forefinger.

'Oh, so it was not a dream then,' I remarked, and Molly wrinkled her brow.

'Not a dream when, miss?' She poked her finger towards her eye.

'Not a dream at all,' I said, nearly as confused as she was, and Molly laughed.

'Oh, miss, how can a dream not be a dream?' She rotated the finger horizontally.

I tried again. 'No, I meant the mouse.'

'But...' Molly licked her finger and thought about the taste of it. 'How can a mouse be a dream anyway?' She had another lick and smacked her lips. 'When Mr Grice—' Molly crossed herself—'caught a mouse in his scrungulater, he didntn't not say,' Molly's voice rose in an uncannily inaccurate imitation of her employer, '*Oh by George, I has encaptured a dream.*'

I covered my mouth and pretended to cough. 'So what happened to the mouse?' I asked, still unclear as to whether it had existed outside Molly's unusual brain.

Molly sniffed. 'I thoughted you'd would of been more worried about what happened to me.' She sniffed again.

I glanced at the grandmother clock and wondered if time were going backwards. 'So what *did* happen to you?' I asked reluctantly.

Molly made a noise that I can only describe as a *snurkle*. 'Well, I swallowed it of course,' she told me, it being inconceivable to her that anyone in their right mind would have done anything different.

'Oh.' I had been driven mad by drugs eighteen months ago and Molly was having much the same effect. 'Is it still in your stomach?'

Molly made a sort of *chundling* sound. 'Still? It aintn't anything but still.' She put a hand to her left bosom. 'It's running about in there like a—' She struggled for the apposite word. 'Gravestone.'

I went into the study where Sidney Grice was sifting through his mail.

'An epistle from Pound,' he announced. 'He has wearied of dealing with Fenland creatures in uniform and taken a temporary posting in Limehouse.'

I adopted a casual pose by the fireplace. 'When does he return?'

'On Thursday.'

My guardian put the letter in the top drawer of his desk and my foolish heart turned over. I was so desperate and yet so afraid to meet George again, and I could not help but remember a time when he would have sent that message to me.

Molly answered the doorbell.

'Probably two callers,' Mr G murmured without glancing up.

'How can you tell?'

'By listening to the footfalls.'

'They could be carrying a third person,' I teased, as he filled his Grice Patent Fountain Pen from his Grice inkwell, which he had not patented as he wished to keep the design a secret.

'I considered that possibility and dismissed it.' He wiped the back of the nib on his blotting paper. 'They would be dragging their boots more.'

'Or in their stockinged feet.'

'Which is why I said *probably*.'

Molly entered, bearing a tray and shutting the door, and Mr G inhaled.

'A well-to-do man and a woman,' he declared, 'to judge from the scents of expensive feminine perfume and masculine pomade, which even Molly cannot completely overpower.'

Molly brought the tray over. 'I swallowed a—' she began, forgetting that her employer was apparently able not just to hear a pin drop but – I sometimes suspected – a pin as it was falling.

'Mouse.' Mr G slid the cards off like a poker player.

'Told you.' Molly folded her arms triumphantly.

Sidney Grice titivated his perfectly pinned cravat. 'Bring them in.' He slipped the cards into one of his many waistcoat pockets.

'Mr and Mrs Wright,' Molly announced, to everyone's apparent satisfaction. It was not like her to get even the simplest of names right.

Sidney Grice shook their hands and introduced me. They were a small couple, short and delicately boned, their faces grey and stretched with anxiety.

I ushered Mrs Wright towards my armchair, but she demurred and sat between me and her husband in one of the two upright chairs that he had dragged over, sitting beside Mr G so that we were all in a semicircle round the hearth.

'Thank you for seeing us,' Mrs Wright began.

'The only gratitude I seek is of a monetary nature,' he told her, so softly that he might have making a pleasantry.

'I shall not beat about the bush,' Mr Wright promised.

'But you are already doing so,' Mr G assured him, with an unnerving light smile upon his lips.

'It is Albertoria, Mr Grice.'

'What is?' He tapped his own left knee to hurry things along and it was just as well that I did not make my guess, which was that they were referring to a monument, because Mrs Wright trembled and told us, 'Albertoria is our daughter.'

'Or was,' Mr Wright whispered.

'Do not—' Mrs Wright sobbed and her husband took her hand.

'I pray that I am wrong.'

Sidney Grice opened his mouth but, for once, he paid heed to my warning cough and glare that this was not the time to demonstrate his notorious lack of tact.

'Is she missing?' I asked.

Mr Wright tilted his head right back and his wife lowered hers miserably.

'Since the night of Saturday the second of August,' she said.

'At what time and where did you last see her?' I tried, though the date was horribly familiar and Mr G had perked up on hearing it.

'She was a vexatious girl,' Mr Wright burst out.

'Not bad,' his wife protested mildly. 'Just high-spirited.'

69

'I do not believe – because I have no reason to do so – that Miss Middleton's interrogation incorporated a supplementary question regarding your incongruously labelled progeny's character,' Mr G remarked, the hand on his knee fluttering rapidly now. 'Perhaps I could entice you to satisfy her curiosity.'

Mrs Wright put her hand into the small satin handbag on her lap. 'At about nine o'clock that night,' she told me, 'she said her wisdom tooth was hurting and she wanted an early night.'

Mr Wright forced his head up as if his neck were rusty. 'At about half past ten, I sent Ann-Jane, our maid, to check if Albertoria was asleep, only to be informed that she was not in her room and her bed had not been slept in.'

'And how did the put-upon Ann-Jane ascertain that last allegation?' My guardian's hand stopped about four inches above his leg.

Mr Wright puzzled for a few seconds. 'Because the sheets had not been disturbed.'

'And your daughter could not possible have straightened them or plumped up a pillow?' Mr G leaped in.

'Well, I suppose—'

'Suppositions are of slight use to me.' Sidney Grice ignored my mouthed entreaties. 'You must approach a greater degree of accuracy if you wish to avail yourself of some of my superlative powers.'

Mrs Wright withdrew a tiny square of white lace from her handbag and dabbed the corners of her eyes, and her husband's jaw muscles bunched angrily.

'Can you describe your daughter?' I asked.

'They would be even poorer parents than they seem if they could not,' my guardian muttered.

'Now see here.' Mr Wright squared up to the detective.

'I see everywhere that can be seen.' Sidney Grice tossed his head.

'Sixteen,' Mrs Wright said, 'about your height and build, but pretty – lovely auburn hair and beautiful green eyes.'

'We shall need some more details if we are to help you find her,' I began.

'And a sweet little freckle here.' Mrs Wright dabbed the left side of her nose and burst out with, 'Oh, I am so afraid.'

Mr Wright leaned over and squeezed his wife's shoulder.

'We must be brave for Albertoria, my dear,' he encouraged her before turning back to the detective. 'You see, Mr Grice, we fear—' His voice cracked but he fought to continue. 'We fear that our daughter may have been found and lost already.'

Sidney Grice seemed lost in thought but his face glowed. I never met a man so entranced by the prospect of death.

15

The Return of the Detective

REDDY DID NOT come out to greet us on our second visit to Amber House but was sitting defiantly with an open book on her lap at Lucy's side when Aellen, the maid, showed us into another sitting room, across the hall from the blue room.

Lucy was working on a piece of needlepoint. She was in a high-backed armchair beside the front window, her feet on a circular pompom and her legs covered with a Cameron tartan blanket.

'In deference to your loathing of greenery,' Lucy greeted us, 'I thought we would convene in pink today.' Sidney Grice curled up his nose and her warm green eyes crinkled in amusement. 'You do not approve?'

'Pink is the colour of dead salmon and under-cooked mammalian flesh.' My guardian lowered his satchel to the floor, reeling out the strap as if depositing an unstable explosive device. 'It is in the eyes of strangled rabbits. Pink is a colour of death.'

'It is also the colour of roses, sunsets and flamingos,' I pointed out and stepped forward to kiss Lucy.

'Even worse.' He doubled up so suddenly that I feared he had been taken ill. But he was only fiddling with his left bootlace, and I hoped that he was not wearing the pair that had crampons hinged into their soles.

'I should very much like Freddy to stay today,' Lucy asserted as we sat on two shepherdess chairs.

Mr G shot up, his hair falling into a long fringe. 'And so should I,' he agreed, with such alacrity that Freddy, who had clearly built up a head of steam for an argument, looked all at once deflated.

'You will take tea?' Lucy enquired as Mr G flopped down again to finish retying the lace.

'No.' He hinged up in an unnervingly mechanical way and, as Freddy shifted to view his capers, I glimpsed her profile against the bright daylight. It reminded me of a photograph I had seen of the actress, Ellen Terry.

Oh, Freddy, I thought. *You must have been so pretty.*

Freddy caught my gaze and I looked away.

'Is something wrong?' She trained her hair forward across her cheek.

'Nothing.' I smiled unconvincingly.

My guardian smoothed out a wrinkle on his sleeve. 'If that were true I would find myself compelled to reappraise my motives for coming here.' He leaped upon a newly created crease. 'For I was given to believe that a great deal was amiss.' And, ignoring their perplexity, Sidney Grice lowered his long, slim, elegant nose into the crook of his right thumb, and his elbow on to the armrest cover of his chair. 'So, Miss Bocking,' he said, just as I was wondering if he had nodded off, 'have you prepared yourself to give me an account of your interesting experiences?'

Lucy's eyes shadowed. '*Interesting?*'

'You do yourself a grave injustice if you pretend that they were dull.' Mr G collapsed again, arms dangling, but, instead of doing up his laces, tied his left boot to the right like a wayward child playing a prank on an adult.

Lucy put down her needlework and picked up an empty lead-crystal posy vase.

'Where shall I start?' She toyed with the vase, the voile-filtered sunshine glittering off its cut-glass facets.

73

'We know how you got to the Golden Dragon and how you smoked opium,' I recapitulated. 'Can you bring yourself to tell us what happened next?'

'If not I might as well go home.' Sidney Grice finished an elaborate knot and sat back, exhausted by his endeavours.

Freddy slammed her book shut. 'Perhaps you should.'

And my godfather regarded her coolly. 'From henceforth I suggest that you speak only when you have something intelligent to say – which is rarely, if ever.'

Freddy flung her book on to the floor, where it landed face down, and its spine cracked. *Sylvia's Lovers*, I read sideways on the cover. 'And might I suggest that you leave? I think Miss Bocking has had enough of your outrageous behaviour, Mr Grice, and so have I.'

There was a clatter and I turned to see Lucy picking her vase off the table, mercifully unbroken.

Mr G sipped his tea, rolling it around his mouth before swallowing. 'You are here under sufferance, Miss Wilde, and what you might suggest is of only peripheral interest to me.'

Freddy kicked the book and it skimmed under a lacquered dresser. 'Tell him to go, Lucy,' she urged.

Lucy Bocking touched her friend's wrist and said quietly, 'That might be best.'

'It certainly might be,' Sidney Grice agreed, 'if you wish to spend the rest of your life in suffering from the insult that has been offered to your person, and in ignorance of the identity of your violator, but as long as there is breath in my body and money in your coffers I shall do almost everything within my powers to save you.'

16

The Peacock Weeping Blood

THE SILENCE WAS broken by Freddy. 'Fine words,' she mocked. She had put some ointment on her face and it glistened.

'I do not have to convince *you*,' Sidney Grice responded pleasantly.

'He *will* do it,' I assured them.

'Your loyalty is touching,' Freddy sneered and Lucy patted her wrist.

'Freddy is very protective of me,' she said. 'I only wish you would not keep distressing her.'

'Surely that cannot be your only wish.' Mr G rubbed his wounded shoulder. 'And Miss Wilde has exhibited a great deal of hostility towards me.'

Freddy bristled. 'If you tried to be a bit nicer...'

'One cannot be nicer if one is not nice to begin with.' Sidney Grice balanced the notebook to stand vertically on the arm of his chair. 'And, since I am not, your exhortation to make an attempt is in vain.'

'In that case...'

'If you two are going to squabble all morning I might as well have stayed at home,' I scolded, taken aback at how much like my godfather I sounded, and Freddy and Mr G froze like naughty children. 'But, since we are here, shall we try to progress with the investigation?'

Lucy Bocking passed the needle up through her work, a peacock on an open-weave rectangle of canvas, his fan yet to progress beyond a saffron skeleton.

'What happened that night?' I urged.

Lucy looped the thread down and up again. 'I was very swimmy,' she said at last and Mr G leaned sharply towards her.

'Define *swimmy*.'

'It was like being intoxicated.'

'Is it an American word?' He clicked his fingers and his notebook fell into his hand.

Lucy touched her damaged cheekbone. 'I do not think so.'

'What a relief.' He conjured up his Mordan mechanical pencil. 'Spelled with two M's?'

'I believe so.'

Sidney Grice regarded her dubiously. 'Proceed with your fascinating account.'

'I fell into a kind of stupor.'

TWO M's he printed in block capitals. 'What kind of stu-por?'

'I was almost asleep but still aware of what was going on.'

'Like an evening at the opera.' He shuddered. 'So what *was* going on?'

It was as if Lucy had not heard the question. She turned her attention to her sewing.

'I am sorry,' I commiserated, 'but we must know if we are to help.'

At that moment Lucy Bocking became fragile and vulnerable. Her hand was unsteady as she continued with her work. Freddy pushed the table aside and kneeled before her friend.

'You *can* do it, Lucy,' she reassured her, 'and you must. Is that monster to go free and repeat his crimes with other young women?'

'Stop.' Lucy took a long unsteady breath. 'I felt myself being pushed backwards,' she continued at last, 'and my skirts being pulled up.' She spoke low and quickly. 'And a man got on top of me.'

'Did you struggle?' Sidney Grice asked and Lucy flared.

'I did not encourage him,' she retorted bitterly.

'Sometimes women are too frightened to resist,' he explicated, 'and the men have believed or pretended to believe this signifies consent.'

'And you think that justifies their actions?' Freddy snapped.

Mr G put a finger to his eye. 'I would not be here if I did.'

'Perhaps you just want the money,' she jibed.

'Some of that sentence was true,' my godfather agreed pleasantly. 'I do want the money but I do not *just* want it, for I do not need it and, if that were my only motivation in life, I would be better off murdering my father who has a great deal of it. Forgive your acquaintance's digressions, Miss Lucinda Sephora Bocking, and react appropriately to my enquiry.'

Lucy grimaced. 'I tried to fight him off, but he was too strong and heavy and I was confused. I did not really believe it was happening at first.'

'Did you see him?' I asked.

'No.' The needle was being worked furiously now. 'As I was trying to explain, my skirts were up over my head.'

'Did he speak?'

'Not then.' Lucy pricked herself and Freddy flinched.

'Did he smell of anything – soap, cologne, tobacco, alcohol, coffee, rendered fat, fish, fresh or stale sweat?' Sidney Grice curled his nose as if being assailed by all those aromas at once.

'No.' A red teardrop welled on to her fingertip and the two women watched it in fascination. 'I do not think so... cologne perhaps.'

'I cannot think of a delicate way to phrase this,' I began.

'Did he violate you?' Sidney Grice broke in, 'I assume you know what violation means.'

'For heaven's sake,' Freddy said in disgust and the drop quivered.

Lucy jerked her head briskly and the drop broke free, fell and burst on to her tapestry. 'Yes, I do, and yes, he did.' A bright stain flooded over the peacock's wing.

'Completely?' Mr G pressed and I could hardly hear Lucy's response. 'Speak up.'

'Yes.' She dropped the needle and let it hang by its crimson thread. 'Completely – and I know what that means too – but even that was not enough for him, Mr Grice. He beat me.'

'Was this before or during the act?' I asked tentatively.

'What the hell does that matter?' Freddy demanded fiercely and Mr G cocked his head away from me.

'Before might have been to subdue his victim,' I explained. 'During indicates a pleasure in the act of violence itself.'

'Dear God, what a world you live in,' Lucy said, with something approaching pity.

'We all live in it,' I told her, 'but Mr Grice and I are trying to do something about it.'

I glanced across and my guardian printed *TRYING*.

'It was during and after,' Lucy replied.

'Open hand or closed fist?' Sidney Grice held out both hands to demonstrate the alternatives.

'Open at first – slapping my legs, then my arms, but only two or three times – and then my face with the front and back of his hand many times.'

'In what manner did he strike you?' He ran the end of his pencil across his lower teeth like a stick on railings.

'I do not know what that means,' Freddy protested.

'You do not need to.' Sidney Grice twisted the handle of his cane six times to wind up whatever mechanism it contained. 'Miss Bocking comprehends and will respond accordingly.'

Lucy collected herself. 'Not wildly at first,' she answered. 'Slowly and deliberately like a parent chastising a child.'

'An interesting simile.' Mr G made a note and overlined it.

'Did he pull your skirts down to hit your face?' I asked and Lucy's shoulders shook.

I half rose to go to her, but my godfather raised an arm to halt me.

'Yes.' She motioned Freddy away as if feeling suffocated, and Freddy slid back but stayed on her knees. 'But I still could not see him properly. The lamps had been extinguished.'

'And then?' I pressed as gently as I could.

'Then he started to punch me – in the body, on my breasts and on my face while he was still—' Lucy stroked the peacock's head to brush away its tears but her action only resulted in smearing them. 'Then, after he had finished with me and I thought everything was over, he became angry and more violent, hammering at me with his fists and, while he was doing it, he spoke – more of a whisper with his mouth close to my ear.'

Lucy looked at the floor.

'What did he say?' I asked at last.

'*Dirty.* He said *dirty dirty girl.*'

'Describe his voice and accent.' Sidney Grice pressed a button and his cane whirred, and a pair of curved calipers emerged through the ferule.

'Angry, quite deep, foreign – perhaps German or Dutch – German, I should say.'

'Indeed you have.' Mr G prodded the plate of biscuits with his device. 'Do you know any citizens of Das Deutsche Reich?'

'I have met a few.'

'You did not recognize the voice?' I asked.

'I did not.'

I tried again. 'Did he say anything else?'

'Yes, later.'

'Then tell us when you reach that point.' Sidney Grice pressed the button again and the claws closed smoothly on a Marie biscuit.

'He stopped for a while,' Lucy said wonderingly, 'and I thought he had really finished, but it was only to take his belt off and to whip me with the buckle.' Lucy recoiled at the memory of the blows. 'And then he stopped again.'

'Bother.' The biscuit snapped, showering crumbs over the tray. 'What next?' he asked absently, his attention seemingly fixed on retracting the calipers.

'He put his belt back on.' Lucy hesitated. 'I think. But even then he was not done. He kneeled astride me, his knees pinning my arms.'

'And do you have contusions on both limbs?' My guardian's voice boomed.

'Yes.' Lucy's voice was weak in comparison. 'Mainly on my shoulders.'

'I should very much like to see those.'

'You shall not.'

'I might.'

I spoke when it was apparent that nobody else intended to do so. 'What happened next?'

Lucy held her right arm protectively across her as if it were in a sling. 'He grabbed hold of my hair.'

'Front, back and/or sides?' Sidney Grice asked eagerly. 'One hand or two?'

'His left hand near the front at the top.' Lucy touched the spot. 'He forced my head back and I saw the glint of metal and I thought—' Lucy covered her mouth.

'Do you wish to stop?' I asked and she shook her head.

'I need to say it while I have the strength. I thought he was going to cut my throat.' She put up a protective hand. 'But he dug the tip of the blade into my forehead and cut me.'

Sidney Grice brought his folding magnifier out of his satchel.

'I am sorry to press you,' I said. 'But again, was this a frenzied act or—'

'It was not a wild slash,' Lucy replied flatly. 'He did it slowly – deliberately, like an incision.'

'I shall take this opportunity,' Mr G got up and slid his feet cautiously as if testing for thin ice, his laces still tied together, 'to examine the laceration, the creation of which you so vividly recollect.'

'Lucy is hardly likely to forget it,' Freddy objected, and Mr G twisted his body, feet firmly planted on the spot.

'Do I have to expel you from this disappointing house before I can get some peace from your incessant jibber-jabber?' He flipped open his magnifying glass. 'You may wish to expose your own brow,' he advised Lucy. 'Rather than give me free rein to rummage through your coiffure.'

Lucy parted and raised her fringe. The scar was in the form of a rough X, the top right arm being foreshortened, wide and white with red, raised edges.

Sidney Grice bent over, his nose almost touching hers as he stared through his glass.

Lucy's lips parted. 'I feel like a butterfly pinned on a collector's board.'

'The resemblance is superficial and fleeting.' Sidney Grice inhaled. 'You do not, *per exemplu*, have any visible wings or antennae. In what directions did this disagreeable man draw his blade?'

'My top right down and then the top left down,' Lucy recalled, and Sidney Grice traced the directions on her skin with his thumb like a priest anointing her for the last rites.

'You are certain of that?'

'Yes.'

'Certain enough that a man's life might hang upon your remembrance?'

'Yes,' Lucy repeated firmly.

Mr G ran his forefinger over the scar again and Lucy closed her eyes, seemingly comforted by his touch.

'Does it hurt?' He reversed directions.

'Not when you do that.'

'It is closing cleanly,' he decided, 'and may well heal completely.'

He brushed his finger along the lines a fourth time.

'Do you really think so?' Lucy sank back, mesmerized.

'I have a minuscule quantity of doubt of it.' My godfather scratched a tiny crust with his fingerplate from where the two lines intersected. 'Though, of course, you shall always be scarred.'

He pulled away and Lucy opened her eyes and, to my surprise, merely nodded.

'What else did he say?' I asked, and whatever spell she was under was broken.

'*Remember who did this,*' her voice rasped huskily.

'Prior, simultaneous or subsequent to him cutting you?' Mr G shuffled backwards to his chair like a flunkey taking leave of his monarch.

'At the same time,' Lucy said.

'As if he were making his mark,' I conjectured.

'It was probably the only signature he could manage.' Freddy's voice hardened with contempt, but her friend was lost in that room now, eyes searching the night for what she could not see.

'Did he speak again?' I asked and Lucy jolted back into the living world.

'Twice. First it was *Had enough?* And I think I said *Yes.* I was too stunned to really know what I was doing. Then he ripped open my dress at the top and said *Scream* and so I did, again and again. By then I was on the floor.'

'You were still on the sofa when he kneeled on you?' I asked. That was not how I had imagined it.

'Yes.' Lucy closed her fringe like the curtains of a puppet show. 'And I still have the bruises to prove it.'

Mr G perked up. 'I should very much like to see those,' he said again.

'You shall not,' Lucy repeated even more firmly.

'For what it is worth, I have seen them,' Freddy volunteered, but Sidney Grice did not even acknowledge her.

'At what stage did you quit the comforts of the sofa?' He printed, as he spoke, over two entire pages *I DO NOT REMEMBER* and shut his book smartly.

Lucy dabbed her eyes. 'I do not remember falling, just being kicked and stamped on and curling up, trying to cover my face.'

'You have had enough for today,' I said firmly and prepared to do battle with my guardian, but Sidney Grice was swivelling in his chair to face Freddy. A beam of sunshine scattered from his glass eye, the spectrum caressing on his cheek.

'Whereas you,' he rotated his wounded shoulder which had benefited little from the hot weather, 'have been what some might regard as suspiciously quiet.'

17

The Pipes and the Pendulum

FREDDY JUTTED HER jaw, but it was so delicate that she looked more like a little girl pouting than an angry woman. 'What an impertinence.'

Sidney Grice intertwined his fingers. 'Let us begin, Miss Wilde, with Miss Bocking's possibly slanderous assertion that it was you who suggested visiting an opium den.'

'I suppose I did.'

He inverted his hands to create a bowl. 'Why?'

'I had taken opium before,' Freddy admitted. 'It helps me forget.'

'Forget what?' my guardian asked, and she chewed her lips and burst out, 'How much of my life do you imagine I wish to remember?'

'Had you used the Golden Dragon opium house before, Freddy?' I asked hurriedly.

'Never.'

Mr G peered, mystified, into the bowl.

'Why did you not use a previous haunt?' I asked and Freddy touched her amulet.

'Two of them had tried to fob me off by mixing talcum powder into the resin.' She looked abashed. 'The third had evicted me after I... misbehaved.'

'With a gentleman?' I asked, as tactfully as I could and before my guardian could be more direct, but he was occupied in pulling his bowl apart.

Freddy blushed. 'I thought he would be as... affected as I was and so...' She swallowed. 'I tried to kiss him. He opened his eyes.' She bowed her head at the memory. 'And he screamed.' She exhaled. 'There – now you have it. I am humiliated and how does it help your enquiry?'

I did not have an answer for that, but Sidney Grice patted his left knee twice to comfort himself and said, 'All truth is important and Miss Middleton has accessed information of which I was previously and dismayingly in ignorance.'

'How many pipes did you smoke, Freddy?' I took hold of my saucer.

'Three.' She gingerly touched her inflamed left eyelid. 'And then I fell asleep.'

'You saw nothing suspicious before that?' I tried my tea but it was too cold to drink with any pleasure.

'Nothing.'

'When did you wake up?'

'When somebody put a bag over my head and I heard him saying *That's an improvement* – though it was more like *zats* or *dats* – and I felt a drawstring being pulled round my neck so tight I thought I was being strangled.' Freddy put a hand to her throat. 'Then I was pulled to my feet.'

'How?' Mr G took hold of his elbows.

'By the cord.' Freddy massaged her neck. 'I was dragged backwards and hauled up so that I had to stand on tiptoes.' She pulled at the front of her collar. 'I found out later that the drawstring had been looped over a hook and I was turned to face the wall and my hands were tied behind me. I could not see anything. I could hardly breathe.' Panic darted around her eyes. 'It was so hot. I thought—'

'I am not very interested in what you thought.' My guardian hugged himself. 'Could you hear anything?'

Freddy worked her fingers under her collar. 'Everything was muffled. I heard bumps and crashes and Lucy screaming.'

'Does Miss Bocking have a unique scream?' Mr G's arms flew apart and the notebook disappeared into one of his numerous inner coat pockets.

Freddy scrunched her brow. 'I do not think so.'

'Then am I to take it that you assumed that the screams, which you claim to have heard, came from her?'

'Of course.'

'Of course.' He savoured the sound of the words before adding, 'Most people would agree that it was a reasonable assumption to make.' He puffed out his cheeks. 'However, I have yet to formulate the desire to enter into concord with you about anything. Proceed.'

'I could not struggle for fear of choking. I tried to call out.'

'What?' Sidney Grice dangled his watch on its chain. 'And why?'

Freddy flushed. 'Just Lucy's name. I do not know exactly why.'

'People do call out to each other in crises,' I interpolated.

My guardian greeted that statement quizzically. 'Do you have personal experience of such a situation?'

Edward! I heard it as clearly as the day I cradled his bloodied face.

'Yes.'

The watch swung like a pendulum.

'Then you may expand upon that remark when you are solitary for nobody else is interested.' Sidney Grice pointed at Freddy Wilde. 'Resume your unusual account.'

'I do not know how long I was hanging there...'

'Then do not devastate my time with conjecture.' My guardian slipped his hunter back into his waistcoat pocket. 'I can calculate for my own secret purposes that it was more than a second and less than a decade.'

Freddy clearly struggled to suppress a retort. 'Eventually I was aware of somebody untying my wrists,' she said as evenly as she could. 'The—'

'Wrists?' Sidney Grice pounced on the word like a snake on a rabbit, chewing it over in his mind before digesting it. 'You told me your hands were tied and I transcribed your statement. Am I to believe—' he produced his notebook and rustled though the pages, jabbing a slopping line of squirls with an accusatory knuckle—'that I have sullied my black, cloth-bound, three-hundred-and-eighty-four-ounce quality paper notebook with,' his voice took on a tone of moral outrage, 'a falsehood?'

Freddy slipped her right fingers under her left cuff as if to check the truth of her own statement. 'I meant my wrists.'

Sidney Grice closed his notebook reverently and clutched it to his heart. 'I once met a woman who was capable of saying what she meant.' His expression became dreamy. 'Though, of course, she never did.' He stroked the smooth spine. 'Discontinue your discontinuance.'

'I—'

'You were rudely interrupted after voicing the definite article,' my godfather reminded her gently.

'The,' Freddy recommenced uncertainly.

'Well done,' he encouraged her.

'The blood rushed back into my hands.' Freddy eyed him uneasily. 'They were burning.'

My guardian balanced his notebook on the tip of his left thumb.

'It was me,' Lucy said.

'You were burning her hands?' Mr G gaped in astonishment.

'No, I mean I untied Freddy.'

'Her hands or her wrists?' He leafed through his notes until he came upon an elongated ampersand taking up an otherwise blank sheet of paper. 'Miss Wilde has given scant evidence of being capable of distinguishing between them.'

'Of course she can,' I snapped, tired of whatever game he was playing now.

'For her sake I hope – though not with any great solicitude – that you are correct in that assertion, Miss Middleton.' Sidney Grice drew a second ampersand inside the first. 'For, if she cannot, she must suffer many varieties of inconvenience. How,' he tipped his Mordan mechanical pencil towards our hostess, 'how did you travel to Miss Wilde?'

'I managed to crawl over.'

'On your knees, or your hands and knees, or forearms and knees, or elbows and knees?' Mr G wagged his pencil almost in time with his words. 'And do not distress me by asking why that matters.'

'Hands and knees,' Lucy replied crisply. 'And I wish you showed the same concern about distressing us.'

'I rarely feel, let alone exhibit, empathy and you have taken centre stage for long enough.' Mr G rubbed his hands together vigorously. 'Kindly be quiet and let your strange housemate hold our attention a while longer.'

'I shall not be silenced in my own house,' Lucy protested angrily.

'But dear, nice Miss Bocking, do you not comprehend that that is exactly what is happening,' he explained nicely. 'Pray recommence your narration, Miss Wilde.'

Freddy looked uncertainly at her companion, who threw up her hands in surrender.

'Lucy put a footstool by my feet and I managed to get one foot and then the—'

'Other.' Mr G covered his mouth in an ostentatious yawn. 'And now, pleasant Miss Bocking, since you are so keen to dominate the proceedings, perhaps you would explain why you have lied to me since the marvellous moment that we met.'

18

Dressing Up and the Dissembleologist

I AM NOT SURE which of the three women in that room was most outraged by Sidney Grice's last remark, but it was Freddy, of course, who sprang to her friend's defence.

'Lucy has told you nothing but the truth.'

'Quite possibly.'

'Then how...?' She stumbled for words.

'Mr Barf Regal.' Mr G's fingers set off on a ramble around his palm. 'The dissembleologist has it that there are ninety-eight varieties of lies, but I have invented – though never utilized – another three. Fortunately for Miss Bocking – since she shall be paying excessively for my time – they can be divided broadly into two classes. The first is a deception based upon a false state-ment – *exempli gratia* if I ask your sex and you tell me you are a man: that is a lie by commission. The second is a deception based upon concealing the truth – *exempli gratia* if you were in fact a man in disguise and neglected to grant me that informa-tion: that would be a lie by omission.' Sidney Grice waited for his information to be absorbed before concluding, 'Miss Bocking stands – though seated – accused of the latter offence.'

'I do not know what you are talking about,' Freddy blustered and he tugged his scarred earlobe.

'I am not fascinated by your inability to comprehend unex-acting statements,' my guardian told her. 'What is important is that your delightful companion knows *exactly* what I am talking about. Do you not,' his cane lashed out, stopping a quarter of an inch from Lucy's neck, 'Miss so-called *Lucy* Bocking.'

Freddy and I jumped at the swiftness of Mr G's movement, but Lucy only blinked and said, 'I wanted to test your powers of observation.'

'And I your candidness,' he rejoined.

'Would one of you like to explain?' I asked tetchily.

And Lucy's hand went to her throat. 'Your guardian is referring to my choker.'

'You always wear it,' I recalled and crinkled my eyes. 'What did that button come from?'

Sidney Grice lowered his cane. 'You may answer the question.'

And Lucy shifted to take the weight off her right side. 'I trust you are not accusing me of anything else, Mr Grice.'

Sidney Grice's eyes crinkled like those of a kindly uncle playing with his niece. 'Oh, Miss Bocking, pleasant young Miss Bocking, wealthy yet wounded Miss Lucinda Seraphora Bocking, if only you knew how many splendid men and gorgeous women had said that to me just before I handed them over to the Met-ro-pol-it-an Police.'

'You go too far.' Freddy slammed her fist on the table, rattling the crockery and splashing the milk on to the cloth.

My guardian looked at me as if I had made the accusation, but said, 'For once you are right, Miss Wilde, but it is only by going too far that one can hope to come back to one's destination.'

'I think I ripped it off his waistcoat,' Lucy burst out.

'How do you know it was not his coat or his shirt?' Mr G crossed his arms on his chest like a corpse in a wake.

'Because my thumb caught on his watch chain.' Lucy Bocking sucked her finger. 'Besides, look at the size of it.'

'Wonderful.' Mr G whisked his feet apart and the knot he had created earlier separated, leaving his laces tied in their customary neat bows. 'Miss Middleton would do well to take note of your observational processes.'

I resisted the impulse to empty the teapot over his head, and addressed Lucy. 'At what stage was this?'

Lucy rubbed circles just above her hairline, as if to ease a headache, and said huskily, 'I think… as I was falling. I grabbed hold of what I could to try to save myself, and when it had ended I found it clenched in my fist.'

Sidney Grice shot to his feet and, for a moment, I thought he was going to take the button by force, but he only said, 'Cross my palm with dentine.' and Lucy obediently withdrew the four gold pins which she had passed through the holes in the button and dropped it into his hand.

'Please, if it is not too much trouble, might I ask if there was any thread attached?' my guardian enquired meekly.

'I wonder at your sanity,' Lucy said, incredulous at the sea change in his manner, and Sidney Grice looked wounded.

'It was a civil and pertinent question,' he pointed out mildly.

'The answer is no,' Lucy told him.

'Do you mean *no*, I may not ask, or *no*, there was no thread?'

'The latter.'

'Not yes?' he pressed hopefully.

'No.'

'Oh,' he mulled quietly. 'A short word but redolent with meaning. I shall retain this carved and perforated disc.'

'Nobody has given you permission,' Freddy objected.

'I did not seek permission.' He lurched across the room some nine limping paces, to stand between two portraits. 'Therefore it cannot be refused.' His head swivelled from one to the other like a tennis umpire. 'Mr and Mrs Clorence Bocking, your putative progenitors. How—' he spun back— 'did they die?'

'Why are you so determined to upset Lucy?' Freddy Wilde raged.

Sidney Grice posed like a blackbird listening for a worm. 'My thirst to bring this matter to a conclusion is unquenchable.' He took one pace to his right. 'And so I must insist upon an answer, and please – for I am ever eager to avoid giving offence – do *not* ask me to explain why my question is pertinent.'

Lucy clenched her needlework. 'I am sure you know the answer already, Mr Grice.'

The detective stretched out his arms to either side until they were parallel to the floor. 'I have perused the police and newspaper reports and am at a loss to know which to disbelieve the most.'

Lucy picked distractedly at the end of a loose red thread. 'My parents were murdered.' She gazed at him steadily. 'It was an act of revenge by Dester Green, the father of Jocinda, a maid.'

'Revenge for what?' I asked and Lucy looked about for an escape route.

'She was caught stealing from Freddy's home and, when her room was searched, it was found that she had taken a lot of our things too, silly trifles really – a napkin ring, silver but not a valuable one, a brass candlestick, one of a matching pair, a hairbrush, lots of little things over a few months. My parents would have let Jocinda go without pressing charges. She had been almost a part of the family, and Freddy's parents agreed – they were kind-hearted people – but her father came to the house and made threats and would not leave, and so the police were called. Jocinda was sentenced to eighteen months in prison and her father was given four months hard labour.'

'But why did he wait so long to retaliate?' I asked.

Mr G was examining Mrs Bocking's mouth in her portrait with his pocket magnifying glass.

'Dester Green attacked a warder in a failed escape bid and was sentenced to another seven years.' Lucy passed her needle up though the fabric.

'Not very bright of him,' I commented.

'He was from the north of England.' My guardian swivelled to meet my glare guilelessly.

Lucy closed her eyes. 'The day after he was released, Dester Green got a skinning knife and attacked my parents on their evening constitutional.'

'I do not remember reading about that,' I puzzled, for I had devoured accounts of gruesome crimes since I was a child, and a double killing like that would normally fill many a yard of newspaper.

Mr G peered into Mrs Bocking's ear. 'The news was swept aside by the floundering of the *Eurydice*.'

And it was not difficult to understand why, for that disaster had dominated the minds of the public for months. A ship manned mainly by young trainees had sped without incident across the vast Atlantic Ocean only to founder off the Isle of Wight in a snowstorm with over three hundred lives being lost.

'So close to home,' Freddy breathed, and I was not sure if she meant the *Eurydice* or the Bockings.

'And, because the investigation was left in the hands of the almost fabulously incompetent Chief Inspector Grundaway,' Sidney Grice turned his glass on to Mr Bocking's neck as if searching for the fatal wound, 'Dester Green was acquitted.'

'But why?' I asked as my godfather limped back towards us.

Lucy Bocking let go of her needlework, leaving it crumpled in her lap.

'It was a dark night and he ran away.' There was such bitterness in her voice now. 'The police traced him through a silver charm shaped like a safety pencil sharpener that he dropped on the scene. It must have been one that Jocinda had stolen. They were so sure they had their man that they did not trouble to search for further clues.'

Lucy lowered her head.

'The defence were able to demonstrate that at least thirty other people had identical charms,' Freddy put in.

'Including one Addrum Droffer, a sacked clerk, who had been heard to threaten Clorrence Bocking in St Lawrence's Church.' Sidney Grice bobbed to pick up the book, without breaking his stride.

I shuffled my feet for I had new boots on and they pinched. 'Do you think Dester Green might have had something to do with the attack upon you?'

'Unlikely.' Sidney Grice tossed his coat up at the back to avoid crushing it as he regained his seat. 'He was axed in the vertebral column in yet another brawl and almost paralysed.'

'I believe he tries to communicate by blinking, but nobody in the poorhouse can be troubled to work out what he is saying.'

I shivered. Wicked though Dester Green undoubtedly was, the idea of being trapped in such a way chilled my blood.

'What did Jocinda steal from your house, Freddy?'

'A yellow dress I had worn to Lucy's parents' garden party the summer before the fire.'

'Shall I continue my account of the circumstances of the assault?' Lucy pressed.

'I have little doubt that you shall,' the detective assured her. 'But kindly do not do so before I have quit the premises.'

He held the book by its spine and shook it vigorously but nothing fell out. I noticed the title, *Endymion*, in pale lettering.

Lucy flushed and wriggled under her blanket. 'If you do not want me to tell you anything else, why have you come?'

Sidney Grice marked a page with an omnibus ticket, though where he got that from I had no idea, for I never knew him to use that means of transport.

'To learn a little of your early lives.' He put the book on his lap. 'Starting with yours, Miss Wilde, since you are usually the one who is cruelly ignored.'

'By you,' Freddy pointed out.

'To whom else would I be referring?' he said reasonably. 'Miss Middleton is almost pathologically kind and Miss

Bocking gives the impression of being overly fond of you.'

'Overly?' they chorused.

'That was nicely listened.' Sidney Grice brushed and slapped his sleeve vigorously as if it were starting to smoulder. 'But, to return to you, Miss Freda Josephina Wilde.' He blew on his left knuckles. 'Prior to the combustion of your parents' reputedly splendid home and its several occupants, did you have a jubilant childhood filled with love and laughter?'

'What on earth has that to do with what happened to me?' Lucy swivelled towards him.

'It might take me days, weeks, months or even years to give that clever enquiry the response which it merits.' Mr G bared his teeth briefly though not cheerfully. 'For I shall not know it until this case is solved and your money snuggling down in my over-stuffed coffers.' He took up the book again, as if about to swear an oath. 'Kindly permit your sometime-irascible companion to answer my question.'

'It was happy enough, I suppose,' Freddy snapped, thereby at least partially justifying my guardian's description of her.

'According to Mr Gringham Heartley, assistant clerk to the Registrar General of the General Register Office of England and Wales in the North Wing of Somerset House,' the detective said, as he replaced *Endymion* on the oval mahogany table at his side, 'you had three brothers, two of whom perished before you were born and one before your first birthday.'

Lucy flared angrily. 'I did not employ you to pry into our private affairs.'

Coffers, he wrote, then said, 'As our ancient foes, the boorish, attenuated and ineffectual French might say, *au contraire*.'

'But only insofar as they concern the attack upon my person,' she argued.

'Oh dear.' Sidney Grice pinched the bridge of his nose. 'Why have so many beautiful women thought they could dictate the course of my investigations?'

Lucy rounded on my guardian. 'I will thank you not to make any more comments about my appearance.'

'I shall not give you grounds for gratitude,' he avowed. 'And so, Miss Wilde, to all intents and purposes, you were reared as an only child.'

'Yes,' Freddy agreed. 'And I believe I nearly died from whooping cough when I was three. I fear that, as a result, my parents spoiled me.'

'I wondered who had,' my godfather murmured. 'You are five months and one day younger than Miss Bocking.'

'Yes, and we have lived almost all of our lives close to each other,' Freddy volunteered.

'That was not a question, but thank you for that unsolicited information,' Mr G said, and she bristled before realizing that he was not being sarcastic. 'Let me direct my attention,' he mimed the washing of his hands, 'to the current employer of some of my unequalled abilities. You lived – did you not? – until shortly after your parents' slaughter, in the unimaginatively and now inappropriately named New House on Abbey Road, adjacent to Steep House, the residence of the menacingly named Wilde family. Mr Gringham Heartley and Miss Freda Wilde separately gave me cause to suspect that you had a brother.'

'Eric.' Lucy pulled her lower lip tightly up. 'He was five years older than me.' Her upper lip forced her lower down. 'Eric died in the fire.'

'Poor Eric.' Freddy took her friend's hand. 'He was a lovely, gentle boy.'

ELTNEG Mr G wrote. 'Oblige me for once by defining *lovely*.'

'Sweet-natured.' Freddy poured milk into three cups.

'And handsome?' I asked, not sure why that was relevant but pleased to hear my godfather humph approvingly.

'Very,' Lucy said without hesitation.

'You have a photograph of him, Lucy,' Freddy reminded her.

And Lucy shifted. 'I am not sure where it is.'

Freddy treated us to a rare brief laugh. 'Lucy is always losing things.'

'That is not possible.' The spring knife appeared in my god-father's grasp but disappeared so quickly that I almost thought I had imagined it. 'Even the most careless person – a title for which Miss Middleton could intermittently compete – must spare the time to perform other tasks.'

All three women groaned.

'And Eric died in the fire,' I recapitulated, shocked at how hard my softly spoken words came out.

Freddy puffed out her lips. 'He broke in to try to save us but was trapped in the front cellar before he managed to rescue anyone.'

'What would have induced him to go down there?' Mr G was trying to balance a gunmetal pen vertically on the tip of his middle finger.

'To escape the flames, I suppose,' Lucy replied. 'And, once he was down there, the only way out was by the stairs into the hall.'

'It was a courageous act,' I mused. 'Was he very attached to your parents, Freddy?'

Freddy avoided her friend's gaze. 'They did not really get on,' she admitted reluctantly.

'Eric's main concern would have been Freddy.' Lucy spoke in a monotone. 'He had a bit of a soft spot for her.'

Sidney Grice caught the pen as it fell.

'It was just a schoolboy thing,' Freddy protested bashfully, 'and I would hate to think that Eric was lost because of it.'

A tear trickled down Freddy Wilde's cheek and Lucy patted the hand that enclosed her own.

'I like to think that he was.' Lucy dabbed her own eyes. 'I like to think that Eric died for love.'

Mr G tried again, the pen teetering on his oscillating finger.

I struggled to ignore his antics. 'How did you get out, Freddy?'

'I do not remember anything between going to bed and waking up in pain.' Her hand hovered over the biscuits. 'Fairbank, the butler, found me unconscious and carried me out.'

She pulled back without selecting anything.

'How...' Sidney Grice glimpsed my expression and put the pen back into his pocket. 'How did brother Eric break in?'

'Through a ground-floor window, I believe,' Lucy said. 'I knew nothing of what happened until I was awakened by the sound of the fire brigade arriving. They said the glass had been smashed from the outside.'

'We shall talk more of this.' My godfather eyed me sulkily for interrupting his game. 'Who has possession of the site now?'

'That is a moot point,' Freddy said wryly. 'My father's affairs were in a terrible state when he died. Apparently he had borrowed money from all sorts of creditors, not all of them reputable, and used our home as security on more than one occasion and so, until the courts make a ruling on who actually owns the property, the insurance company will not pay out.' She plucked at her dress. 'And so Steep House still stands in ruins.'

'Which company?' Mr G walked his fingers through the air.

'If we could actually talk about why I employed you,' Lucy tried.

'Of course you can.' Sidney Grice jumped to his feet. 'You and Miss Wilde may talk about it until your tongues cleave to the roofs of your mouths.' Mr G slouched back, as if about to take a nap, but all at once tipped forward and on to his feet in one smooth movement. 'Come, Miss Middleton, you have given enough offence for one day.' He grasped his startled client's hand. 'How chill your dear little fingers have become. Goodbye, Miss Bocking. I hope we meet again.'

'But I thought...' Freddy pressed the bell in confusion.

'There you go again,' my guardian told her. 'Imagining that I care what you think.'

'I am sorry,' I apologized to them both.

'They are polite ladies,' Sidney Grice told me, 'and if they cannot forgive you they will at least pretend to do so.'

'I was apologizing for—'

'Best not to remind them,' my guardian advised and, shouldering his satchel, made a stiff bow of the head. 'I bid you brace of spinsters farewell.'

Mr G trotted backwards to the open door and, spinning half a circle in mid-air, jumped with both feet, like a child over a puddle, into the hall.

Freddy came racing after us.

'You cannot keep treating my friend like this.' She clenched her fists furiously.

'Oh, Miss Wilde, I can only apologize,' Sidney Grice bowed his head, 'if I have given you grounds to believe that.'

Aellen handed me my cloak. 'If you give me warning in future I can have a cab waiting for you, sir.'

'That is a kind thought,' Sidney Grice remarked, 'and so I decline it.'

'Why?' I asked as we stepped into the square and three hansoms edged past, all occupied.

'The day we accept kindness from our servants we become beholden to them.' Mr G stuck out his cane, but we were beaten to it by an elderly gentleman in a towering beaver-skin topper. 'And that is an egg's eyelash from *equality*. The moment you bridge the gulf between ourselves and the lower orders they will swarm across it and storm the citadels of our privileges.'

'No need ter totter with a good boot on yer trotter,' came from across the square, competing with a girl's 'Buy my lovely fresh flowers'.

She waved a wilted fistful under a frock-coated gentleman's nose but he batted it away, the head flying off in a faded shower.

A gentleman in a green paisley waistcoat and pinstriped grey trousers was stamping his black, side-buttoned boot. 'Now see here, my good fellow.'

An empty hansom came along the opposite side and seemed about to go ten yards on to a young man in a short sand-coloured coat, jumping up and down and waving frenetically.

'Oyah!' I bellowed and the driver hauled on his reins and wheeled his cab across the traffic to pull up alongside us.

'Why, March,' my guardian said, 'when it comes to social bridge-building, you are a veritable Mr Isambard Kingdom Brunel.'

19

The Style Street Slaying

THERE WERE TWENTY-FOUR cadavers laid out on trolleys under formalin-soaked sheets in the dissection room of the anatomy building opposite number 125 Gower Street, but all the living occupants were congregated at the far end of the room when we entered. Professor Duffy was bent, a hooked Pirogov retractor in hand, over a long marble-topped table behind a tin bathtub. And half a dozen students, their long laboratory coats encrusted in dried body fluids, stood round the table, sorting through a selection of human fingers in two kidney dishes.

He glanced up. 'Mr Grice and Miss...' His voice and interest in me trailed away. 'Meet my human jigsaw puzzle.'

There was a man's head on the slab, badly gouged, as were his limbs. The rest of him was still in the tub, a mess of torn bloodied flesh with projecting bones still waiting to be reassembled.

'Style Street?' Sidney Grice picked up a thumb with some tweezers.

He put it under his nose and, for a horrible moment, I thought he was going to pop it in his mouth but he sniffed appreciatively and put it back in the bowl.

'What happened to him?' I asked, hoping I did not look as queasy as I felt in the midst of such masculine company.

'He was passed through a rag shredder.'

'Was he still conscious?'

'Not when he came out of the other end.' A tousle-haired pimply student guffawed and his companions chortled, partly at his joke but mainly at me.

'It is impossible to tell,' the learned professor explained for the benefit of the simple girl who had asked the question.

'Have you considered the possibility that Miss Middleton was merely curious as to whether you had calculated the answer for yourselves?' my guardian enquired with touching, though unjustified, loyalty.

Professor Duffy unsuccessfully suppressed a snigger. 'Indeed?'

'Perhaps you would like to explain your methods for the benefit of these *gentlemen*,' Mr G invited me, mouthing the last word like a bad taste.

No, I damned well would not, I thought, but I forced what I hoped was a confident smile and murmured, 'Surely they have already worked it out for themselves.'

'Not yet,' a reedy, red-eyed youth sneered.

'Well, the patterns of bleeding...' I floundered, and felt my godfather's cane press into my boot. 'Are irrelevant,' I added hastily.

The students folded their arms to watch me make a fool of myself and I obligingly walked slowly round the table whilst I played for time. Sidney Grice wandered away behind the group, leaving me alone.

'I fear your master overestimated your powers.' Duffy smiled patronizingly as Mr G popped up behind him, miming an orchestral conductor, rather unhelpfully, I thought.

'I have no master,' I retorted.

Mr G rolled his eye and repeated the manoeuvre, nodding and shaking his head, arms waving and twirling, and then I realized – he was tying an imaginary rope.

'He was dead or at the very least unconscious,' I declared.

The professor eyed me suspiciously. 'Explain,' he commanded, as if I had joined his unsavoury band.

My mind raced. 'The arms and legs are severely lacerated but there is enough skin visible to be confident that there are no rope marks, and you could not make a conscious man lie still on the conveyor belt to be fed into a shredder without tying him up.'

'Hmmmm.' The professor considered my proposal dubiously and my guardian, still behind him, threw back his head in despair and tried again, this time very slowly. He held out his right hand like a claw and drew it down in a wavy motion, shaking his head. He repeated the process in a straight downward line, nodding vigorously. And then it clicked.

'Let me make it simpler,' I continued, to my guardian's approval. 'The striated wounds, caused by the shredding teeth, run in straight parallel lines. No matter how well you restrained your victim you could not stop a sentient man from writhing in his agonies.'

And, from the back of the room, Sidney Grice applauded silently.

'I was going to let my fledgling colleagues work that out,' Duffy declared unconvincingly. 'What is the purpose of your visit, Mr Grice?'

'Mr Jonathon, alias the Walrus, Wallace,' my godfather announced.

'Oh yes.' The professor indicated a covered mound to his left. 'Haven't had a chance to look at him yet. I had forgotten he was one of yours.'

'I do not and never have possessed Mr Wallace, nor have I constructed a scheme to do so,' Mr G assured him, and we went over and, walking down each side, peeled the saturated sheet back.

Johnny looked smaller than when I had last seen him. It was not just that he was lying down or that he was naked, but there is something about death that diminishes a person – as if the flight of the soul physically shrinks a body. Sidney Grice huffed noisily.

'Some cack-handed fool has already interfered with him,' he snarled, and I looked to see that the dome of the skull had been sawn clumsily so that the neat bullet wound was now a jagged hole some four or five inches in diameter. 'And, from the determinedly innocent look on that pallid Habsburgian boy's face, it is clearly his doing.' Everybody looked at the pale student, who had a projecting lower jaw, though I thought it unkind of my guardian to remark upon it. 'I would advise any gamblers amongst you to wager that it was he.'

The pale youth paled further. 'I was just looking for the bullet.'

Sidney Grice held out his hand and the student reluctantly reached into his laboratory coat and surrendered a grey lump.

'I wanted it as a souvenir,' he mumbled.

Mr G turned the bullet over, a shapeless, squashed lump of lead now.

'With what did you remove it?' he demanded. 'The truth, boy.'

The pale student paled some more. 'My fingers, sir. It seemed easier than poking blindly with forceps.'

'You are sure?'

'Yes, sir.'

'No metallic instruments at all?'

'No, sir.'

'Good boy.' Mr G snapped his fingers and a sixpenny piece appeared between them. 'Here.' He spun it high in the air. 'Use that to induce a barber to relocate the untethered ends of your oleaginous hairs closer to your scalp.'

'I do not know why you are interested in Wallace.' Duffy was clearly discomfited at he and his students being belittled. 'You already know how he died.'

'Oh, Professor.' My godfather went down on his haunches to scrutinize a tattered lung that had been deposited in an enamelled bowl on the floor. 'One of the few things we have in common,' he parted two spongy lobes with a steel spatula, 'is that our interest in people is only increased by their demises.' Mr G poked the instrument into the opening of a large bronchus and scooped around it. 'The man who once possessed this cadaver came recently from a rural area. He had a chronic inflammatory pulmonary condition which I have oft observed afflicts those who deal with hay.'

'We called it *farmers' chest* in Lancashire,' I recalled.

'I suspect it is a reaction to the dust created in the production of fodder. His lungs are choked with it.' Sidney Grice held out the spatula coated in phlegm speckled with off-yellow particles.

An alternative to his theory sprang to mind but I refrained from voicing it amongst such would-be superior beings. Professor Duffy had no such qualms, however.

'Tens of thousands of people in London deal with hay every day,' he objected. 'Ostlers, carters, stable lads and grooms, for example.'

'And inhale the soot-laden air with every breath,' my guardian reminded him. 'You have performed enough autopsies to have observed that their alveoli are clogged with carboniferous deposits. Scalpel, Miss Middleton.'

I passed one handle first – as often I had placed one into my father's hand before the world made me old whilst I was still young – and Mr G sliced deep into the tissue.

'Quite pink,' I vouched. 'So probably not a smoker either.'

'Come, Miss Middleton.' Sidney Grice rose and made for the exit. 'Oh, and that right middle finger does not belong to the same man. It is too short and smells of tobacco tar.'

'Anything else?' Professor Duffy asked tersely.

'I think that will do for today,' my guardian assured him, lifting the corner of a sheet idly to inspect a partly dissected foot.

'Perhaps you would care to give our man a name,' the professor suggested sarcastically.

'Simon,' I said, and he gaped at me. 'It is a nice name,' I continued, 'but not necessarily his.'

'Goodbye, Professor.' Sidney Grice tipped his hat as he ushered me out. 'I cannot agree.' His lips were as immobile as a very good ventriloquist's. 'With your inflated puffery for that appellation. It tastes of pork. Acwellen is a far superior name. It is Anglo-Saxon and means—' we passed back out on to Gower Street—'*Kill.*'

20

The Street of Seven Dreams

THE LIMEHOUSE BASIN was crowded as always and a great steamship was being unloaded, stevedores lowering long full sacks into barges for transfer along the Regent's Canal, thence to be transported throughout the country. Lascars in pantaloons and baggy jackets, heads covered in flat cylindrical skullcaps, dragged a rope as thick as their arms, working it into a giant coil. A gang of perhaps twenty black longshoremen, stripped to the waist, torsos glistening in the blaze of the sun, hauled the *Alice Rose*, a four-mast windjammer, back to the pier that she had overshot. Land and river swarmed with activity, and countless voices in dozens of different languages and accents competed to be heard above each other and the crash of cargo being dumped on the quayside.

'Is it not inspiring,' Sidney Grice shouted above the hubbub, 'to think how many of these creatures could die without anyone caring.'

He threw our fare up to the driver, who put it in a cloth bag under his straw hat.

'They could have someone who loves them,' I argued, taking his arm to clamber on to the cobbles.

There was a strong stale smell coming from the river and I dreaded to think what it must have been like in the days of the Great Stink when the Thames was an open sewer, before Joseph Bazalgette built his drains and pumping stations.

'Nonsense.' Mr G tidied his coat. 'Who, for example, could care about this loathsome specimen?' He poked a ragged but otherwise presentable youth in the chest with his cane.

'Oy!'

'His mother.'

'I doubt he ever had one.' Sidney Grice led me up a narrow street into a short alley with a strong smell of rancid butter, and then into a long one stinking of cats, then a series of passage-ways, each narrower and less salubrious than the previous, the doors either side of us going from painted to patchily painted to unpainted to broken, to being replaced with sacking hooked over rusty nails. And then we were in a court, deserted except for five women squatting in the corner some forty feet away, shelling peas from a sack into a bucket and dropping the pods into their grubby aprons.

'Never mind 'er, darlin',' one called out. 'I can give you a better time.'

'The only thing you could give him would be infectious,' I called back and my guardian paused to consider my comment.

'Pulmonary tuberculosis and scabies being the least troubling of her afflictions,' he pondered.

'Who you calling scabby?' the woman spluttered chestily, while her companions clucked in sympathy.

'I am unfamiliar with her cognomen and have no desire to familiarize myself with it.' Mr G raised his stick in salutation. 'Goodbye, repellant and plebian females. May your lives be abbreviated.'

He took my arm and we turned left down a winding lane.

'A proper gent,' I heard the woman say as I dodged a piglet scampering straight towards me.

'Gawd, which rag-and-bone man did 'e pick 'er up from?' one of her companions croaked to more cackling than any joke ever told before could possibly have merited.

'There you go, causing trouble again,' my godfather scolded

as we turned down yet another alley, this one hung with lanterns and the first property bearing a sign with red Chinese symbols arranged round the words *Golden Dragon*, also in red.

The front door was painted red too and I was beginning to think the theme somewhat overdone before the door was opened – in response to Sidney Grice's complicated rhythm of knocks – by a Chinaman, very tall compared to those I had seen slaving on the docks, and clad in a red kimono. He bowed and admitted us into a waiting room – the walls, floor and ceiling, the bench and the two armchairs all coloured deep and dark vermilion. Had there been any windows in this lamplit room, I had no doubt what colour the drapes would have been.

'Mr Glice.' the Chinaman put his hands together, hardly visible amongst the voluminous sleeves of his robe.

'And Miss Middleton,' I added, in the unlikely instance of anyone being interested, and the Chinaman bowed so low that I could see the long pigtail braided down his back.

'An honour.' He came up gently. 'What bringee you to my humble home?'

'Save the theatricals for your customers, Jones,' Mr G told him sharply. 'Your humble abode is a thirty-four room mansion in Primrose Hill, and even Miss Middleton would not be taken in by your counterfeit orientalism.'

I had more pride than to admit that I had been.

The apparently fake Chinaman smiled serenely, his moustaches hanging like bootlaces almost to his chest.

'Pleasee, Mr Glice. In Plimlose Hill I may be who I choose. In the Street of Seven Dreams I am Chang Foo.'

'This is Grey Dog Lane,' my guardian pointed out

'To you pah-haps,' Jones/Chang conceded.

'But your eyes,' I looked into them and they returned my gaze placidly. 'They look oriental.'

'I was born with droopy eyes.' Jones gave up his pretence.

'Ocular ptosis,' I realized.

'Is that what it is?' Our host smiled ruefully. 'The other children used to call me names.' His mouth tensed as he remembered. 'There was nothing I could do so I decided to put it to my own advantage. I've always been interested in opium since my grandmother introduced me to the habit, but nobody buys from an Englishman.'

'You are very well spoken,' I observed.

'Another fraudulent device,' Sidney Grice told me. 'Jones was born and raised not thirty yards from here.'

'We are none of us who we pretend to be,' Jones said.

'I think I am,' I objected.

'You probably are,' my guardian conceded. 'Whereas I do not *pretend* to be anyone.' His cane shot up under Jones's chin. 'Miss Bocking.'

Jones jumped but instantly readopted his inscrutable image. 'I don't know nuffink abart that.' He reverted to his native Cockney.

'You must know something,' I reasoned, 'or you would have asked who Mr Grice meant.'

'A rational remark,' my godfather approved.

'Well, I know she came with 'er friend and left with 'er friend, but they nevva said nuffink to me.' Jones flapped his wing-like sleeves and Mr G blanched but held his ground. ''Er friend wore a veil but lots of women don't want to be recognized.' He sniggered breathily. 'Once 'ad a muvvah sittin' next to 'er daugh'a and neevah nevvah knew it.'

'And you did not notice anything unusual on the night Miss Bocking came?'

'Did he not?' Mr G wandered to a red-lacquered table in the corner and tried the drawer.

'That was a question.'

'Then be so charitable as to phrase it as one.' Sidney Grice pulled off his gloves, drawing his breath in sharply as if the process were distressing.

'Did you notice anything unusual?' I tried again.

'Nuffink,' Jones folded his arms inside his sleeves, 'is unusual round 'ere.'

'What about the men who were with her?' I persisted.

'I didn't notice them,' Jones assured me placidly, and glanced over his shoulder. 'That drawer is locked.'

'I have ascertained that already.' Mr G wheeled round. 'We shall look downstairs now and you shall remain, seated.' He rattled the back spokes of an upright wooden chair. 'Here.'

''Ere 'oo said yer could poke around my place?' Jones objected indignantly.

My guardian licked his finger and held it up as if checking the direction of the wind.

'I was not aware that anybody had,' he answered. 'And I certainly did not ask anyone to do so.' He swept off his hat and dropped his gloves one by one into the upturned crown.

I scrutinized a red tassel which dangled from an oil lamp hanging from the ceiling, and sniffed it in an attempt to look as if I was doing something, but neither man was paying me any attention. It smelled, as the rest of the room did, of a sickly perfume.

'How many police officers would you like to visit you tonight, Dr Jones?' Sidney Grice stood on tiptoe to look him in the eye.

'Dr?' I repeated incredulously and, now that I had their attention, examined the tassel again.

Jones shifted his feet. 'This is an easier and more lucrative living,' he admitted bashfully before stiffening his sinews.

'He is not qualified other than in the art of cheap swindling.'

'Cheap?' Jones ruffled his robes. 'That certificate cost me a fortune.' He tightened the wide silk belt around his waist. 'Look, Mr Grice, I pay to be left alone.'

'But you do not and never shall pay me to do so,' my guardian reminded him.

Jones swished his pigtail crossly. 'Oh, very well.' He flapped a wide sleeve. 'Behind the head.'

A golden dragon smiled toothily all along that bamboo-lined wall, carrying the world in its claws in a pose more reminiscent of an underarm bowler approaching the crease. I slid the end screen aside to reveal a door and Dr Jones turned sulkily away. 'The honourable gentleman will not find anything of intelest,' he prophesied in his best cod Mandarin.

'I have only ever been to nineteen places where I found absolutely nothing of interest.' Sidney Grice took a hair off the fabric. 'And in every instance bar one I was asleep.' He compared the hair to mine, put it on his palm and blew it away. 'The last, of course, was Paris.'

I opened the door, to my guardian's unconcealed chagrin. He had a fondness for doing so in theatrical manners, but I had endured more than enough of his public displays recently. A steep narrow staircase, with solid walls to either side, led down away from us.

'You will not lock us in,' I said. 'And that was not a question.'

'Never entered my 'ead.' Jones jerked his neck forward like a strutting chicken.

'Then present me with the key,' my guardian said firmly.

Jones seemed about to protest but, realizing there was no point, brought a hand out of his voluminous sleeve and handed it over.

'One word of warning.' Mr G paused with his foot on the top step. 'If anything unpleasant should befall myself and my assistant down there, it will be very much the worse for us.'

And, with that encouraging thought, I followed him down.

21

Into the Dragon's Lair

THE STAIRS WERE unlit as was the room into which we descended, but Sidney Grice soon had three oil lamps lit and the more my eyes became accustomed to their glare, the more dingy our surroundings looked. True, it was decorated, as my guardian had predicted, in supposedly erotic murals, but they were clumsily drawn and peeling in the damp that infests all London cellars. The four sofas were upholstered in balding velvet with the grease marks of a thousand heads on their backs and arms and peppered with countless burns. Each sofa had a long low table in front of it, the red paint marked and blistered by the heat of innumerable pipes. The furniture stood on a large square rug – red, of course – which looked fairly new but could not disguise the hardness of the stone floor beneath it.

Mr G pulled back another drape in the far left-hand corner to reveal a plain plank door, locked, with the key removed. He pressed his ear to the woodwork and rapped once with his knuckles.

'What are we looking for?' I asked, hoping he would not say something as vague as *clues*.

My guardian glanced at the ceiling, stained with smoke and dotted with hundreds of ochre splots that were probably meant to be suns.

'Oh, for goodness' sake.' He reached into his inner pocket. 'Do I have to write you a list?'

'No,' I replied, taken aback by his sharpness, but apparently he felt he did, for he was scribbling away industriously in his notebook and cringing at the desecration as he tore out another page.

'Take this.' He pressed the folded the paper into my hands. 'And go and read it under that oil lamp.'

He pointed to the one at the foot of the stairs, and I was about to insist that I could read it just as well where I was when I felt his toe tap mine.

'Very well.' I went over and unfolded his missive.

1 Do not say anything.
2 When I say the word 'fascinating' you are to re-enter the reception area as quietly as your ungainly construction permits – remembering as you should have observed during our descent that the ninth tread on your ascent crepitates – so as to present yourself unexpectedly to Mr Thomas David Jones.
3 Pay particular attention to what he is doing. He will be doing something. The Welsh are always doing something.
4 Exercise one of your few skills by devising a convincing untruth for your unexpected appearance.

Mr G dropped on to his haunches and tipped his head like a blackbird listening for worms.

'This is not fascinating,' he said.

I clamped my jaw tight just in time to choke back my instinctive reply and set my foot upon the first step. The stairwell was so narrow that my dresses rustled noisily against the wall.

'The police will not be intrigued by what I have found,' my guardian declaimed, never quite able to bring himself to tell a lie.

I was on the third step as he boomed out, 'For I shall not, having no motive to do so, grant them such information.'

Another step, holding my skirts in as best I could.

'I have not not seen the like of this unenchanting... *thing* in nineteen years,' came after me, by which time I had reached step six of about fourteen.

'Blimmit,' I cursed quietly as my hem snagged on a splinter.

'Language,' my godfather responded automatically, but it was all I could do to restrain my tongue as the lining ripped when I pulled it free.

It was a light blue dress and not new, but it had given me good service and had a useful secret pocket just large enough for my spare cigarette case.

'My word, this is not markedly different from the last one I came across.' Mr G struggled to continue as the stair squealed under me.

'Sorry,' I hissed. I had thought I was on the eighth step.

'Oh, just get a move on,' he rapped, and I galloped up the remaining five steps like a herd of Mollies in full stampede, almost wrenching the screen off its runners as I stumbled through the opening at the top.

Thomas Jones was intent upon his inkwell as I burst into view. 'What are you doing?' he demanded.

'What are *you* doing?' I demanded. 'You are supposed to be in that chair.'

He snapped the lid back down. 'Nobody tells me what to do in my own establishment.' His face was flushed and looking less oriental now.

'Mr Grice does,' I assured him.

Footsteps sounded on the stairs and Jones hastened back to his chair. 'You won't say anything?' he pleaded, now a naughty child trying to do a deal with nanny.

'I always say something,' I told him.

'Oh, be a sport.' Jones hitched up his robes, showing off a rather flashy pair of embroidered pink slippers that I would not have minded for myself.

'He was bent over his desk,' I announced as my guardian appeared.

'Have you even heard of the word "circumspect", Miss Middleton?' Mr G took a constitutional round me, then swayed and dropped to the floor. He could not have tripped and it was not a faint. People who swoon crumble at the knees but my godfather crashed like a statue being toppled from its plinth on to his shoulder. His eyes were still open. Was he having some kind of a fit? I was about to kneel and check when he rolled on to his back, sat up and sprang acrobatically to his feet. 'Indeed,' he told himself, scooped out his gloves in his left hand, whipped up his hat with his right and went to the exit, apparently none the worse for his experience.

'I think it comes from the Latin, *circum* and *specere*,' I told his back, determined not to be as nonplussed as I felt.

'I am elated to find evidence of you thinking at all.' Sidney Grice opened the door in a disconcertingly normal manner.

'Oh,' I said lamely as he marched straight out. 'Goodbye, Mr Jones.' My godfather was five yards away by the time I got outside. 'Wait for me, Mr Glice,' I called after him.

*

There was a message on the hall table when we got back to 125 Gower Street, a letter with the familiar blue eight-pointed Brunswick star crest on the envelope.

'You open it.' My guardian was preoccupied in rearranging his canes.

'A body had been found which might be of interest,' I read out and Sidney Grice jabbed his finger at the missive.

'Why was it not in my tray?' he demanded of Molly and she chewed her lower lip.

'I dontn't not think a body would fit in there, sir,' she decided. 'Ohhhhh.' Molly clutched her stomach.

'Whatever is the matter?' I asked.

Her face was pale and clammy. 'Oh, miss,' she moaned, seeming to think that was sufficient explanation.

'Are you ill?'

'Of course she is ill.' Mr G opened another letter. 'If a servant is healthy, he or she – or, in this wretched creature's case, *it* – is not working hard enough.'

'I think it might be the poising I drank.' Molly staggered towards me but, mercifully, did not collapse into my arms. 'To kill the mouse a bit.'

'You took mouse poison?'

'Only all of it.' Molly flopped her arms weakly.

Her employer headed towards his study.

'But where did you get it?' I considered whether to summon a cab or try to get her up the road to the hospital by foot.

'From that cupboard what Mr Grice told me never to touch what got accidently unlocked.'

'Oh, Molly,' I cried. 'He keeps acids and all sorts of things in there.'

'Not all sorts.' Molly flapped a hand weakly. 'He dontn't not keep no chocolates or beer 'cause I've looked.'

'But what did you take?'

There were beads of sweat on her downy upper lip.

'Look at the lumpen wench's tongue,' came out from the study.

'This.' Molly delved in her apron pocket and handed me a brown bottle.

'Vermilion,' I read from the label.

'Verminions is rats and mice and liberals,' she explained, leaning heavily on the hall table. 'Mr Grice told me that.'

'Dye,' I continued.

'I'm trying,' she retorted irritably.

'It is a stain,' I explained and saw, too late, that her tongue was bright red.

'Oh, bless.' Molly clamped her paws together. 'Mrs Mouse will look ever so pretty now.'

'You have not swallowed a mouse,' I assured her wearily.

'Oh no?' Molly plonked her fists on her substantial hips. 'Well, how come I've stained her red then?'

'Tea,' Sidney Grice barked, and she scurried off, her logic irrefutable.

22

◆━◆◈◆━◆

The Body in the Mud

SERGEANT HEWITT WAS a sturdy, weather-beaten man with a slight roll to his gait, as one might expect from a seafaring man, but, though he spent much of his time on the water, Hewitt's duties in the Thames River Police never took him further than the coast.

'Not a pretty sight,' he warned as he came along the quay from where his launch was moored.

'She does her best.' Sidney Grice defended me and the sergeant guffawed, under the impression that my guardian had made what he never made, a joke.

'March Middleton.' I shook his hand, hardened and scarred by a tough outdoor life.

His left thumb was missing. 'Caught on a capstan,' he told me in response to my glance down.

Mr G whipped out his journal to make a note. 'Do you still have it?'

Sergeant Hewitt looked puzzled. 'My thumb? No, why?'

'It might be evidence,' Sidney Grice pondered.

'What of?' the sergeant asked, striding past us and up a ramp towards a tarred wooden shed.

'Of what?' Mr G corrected him.

'Where was the body found?' I asked as the two men stared at each other.

Hewitt shook his head like a swimmer trying to clear his ear.

119

'Down in the estuary, washed up in the marshes near the Isle of Sheppey.'

'That must be about forty miles away,' I estimated.

'Nearer fifty,' the policeman calculated. 'Miss that and, unless you ground at Margate, you're bobbing about feeding dogfish in the North Sea.'

'By whom and under what circumstances was it rescued?' Sidney Grice whipped out his magnifying glass to examine a curtain of dried seaweed hanging down a wooden post.

'A Squire Boweley from Basingstoke.' Sergeant Hewitt inserted and turned a key in a chunky padlock. ''E was 'untin' lugworms – one of those daft beggars what writes books on 'em – when 'e spotted 'er stickin' out of the mud. Thought it was just an old sack until 'e got close. The eels 'ad taken a few dinners off 'er by then. We only identified 'er by the report of 'er bein' missin' and 'er locket.'

'Do you have the locket?' I asked and the sergeant brought it out of an inside pocket of his cape.

The locket was gold on a gold chain, and it was fortunate that the body had not been found by mudlarks, for they would have been unlikely to have handed in such a treasure. The front was embossed with a rosebud design and the back engraved with the words *To our darling Albertoria with love from Mummy and Daddy*. I pressed the catch and the two halves sprang apart like a clamshell to reveal Mr Wright's face in the left section and his wife's in the other.

Sidney Grice took it from me and handed it back without comment.

'Can I keep it?' I asked. 'I shall be visiting them later.'

Sergeant Hewitt took told of his mutton chops. 'I suppose I can trust you.'

'I wish I had your faith,' my guardian muttered.

'What's that you say?' The sergeant tugged his whiskers.

'Mr Grice wishes he had your face,' I lied.

'Oh.' Sergeant Hewitt simpered. 'Thanks very much.'

I slipped the locket into my handbag. 'Shall we?' I tipped my furled parasol towards our destination.

'Right.' Hewitt opened the lock and hesitated. 'Sure you're up to this, miss?'

'I *have* seen bodies before,' I assured the sergeant and he puffed.

'Not like this, you ain't.' He heaved the right hand of the double doors open and stood back. 'I'll wait out 'ere unless you need me.'

Sidney Grice brought out a black cloth, crumpled it into a ball, sprinkled it with camphor from a dark blue bottle and clamped it over his thin and elegant nose. It was not like my godfather to be squeamish – usually he relished the gruesome – but, as soon as I stepped into the shed after him, I understood why he had done it. The air was thick with decay. I snatched the bottle from his outstretched hand and hastily followed suit.

It was a good-sized shed, perhaps forty feet long and half as wide, and fifteen high at the apex of roof. It must have been a boathouse once, but there was a jig-saw powered by a small steam engine in a far corner and some other machinery covered in sacking against the wall, so it must have been used as a work-shop since then, which was why two long skylights had been put into the ceiling for light and ventilation, though they were locked now.

A trestle table had been set up in the middle of the concrete floor and on it was what I could only describe as a *thing*. What we had been told might be the mortal remains of Albertoria Wright was scarcely recognizable as human. A long dark mound bound in rags had been placed upon those boards. At the far end was a tangle of what I took to be hair, but there was nothing resembling a face framed in it. The whole head was a ball of matted brown slush. Most of the mud had been hosed from the body but it still clogged the cavities which would have recently housed the eyes, nose and mouth of a pretty young girl.

Sidney Grice stood at her feet, peering over the top of his cloth, his cane held vertically like a guard shouldering arms, and I edged along the side of the boards, forcing myself to look and to breathe as normally as I could, for the stench of rottenness seeped even through the penetrating mothball vapour. A bare arm jutted over the side but it was so slimy that I could not touch it. The fingers were blackened and fanned out and the whole limb was caked in something like flour.

'What is that powder?' I managed.

'Salt,' came the muffled response, 'to kill the leeches.'

The torso was bloated and bulging through the ripped remnants of a striped dress. I found an intact patch near the hem and cut out a square of it with my nail scissors, dropping it into a pouch that Sidney Grice held out for me.

My guardian set off up the other side of the table, stopping at where her waist might have been to face me over the muck that was once a woman.

'The cadaver is too decomposed to lift, let alone turn,' he stated. 'And corruption is far too advanced to give us any hope of verifying or dismissing her claim of having been despoiled.'

We continued counterclockwise until he was at the head and me at the foot. Her right leg ended at the ankle, the sheared-off ends of the oval tibia and more slender fibula clearly exposed.

'From the cleanness of the de-pedification, the stretching and rips in her clothes, it seems likely that she was caught at some stage on a propeller,' he proposed, his voice more distant than the covering of his mouth seemed to warrant.

'I cannot see any other jewellery on her,' I said. 'No rings or bracelets or earrings.'

'I know what jewellery is,' he said sharply.

'Stop it,' I cried and, to my surprise, he mumbled, 'Very well.'

I turned back to the business in hand and gingerly took a

loose strand of hair hanging over the end, wiped a tarry coating off with my spare handkerchief and raised the tress towards the light.

'I suppose she could have been described as auburn,' I said.

'I would say so,' Mr G concurred.

'Unfortunately, there is no nose for us to find a freckle.'

'Quite.' Mr G puffed his cheeks. It always annoyed him when I observed the obvious but equally when I failed to do so. 'Which leaves us with?' He nodded towards me.

'The wisdom tooth,' I recalled. 'Shall I fetch some water to wash the mud out?'

I surprised myself by the matter-of-fact way I made that suggestion. I might have been offering sugar to a guest.

'Who knows what we might accidentally wash away?' Sidney Grice reached into his satchel and brought out a silver spoon, dipping it into the deposit as a man might sample his dessert. He tapped out his first spoonful on to the table and raked through it with the rim of the bowl. There was nothing recognizable as lips in front of the still-white teeth nor gums around their necks. 'And what is your opinion?'

'It is an adult dentition,' I observed.

He dug a few times more.

'Quite a young adult, I would think,' I continued. 'The crests of bone between the teeth are still quite high and sharp and there is not much sign of abrasion.'

'Good.' He ladled out something like old liver and I realized with horror that it was putrefied portions of tongue. I retched and my guardian looked at me before asking, 'Do you want to go outside for a while?'

'Do you?'

'No.'

'Then neither do I.' I fought my churning stomach. Nothing would induce me to admit that I was more squeamish than he, not even the dizzy swirling in my head. 'Kindly clean the back teeth.'

Sidney Grice grunted. 'Very well.' And he scraped away what he could before wrapping his spoon in a cloth and delving about deep in the cavity. He pulled the soiled cloth out and I peered in. My eyes did not want to focus but I made them.

'The lower right wisdom tooth is tipped forwards and impacted against the second molar.'

'Would that cause pain?'

'Probably. It is half-erupted and that could have made the gum very inflamed, especially as the upper tooth is over-erupted and would have bitten down on it.'

'Anything else?'

I twisted down, trying not to cast my shadow over the cavity and not to focus on that scooped-out root of tongue nestling in the entrance to the throat like a giant slug.

'The left wisdom teeth are completely buried under bone so I doubt they would have hurt her.'

Sidney Grice bobbed briefly and rose slowly, and I reluctantly did another circuit. I did not expect to find anything but I felt I owed it to the dead girl and her parents to try, and I had nearly joined Sidney Grice when I slipped. The liquids of putrefaction had oozed from under the trestle into a greasy puddle on the floor. My godfather's arm shot out and I grabbed it but, with the heaviness of my fall, it bent. My guardian grunted with the effort and stopped me, my face half an inch above hers.

'Oh, dear God!' I choked on my involuntary inhalation.

He rushed round and helped me to regain my balance without touching anything.

'Thank you,' I gasped and stepped carefully away over the slippery concrete to the door, the sunlight and a welcome river breeze.

'Didn't think you'd last that long,' Sergeant Hewitt conceded, openly impressed, until I took the handkerchief from my mouth and saw that it had dipped into the sepia fluid that had bathed Albertoria Wright's rotting flesh. I rushed away and, doubling over the low wall that separated the ramp from a drainage gulley, evacuated the contents of my stomach.

'I did that,' the policeman confessed. 'So did my constables, and we've fished out many a carcass in our time.'

I uncorked my blue bottle of sal volatile and let the ammonia fumes flood my nostrils and their sharpness jolt me out of my giddiness.

'Come, March.' My guardian took my arm and led me gently away and, when we were out of earshot, said, 'If you have your father's flask with you, I would not object to you using it.'

I opened my handbag but no sooner had I found the flask amongst the numberless other essentials than I let it go again.

'I cannot go to see the Wrights stinking of gin.'

'I can go in your stead,' he proposed. 'At least I will not get emotional.'

I took a parma violet and said, 'Which is exactly why I shall do it.'

'Very well.' Mr G accepted my offer of a sweet. 'Then we had better get you home to bathe and change and I shall arrange for the remains to be sealed in a lead coffin.'

'That is a kind thought.'

'I hope Mr Wright concurs with that opinion when I present him with my account.'

Sidney Grice patted my hand and we walked on, clearing our lungs in silence, and we were still arm in arm when we found a cab ten minutes later.

23

The Old Man of Great Titchfield Street

GREAT TITCHFIELD STREET ran long and straight from Greenwell Street in the north – with its excellent George and the Dragon pub – to Oxford Street, with its stalls, stores and bazaars, in the south.

It never ceased to fascinate me how the character of London could change so rapidly, and rarely was this better demonstrated than along this road. Once a pleasant thoroughfare constructed by the Duke of Portland, the desirable houses were gradually broken into rented rooms or cheap clothing shops, driving property prices down and the original residents out.

Now, however, the street was being reclaimed by the well-to-do. Crumbling dwellings were demolished and more salubrious properties built, starting at the Oxford Street end and steadily stretching northwards so that there was no indication, when one approached the smart, well-kept properties, that one only had to continue up the street to find oneself in the midst of appalling deprivation and degradation – malnourished mothers and children, unemployed men and habitual criminals jostling within a short stroll of luxury.

The Wrights, needless to say, lived in the better area – for nobody in the worse could have afforded even a consultation with my guardian – and, twenty yards up the road, I made out a high barred gate and two uniformed watchmen whose sole purpose would be to keep the two worlds apart.

An elderly maid answered the blue-painted front door and admitted me to a pretty hall – a sage oilcloth on the floor and lemon wallpaper with wispy swirls of green foliage.

'Are you Ann-Jane?' I placed my card on a silver tray.

'Yes, miss,' she replied, a touch warily.

She was even more petite than her employers.

'So it was you who found that Miss Albertoria was missing?'

I glanced round the narrow hallway. It had three doors, all painted in a fresh cream colour, two to the left and, just visible as a frame to the right behind a steep cantilevered staircase, the third, which must have led to the domestic quarters for there was no cellar beneath the house.

'Yes, miss.' Ann-Jane looked around nervously. 'But I know nothing else about it.'

Her accent was unusually well-cultivated for one in her employment and I wondered how she had fallen so far in position.

'Did Miss Albertoria ever confide in you?'

In one section of the cherry-wood umbrella stand was a nice Prussian blue parasol with a frilled border, and it occurred to me that it might have matched the muddy shreds barely clothing the remains we had viewed earlier, and that the owner would never set out with it again.

'Nothing of consequence, miss.'

'No gentlemen friends?'

'Not that I know of, miss.'

She shuffled her feet.

'Or girlfriends who might lead her astray?'

Ann-Jane swallowed. 'We never talked about that kind of thing, miss.'

I took a step back and walked a quarter way round the maid. It was something I had seen Sidney Grice do many times to unsettle people and it seemed to work rather too well for me, for Ann-Jane emitted a squeak.

'I mean you no harm.' I hurried back to face her and Ann-Jane was quivering when I put my hand on her arm – a gesture of familiarity that would have appalled my godfather. 'What are you afraid of?'

'Nothing, miss.' But a flick of her eyes told me that whatever frightened her was behind that first door, and almost immediately I saw the white porcelain handle turn.

'Who is it, Ann-Jane?' Mrs Wright poked her head into the hall like a mouse checking if it was safe to venture out of her hole. 'Oh, Miss Middleton, I thought it must be you. Please come through.'

Mr Wright was getting to his feet as I went into the cosy pink and blue sitting room. They had been having tea.

'You have a pretty house,' I began, instantly regretting that my pleasantries might have lulled them.

'All Albertoria's choice.' He shook my hand and guided me into one of the two remaining chairs, my back to the hearth, decorated with a fan of peacock feathers. 'You have news.' He went to stand behind his wife's chair.

'Awful news, I fear,' I began.

'No,' Mrs Wright corrected me mildly.

'You only fear?' A ray of hope came from Mr Wright and I wished I had not put it there.

I reached into my handbag and brought out a white cloth bag. 'Do you recognize this?'

Mrs Wright took the locket from me with trembling fingers and fumbled the catch open. She gasped in pain and cupped her hands around it.

'It is Albertoria's,' Mr Wright confirmed. 'We gave it to her for her sixteenth birthday.'

'Where did you get it?' His wife put the gold locket to her cheek.

'If I might ask you first...' I struggled to proceed. 'You mentioned that your daughter had trouble with a wisdom tooth—'

'Her lower right,' Mr Wright broke in. 'What of it?' He eyed me warily.

'I am very sorry to tell you that we believe a body that was found on the Isle of Sheppey is that of Albertoria,' I told them as steadily as I could.

'No.' The word came more sharply from Mrs Wright this time.

'Because of the locket and her tooth?' Mr Wright pressed me.

'And the dress,' I brought out the scarp of fabric, as clean as I had been able to get it.

'Somebody could have stolen the locket and dress,' Mrs Wright said quickly. 'Describe her.'

'She had long auburn hair,' I tried.

'Plenty of girls match that description,' she burst out. 'Is that the best you can do? We gave you a detailed description of our daughter and that ridiculous little man scribbled it all into his silly little notebook.'

In happier times I would have laughed to hear my godfather so described, but I was beginning to wish I had let him perform this duty.

'As far as we could tell, she matched every detail of Albertoria that you gave us,' I said as confidently as I could.

'Did she have a dimple in her chin and a freckle on her nose?' Mrs Wright asked eagerly.

For once I knew I could not lie. 'I am sorry but her skin has deteriorated from being so long in the water.'

'What colour were her eyes?'

'It was difficult to tell.'

'Difficult?' Mrs Wright's voice rose. 'Difficult to tell what colour a girl's eyes are? You are supposed to be professionals.'

Mr Wright put a hand on his wife's shoulder but she shook him off.

'I am very sorry but the body was that of your daughter,' I insisted.

Mr Wright made a mask of his hands and took in four rapid shallow breaths. 'I knew it,' I heard. 'I knew it but I still hoped.' He pulled the mask down to reveal an older man.

'You are hiding something,' Mrs Wright accused me. 'You are lying. You have not been to see her or you did not look properly. She has such distinctive eyes you could not mistake them.'

'My dear,' Mr Wright said softly, and I knew that he understood, but Mrs Wright was up, her dress sweeping her half-drunk cup and its saucer on to the circular Indian rug, the remaining tea set vibrating on the table.

'I do not believe you, and I shall not believe you, until I have seen her with my own eyes.'

I stood to face her. 'I really do not think that is wise.'

She screwed her body up in a furious grief. 'I am not interested in what you think. You are paid to know and you do not seem to know anything.'

'Her body is being sealed in a lead casket,' I tried desperately and a rage burst out of her.

'You dare? What? I am not allowed to chose my own daughter's casket now.'

'It can be placed inside one of your choosing,' I assured her.

Mr Wright was swaying worryingly. He grasped the back of the chair.

'And how will I know it is her and that I am not paying to bury another woman and mourning at a stranger's grave?'

'It *is* Albertoria,' I insisted. 'I promise you, Mrs Wright.'

'And what is your word to me?' She waved the locket in my face. 'You are grubby professionals feeding off the grief of others. No doubt you are off now to tell some other unsuspecting parent that you have found their daughter too.' She threw her arm out blindly, catching my throat. I stepped back, choking. 'For all I know the casket could be empty.' Mrs Wright stepped clear of the table, cracking the saucer underfoot. 'I *shall* see my beautiful Albertoria. What mother does not know her own child?'

I rubbed my neck and caught my breath. 'She is in no condition to be seen. I am sorry,' I tried desperately.

But Mrs Wright's fury did not so much cool as become an icy rage. 'If you can see her, why cannot I?' she reasoned. 'Do you think I have not seen a body before? I must have seen a dozen, probably two. Albertoria, if it is indeed her, cannot be laid to rest in wet rags. I must put her new chiffon dress on her and her matching pink slippers with buttons and, after I have punished Ann-Jane, she shall help me put up my little girl's hair.'

'I am sorry,' I said gently and put out a hand, but another swing of her arm swept it away and the rage exploded.

'Stop it!' she shouted. 'Stop saying that you are sorry.'

'My dear,' was still all Mr Wright could manage.

'I *shall* see her and if it is her, I *shall* say goodbye to my daughter.' She leaped forward, pushing me aside so violently that I toppled, sprawling with my elbow into the table, narrowly missing sending the whole tea tray flying after that cup.

'Wisporia.' Mr Wright rushed after his wife and grabbed her sleeve as I struggled to my feet. 'Listen to what Miss Middleton is telling you.'

'Let me go.' Mrs Wright wrenched herself free but her husband got hold of her again. 'Albertoria needs me.'

'You cannot help her now, Mrs Wright.' I straightened myself up.

'How dare you?' Mrs Wright made towards the door, dragging her husband with her. 'Who in damnation do you think you are to tell me I cannot see my own daughter?'

'Please listen, Wisporia,' he begged. 'Albertoria has gone and there is nothing we can do except to put her in the earth.'

Wisporia Wright seemed to weaken and her husband tried to turn her to him.

'I *shall* see her,' she said firmly.

'No,' he insisted.

'And you shall not stop me.'

'Do I have to spell it out?' Mr Wright closed his eyes, unable to look at the effects of his words. 'She has been three weeks in that stinking river, Wisporia.'

'Then I will take things to wash her clean.' She raised her chin. 'Soap and those flannels with her initials.'

'For the love of God, woman,' her husband shouted, fists clenched against his temples. 'She is in a lead casket because she is rotting.'

Mrs Wright stopped and was all at once calm. Her fingers went to her right cheek and then to her husband's left. They bent and blanched at the tips as they drew down, nails raking deep into his flesh.

*

'Pour two large brandies,' Sidney Grice instructed after I had described what had happened.

'But you do not take alcohol.'

'I will nurse mine whilst you drink yours.' My guardian finished stacking his correspondence into three piles. 'And then we shall swap and I will stare into the empty glass.'

Waterdale Assurance Co. Ltd, I read on a top envelope.

I went to the sideboard to fetch the decanter. 'Do you never get upset about death?' I pulled out the stopper.

'Only life disturbs me,' he declared. 'Death is nothing.'

'Dear God, when we catch the man who drove her to such despair...' I burst out.

'There are almost innumerable unproven assumptions in that truncated display of emotion.' My godfather crossed his ankles. 'But we shall content ourselves with a brace of them, the first being your need to substitute the adverb *when* with the conjunctive *if*. The second being your unspoken assumption that somebody must be punished for her death.'

'But he—'

'That was your fourth error of logic. We cannot even be

certain that a man was involved.' He flexed his feet one at a time.

I ran silently through my words. 'Very well,' I challenged. 'What were the other mistakes?'

Mr G checked the list off on his long slim fingers. 'We do not know that God exists. We do not know that he is dear. We do not know if there is anyone to be caught, or if he or she or they will be, or if we will be the ones to entrap that person or persons. We do not know that anybody did anything untoward to Miss Wright. She might have been a fantasist. She might have willingly engaged in or even have initiated acts of which she later became ashamed. We do not know that she intended to self-immolate.' He took a breath. We do not even know if that pasty-faced Father Seaton was telling the truth and that he did not murder her himself.'

He took a breath.

'That will do for now.' I jumped into the pause and the door flew open.

'Dinner is swerved,' Molly announced and, for the first time, I was glad that it was vegetarian.

24

<hr>

Crook and the Tilbury Typewritist

LIMEHOUSE POLICE STATION was as dreary inside as out, with three rows of backless wooden benches facing the desk. I had met the duty sergeant once before when we had captured the Tilbury Typewritist. The policeman had taken exception on that occasion to a female pointing out that he had released the same criminal only a fortnight previously, and he did not seem any the more thrilled to see me this time.

'Good afternoon, Sergeant Crook,' I greeted him. I occasionally wondered if the mockery his surname must arouse had made him such a sour person and, if so, why he had not changed it or his profession. 'We have an appointment with—'

'I know.' The sergeant glowered at us. 'Sit over there, girl.'

I had been about to settle exactly where Sergeant Crook was directing me but I immediately straightened up. 'You have a vivid imagination, Sergeant, to think that you see any girls here.'

'Well, you ain't a bloke.' Crook snickered at his own wit.

'I would have thought all your years of experience in the force would have taught you to recognize a lady when you see one,' I retorted. 'I have no difficulty whatsoever in identifying an obnoxious oaf.'

''Ere,' my good friend bristled. 'Who you calling a noaf?'

'There are three people in this room.' I smiled sweetly. 'So I shall give you four guesses.'

Sidney Grice ambled to the desk. 'From where have you acquired additional income, Crook?' he demanded.

'Dunno what you're talkin' abart.' The sergeant touched his moustaches.

'You have just put your finger on it,' my guardian told him. 'Literally.'

'Eh?'

'Your ridiculous and over-exuberant facial disfigurement has been waxed with Bowtree's Preparation and your sparsely thatched parasitized scalp dressed with Sniff's Macassar Oil, neither of which is to be had legally for under a guinea a bottle, scarcely affordable on your meagre though undeserved salary. Even Miss Middleton is unlikely to indulge in such extravagance.'

I was about to point out that I had no use for either product, especially the former, when a door to my left opened.

'Good afternoon, Mr Grice.' I did not need to turn to recognize the voice as Inspector Pound stepped in.

He took my hand gravely. 'And Miss Middleton.' His clear blue eyes met mine uneasily, I thought.

I had been *March* and even his *Dearest* at one time, but I tried to push that memory aside and returned his greetings politely.

'You are looking very well,' I commented, for George Pound had improved markedly in the nine months since I had last seen him. His posture, which had become stooped under the weight of his injuries, was upright again and he had regained some of the weight he had lost. His once-sallow complexion had taken on a healthier glow. Admittedly his black hair was lightly peppered with grey, but that only made his always-dignified appearance all the more distinguished.

'I am,' he assured me.

'I am very glad to hear it.'

George Pound released his grip.

'Mr Grice.' They shook hands.

'I see you have taken up transporting yourself on at least one of John Kemp Stanley's so-called safety bicycles.' My godfather wiped his hand on a white rectangle of cotton. Often he seemed more squeamish about touching the living than the dead.

The inspector glanced down. 'Do I have oil on my trousers?'

'Not visibly to the naked eye,' Mr G assured him. 'But the faint stretching and traces of a crease above each ankle indicate the wearing of clips to prevent one's apparel becoming entangled in the chain.'

'Come through.' Pound laughed. 'I had a lesson from a salesman who tried to convince me that my constables should ride them.' The office he led us into was cramped, floored with cracked linoleum, and gloomy, as the gas mantle was broken and the window frosted and barred. 'He reckoned that my men could travel much more quickly than on foot and get down alleys too narrow for a mounted policeman to pass along.'

He directed me to the only chair, a simple pine upright behind his desk, but I remained standing with the two men.

'You were not impressed,' I gathered from his manner.

Sidney Grice was leafing, uninvited, through a stack of paperwork.

'A policeman should look dignified.' Pound whipped a file out of my guardian's hands. 'Not like a child on a hobbyhorse.' He went behind his desk. 'Besides which, I don't need to tell you two how potholed the back streets can be.'

'Then kindly do not trouble to do so.' Mr G eyed the file like a boy hoping for a gift.

'And, as one constable proved painfully to another, it just takes a kick at the wheel or a stick between the spokes to send the rider sprawling.' He slipped the file into the middle drawer and locked it, and Sidney Grice made a tiny disappointed noise.

'Miss Albertoria Wright.' My guardian tapped the floor with his cane like a magician I saw once, but, unlike Monsieur

Magico, Sidney Grice did not disappear in a puff of yellow smoke.

Pound grimaced. 'Have you seen her body?'

'Possibly,' Mr G said cagily. 'The corpse matched her description in nine ways – sex, approximate age, build and height; hair length and natural colour; what limited dental information we have; clothing and jewellery – though, of course, those last two are easily changed.' He let the papers he had picked up fall back on the desk. 'I would need at least nine more corroborating factors to make a completely confident positive identification.'

'Have you any idea who drove her to this act?' I asked, and my guardian opened his mouth. 'Yes, I know,' I said hastily, 'that I have made a hundred unsubstantiated assumptions such as that it was Albertoria and that she did commit suicide and that she was driven to it by somebody.'

Sidney Grice yawned. 'You are too hard on yourself, Miss Middleton. You have only made forty-eight errors.'

Inspector Pound scratched his chin. 'Oh, I don't know,' he said. 'I can think of a couple more.'

Mr G considered the statement. 'I assume you are not including any of the ninety-three subdivisions. Oh, I see—'

I was not the only one who had caught what she had never thought to see again, a brief but very welcome twinkle in the inspector's eyes.

'A joke,' Sidney Grice said glumly.

25

The Axminister Axeman

SOMEBODY KNOCKED ON the door.

'Go away,' Sidney Grice called and we listened as the heavy footfalls faded.

'That might have been important,' Inspector Pound objected.

'But not to me,' my guardian pronounced, which, to his way of thinking, should satisfy everyone.

'Actually,' Inspector Pound held up the key to taunt Sidney Grice, 'we do have information about a man she was seen leaving the White Unicorn with.'

'With whom,' my guardian corrected automatically.

'A number of witnesses saw her arguing with him at the bar,' the inspector ploughed on.

'How many?' Mr G demanded.

'We spoke to five.'

'A small but prime number then,' my godfather muttered.

'Enough for us to piece together a reasonable description. It was generally agreed that he was a tall man, a foreigner with military moustaches, middle-aged, close-cropped hair and a scar on his left cheek.'

'Schlangezahn,' I breathed. 'The man who attacked Geraldine Hockaday.'

Sidney Grice put down a stone paperweight with which he had been toying. 'Possibly the prince who was allegedly the man who allegedly committed that alleged crime.' He whisked up a paperknife.

'We have one more piece of evidence that makes one of those allegedlies a bit less alleged.' The inspector took a rectangular taupe envelope from the letter rack on his desk and emptied out six torn pieces of stiff white card.

Sidney Grice flipped two blank pieces over with the knife to show the elaborate printed letterforms.

'A customer picked it up,' George Pound explained. 'Harry Stewart – he used to be in the force.'

'London is becoming devoid of men who did not used to be policemen but are not now,' Sidney Grice commented labyrinthically.

'He became concerned when he saw the man trying to drag her out of the door but, when he intervened, the man became so menacing that Stewart backed off.'

'So he just sat back and let it happen?' I said incredulously.

'The whole pub let it happen.' Pound clearly took my disbelief as a slur on his force. 'Step into the White Unicorn any time and you'll see a dozen women being mistreated. Most of them earn their living that way.'

'Is it the same Harry Stewart who was attacked by the Axminster Axeman?' My guardian clinked his right eye with the tip of the knife. 'He lost both hands and his left leg above the knee.'

'I am sorry,' I said.

'If there are any conclusions to be jumped at,' my guardian explained, 'Miss Middleton is a regular Springheel Jack.'

George Pound brought out his meerschaum pipe. 'Do you like jigsaw puzzles, Miss Middleton?'

'Not since I was a child.' I stepped to the desk. 'But I think I can manage this one.'

Two of the pieces were upside down but I did not need those to work out the name. Ulrich Schlan....

'Have you spoken to him?' Sidney Grice enquired.

'They don't send a lowly inspector to interview a Prussian nobleman.' Pound watched my guardian's antics cagily. 'The Chief Constable had a word and came away none the wiser.'

'The Germans owe Mr Grice a favour,' I recalled. 'So the prince might speak to him.'

'He will be speaking for himself tomorrow.' Pound slipped the keys away. 'He has volunteered to appear at the inquest.'

'Volunteered?' I echoed.

Pound nodded. 'You don't subpoena a cousin to King Wilhelm.'

'Kaiser,' Sidney Grice corrected him.

'Really?' The inspector raised his eyebrows. 'I thought his name was Wilhelm.'

And, turning from my godfather, George Pound gave me a wink.

26

⊙✦⊙

The King of Kings and the African Sun

I WENT TO CHRIST the King. Peter Hockaday had taken a job researching the family history of the elderly Reverend Zedobiath Darwin, who was anxious to prove that he was not even remotely related to the infamous Charles. For a small monthly stipend Peter would go to the vicar's house in Byng Place and trawl through an enormous, disorganized collection of papers, many of which had no bearing on the gentleman's ancestry at all, but Zedobiath was adamant that they had to be checked and filed before he would be satisfied.

The Reverend Darwin always attended an afternoon liturgy at the Church of Christ the King, a few dozen yards away, and Peter would escort him there and walk briskly round the square for twenty minutes before collecting him. For once my timing was perfect and I was just in time to witness Peter handing his enfeebled charge over to a verger before making off.

Geraldine's brother was a tall man, and his military training showed in his erect gait and the way he carried his cane tucked under his arm as a swagger stick.

'Good afternoon, Miss Middleton.' He lifted his hat. 'Are you attending the service?'

'I do not need to go in there to find God,' I said, and he let his hat drop back.

'You are lucky to find him at all,' he told me. 'I lost him under the African sun and I have never quite found him again.'

141

That was the first time I had known Peter Hockaday to refer even obliquely to his time in the Sudan. I knew from Geraldine that he had been present at the battle of El Obeid, a terrible slaughter with eight thousand Egyptian troops killed by the Mahdists and only a handful of their British officers surviving. He was lucky to escape with only part of his left earlobe missing.

'Perhaps he will find you again one day,' I suggested.

Peter Hockaday did not look convinced. 'But I must not talk like this on hallowed ground.' He tried to look abashed. 'Will you take a short walk with me?'

'It is you I have come to see, Mr Hockaday.' I took his proffered arm. 'I am worried about your sister.'

'You are right to be.' He paused to tickle a stray dog's ear. 'Oh, Miss Middleton...'

'Please call me March,' I urged. 'It saves three syllables.'

'If you will do the same,' he told me and became flustered. 'I mean, call me Peter, of course.'

I laughed and then remembered. 'You were about to say something.'

'Only that I wish you had known Geraldine before... all this.' We turned left into Gordon Square, a pleasant rectangle of greenery surrounded by superior soot-dabbled houses, the dog ambling at Peter's heel. 'She was so *alive*,' he continued. 'Her eyes, I cannot tell you, March. If they could have been mounted they would have graced the Crown jewels. Oh...' Peter stopped and his new friend stopped too, sitting obediently at his feet. 'I hope you do not think I was making fun of Mr Grice's eye.'

'I shall not mention it to him,' I vowed, and we set off again.

Peter had long strides and, though he tried to accommodate his pace to mine, I found myself almost breaking into an intermittent run.

'I hope you do not mind me saying that Geraldine does not

like your guardian,' he told me, as we skirted a group of boys kicking a rag ball. 'And, if truth be told...'

'Neither do you,' I broke in. 'Not many people do.'

Peter hesitated. 'Would it be impertinent to ask...'

'When I was imprisoned Mr Grice came to see me.'

'I should hope so.' He patted the dog.

'He was my one comfort,' I said. 'I know that is difficult to believe.'

Peter squeezed my arm with his. 'He does not seem the most sympathetic of men.'

'He asked me to marry him.' I glanced up and saw that my companion was shocked. 'But that was only so that he could control my money.'

I shut my mouth. It had not been exactly like that, had it?

'Is he making any progress on my sister's case?' Peter asked.

'Very little.' I reached towards the dog but it shied away. 'I did make an offer to Geraldine to refund your money if she wanted us to drop our investigations.'

Peter crushed my arm against him. 'You will not abandon her? You cannot.'

'I do not know what else to do,' I confessed.

'And Mr Grice – has he given up?'

We stepped on to the road to get round an artist chalking a good likeness of Lord Nelson on the pavement.

'Mr Grice never gives up,' I asserted, though I sometimes believed he had given up on me.

We turned right, along the short side of the not-very-square square.

'I shall give him a week,' Peter declared.

A hurdy-gurdy man was jigging wildly as he cranked his instrument. Some of the strings were broken, I noticed, but he still managed to produce such an ear-splitting wailing noise that the dog darted in front of Peter, hackles raised, ready to protect its new master.

'And then you will want your money back?' I clarified.

Peter puffed. 'I shall have no use for money then and neither shall the man who hurt my sister.'

The dog jumped backwards, nearly tripping us both over it.

'What will you do?' I asked in alarm.

'I think you can guess.'

'Stop thief!' We turned to see who was yelling. 'Those two,' an elderly man in a tattered naval uniform bawled from across the road. 'They be stealing my barker.'

The dog, on hearing his true master's voice, cowered and tried to hide behind my skirts, but the old seaman came rolling over, miraculously avoiding being run over by a phaeton weaving round a covered cart.

'I assure you,' Peter began, but the man was reeling a length of rope out of his pocket and looping it around the dog's neck.

The dog crouched.

'How do I know it is yours?' I demanded.

'Well, it ain't yours,' he replied and dragged the dog away, its claws trying desperately to anchor it to the spot.

'You are choking it,' I protested, but the dog gave up the fight and slunk miserably beside him.

I knew this was a trick to make us buy the animal, but neither of us could adopt a dog.

'You will not take the law into your own hands?' I asked anxiously, but Peter did not reply at once.

A cat ran by with a flapping grey pigeon in its mouth and a clock bell sounded far away.

'Geraldine left it in the hands of the police and I placed it in Mr Grice's.' His clear blue eyes darted away from me. 'And what good has it done her, March? If we cannot have justice, we shall have revenge.'

'I may have a better plan.' I saw the pigeon's beak open and close in a silent plea for the mercy it would not receive.

He checked his half-hunter. 'I am sorry. I must return to my employer, but can I meet you to discuss it?'

'Do you know where the Empress Cafe is? Tomorrow at ten?'

'I shall be there. Will you be all right if I leave you here?'

'I came alone,' I reminded him, and Peter Hockaday inclined his head.

I stood for a minute, watching him march away, a good head above the crowd, so tall and strong that I was frightened for him.

27

The Count and the Coroner

I HAD SEEN MORE imposing edifices than Limehouse Town
Hall, but there was a modest dignity in its square two-
storey exterior with high arched windows and matching
pillared portico. The entrance hall was pleasant enough,
mahogany fittings and a rosewood grand piano showing that it
was not built only for bureaucratic functions.

The inquest was held on the first floor, up a wide, iron, grand
staircase, rising to a mezzanine before splitting to continue
upwards and back on itself. At home my guardian had a habit
of trudging up the stairs like a condemned man to the gallows
but, as so often when we were out, he sprinted and was up the
right arm two steps at a time, leaving me to climb the left as
quickly and elegantly as my garments permitted.

The Grand Assembly Room seemed too cheerfully lit for the
occasion by its full-length windows and it was a pity that nobody
had seen fit to open them and let in a breeze from the river for,
even with no more than a couple of dozen people present, the air
was oppressively stuffy.

Sidney Grice brushed by a dark-blue uniformed elderly usher
– who was trying to enquire as to his business there – and settled
on the front row, dwarfed by the figure of Inspector Pound to
his left.

'If miss would care to sit with sir she will be out of the
direct sunlight,' the usher told me, his voice rustling like

autumn leaves, and I was tempted to follow his suggestion but I slid into a reddish-brown morocco-covered chair in the back corner behind a hefty fellow who looked and smelled like a cowman. If I craned my neck I could just about see the proceedings, but was confident that I was unobtrusive under my wide-brimmed bonnet.

The room itself was pleasant enough, with huge Persian rugs on the polished oak floor. A low dais had been constructed at the front with a desk, behind which sat the coroner, a plump, jolly-looking man, with his clerk, a thin specimen of his sex, whose general demeanour might have led one to believe that it was he who had been bereaved. The clerk's skull fascinated me with its patchworked geometrical shapes like the papier-mâché puppets I used to make as a child.

The coroner gave a preamble about why we were there and the scope of his hearing, and called upon his first witness, Father Roger Seaton, the blonde-haired cherubic curate who had seen and spoken to the girl answering Albertoria Wright's description, on Westminster Bridge. He said little that I had not previously read in the *Daily Telegraph*, expressing his devout hopes for her immortal soul and reiterating that he could not say for certain whether she had fallen by intent or accident. Strangely, for a man used to preaching to hundreds, his voice was low and indistinct and he had to be urged courteously three times to speak up.

Sidney Grice appeared next, very distinguished in his charcoal frock coat with matching cravat. He concisely summed up the reasons for believing the body in all probability to be that of Albertoria and was gracious enough to acknowledge my role in the examination. The coroner expressed his shock that a lady should have performed such a task and I was not called upon to give my account.

Sergeant Hewitt of the Thames River Police could not be present, as he had been crushed when he slipped between his launch and a barge he was about to search for contraband. The coroner expressed his hopes for a speedy recovery and allowed the clerk to read out a short statement about how the body had been found.

Inspector Pound came next, smartly besuited, his moustaches – which I had once ravaged in an attempt to tidy them whilst he was ill – neatly trimmed, his lips full red, his eyes clear blue, his strong square features beautiful in the sunlight.

He gave his evidence clearly and concisely and, though I no longer had any right to be, I was proud of my onetime-almost fiancé. George Pound recounted what he had been told by the customers of the White Unicorn. He was at once authoritative and yet so vulnerable that I wanted to rush up and hug him.

The last witness was a tall, well-built man, stately in his deportment and dressed in a frock coat, and it was no surprise to me when he introduced himself as Prince Ulrich Klaus Sigismund Schlangezahn, Colonel of a regiment of Prussian Hussars. He was a striking man, with close-cropped hair so black that I suspected he encouraged the coloration. His face was precisely and symmetrically carved, with a long, slightly hooked nose, immaculately waxed, upturned military moustaches, pale lips pulled down a little severely and eyes so deep-set under a prominent brow that they flashed almost jet as he directed them round the room. His left face was divided by a clean white scar, running from above his eye and down his cheek to just above the corner of his mouth.

He spotted Sidney Grice and inclined his head a fraction in formal recognition, but my godfather was too intent on the witness to consider what he rarely worried about – social niceties – and his posture remained rigid.

The prince's voice was loud and unfaltering with the authoritative ring of a man used to commanding others. He did not attempt to deny meeting a girl who he now believed to be Albertoria Wright, nor that he had spoken to her, but he declined to reveal what they had spoken about. Yes, he had given her his card and, yes, she had torn it up and, yes, he had taken her arm to lead her from that public house. He called it a *bier keller*, which gave rise to some merriment amongst the scant audience for which the coroner gently admonished them. He had taken her outside, but she had run away and he had not followed. A gentleman does not chase girls along the streets.

His manner was aloof and spoken as if we were all unpleasant aromas.

The coroner listened with polite scepticism. 'Is there anything else you can tell us, Your Highness?'

'No.' Schlangezahn bowed stiffly to the coroner and marched away.

*

'Cold fish,' Pound murmured afterwards. 'Makes you seem the picture of charm, Mr Grice.'

'Charm,' Sidney Grice pushed me out of his way, 'is like a beautiful woman – superficially attractive but, beneath the surface, there is always gristle and offal.'

'What a horrible image,' I objected.

'I see no mirrors,' he said laconically.

28

The Breath of Angels

THE ROOM WAS dark, lit only by four tiny oil lamps, brass with stumpy glass chimneys. I had seen their like before – those long nights in Cabool. The flames were so short that they hardly broke the darkness enough to cast shadows on the low tables where they stood and I could barely make out the two men already reclining on the other couches. One of them leaned forward, dipping his bleached face into the yellow pool. He was a young man with straw-coloured hair and Prince Albert moustaches, and he did not even glance at me with his drooping eyes as he set about his task.

The boy showed me to my couch, velvet-covered with a tartan blanket. 'You need help, mistress?'

'No.' I gave him a shilling and he left. Already my eyes were gathering the gloom. The basement ceiling was low and the walls much as I remembered them – garish scenes of corpulent men and their impossibly curvaceous concubines in awkward and unappealing poses.

A lacquered tray had been set up with its lamp and paraphernalia. I lifted my veil and, turning my attention to a white porcelain dish, selected a tablet from the six arranged round a rampant dragon on the base. The paste was too damp. I impaled it on a long silver needle from an ivory thimble and held it well above the flame, watching the steam rise as I rotated the tablet.

It reminded me of cooking potatoes on a bonfire when I was a child in Parbold so impossibly long ago.

I lowered the tablet and watched it turn from light to dark brown to rich gold. It should be sticky enough now. The pipe lay beside the tray, about two-foot long and made of dark-stained bamboo, ornamented with stamped copper rings. I pressed the softened tablet into the doorknob-shaped clay bowl and lay, propped up on one side, putting the bowl on to the flame, just long enough to vaporize the resin without burning it.

Reclining, I put the open end to my mouth and sucked, drawing the incense deep into my lungs, holding that familiar coolness as long as I could until exhaling through my nose to gather the last of its essence before it wisped into the darkness.

The effect was immediate – a complete unfathomable happiness, an intense sense of hope, a great surge of bliss. I was aware that the men were watching me, but I felt nothing other than the profound wonderment that comes over all indulgers of the sacred flower.

How could I have forgotten how paradise seeps from the bulb of a poppy? I sucked again and let the breath of angels flood into my body, drawing me back into my pillow, sinking me into myself, closing my eyes with such a delicious drowsiness that I hardly heard the key turn in the door.

Somebody spoke. 'Turn up the light.' And as the gas flared I opened my eyes to see silhouettes taking form, blurred shapes coming into focus, one tall and wiry, blond with a tanned complexion, the other even taller and barrel-chested, more mature, both standing looking at me. The second man's lips were full and sensual, the upper carrying waxed military moustaches, his hair black and cropped short, and I tried to tell myself that it was just my pipe and the poor light that made him look handsome. I smiled sleepily.

The second man did not smile back. He walked up and

looked down at me as one might assess a prize pig. '*Mein Gott*, she is a plain one.'

And, all of a sudden, he did not seem quite so attractive, his leer forking off in a livid scar. He prodded my waist with his cane. 'Not much meat on her.' He turned to his companion. 'You vill have to do better than this if I am to use you again.'

The younger man flapped his hands. 'It is like fishing. Sometimes you pull out a Dover sole, sometimes a lamprey.'

'Next time catch me a salmon, something I can get my teeth into.'

The older man sniffed and reached down to stroke my cheek with the back of his hand. I slapped it away.

'Do not touch me.'

He grabbed hold of my hair. 'She has spirit. I like that better than the vilting English roses they usually bring me, who beg and veep and svoon. You will give me a bit of a fight, vill you not, my little one?'

He grasped under my head and pulled me up, his face so close I could smell his cologne. Few Englishmen would have worn that.

'Let go.' I clawed at his face but he grasped my wrist, pulling me easily away.

'That hurt a little.' He dabbed his nostril where my nail had caught it. 'Do you like pain, girl? I can supply it in plenty.' His fingers clawed into my hair and twisted it and I winced, but I would not cry out. He let go and I fell back.

'I think that is enough.' The young man's voice took a hard edge.

The Germanic man blinked like a lizard. 'Getting a fit of conscience?' he mocked. 'Vell it is late for that, my fellow. Your money is on the mantle shelf. Take it and go. Vee shall never do business again.'

The younger man looked at him coolly. 'You will leave her alone *now*.'

The tall man laughed. 'And how vill you make me?'

'Before you start a fight...' I pulled my skirts just above my knee. The younger man averted his eyes in embarrassment but the other appraised me critically.

'Nice legs,' he purred.

I found my garter – 'Thank you' – and whipped out my revolver, the one I had taken from Johnny Wallace.

The German raised his eyebrows and depressed his moustaches. 'Do you know how to use that?'

'Enough to put a bullet through your heart,' I bluffed, and he eyed me with amusement. 'Or brain – if you have one.'

'This is ridiculous,' he said calmly and jerked his head towards the younger man. 'If you vant more we can negotiate.'

I got to my feet, keeping the gun aimed straight at him.

'We can negotiate better at the police station,' the younger man told him.

The tall man frowned. 'You are not looking like a – vot do you call them? – peeler.'

'That is because I am not.'

'Vot then?'

'Your nemesis,' I said.

The German man looked momentarily nonplussed but he recovered quickly. 'My men are up the stairs and they are many and armed. Do you think you can take me out of here and through the streets of London like a valk in Hyde Park – you, a girl and he,' he vibrated his lips, 'hardly more than a boy?'

'Yes,' I said.

The young man clenched his jaw. 'Shall I take the gun now?'

Two of the lamps burned out in quick succession.

'No, thank you, Peter.'

'I had a servant called Dieter.' The older man tipped his head back. 'He displeased me and I had him flogged.'

'Why, you arrogant...' My companion bunched his fist.

'I have a servant called Molly,' I told the older man. 'She is a good-hearted woman and might even visit you in prison.'

'You are making a stupid mistake,' he sneered.

'It is you who have made the mistake,' Peter assured him.

'And if I even think you are signalling to anybody...' I linked my left arm through the German's, pushing the barrel under my cloak into his ribs and trying not to look unnerved by how much he towered. 'I must warn you that I have a very nervous finger, Your Highness.'

The German man's lips drooped. 'You are knowing me? That could be very awkward.' He blinked lazily. 'For you.'

'We have known you for a long time, Prince Ulrich,' my companion said. 'But we never had any proof.'

The prince reappraised me. 'Pity,' he said. 'You may be plain but we could haff had such sport.'

'My sister is still housebound because of your *sport*.' Peter came towards him. 'My God, if I had that gun!'

Which was exactly why he had not.

'Better to let him live,' I reasoned, 'and suffer for what he did.'

'Vich one voz she?' Schlangezahn enquired as one might discuss a mutual acquaintance.

'The one who will put you behind bars,' I told him. 'Now, perhaps you could escort me to the police station.'

The prince's face was impassive and he bowed from the waist. 'The pleasure, dear lady, is all mine.'

'Move, damn you,' Peter urged impatiently.

'Haff some respect,' the prince reproved mildly. 'There is a lady present.'

29

The Stairs to the Stars

THE STAIRCASE PRESENTED our first problem. It was steeper than I remembered and ran straight up a narrow gap between two walls. There had hardly been room for me to pass down in my flounced-out skirts and bustle, let alone walk two abreast.

'I shall go first,' I decided, 'and you shall bring up the rear, Mr Hockaday.'

'Hockaday,' Prince Ulrich mused. 'I rarely know their names but this one caused me trouble.'

'She has hardly begun,' Peter vowed, as I put my foot on the first step.

We moved up crabwise so that I was up three steps before my prisoner was on the first. His face was slightly lower than mine and I could look into his eyes, deep and dark with a hint of amusement.

Muffled voices came down the stairwell.

'I do not believe you vill kill me.' His lips pouted disdainfully.

'There is one sure way to find out.' I edged up another step.

The prince stumbled and I dug the muzzle in.

'I believe you,' he promised hastily.

The talking grew louder, men's voices raised in banter and breaking into laughter. My right shoulder touched the door at the top and I realized that I had a problem. The door had a round wooden handle. Obviously I could not turn that with my elbow and I could not use my right hand.

'Do not put me to the test,' I warned and unlinked my arm from his, keeping the gun firmly in place.

'If you shoot me, my friends will kill you both, and they are cruel men,' Prince Ulrich assured me.

'Then you had better behave,' Peter Hockaday warned, 'or we shall all die.'

I twisted my torso, not taking my eyes off the prince. 'You will speak English.' I found the handle with my left hand. 'Here goes,' I breathed, mainly to myself, and twisted the handle.

The door creaked and I linked my arm through his again.

'Ulrich,' a deep voice cried merrily. Sidney Grice would have been able to translate his next remark but I did not have much German. I think he commented how quick the prince had been, and that another voice asked if he'd had good sport.

'Speak English in the lady's presence,' the prince instructed.

The door swung open and I saw three of them, two sitting, and one standing over the 'Chinaman' at his desk. Foo/Jones stared at me and wet his lips, nonplussed and then amused. He put his hands together and bowed.

'Aber voz...' A striking redheaded young man in a long maroon cloak eyed us in surprise.

'It is all gutt,' the prince assured them. 'Vee are just going for the valk.'

'Aber,' the young man began again, and then some more. I understood none of it but his tone was clearly suspicious.

We shuffled up.

'Nein nein,' Prince Ulrich assured him. 'Vee go alone.'

We were in the room now and it was obvious from their uneasy glances that they were suspicious. Peter Hockaday came up after us.

'Guten abend herren,' he greeted the group cheerily and their puzzlement increased.

I got to the door with my prisoner and he pulled it open. The red-haired man grabbed Peter's arm.

'Vot is going on?' he demanded.

'We are.' Peter tried to shrug him off but the man tightened his grip.

Jones did his best oriental inscrutability, but I saw him slide open a drawer without taking his brown eyes off me and I was not going to wait to find out what he kept in there.

'We are leaving,' I insisted quietly. '*Now.*'

'Release him,' Prince Ulrich commanded his companion and the red-haired man let go of Peter. 'Oh, I nearly forgot.'

He reached into his coat pocket and I dug the muzzle in, but the prince produced a black cloth bag with a drawstring, and I heard the coins clink as Jones/Chang caught it.

The moon glowed full that night and countless stars burned unimaginably far away, but all the lights of heaven could not penetrate the black misery that went by the name of Limehouse.

30

The Old Biscuit Warehouse

I KNEW THAT WE had almost no hope of hailing a cab in that area, which is why I had arranged for Gerry Dawson to take us. Gerry was an ex-policeman and one of the very few drivers I could rely upon completely. My trust was not displaced for, as we rounded the corner to the site of the old biscuit warehouse, I saw his hansom still waiting by the half-tumbled unloading bay, his piebald mare, Meg, in harness. Her back was sagging and she stood with her front left leg raised from a strained hock. It was not that he treated her cruelly – for his wife joked that he loved his horse more than her – but Meg was getting old and a life of hauling heavy loads was beginning to show.

Gerry looked down from his high seat at the back. 'Didn't know you was reelin' in such a big bloater. We'll never get the three of you aboard.'

'We cannot leave Miss Middleton here unaccompanied.' Peter Hockaday hesitated. 'But I am worried about her riding in your cab with him.'

Gerry Dawson pulled the lever to unfasten the flaps. 'Don't you worry about the Frenchy. I can deal with him.'

'I am a Prussian officer,' Prince Ulrich expostulated, 'of noble lineage.'

Gerry shrugged. 'It's all the same to me. Foreigners are Scots or French and you ain't wearing a kilt.' He gestured with his whip handle. 'Hop on.'

I let go of the prince's arm and he heaved himself on to the footboard.

'If anything should happen to Miss Middleton...' Peter warned our prisoner, but Prince Ulrich sneered.

'It is not I who vill be afraid ven my friends find out vot has happened.'

'Those posturing dandies?' I scorned, ignoring the hand he put out to help me aboard and keeping my revolver trained on my captive.

'Is that weapon loaded?' Gerry leaned away.

'It certainly is.'

'Only you won't shoot Meg?' he asked uneasily, having heard about my expertise with firearms.

'I have had lessons.' I scrambled aboard, slightly ashamed at how easily the lies tumbled out.

The prince looked about. 'Who is Meg?'

'Your kind of girl,' I told him. 'Black hair halfway down her back.'

He pursed his lips. 'I prefer blondes.'

I squeezed in beside him, pulling the flap shut after me. Gerry double-clicked his tongue and we edged into the cobbled square.

'Don't go wanderin',' he cautioned Peter. 'Stand under the shelter. You won't be seen there and I'll be back before you can spit.'

'Be careful, March.'

'It is not me who will need protection when we meet again.' I wagged a finger. 'Lamprey indeed.'

'Sorry about that.' Peter grinned boyishly, tipped his hat and disappeared into the shadows.

'Do not worry,' the prince said. 'I shall be making very good care of you both.' And there was nothing boyish or reassuring in *his* smile.

31

The Curious Case of the Coughing Dog

EARGENT HORWICH WAS on duty as we made our way into Marylebone Police Station.

'Gerry,' he called brightly, though it was after three in the morning by the clock behind his counter. 'Come to rejoin the force?'

'Not likely.' Gerry Dawson grinned. 'I'd rather enjoy a pint with people than arrest them.'

We all knew that Gerry had not touched alcohol since Sidney Grice had rescued him from sleeping in doorways.

'Miss Middleton.' The sergeant greeted me warmly for Mr G and I had kept him from ruin too. He eyed the way I stood arm-in-arm with the prince in surprise. 'Who's the gentleman friend?'

'Neither a gentleman nor a friend,' I replied.

'You will be all right now?' Gerry asked me.

'I am sure Sergeant Horwich will look after me. Thank you for getting us here, Gerry.'

'I'll go back then.' He nodded to his old colleague.

Was there a wistfulness in the way Gerry Dawson viewed his old haunt as he set off? I thought so, but I was busy keeping hold of my prisoner.

'I wish to press charges,' I told the sergeant, 'against this man for attempting to violate me.'

The sergeant studied us both. ''E don't look that desperate.'

'Nor am I,' the prince said coldly. 'I am Prince Ulrich Albrecht

Sigismund Schlangezahn, cousin to Kaiser Wilhelm, Emperor of Prussia, and, if you release me this instant, I shall ensure that you do not lose your job and pension on my account.'

'Blimey, 'e don't 'alf talk funny,' Sergeant Horwich commented and picked up his pen, the wooden handle stained blue but a new brass nib on it. 'Name.'

The prince stood erect. 'I haff already told you.'

Horwich dipped the pen. 'Yeah, but you'll have to spell it for me. All those Rooshan words sound the same to me.'

'Prussian,' Prince Ulrich insisted vehemently.

The sergeant shrugged. 'Same thing.'

There was a commotion at the entrance and a large black dog burst through the door, dragging a disarrayed Constable Perkins by a rope around its neck. They were followed by a ruddy-faced woman, and it did not take my guardian's skills to deduce from her bloodstained apron and the strong aroma that she worked at a fishmonger's.

'What's all this?' Horwich bellowed in his best military manner.

The door swung shut and flew open again, and a thin man rushed in breathlessly.

'Arrest that woman, Constable,' he squealed and the sergeant stiffened indignantly. 'She's poisoned Nero.'

'Poisoned?' the woman shrieked. 'That mangy mongrel snaffled an 'ole cod 'ead and 'e won't pay for it.'

'Snaffled?' The man went purple. 'She fed Nero a rotten fish 'cause 'e nipped 'er bleedin' tabby.'

The dog started coughing.

'Nipped?' The fishwife howled. I was getting bored with their habit of repeating each other, but apparently they were just getting into their stride. 'Nipped? That stinking fleabag near bit my Queenie clear in 'arf last week and today 'e charges in like Nelson at Waterloo and—'

The dog quivered.

'Silence,' Sergeant Horwich bellowed. 'You,' he jabbed his pen, splattering the man's shirt in royal blue ink, 'will buy 'er a new cat if 'er old one can't be mended. You,' the pen shot towards the woman, 'will pay for 'is dog if it pops its paws. And General Nelson was not at Waterloo.' He scratched his head with the pen handle and ended weakly, 'I don't think.'

The dog appeared to be choking.

'See, 'e's dyin',' the man cried. 'I want annuva black one what can sing for the queen. Show them, boy.'

And Nero stretched out his neck, but instead of obliging us with a tune, convulsed and vomited over Constable Perkins's boot.

'Ruddy 'ell.' Perkins shook his foot in disgust.

'There you are!' the man exulted. 'There's your 'ead back.'

'What on earth is that commotion?' Inspector Pound came out of his office.

32

The Hound of Marylebone

THE INSPECTOR WAS not quite his usual dapper self. He must have been working many hours by the time I met him that night for his necktie had been pulled down and his collar unbuttoned, and – though I rather liked the stubble – he was in need of a good shave.

'Miss Middleton,' he greeted me formally. His clear blue eyes looked at my prisoner. 'And Prince Ulrich.' Pound acknowledged him icily.

'Inspector Pound.' The prince touched his own cravat as if to emphasize his sartorial superiority. 'I thought I saw the last of you.'

'I hoped the same,' Pound told him and turned to me. 'What is your business with this man?'

'Is that Eric with a U?' Horwich picked up his pen.

'Prince Ulrich attempted to force himself upon me.' I indicated the prince with a tip of my head and in an instant Inspector Pound's cool blue eyes took on a glow.

'And what have you to say to that?' he asked the prince sharply.

'I am a member of His Imperial Majesty Kaiser Wilhelm's delegation here on diplomatic business,' Prince Ulrich responded contemptuously. 'I do not answer to you.'

Pound's eyes flared. 'I am an officer of the law of this land and no man is exempt from it.'

'However,' Ulrich met his glare insolently, 'since you are clearly acquainted with this peculiar woman, you might ask her to remove her pistol from my person.'

I had almost forgotten that the revolver was still poking into the side of my captive's chest and unhooked my arm from the prince's to bring out the gun.

'Blow me,' the man said and, snatching his dog's lead from Constable Perkins's grasp, scarpered on to the street. The fish-wife had beaten him to it.

'Not your usual style.' Pound raised his eyebrows as he eyed my weapon. 'I would be grateful if you could point it at the floor.'

I did so and the inspector took my weapon by the barrel, carefully lowering the hammer and passing it to the sergeant. 'Put that in the safe.'

'It is not loaded anyway,' I assured him.

The prince laughed. He had strong white teeth and was, in an instant, altogether less forbidding.

Inspector Pound greeted my announcement with something close to despair. 'Keep this man here but do *not* arrest him,' he instructed Horwich. 'I will take a statement from Miss Middleton in my office.'

I followed him down the corridor. 'I was not expecting to see you here,' I told his broad back.

'They are very short with injuries and a resignation,' he told me gruffly over his shoulder, and I pondered on the irony of that, for it would have been much easier to have taken my prisoner to the Limehouse Station had I not been trying to avoid this meeting.

I had first entered that room the day after I came to London, when Sidney Grice had questioned William Ashby for the stabbing to death of his wife, Sarah. Inspector Pound had a contempt for paperwork which was to earn him more than a few reprimands from his superiors over the years and the room had been in chaos, but whoever had used it in George's absence had been exemplary in his tidiness for there was not a document on the floor, not a chair piled high with files.

'Take a seat,' he instructed rather than offered and I sat on the edge, my bustle against the back spindles, whilst he perched on the corner of his desk.

'So what is this about?' His tone remained official.

'I am sure you remember Geraldine Hockaday,' I began.

'I am unlikely to forget that case,' he replied grimly. 'Schlangezahn got off without charge and the German ambassador demanded that I was dismissed. If he had not been so high-handed and got the Home Secretary's back up, I would have been looking for another job.'

George Pound rebuttoned his collar.

'Well, you have two witnesses who will not be intimidated this time,' I assured him.

'Two?' He straightened his tie.

'Peter Hockaday was there with me.'

'Her brother?' he clarified in surprise, brushing some dust off his knee.

'He pretended to be a procurer.'

Pound's eyes narrowed and I knew that look. 'This sounds dangerously like entrapment.' His hands rose and for a moment I imagined they might cup my face but he only tugged his coat sleeves down over his wrists.

'He approached Peter.'

'In front of witnesses?'

'None that would come forward,' I admitted. 'It was in the lounge bar of the Waldringham Hotel.'

Inspector Pound exhaled heavily through his nostrils. 'What does Mr Grice think of all this?' He tapped his right heel three times against the desk. 'And why is he not here?'

I swallowed. 'I have not told him yet.'

Pound blew out through his lips and I could not help but

remember how they used to mould to mine. He rocked forward on to his feet.

'When I came into the lobby there was an angry mob baying for Schlangezahn's blood, with a ferocious black hound straining to savage him,' he decided. 'I shall detain Prince Ulrich here for his own protection and to maintain public order. You will go home and return immediately with Mr Grice, and we will see what we can sort out of this mess.' He opened the top drawer of his desk and brought out a full whisky bottle. 'Perhaps he will be a bit more conversational over a drink.' He rooted about for two almost clean glasses.

'I doubt it,' I said.

'So do I.' Inspector Pound huffed. 'Go.'

33

The Nightwatchman and Identical Twins

THE NIGHT WATCHMAN was hurrying down steps to knock on basement doors as I returned to Gower Street. In poorer areas he would have tapped with a bamboo pole on upper windows, but in this part of Bloomsbury it was the servants who were roused, not the householders. The latter could have an extra hour or so in bed while their water was heated and breakfasts prepared. My guardian would not pay the penny a day for this service. He expected our maid to wake herself without the benefit of this or the expense of an alarm clock. After all, he always woke up at exactly whatever time he had decided upon.

Molly did not look like she had been up long when I tapped on the door and she was in the process of pinning on her hat when she answered my call.

'Yes?' She peered blearily though the gap.

'It's me, Molly.'

'But you're in bed,' she objected.

'As you can see, I am not.' It was starting to rain.

Molly wrinkled her nose. 'How do I know you ain't not your own identical twin like Gasper Square in *The Shade of Merry Murray*?'

'Squire Jasper,' I corrected, as if the name mattered. I had long given up trying to convince her that I had invented the story for amusement. 'If you think I am not me, go and see if I am in my room.'

Molly considered my suggestion.

'All right, I shall abmit you.' The idea of running back upstairs cannot have been attractive to her. 'But, if you aintn't not you, you'll be fearious when you find out.' She took the chain off. 'And you dontn't not want to get on the wrong side of you, I can tell you, miss – if you *are* you.'

'Oh, for goodness' sake.' I rammed my cloak into her arms and marched into the study.

'He's out,' Molly called after me. 'Infestigating why Nelsong's Columns aintn't not been stolled.'

I went upstairs to tidy myself up. It had been a long night and the effects of the opium had still not worn off. I sat on my bed and the next thing I knew, there was a face pressed against mine and Molly was saying, 'If you aintn't not the other one, he wants to see you immediantley and that means without not no delay.'

I got up, straightened my clothes as best I could, and trudged down after her.

Sidney Grice sat at his desk perusing his copy of Jacob Cromwell's *Secreta Botanica*, the infamous book of poisons, which was one of his greatest treasures. There were only four copies known to be in existence.

'Explain,' he said without looking up.

'How much do you know?'

He turned a page with an exquisite float of the fingers. 'You do not imagine you can go in and out of people's lodgings without such visits being drawn to my attention – especially those of Lieutenant and Miss Hockaday?'

'Gerry has spoken?'

My guardian scribbled a note on a sheet of white paper and suddenly I felt like the little girl I had been, on one of the very few occasions her father had scolded her.

'Dawson has nineteen faults of which I am aware.' He leafed back. 'One of which is his loyalty.'

"Is that a fault?'

'To me, no: to you, no: to you in preference to me, yes.' He ran his white-gloved finger lightly under a line and whispered *helleborus niger*, as if it were sacred.

'I knew that you use street urchins to supply information but I did not imagine that you employed them to spy upon me,' I said indignantly.

'And yet…' Sidney Grice looked up. He had a black patch on, but his good eye seemed to drill into me. 'You have such an invigorated imagination as a rule.' He placed his pencil parallel to his blotter. 'Explain.'

'Peter was set upon killing Prince Ulrich, but I persuaded him that it would be better to bring him to justice.'

Mr G took off his pince-nez and polished both lenses, though only the left was of any use to him. 'Continue.'

'We decided between us that the best way was to catch him in the act.'

'And so you used yourself as bait?'

'Yes.' I looked down.

'It seemed to you that the best way to apprehend a criminal was to trick him into committing another crime?' He clipped his eyeglasses back on to his long thin nose.

'Put like that…'

'Put like that, does it seem foolish?' My godfather slapped his desktop. 'I devoutly hope it does, because it was. It was also reckless and immoral.' He raised his hand to forestall my defence. 'Where is he now? And, if I were a praying man, I would be petitioning God for you to tell me truthfully that he is not in Marylebone Police Station.'

'You prayers would not be answered,' I admitted. 'I left him with Inspector Pound.'

Sidney Grice clicked his tongue meditatively. 'And was he delighted with your actions and the position in which you have placed him?'

'He was not,' I conceded. 'In fact he asked me to fetch you at once.'

'Am I a rubber ball or a stick that I should be *fetched*?' my godfather asked indignantly. 'Do not answer for it should he obvious, even to one as mutton-headed as you, that I am not. Give.' He upturned his palm.

'What?'

'Give,' he repeated firmly, and I took an oval ivory box out of my secret pocket and placed it in his beckoning hand.

There had been three cubes left and it seemed a shame to waste them.

'I only—' I began, but we both knew I had not *only* done anything.

'Proceed instantly into the hall.' Although we were the same height, my guardian somehow managed to tower over me. 'If that is not too challenging for your so-called intellect. Tell Molly to stop eavesdropping and to prepare my Grice Patent Insulated Flask of tea. Run the flag up and await me there. I shall join you in one minute and forty seconds when Mr Cromwell has revealed what he proposes as an antidote.'

The doorbell rang and I heard Molly clatter the short distance to the front door. There was a faint buzz of voices and she clumped into the room.

'You know that man?' she announced. 'It's him.'

'Tell Dawson I shall be with him in one minute and thirty-two seconds,' her employer commanded and returned to his book.

'Leave this to me, Molly,' I said and went out into the hall. Gerry stood on the doorstep in the rain and he did not look happy.

'Where's the guv'ner?' he asked urgently. 'That pal of yours is nowhere to be seen.'

34

The Mexican Tailor

SIDNEY GRICE WAS in the hall before Gerry had finished speaking.

'Flask,' he barked at Molly.

'I've only got two pairs of hands,' she grumbled, thundering into the basement.

'Cloak,' he snapped at me. 'Where did you leave him?' he rapped at Gerry.

'The old biscuit warehouse on the corner of Grady Street...'

'And Durrent Road.' Mr G whipped his Ulster coat off the stand. 'You left him there alone?'

'Not much choice,' Gerry protested. 'I told him to hide and went back soon as I could. Been up and down Limehouse all night, I have.'

My guardian donned his hat. 'Was he armed?'

'No,' I confessed and put on mine.

He pulled on his gloves and selected a cane, which I recognized as one of his sword sticks by the curved gouge along the shaft, caused by his fight with the Mexican tailor in *The Mystery of the Unsmoked Bloater*.

Molly came galloping back with her employer's bottle of tea.

'Marylebone Police Station,' he instructed Gerry.

'But we must go to Limehouse,' I protested.

'Is there something that fascinates you about that area?' He pushed the cork in more firmly. 'Or do you hope to relive your escapade?'

'But that is where Peter is.'

'It is where you left him.' He rammed the flask into his satchel. 'But, if you were listening, you would know that your accomplice has quit his post – whether voluntarily or under duress remains to be established.'

'But we must go to look for him,' I protested.

'Do you know the area better than Dawson?' Mr G demanded. 'Even assuming your accomplice is still there, the courts and alleyways would have to be drastically simplified before they could begin to be classified as a maze, and you cannot buy information there, not even for money.'

I knew that my godfather was right and that we could trawl Limehouse for a month and achieve nothing, but I could not help feeling we should be more actively searching.

35

The Sword of Honours

INSPECTOR POUND LOOKED even more harassed than when I had left him.

'Take a look at those.' He thrust a fistful of telegrams at my guardian.

'Good morning, Inspector,' Sidney Grice greeted him and skimmed the contents.

'Congratulations, Miss Middleton,' Pound snarled. 'I am currently being vilified by Sir William Vernon Harcourt, the Home Secretary, for causing an international incident. You are aware – are you not? – that this man is related to Her Majesty the Queen.'

'Does the German Embassy know that Prince Ulrich is here?' Mr G asked.

'Of course.' The inspector grimaced. 'The envoy has just left and only to fetch the ambassador in person.'

'Has he spoken yet?' I enquired.

'No, nor will he,' Pound replied, 'except to insult my men by telling them they are pigs and dogs.'

'This came as a surprise to them?' Sidney Grice clipped on his pince-nez to decipher a scrawled missive.

'Where is he now?' I asked hastily.

'In an interview room.' Pound bottled up his indignation at my guardian's remark. 'He's so objectionable I'd have throttled him if I'd kept him in here, but it has been impressed upon me that it could be construed as an act of war if I locked him in a cell.'

'He will be in one soon enough,' I forecast.

'Not on the evidence that you have produced, some might say *manufactured*.' Mr G took off his pince-nez but continued reading.

'However Prince Ulrich came to be at the opium den—' I began.

'Opium? Oh, for heaven's sake,' Pound protested.

'He tried to assault me,' I persisted. 'At least he cannot deny that fact.'

'It is a popular – and therefore fallacious – belief that facts speak for themselves.' My guardian let the papers float one by one, some on to the desk but most on to the floor. 'If they did, I would not be obliged to spend many of my conscious hours speaking on their behalf. That you have caught His Highness in a trap is almost indisputable, but there are two obvious escape routes. The first I have already alluded to. He can simply deny everything and then it is just your word against his – especially as your one witness has yet to re-emerge.'

'Do you think he will?' I asked worriedly.

'Of course he shall,' my godfather reassured me. 'One way or another.'

'You do not think he is—' I cried.

'I have no reason to believe that Hockaday is dead,' my godfather hastened to reassure me, 'or alive.'

I stepped back.

'I will send a man to look for him,' Pound promised.

'One man?' I threw up my hands.

'Which is one more than I can spare,' the inspector told me stiffly, and I lowered my arms for I knew the force was over-stretched, with officers being seconded to Limehouse and the search for the Soft-Hearted Strangler, who had struck again in Soho. 'And I am tied up at present with a very angry German, and running out of reasons to hold him.'

'Well, I am not afraid to be cross-examined in court.'

'Then allow me to be afraid for you.' Mr G speared a ball of paper. '*I* have a deserved reputation for truthfulness, but you are a girl and what judge in his right mind would take your word against that of a Prussian officer, gentleman and aristocrat?'

'First, I am a woman.' I banged my fist on the wall and wished I had not. 'And, second, my word is as good as any man's any day.'

Mr G looked at me pityingly. 'Shall I give examples of your deceitful behaviour since you lumbered so gracelessly into my home? Shall I mention your clumsy untruths regarding your inhalation of tobacco-leaf smoke, your ingestion of ethyl alcohol, the company you keep? Shall—'

'What is the other way?' Pound broke in.

'Simply denying the facts gives me the opportunity of proving them and, if Prince Ulrich knows anything about me, which he does, he will know that it is my job to prove facts and there is none better at it than I.' He folded the last telegram five times. 'The second route is more elegant and almost unanswerable, and therefore he will take it.' He tossed the paper over his shoulder without troubling to flatten it for inspection.

I looked towards the inspector for clarification but there was none forthcoming.

'And that is?' I enquired.

'He has an excuse.'

'What possible excuse could there be?' I railed at the very idea.

Mr G raised his left eyebrow. 'Why do we not ask the man himself?'

'He will not talk to anybody,' Pound insisted. 'I tried for two hours.'

Sidney Grice pirouetted. 'He will speak to me.' And he marched out of the door.

175

36

Scars, Scraps and Salvage

T HE STAGE THAT was interview room three never changed. Only the actors came and went. The long pine table still stood at right angles to the wall, which was still in need of whitewash. The tall grilled window had been boarded over, though, after – as Inspector Pound had told us on the way – being smashed by an inebriated bottle seller with one of her wares.

Prince Ulrich sat at that table, straight as a broomstick, with a constable behind him.

'Stay seated,' the constable commanded, but the Prussian snapped smartly to his feet and held out his hand, horizontally as if to kiss mine. I did not offer it in return but sat in one of the three wooden chairs facing him.

The men remained standing, sizing each other up – the prince lazy-eyed and the inspector coolly – and my guardian might have been a referee between two prizefighters.

Sidney Grice stepped back, clipped his pince-nez on the bridge of his long thin nose, and looked the Prussian up and down. 'I wonder if you are as false as your duelling scar.'

Prince Ulrich tilted his head in acknowledgement of the observation. 'How can you tell?'

'For the slash of a sabre to have cut such a straight line it would have to have smashed through your zygomatic arch and you would have a permanent indentation,' Mr G explained.

'You have none, therefore the scar was caused by a careful incision.'

'They were quite the fashion when I was a cadet,' the prince admitted. 'But they had to run up to the eye for the correct effect, a dangerous feat and difficult to pull off with a sabre, and zo I haff a bottle of schnapps and my friends perform the operation with a bayonet.'

'I am glad I do not have such friends,' I commented.

'But you haff not introduced me to yours,' the prince reminded me.

'Mr Sidney Grice,' I said shortly.

'I recognized you at the inquest.' The Prussian clicked his heels in a way that I had only seen on the stage before. 'But for us to meet in person is an honour.' He bowed his head stiffly.

'It is,' my guardian agreed.

'For whom?' I enquired, but Sidney Grice waved me to be quiet.

'May I see your hands, Prince Ulrich?' he asked, a great deal more politely than he would of most suspects, and the prince held them out palms up. Mr G bent until he was almost touching them. 'Excellent.'

'I am glad you are approving.'

'And the backs, if you please.' Prince Ulrich rotated his wrists.

'Do you cut your own nails?' Sidney Grice sniffed them.

'Do you?'

'I am not here to be questioned by you.'

'Nor I by you.'

'Kindly expose the soles of your boots to my inquisitive gaze.'

The German flared his nostrils but, nonetheless, turned his back to raise his left foot and then his right.

'Hauenstein leather,' Sidney Grice observed. 'And the left again, please.' He brought out a pencil and scraped a fleck of dried mud on to the cover of his notebook, holding it up to the window and smelling it. 'Pity.' He blew it away. 'Please be seated, Your Highness.'

The prince glided back on to his seat and the other two sat either side of me. 'Pound,' Prince Ulrich said thoughtfully. 'I knew a Herr Pound. He was a vulgar fellow.'

The inspector bristled. 'If...'

But I was used to the prince's trick by now. 'I know a Prince Ulrich,' I put in. 'Odious specimen. He attacks women.'

The prince sniffed. 'A gentleman seeks his pleasure vere he can.'

'So does a street dog,' Pound told him.

Prince Ulrich raised a hand as if to slap the inspector with the back of it.

'My Gott, if you spoke to me like that in my country—'

'Unfortunately for you, this is my country and, if you do not lower your hand immediately, I shall charge you with threatening a police officer in front of three witnesses,' Pound said angrily.

'Schweinigel,' the Prussian hissed, but pulled his arm down.

'Well, this is jolly.' Sidney Grice whipped off his pince-nez and jabbed them to within half an inch of the Prussian's left eye. 'You were apprehended allegedly in the process of purchasing a woman for the purpose of outraging her against her will.' My guardian made a quick note in his own shorthand.

'And what a poor purchase she was,' Schlangezahn sneered. 'I haff seen better scraps thrown to the butcher's cat.'

Inspector Pound drew a sharp breath but I touched his sleeve quickly.

'You thought you had paid for me?' I enquired. 'You have not begun to pay for me yet, Prince Ulrich – nor any of those you have abused.'

The Prussian half lowered his eyelids and he tilted his head back. 'I haff not been charged with any others.'

Sidney Grice snapped his notebook shut. 'You have an excuse.' And the prince eyed him indolently.

'I do not make excuses.'

'Whatever you call it.' Mr G flapped his hand irritably. 'Let us hear it and then we can all go home for a nice cup of tea.'

Prince Ulrich curled his lip. 'Only the English could regard leaves soaked in water as the height of sophisticated pleasure.' He yawned behind the side of his fist. 'Very vell. I too am appalled by the accounts of the fates of your vomanhood. Your police have proved to be impotent and incompetent—'

'This had better be good,' Pound warned. 'For you won't have a comfortable night if we put you in the cells.'

'And zo,' the prince continued, 'I decided to set my own trap, use the services of a...' His long fingers combed the air for a word. 'Procurer. And, once he had taken my money, to hand him over to the authorities. I voz no more to know that the procurer was trying to catch the villain than he voz to know I was doing the same.'

'But you pulled my hair,' I remembered.

'I played my part as you played yours.' The prince batted my accusation away like an annoying bluebottle.

Mr G slipped his notebook away and stood up. 'Good day, Oberst.' He nodded.

'You will wait in my office, Mr Grice?' Pound's voice was icy.

'I shall,' my guardian concurred. 'But not today. Farewell, Inspector.'

'That was not a question.' I had never known George Pound to exhibit such bottled anger.

'I beg to differ.' With a swish of his Ulster overcoat, Sidney Grice was gone, his ward trailing sheepishly back up the corridor.

37

The Feet of Friends and the Power of Steam

L IMEHOUSE DID NOT seem so menacing in the light of
day. It bustled with dock life and there was even the
consoling sight of a policeman ambling through a group
of black sailors, who, to judge from their reeling gaits, had not
long been on dry land and, from the way they swayed along in
straight lines, had not yet visited a bar.

Gerry Dawson guided Meg up a street leading away from the
water and we negotiated a series of sunlit alleys, barely recognizable as those that we had edged along at night.

''Ere we are.' We stopped by the loading bay.

Five urchins tumbled through a doorway across the court. I
gave them a penny each and they loitered nearby, watching us
curiously.

'Lost yer nosebag, missus?' one called, to his friends' hilarity,
making me very glad indeed that I had been kind to them, especially as I could not be so cruel as to mock their wretched
appearances. Every one of them had the bow legs and bulging
brows of rickets.

'Shove off.' Gerry waved a threatening fist and they backed
a pace or so but did not scatter.

'The little rascals,' my guardian said, with a benevolence that
he reserved almost exclusively for people who were rude to me.

The bay was no more than a tumbledown rotting wooden

shelter, attached by one long side and one short to a crumbled brick wall, the other corner once supported by a post which was now snapped and hanging loose, so that the roof sagged from about eight feet high at the wall to three feet at the unfixed corner. Old soiled straw on the cobbles indicated that a pony or donkey must have been housed there sometimes.

'Well, he ain't here now,' Gerry observed.

'If only I had an opening for another assistant,' Mr G muttered, 'I could reject you for it without an interview.'

'Not so pretty as your present one,' Gerry said, more gallantly than truthfully.

'Miss Middleton's unfortunate appearance is none of your concern,' my guardian scolded.

The ground was trampled with a jumble of bootprints and hoof marks.

'I suppose it is too much to hope you are capable of recognizing your friend's impressions.' Mr G ran the ferule of his stick round the smudged outline of a heel.

'Would you recognize yours?' I challenged.

'If I ever had a friend I most certainly would.'

'Wouldn't recognize my own in all that mess,' Gerry contributed.

And Mr G dropped his eye into his hand and straight into his waistcoat. 'Yet another reason why I shall not be offering you the imaginary position.'

He raked about in the straw with the ferule of his cane, uncovering nothing other than more muck. 'If you were to kneel and sift through it with your fingers, Miss Middleton—'

'Perhaps you would like to show me what you mean,' I broke in, but neither of us seemed inclined to follow the other's suggestion.

Sidney Grice leaned in as far as he could and puddled his stick around.

'Found anything?' Gerry asked over my shoulder.

'I have found almost innumerable things,' Mr G answered testily, 'most of them being the end products of equine digestive processes, though at least two canine and four feline visitors have made generous contributions, not to mention a difficult to ascertain number of *Mus Musculus*—'

'Who?' Gerry queried.

'Mice,' I translated.

'And *Rattus Norvegitus* visitors.'

'I can guess that one.'

'And,' Mr G's voice rose indignantly, 'the young of a species unworthy of classification as *Homo Sapiens*, indeed scarcely describable as *Homo*.'

If the children knew that he was disparaging them they showed no sign of it, merely calling out helpful suggestions to my godfather not to slip, along with a toothless boy's insistence that any *tin* dropped in there must have been his.

Sidney Grice pulled his head out and straightened up. 'Got a rag, Miss Middleton?'

The filth began to steam and, in places, bubble, slurping and popping with his vigorous stirring.

'I have this.'

'It will have to do.' He wiped his cane clean on my pink silk handkerchief. 'Want it back?'

'No.'

He dropped it in the gutter and leaned in sideways to scrutinize the brick wall to his side.

'Ummm humph,' he said – or words to that effect before repeating the sounds backwards. 'Aha.' He took hold of the corner and leaned in sideways. 'Interesting.' He re-emerged. 'Possibly.' And fiddled with the handle of his cane.

'Is that the cane with your clockwork fingers?' I asked.

They had not been a great success at picking up biscuits.

'A similar but manual device.' Mr G pressed a button, the ferule retracting to expose two flattened prongs which, when he twisted the handle, closed together like miniature fingers, hinging apart with a counter-twist.

'Excellent,' he grunted, and reached in and upwards to something just under the roof. 'Steady,' he instructed himself. 'And... Got you.' He emerged triumphantly with what looked like a piece of fur in the grip of his prongs. 'What colour would you say Lieutenant Peter Lewis James Hockaday's hair was or – to cut to the chase – would you say it matched this?'

I looked over and saw a clump of yellow hairs.

'Very similar,' I said with a sinking feeling. 'Oh dear Lord.'

As Sidney Grice rotated his find I saw that attached to the underside was an area – about the size of a postage stamp – of scalp.

'Looks like he had his head banged good and hard on the wall,' Gerry contributed.

'If we could find a board I can get a proper look without soiling my boots,' Sidney Grice mused. 'It is quite dark in there but I am fairly certain that there are another three pieces and, lower down,' he indicated with his stick, 'are twenty-six stains, six of which bear seven striking resemblances to blood.'

'A violent struggle,' Gerry pronounced gravely.

'I appear to have a new professional rival.' My guardian dropped his sample into a wide test tube.

'Thruppence to the boy who brings us a wide plank,' I called across the court and there was an immediate stampede.

'And a free night in Commercial Road Police Station if I discover that it is stolen,' Sidney Grice called after them.

'Well, they ain't gonna go to the plank shop and buy one,' Gerry Dawson snorted.

'No, but they might be able to borrow one from a carpenter,' I said hopefully.

''Ere you come back wiv that, you likkle bleeders,' a woman shrieked over the clatter of clogs returning at full pelt.

—◦•❖•◦—

38

The Dancing Needles

MRS FREVAL WAS cheerier when she answered the door that morning and I wished that I could share her mood. 'Ooh, 'e reeely reeely loves 'is noo cap.' She swirled her skirts.

Turndap had something that might have been an old paisley pincushion tied with a tartan ribbon under his chin, and I never believed that a dog actually felt embarrassment until Mrs Freval's mongrel proved me wrong.

'You look very smart,' I said, but he avoided my gaze and backed shamefacedly away.

I climbed to the top floor.

'Is that you, Peter?' Geraldine called in response to my knock.

'It is March.'

'I am coming.'

A floorboard creaked and the door came open a crack.

'Oh, it *is* you.' Geraldine let me in, locking and bolting the door after me. 'I have been knitting,' she announced, as if she did anything else.

'What will it be?'

'A scarf for Peter for when the winter comes.' She settled back into her armchair and picked up the wool. 'He feels the cold more after his time abroad.'

'That is a kind thought.' I sat in the only other armchair.

The drapes were drawn as they often were, especially if Geraldine were alone. She felt safer in a cocoon.

'He is very good to me.' She slid a needle through and looped her brown yarn around it. 'He does not like to wear bright things.'

'A lot of men do not.'

'Mr Grice is very—' Geraldine Hockaday struggled for the right word. 'Colourful.'

'In more ways than one.' I hesitated. 'Geraldine—'

'I have not asked you,' she admitted, 'because I can tell by your face something is wrong.'

'It did not go well,' I confessed as she watched me with her quick nervous eyes. 'We caught Schlangezahn as he was about to assault me.'

'But that is exactly what you hoped to do,' Geraldine cried, her triumph mixed with consternation.

'But we had to let him go,' I said flatly. 'The police were under a lot of pressure and I had no real proof.'

'But you had Peter as a witness, surely, and Peter is an officer and a gentleman. He has three medals.'

I took a breath. 'I am afraid that we do not know where Peter is.'

Geraldine's eyes flickered wildly as if searching for her brother in that stuffy, dark room. 'Why not?'

'We had to leave him in Limehouse.'

'Alone?'

'I am afraid so.'

Geraldine hunched over her work, needles dancing around each other but the scarf not noticeably any longer. 'It is I who am afraid. Have you heard nothing from him?'

'Nothing,' I said, and Geraldine curled herself deeper over.

'Then you must find him,' she said. 'It is as simple as that. Find him.' Her voice rose in pitch but was still low in volume as the words rattled out of her. 'Find-find-find-him.'

'We will do everything we can,' I vowed. But I had no idea what we could do.

39

Snakes, Teeth and Castles in the Air

SIDNEY GRICE SPRAWLED diagonally in his armchair, his feet on the coal scuttle. He was browsing through a thick document. *Bocking* v. *Bocking* I read on the cover.

'Scrutinize this,' he greeted me, delving in a waistcoat pocket to show me something like a small biscuit for a good dog.

'Is this the button you took from Lucy?'

'About which you have shown a singular and eldritch absence of curiosity,' he confirmed accusingly.

I refused to admit that I had forgotten all about it. 'Can I see?'

My guardian spun the button high in the air and I caught it in one hand – cream ivory with some symbols carved on it in cameo.

I squinted. 'It looks like a beer barrel tied in a rope.'

Mr G held out his pince-nez. 'Perhaps you should consider getting a pair of these.'

I got up and helped myself to his silver-handled third-best magnifying glass on the desk and went to the window for the better light.

'Rotate it ninety degrees anti-clockwise,' my guardian advised. 'Where is that slattern? She went up twenty minutes ago.'

'Perhaps she did not hear the bell,' I suggested.

'She heard it. There was a three-second pause in her activities.'

'A castle.' I moved the glass out to sharpen the focus. 'With a snake wrapped around it.'

'In which era and at what location have castles been constructed with twin roots?' He let his pince-nez dangle on its pink cord. 'It represents a lower molar.' He put his fingertips together. 'How is your German?'

'As good as my Japanese.' I replaced the glass, gave him back the button and sat to face him again.

'Tooth translates as *zahn* and snake as *Schlange*.' I could not help but notice how he sat more erect when he spoke German.

'Schlangezahn,' I realized, not very cleverly.

Sidney Grice yanked on the bell pull again. There was a distant cry and Molly came clattering down the stairs.

'Surely that is proof enough that he attacked Lucy?'

'Is it?' Mr G inclined his head.

'I suppose somebody else could have worn his waistcoat,' I conceded, as Molly cantered along the hall.

'That is one of forty possible explanations and only the sixth most likely.'

Molly burst into the room.

'You are late,' her employer scolded.

'Better late than later,' she responded brightly but, seeing that did not go down very well, tried again with, 'I'm sorry, sir, but I was just giving the cat a bath.' She struggled to straighten her apron but managed to twist it more askew.

'You were doing what?' I exclaimed in horror. 'Is she all right? You have not drowned her?'

I jumped out of my chair but Molly slapped her knees in merriment.

'Bless you, miss, I didnt't not put no water in. I gave Splirit the bath to play in with Mr Grice's sock what he don't not know she chewded up last week.'

'I think he does now,' I told Molly, and she clamped her hands over her mouth one at a time.

'Oh, miss, you didntn't not tell him?'

'No, you just did.' I sat back. 'And her name is *Spirit*.'

Molly's arms windmilled, nearly catching her employer in the face as he whisked away.

'Oh, bless you, miss, I know that, but she laughs like a spider when I call her that.'

'You took Molly on,' I reminded my guardian and he rolled his eye.

'So you did, bless you, sir.' Molly smiled affectionately.

'That is three blessings in two minutes,' he complained. 'Any more and I might as well have employed the Pope.'

'I didntn't not think you cared for Roaming Cathlicks.' Molly folded her arms with the air of a doorman who had been instructed not to admit me.

'I do not care for anyone,' he reminded her.

'You liked Mrs Dilligent,' she reminisced, 'and the doctor lady.' Molly rested a hand familiarly on the back of her employer's chair and he flinched, his mouth working towards an explosion of abuse. 'And the Gorestring woman what we stayed with.'

It had been one of the most terrifying nights of my life, but Molly was clasping her cheeks as one might recollect a romantic dinner.

'Tea please, Molly,' I put in hastily, and she looked at me dolefully.

'Me and Mr Grice was having a good old chinwag,' she reproached me, catching her employer's expression as she bent to pick up the tray. 'Oh, and now look, you've gone and upset him and he's so difficult to upset normanly.' She stumbled on the hearthrug. 'Not to worry, sir. We'll catch up later.' She began to curtsy, but thought better of it as the tray tipped thirty degrees. 'Bless him,' she crooned as she left.

'But we do know that the button belonged to Schlangezahn,' I recapitulated.

'It certainly resembles a button which Prince Ulrich Albrecht Sigismund Schlangezahn might wear.' Mr G shook open a folded square of chamois.

'So shall we pay him a visit?' I suggested.

'Not yet.' He polished his eye.

'Why not?'

'There are turnips for dinner.' Sidney Grice reinserted his eye. It was not, but it looked upside down. 'And I have yet another telegram to send to that not especially mysterious, though doubtless parasitical solicitor, Mr Silas Spry.'

He went back to his reading.

'Good heavens,' he cried. 'I have yet to reach the thrilling climax of this account but, from Miss Bocking's testimony of how she invented her safety pencil sharpener, it would appear that the design was indeed stolen.' He waved the report accusingly. 'From me.'

40

The Ruins of Abbey Road

WE HAD A good drive, our horse getting into a steady trot and tossing its head joyfully at the unaccustomed exercise along Marylebone Road past the new Madame Tussaud's with its verdigris dome.

'Perhaps they will put you in their chamber of horrors one day,' I teased.

'I would be in familiar company.' Sidney Grice struggled to extract the cork from his flask. 'Apart from capturing three of the murderers represented therein, I have shaken the hand of both Messrs Calcraft and Marwood, the executioners.'

It was another hot day and I was glad of my new bonnet but, though I had brought a new parasol to complete my outfit, I dared not open it in the presence of my guardian.

Families, gaggles of girls and gangs of youths were heading for Regents Park.

'It is salutary to recall that forty skaters drowned in that boating lake when the ice broke eighteen and half years ago,' my guardian said grimly. 'Yet another example of the perils of seeking frivolous pleasure.'

'You take pleasure in some things,' I pointed out.

'None frivolous,' he parried as we whisked by, the sounds of the city almost too faint to hear. 'And very little pleasure.'

London has always been a city of contrasts – poverty cheek by jowl with opulence – but I never ceased to marvel how the urban bustle of Gower Street could give way to near-rural tranquillity still within the borough of Camden. Gower Street ran largely between two rows of terraces, the only vegetation being in the occasional window boxes. Abbey Road boasted imposing villas set back in large plots. The pavements were dotted with plane trees and the gardens profuse with shrubberies and well-clipped lawns.

Four young men crossed in front of us. They had long and unkempt hair.

'Such poverty even here,' I sighed. 'That one has nothing on his feet.'

My guardian clucked. 'He can afford to smoke cigarrrrettes, though.' He rolled the R's in a distinctly feline purr.

It was not difficult to spot the site of Steep House. The line of precisely trimmed privet hedges to our right was herniated by unkempt bushes bulging into the pavement and overhung by branches.

'Halt,' Sidney Grice commanded and the driver hauled on his reins with a gentle, 'Whoah.'

The horse slowed reluctantly, snorting and stamping its hooves at having its fun curtailed.

'There, you unattractive fool.' Mr G stamped both feet at once and we pulled up. 'Reverse your vehicle immediately.' The horse edged uneasily backwards until we were alongside the gates of the previous property. 'Stop-stop-stop.' My godfather could not have yelled any more urgently if we had been about to reverse over a cliff, and the horse obeyed instantly, slithering slightly on the cobbles.

The name on the brick pillar gatepost had been freshly repainted.

'Finkin' of movin' awt 'ere?' Our driver lowered his hand for his fare. 'You won't find a decent tiger for miles.'

'Is he speaking an obscure Hindoo dialect?' my guardian pushed open the flap. 'If so, it is not one that I have studied.'

'It is rhyming slang for *pub*,' I interpreted. '*Tiger cub/pub*.'

'It is wonderful to know that your time in such establishments has not been entirely fruitless.'

We clambered out and I just had time to give the horse a raw potato before the sting of the whip on its flanks set it off again, wild-eyed and sweating with exertion.

'Pay attention,' my guardian snapped as if I had run off to pick wild flowers, and we stood side by side, gazing through the high railings at the childhood home of Lucy Bocking.

New House stood on a wide raised terrace at the end of a thirty-yard gravelled drive, with a carriage turning circle cut into closely clipped lawns, still lush despite the summer's drought. The house itself was wide and clean-lined and stood three storeys, white-painted with a central door and rounded bays at either end. The long windows were divided into small panes. It was an impressive and elegant building, but the crowning glory of New House was a great dome on the flat roof, an upturned cast-iron basket filled with glass glittering in the August sun.

'Very nice,' I commented.

'It is what it is,' my guardian told me.

'So is everything.' I wondered if the fountain in the circle had any fish in it.

'Except art, money, power, chocolate-coated biscuits and people,' he told me. 'Come.'

We made our way back up the road past the privet hedge, rule-straight on one side, unkempt and ragged on the other. The wrought-iron railings flowed on but were eroded in places and brown with rust, and here the spikes were topped by heavy rolls of viciously barbed wire. The gate was chained and secured by a chunky cast-heart padlock.

Mr G slid the cover up.

'Brass workings,' he remarked in satisfaction. 'So they will not have corroded.'

He set to work with his picks, whistling a short low note over and over again, while I watched a grey squirrel chase itself round the trunk of an elm tree.

Just as I was battling with an urge to beat him into silence with my parasol Sidney Grice stopped chirping.

'Got it.'

There was a clunk and he hinged the shackle away to force the gate open with some difficulty, as the hinges had not been so resistant to the elements and fought noisily to resist him.

The top of Steep House was just visible above a crop of giant cow parsley or *Heracleum mantegazzianum*, as Sidney Grice classified it. The roof had gone, apart from the back left-hand corner where a gable of charred beams supported a patchy tent of grey tiles.

The ground had not been tended for years and we slashed our way through the undergrowth with the vigour of two Stanleys hot on the trail of Dr Livingstone. Any thoughts I might have had were interrupted when I became ensnared in a heavy spider's web. I plucked it off my face, stumbled over a tree root and barked my shin.

'Blimmit,' I cursed and my guardian paused in concern.

'I cannot help feeling that I failed you.' He watched me struggle to my feet. 'By not impressing upon you forcibly enough that profanities are *never* acceptable from the mouth of a lady in any but three circumstances, none of which are pertinent to your situation.'

'But it does not mean anything,' I argued.

'The vilest obscenities never do. Duck.' He let go of a bramble and I moved just in time to save my bonnet from being whipped away.

I brushed myself down. 'You have still not explained why we are here.'

Sidney Grice set off again, hacking his way through a splendid crop of nettles. 'Who owns this territory?' he challenged.

'Freddy Wilde, of course, and all the people her father

borrowed from probably.' A creeper had managed to wrap itself round my ankle and I ripped it away, shaking the cherries off a no longer ornamental tree like a tempest.

'And whose companion is Miss Wilde?'

'I hope this game will not last very much longer.' I inspected the blackberries but they were still green and hard. 'For we both know it is Lucy Bocking.'

'Then I need not enquire if you are aware that Miss Bocking is currently employing our services.' He paused to scrutinize a leaf as if he had never seen one before.

'Indeed you need not,' I agreed. 'But what has this got to do with her case?'

Mr G mumbled about something-*iculae vulgaris* and released the leaf. 'Now you have changed the format of our intercourse from me asking you questions to which we both know the answer, to you asking me questions to which neither of us have a solution.'

He pulled apart a drape of dead ivy dangling from the branch of an ancient oak and there stood Steep House, a blackened shell of once-red brick, scabbed with patches of what had probably been a cream render. It stood full height at the rear to the right where a bay supported itself, the house having fallen away to leave it stranded as a tower, perforated by oblongs where the windows would have been. The other bays had collapsed outwards, the front left sprawling towards us.

We stepped up and the ground became firmer. The raised terrace was buried now and the undergrowth too high and dense to enable us to walk round the sides of the house.

It would have been possible to have seen straight through the ruins were it not for the sycamores and birch trees already established in the interior. Chimney breasts rose only a foot or two above their ground-floor hearths, one near the middle three fireplaces high, and I could not help but note how what must have been the servants' quarters had by far the smallest grate.

'What do you hope to find?' I asked.

'The truth.' Sidney Grice crouched by where the front door had been. 'There are few things more tragic than a dead house.'

'A dead person,' I suggested and he sniffed.

'People must expect to die, but to see a building cut down so cruelly in its prime is a calamity on a par with giving the vote to any coarse commoner with ten pounds to his name.'

Mr G shook his head sadly and, though I could not agree with his priorities, I could not help but share his sadness, not just at the destruction of a beautiful house but more especially since we knew that Freddy Wilde's family and their servants had been lost there during that terrible Christmas.

I had read what I could find about the fire in my guardian's vast repository of newspaper cuttings, but I could not imagine the terror of the occupants that night. Did Mr and Mrs Wilde run through the flames looking for their daughter? Perhaps Lucy's brother Eric did. Were the maids trapped in their attic rooms, begging for help? How badly was Fairbank, the butler, injured when he carried Freddy out?

'I am always surprised how quickly nature reclaims her own,' I said, trying to blot out the memory of another fire at the end of an aristocratic dynasty.

'If you had troubled to peruse Hamish Vixen's *Differential Rates of Soil Incremental Deposition and Colonization* you would be less astonished and better informed.' He selected a broken tile out of the dozens strewn there.

'I think I would prefer to be surprised.'

I paced the frontage of the house as evenly as I could over the rubble and weeds. By my feet was a grating over a light well and behind that the blackened remnants of a window frame, little more than charred marks on the wall. Was this where Lucy's brother, Eric, had been trapped and died? I resolved to find out. Such a site should not go unnoted.

From left corner to right, it was a matter of forty-six strides which, at about thirty inches each, made the width of the house some one hundred and fifteen feet and, as far as I could judge, the depth was even greater.

'One hundred and twelve feet,' my guardian confirmed without looking up. He was rooting through the detritus with the end of his cane.

'How can you tell?'

'There is no point in having distances if you cannot judge them.' He sprang up. 'From Miss Wilde's scanty description where would you say her bedroom was?'

'Well, nobody sleeps on the ground floor from choice and the top floor would have been the servants' quarters and the attics,' I reasoned. 'And Freddy said she could see Lucy's house and the driveway from her room. So I would say the first floor of this left-hand bay.'

'So would I.' He limped towards it. 'And, conveniently for us, it has collapsed.'

'Why *conveniently*?'

He tore a tangle of weeds away. 'Because we can see the damage to every level without having to ascend an unstable structure.'

'But there is nothing left of the floors,' I objected and he bfffed.

'There is always something left of everything. It may be a puff of smoke long dispersed into our soiled atmosphere and therefore untraceable, but for as long as this deformed globe hurtles elliptically round the sun it remains.' He bobbed and scraped the moss from a chunk of bricks and cement lying flat on the ground. 'Nonetheless,' he concluded, some time after I thought he already had.

'So her parents must have slept on the right-hand side,' I calculated. 'Freddy said they liked the sunrise and that must be the east.'

'South-east,' he corrected mildly.

I walked alongside the bay – its structure increasingly scattered as I approached the apex – and glanced back to see Sidney Grice shuffling on his haunches to the footings of the house where the outer wall rose three or four courses high. 'Fascinating,' he cried. 'See how everything is piled up.'

'Well, it would be,' I replied automatically, my eye caught by a leg sticking out from under a stone plinth.

41

The Bucket, the Bat and the Broken Glass

S IDNEY GRICE CAME over.

'What have you found?'

I kneeled. 'A doll.' The plinth had fallen against the edge of a rockery so that it lay tilted about thirty degrees from the ground. I drew back my hand. 'It must be Freddy's, the one she talked about.'

'Possibly,' he conceded. 'Stand clear.'

Mr G bent at the knees and, keeping his back straight, ran his fingers under the propped-up end of the stone. The other end was submerged under a heavy net of undergrowth. He braced himself and strained, the wiry roots ripping as he wrenched the plinth, soil scattering, a herbaceous periwinkle torn from the ground with it, violet-blue flowers tumbling away. He was a small man and not sturdily built but he had great strength.

'Can I help?' I stepped forward.

'You most certainly can.' My guardian's face was purple. 'But you most certainly shall not.' He heaved with all his might – his neck muscles about to burst his starched collar – and the plinth hinged up, reached the near vertical and, with one final strain, toppled diagonally into the long grass of a shallow depression. Mr G breathed and rotated his shoulders.

'What a world exists beneath our feet.' He massaged his right upper arm.

And, craning over him, I glimpsed a myriad of woodlice

scurrying for cover, a fat earthworm contracting indignantly, centipedes and millipedes writhing, tiny round white eggs, a spindle-legged spider strutting its suddenly sunlit domain. The doll was uncovered now, fine porcelain lying supine on the soil, her face towards me, politely listening to our conversation. A few shredded strips of dark dress material were draped around her waist and legs. A disgustingly swollen slug slid lazily over her chest. She must have been pretty once. Her left eye was closed but the other still glinted through a layer of dust and long curling lashes. Her cheeks were rosy and her lips deep ruby despite the earwig ambling in the valley between them. And she had thick cascading hair which I had no doubt would be golden if it were washed – one of the reasons I never liked dolls for, not only were they pretty, but they always looked like they knew it. The only damage I could see was a crater in her left temple, big enough to put two or three fingers in and for the large garden snail that had made its home in it.

'Broken,' Mr G observed, rather obviously for him.

'Are you surprised after it was in a fire, fell so far and was crushed by a block of granite?' I pulled a twig from her hair.

My guardian polished his eye on his sleeve and then on a scarlet cloth from his satchel.

'For your benefit I should have said *only broken*.' He reinserted his eye. 'And it was limestone.' He wiped his hands on a blue handkerchief.

The doll's body was chilled from more than a decade in the shadows and most of the remnants of her dress fell away as I picked her up. In the hollow left by her body, countless creatures burrowed from the light.

I shook the dirt out – thin black beetles scattering with it – and her right eye sprang open, sapphire blue sparkling in the August sun. The snail's shell was empty.

The doll was too big to fit with all the other paraphernalia inside my handbag so I wiped her down and sat her on top of everything else, her arms over the sides of the bag as if she were taking a bath.

'Come, March.' He gave me his hand to help me to my feet and kept holding mine until we were back on level ground.

'Thank you,' I said, touched by his unusual concern.

'I should not like you to fall and sprain or fracture your wrist or ankle,' he told me, 'or burst your nose or crack a rib or concuss yourself on something harder than your skull. It would be almost irritating.'

We reached the house again where his cane stood against a section of wall which was still papered though stained.

'What is the trowel for?' I asked.

'Trowelling,' he replied. 'Where was the main staircase?'

I surveyed the wreckage. 'Over there,' I decided. 'By the central chimney stack. There are the parts of some treads sticking out of the wall and you can see the marks where the rest would have been inserted. It must have gone straight up...' I counted the bricks. 'About four steps to a small mezzanine before it split to the left and right. I can almost make out the rectangular areas where they must have collapsed.'

'Either you can make them out or you cannot,' Mr G said shortly and I narrowed my eyes.

'I can just about, but the outlines are not clear.'

'That which is clear,' he screwed the trowel on to the ferule of his cane, 'is very often not.'

'Patented?' I enquired of his device.

'Pending.' Sidney Grice leaned forward, shovelling an inch-thick layer of debris aside. 'No sign of any rot or woodworm yet,' he decided and tapped the exposed floorboard. 'And, despite being American, the oak sounds solid enough.' He stepped over the wall.

'Be careful,' I warned and my guardian snorted as he inched away.

'According to Biedburger's prolix 1877 edition of *A Study of*

Social Converse in the Western Home Counties that is the fourth most common piece of advice given by women to men.' Mr G raised his right leg like a strutting cockerel. 'In my experience it is the seventeenth, but then most women I have come across would not be distressed.' He placed his heel with great precision. 'In fact they would be delighted if anything adverse happened to me.' He lowered his toe. 'Pay particular heed to the next event.'

A sheet of broken glass shattered under his sole.

'Was that it?'

Sidney Grice went down on his haunches. 'Yes.' And scooped a curved sliver of glass and three samples of speckled dust into four test tubes to tuck them into the special tiny pockets in the canary lining of his coat.

'Shall I pay less particular heed from now on?'

My guardian rose in that effortless hydraulic-power-company way of his and leaned on his front foot to test the next section. 'I expect so.' He edged further out.

'What is that?' I pointed to a metal pipe sticking out of the debris, and he shuffled sideways towards it.

'A splendid tribute to English steel manufacturing.' He pulled out the shaft of a garden shovel with all but a stump of the wooden handle burned away. 'Discoloured by heat but otherwise in excellent condition.' Sidney Grice turned it this way and that.

'But why would it be in here?' I pondered.

He put it back down. 'If I were in the mood for speculation I might cobble together a theory, but I shall leave you to work one out.'

'Thank you.' I swept out my hand in a mock bow.

Mr G stepped over a mound and stumbled.

'Be careful,' I cried, adding hastily, 'I am sorry, that slipped out.'

'Babbage with his difference engine would have been hard-pressed to calculate the number of words that escape unchecked from your lank throat.' Sidney Grice bent to toss two bricks and several smaller fragments aside and dug in with his trowel. 'The boards are distinctly less solid here,' he announced, 'not through the actions of insects, nor mould nor rodents, as far as I can ascertain at a glance, but as a result of aqueous precipitation tending to pool in this area.'

'I shall not repeat my advice,' I promised.

'It might be more pertinent now.' He took another step and wobbled. 'If this gives way and I die, I have left instructions in my study regarding the disposal of my corpse filed under *NDM* for *National Day of Mourning*.'

'Only one day?'

'More would be vulgar.' There was a loud crack and he tipped sideways. 'A prudent man might make a retreat and I may be discovered in that category.' Mr G jumped back over the pile just as it slid forwards in a miniature landslide. The floor where he had been standing collapsed and the rubble crashed through a crater five or six feet in diameter, clattering into the cellar and exploding into dust.

'Are you all right?'

Sidney Grice coughed. 'Of course.' He wafted the air with his wide-brimmed hat and peered into the precipice at his feet. 'Well, that was stimulating.'

'Will you come back now?' I begged.

'I shall return,' he vowed, 'but not immediately.' He stuck out his left leg and tested a joist.

'You are not thinking...' I began as he slid his foot along.

'Thinking and doing,' he said. 'Hush.'

My guardian placed his other foot on the beam but I could not see through the clouds of dust whether it sagged or not. He extended his cane to some six feet or so and held it horizontally, as I had seen in a photograph of Blondin crossing the Niagara Falls.

'What are you doing?' I demanded.

Mr G turned his head to look back at me and I wished he had not, for he wobbled alarmingly. 'I believe that *hush* is generally recognized as an injunction to hold one's tongue but, since you ask, I am crossing a seven-foot-four-inch wide chasm by means of a conveniently affixed oaken beam.'

'But why?'

'Because it is too far for me to jump from a standing start.'

I decided that it was safer to let him concentrate on the task in hand. His shortened right leg did not make his task any easier and he tipped worryingly every time he put his weight on it. At last he neared the other side.

'The floor does not look robust enough to support me,' he announced and dipped so suddenly that I thought he had fallen.

'Be careful,' I squeaked before I could stop myself, but Mr G gave no sign of having heard me. He was on one knee, his cane balanced across the beam, and rooting around in his satchel. He had his knife out and seemed to be scraping at a broken board jutting from the other side a foot or two over the abyss. I could hear scratching noises but he had his back to me and all I could see was his arm going to and fro. A test tube appeared and disappeared.

'Intriguing,' my godfather said and got to his feet, reversing cautiously as he avoided the projecting rusty nail heads.

'Shall I come and help?' I offered.

'You shall not.'

But I had already hitched up my skirts and stepped into the house.

The floor felt less solid than I had expected as I tried to follow my guardian's footsteps. The rubble shifted and I was glad I had my parasol to steady me. I could see the side of his face as I rounded the mound.

'Get back.' He froze.

'What is it?'

I had been with my guardian when people had died in unspeakable agony but had never seen such a look of horror on his face. It drained of blood in an instant and his right eye fell unheeded, bouncing off a lathe and clinking on the cellar floor far below.

'Underneath the beam.' He gasped. 'Bats, dozens of them.'

I craned my neck and saw them. He had not exaggerated their numbers for the whole joist was thick with them, clinging to the undersurface, rats wrapped in leather wings.

'Ninety-six at a glance,' he calculated.

'But why did they not fly away when their ceiling broke and all the light flooded in?' I wondered.

'Perhaps you would like to write a paper on the motivations of chiroptera,' he suggested acidly. 'I can wait here whilst you equip yourself with the requisite materials.'

'I believe they are dead,' I proposed. 'Bats' feet lock so that they do not fall from their perches when they are asleep and the same holds true when they have died.'

Mr G shivered. 'I did not know you were such an expert.'

He took another careful step back and one more until he was within a foot of the edge. Something twitched under the floor close to the plank he had examined.

'Close your eye,' I shouted.

'What?'

But for once Sidney Grice did as he was told. He crossed his arms defensively in front of his face and a solitary bat shook itself free, flying up through the hole, rising through the dust, swooping around his head, and I knew that if he sensed it swirling about him like a moth near a lamp post, my guardian would fall. I darted towards him, flailing with my parasol and caught him on the upper arm.

'What are you doing?' he demanded.

'Defending you.'

'Do *not* tell me from what,' he begged.

I had never known him so helpless, this man who faced death with a calmness that would do credit to a regiment of guards. I waved my parasol again and the bat whirled away.

'You are safe now,' I said.

Sidney Grice opened his eye, swivelled, and took hold of the end of my parasol, and I led him like a blind man off that beam, back across the floor, through the window and out of Steep House.

42

The Terror of Seeming

SIDNEY GRICE WAS shivering as he set foot on the mossy flagstones by the site of the front door, and I would have offered him my flask but I knew that he would refuse it.

'Do you want to sit down for a while?' I asked.

'Why on earth would I be standing if I did?' he replied sharply, evidently having composed himself again.

His hand was steady as he poured out the last of his tea.

'What did you find over there?' I beat some dust off the sleeve of my dress.

Sidney Grice swallowed his beverage and drew the test tube out of his top waistcoat pocket. 'What do you make of that?'

The doll leaned over with me, winking suggestively.

'It looks like shavings of wood.' I wiggled the tube to separate its contents. 'With flakes of dark brown paint.'

Mr G drained his cup. 'Not paint, March.' His voice rang through the forsaken lands and the ruins of Steep House. 'Varnish. Do you not see? The floor near the main staircase had been varnished.'

'But most floors in good houses have been treated with something.' I handed him back his find.

My guardian slipped the test tube into one of the leather sleeves sewn inside his satchel. 'Yes.' He loosened up his shoulders. 'But some of it has been burned off.'

'But it would be – in a fire.' Not for the first time I was baffled.

Mr G raised his hands like an Old Testament prophet. 'Have you learned nothing under my masterly tuition?' His voice fell accusingly. 'It is in the ordinary that most extraordinary is to be found. That is Grice's fourth law.'

'I thought it was the ninth,' I said.

Sidney Grice sniffed. His face was as coated as a miller's at the end of a morning's work. 'I have upgraded it.'

The doll and I looked at each other and her eyes rolled back into her head.

A velocipede stood against the trunk of a chestnut tree. The tyres had perished and ragweed wound between the spokes. Perhaps Eric had left it there carelessly when he had raced to the scene, an unthought of action that lived beyond him and his parents.

Mr G got out a folded patch and tied it.

'You do not have a spare with you?'

'I am tired of wearing it.'

'Does it hurt?' I asked in concern, though the socket looked a great deal less inflamed than I had known it to be.

'Always.' My guardian's head went down, the weight seemingly too great for his neck. 'Come, March.' His head rose slowly. 'Our work here is done.'

Through the poplars on the western boundary I spotted the slate roof and two chimneys of New House, and we deviated from our path to get a better view but could still see no lower than the upper floor.

'So Lucy must have had a bedroom in that corner.' I pointed to the front.

'If their descriptions are to be believed.'

'Shall we call on the way home?'

'I have no craving to do so.'

'Then I shall.'

'As you wish.'

We skirted an ornamental pond. Flame-blue dragonflies

darted and dipped over it and my guardian blenched but forced himself to continue. 'My fear of things that flap is rational,' he explained stiffly as he relocked the gate. 'The fact that you do not share my fear is merely an indication of your irrationality.'

I did not reply, for this was one thing I did not want to argue about. He knew it was a weakness, but the anxiety he had exhibited was nothing to the terror Sidney Grice had of seeming to be human.

43

Heels, Wheels and Lemonade

LUCY AND FREDDY were out, Aellen told me, and I clucked in annoyance. If Sidney Grice had waited a minute he could have given me a lift home.

A whippet was chasing its tail round a man in tails and an opera hat playing 'I Adora Flora. Why Don't She Notice Me?' on the harmonica. The man clicked his fingers and the dog went up on to its hind legs. I often worry how cruelly animals have been trained, but this dog was wagging its tail and looked, if anything, a bit too well-fed.

I reached for my purse and was so engrossed in watching as I left Amber House that I stumbled on the kerb and heard a snap. 'Blimmit,' I cursed as I put out my parasol to stop myself tumbling under the front wheels of a brougham speeding along.

'Take a bit of water with it,' the driver shouted as they clattered past.

'Take a lot and drown yourself in it,' I yelled back, thankful that my guardian was not within earshot. 'Oh blart.' I nearly stumbled again as my heel came adrift.

'This is your lucky day.' The bootmaker materialized at my side. 'And mine.'

He looked so pleased and I felt so stupid that I almost stalked off, but it is difficult to march with dignity when one heel is hanging by a thread.

'Can you fix it?' I asked, and he smirked.

'Well, I ain't a clock mender.'

'Do I need to take it off?'

'Not if you don't mind showing a bit of fetlock.'

It would be a great deal easier than unlacing, taking off, replacing and relacing my boot, I decided.

''Ang on to the lamp post then,' he instructed, and I leaned my parasol against it before taking a grip on the hot green-painted iron. 'Foot up.' I bent my knee and he took my ankle between his knees as a blacksmith might shoe a horse. 'That's lucky. The 'eel is broken.'

'I know it is,' I retorted irritably.

'No, I'm sayin' the 'eel is snapped froo, not orf. If I jest bang a nail in, it'll tide you over nice.' He clinked about in his canvas bag. 'That'll do it.' More clinking. 'Now, this won't 'urt a bit.' He started to tap, whistling along with the verse that went *Oh Flora don't ignora me todaaaaay*, and five knocks later he wiggled the heel about and lowered my foot to the ground. 'That'll get you 'ome if you don't play 'opscotch on the way.' He waved his hammer like a flamboyant auctioneer. 'Bring 'em back when you've got anovva pair on and I'll set you up wiv two noo heels. Those ones are rubbish.'

I did not tell him I had paid six pounds for them three weeks ago. 'How much do I owe you?'

The bootmaker scratched under his cap as if solving a complicated calculation.

'Five spinners,' he decided, and I ran through every possible rhyme in my head. 'Spinnin' Jennies – pennies,' he explained.

'You made that one up,' I accused and he wrinkled his nose.

He was a much smaller man than I had thought, I realized, now that he was close – hardly any taller than me and slightly on the plump side, and his skin was almost as smooth as Sidney Grice's. He still had a brown stain on his upper lip and a trace on his lower, like a child who hadn't had his face washed after eating chocolate – a birthmark, I decided.

'P'raps.' He grinned mischievously. 'But they'll all be sayin' it this time next week, just you wait and see. Like sheep, they are. Baa baa baa,' he mimicked.

'Fivepence for a nail?' I complained mildly. 'I doubt you pay a penny a dozen for them.'

'Great Aunt Edif, you've got a cheap ironmonger,' he countered. 'Give me 'is name and you can 'ave that one for free. Or – tell you what – I'll just take the nail awt and we'll call it quits.'

I gave him a sixpenny piece.

'I ain't got nuffink smaller,' he warned.

I nearly suggested we looked for a cafe, but few places were happy to give change unless I bought something so it hardly seemed worth the trouble.

'You can knock it off my next bill,' I told him, and he threw out an arm.

'Oh fanks, miss, you're an ops-a-daisy.' His hammer went flying out of his hand, skidding along until a flower girl put her foot on it.

'Oh Lor',' she cackled. 'Do anyfink for a giggle, 'e will.' And she toed it back along the pavement towards him.

'We could do wiv you in goal for Spurs, Peggy.' The bootmaker clapped appreciatively and she hooted in merriment.

Most comedians would sell their mothers and throw in their souls for free to have an audience like her, I pondered, as I crossed the square. I would have given a great deal at that moment to be able to jump into the Serpentine to cool off, but instead I had to gently steam under my layers of cotton and be grateful that the Rational Dress movement had banished the corset from everyday wear.

'Ice-cold lemonaayade,' a shaven-headed boy called out. 'Satcha treat in the 'eat. Lovely r'freshin' ice-cold lemonaayaay- aayaayaayade.'

That sounded too good to miss, so I risked and wasted a penny. His product was warm, cloudy and fusty, served in a cracked cup dipped into the sediment at the bottom of a barrel. I handed it straight back.

'I could get better from a horse trough.'

'No, you could'n'.' He flinched from my barb. 'It'd be 'xactly the same.'

44

❖•❀•❖

An Inspector Calls

I WAS CHECKING THROUGH my account of the strange case of the woman who lost a sandal in Bohemia when the doorbell rang. Molly thundered along the hallway and I heard an *Oh it's you*, and I hoped it was somebody who she was entitled to address in that way. She had once spoken to the Prince of Wales's equerry in an even more familiar fashion. I did not have to worry long, however, because she came bursting in with *'Spector Pound*, flinging out her arm as if introducing a trapeze artist.

'Thank you, Molly.' I got up from the desk. 'Good morning, Inspector. If you are looking for Mr Grice, he has been called as a professional witness in the trial of Beryl Cornette.'

The inspector looked uneasy, I thought. Did he have bad news?

'Actually, it is you I have come to see,' he said, and Molly winked.

'Aye aye.' She gave him a big nudge.

'Go away,' I said in my most Gricean tones.

'But he's only just got here.'

'I was talking to you.'

'Ohhhh.' She tangled her fingers.

'And do not eavesdrop,' I warned, waiting for her to ask me what an eave was and if it would break when she dropped it, but she only gave another pained but briefer *Oh*, tied her fingers into granny knots and clumped back towards the lower stairs.

'I have some good news,' he told me.

'You do not look like you have.'

His face was pinched and anxious. Was he going away again? I realized with a pang that it was none of my concern any more.

'I am to be promoted,' he announced, 'in about two weeks' time. Newburgh is retiring at last and I am to take his place.'

'Chief Inspector?' I resisted the urge to throw my arms round him. 'But that is wonderful.'

'I shan't be sorry not to be posted back to Limehouse.' He managed a fleeting grin.

'Quigley must be eating himself,' I crowed. 'He thought the job would be his.'

'He will have to accept it.' Pound shrugged. 'Or leave.'

'The latter would be too much to hope for.' I touched his hand. 'Oh, George, that is marvellous news.'

He smiled again but still nervously. 'I hoped you would be pleased.' His clear blue eyes – the ones that Harriet said she go could boating in – were troubled.

'Are you not?' I asked in consternation, and George Pound cleared his throat.

'I have been a fool, March.' He called me by my Christian name for the first time since we had separated at that graveside. 'A damned fool.'

'What have you done?' I asked, praying that he had not gone off and married some horrible woman.

'Would you like to sit down?'

'No.'

'I let you go, March.' He looked at his feet. 'And when you tried to come back to me, I turned you away. I was a damned fool.'

At this point Mr G would have reminded the inspector that he had already established that point, but I only said, 'What are you telling me?'

'I was worried about the gulf in our affairs but mine are much improved now, though I will never be a wealthy man.' He glanced into my eyes.

'I do not care about that.'

'I know.' George Pound searched my face and his big hand went to my cheek. 'When I thought I had lost you—'

I put a finger to his lips. 'You never lost me.' And for the first time I saw those eyes glisten.

'I love you so much.' He went down on one knee. 'March—'

'Don't,' I said, and he looked at me in bewilderment. 'Do not say it unless you mean it – really mean it – and mean it forever.'

'Will you marry me?'

'Oh, you bloody fool.' I fell down on my knees and cradled his big, wise, strong, gentle face. 'Of course I will.'

And the tears ran down George Pound's cheeks and I kissed each one away until I could not see them for my own.

'Oh Lor'.' Molly materialized with unnerving stealth. 'Has she fallened over again? What a cry baby.'

*

Molly served us tea on the first floor. George did not feel comfortable with the idea of sitting in Sidney Grice's armchair, and there was a sofa in the sitting room where we could sit together and look out on the street, but mainly at each other.

'I shall get you well again,' I promised, toying with the ring on my third finger.

'I am quite well now,' he reassured me. 'My wound burst and it seemed that I would die, but the poison drained and now it has completely healed.'

I should have been there with you.

'I shall make you *very* well,' I told him. 'You have lost weight. I shall feed you up with beef and kidney pies and puddings and foaming pints of stout.'

'It will be me that is stout,' he warned.

'I hope so.' I squeezed his hand. 'And I shall cut and rub your tobacco and fill your meerschaum pipe, and take you back to Parbold and introduce you to my old friend Maudy Glass, and show you all my childhood haunts.'

George snuggled closer. 'I shall ask Mr Grice this evening,' he vowed.

'Let me speak to him first.' I kissed George. 'You know what he is like.'

'All too well,' George agreed ruefully, and pinched his philtrum.

'Strictly speaking, he cannot forbid it,' I said, 'for he is not my legal guardian, but I should like his blessing.'

'And so should I,' George agreed heartily. 'I have a very high opinion of your godfather and I should not like to come between you.'

'Your sister will not be happy,' I predicted.

'Lucinda will come round to the idea.'

'I doubt it very much,' I argued, with some feeling, for I did not care for Lucinda and she detested me, blaming me – and not without reason – for her brother's being stabbed.

He separated his thumb and forefinger to run them under his moustaches. 'She knows that I care for you, and I shall let her stay in our uncle's house. We can find somewhere to rent.'

'I cannot promise to be an obedient wife,' I warned and George Pound put his arms round me.

'I should not believe you if you did.'

'And I still want to be a personal detective.'

'And I shall do everything I can to support you in that,' he said, and I knew that he would.

We sat a while, me nestling into his embrace.

'Shall we have children?' It occurred to me that I did not even know if he liked them.

'Twenty.' He hugged me. 'Well, at least one, I hope.'

'Two would be nice.' I kissed his palm. 'It can be lonely, being an only child.'

'Siblings are not always a blessing,' George told me ruefully. 'But, if you want two, then two it is.'

An omnibus drew alongside with a Sikh in crimson robes and matching turban at the back of the top floor in splendid isolation, a warrior king aboard his chariot.

'I know how desperately you miss your fiancé,' George said carefully. 'Your first fiancé, I mean. But I want you to make a promise to me, March. If anything happens to me—'

'I will not let it.'

'If it does,' he insisted, 'you will not keep a shrine to me.' George put his hands to my face and turned it to look at him, and his gaze searched mine.

'I promise,' I said. 'No shrine. And, whilst we are on that subject, you asked me once what I would do if Edward could return.'

I felt his fingers tighten. 'It was not a fair question,' he mumbled and glanced out of the window.

The Sikh stroked his beard and was gone.

'You had every right to ask it,' I insisted, 'and I told you that I did not know. But I would like to answer it now. You are not a substitute, George Pound. You are not second best. If I had to chose between you, it would be you without hesitation.'

I had thought that I would feel guilty saying that aloud, for I had loved Edward with all my heart, but that heart had been broken and George Pound had mended it, and now it almost burst with love for the man with whom I would share my life.

45

The Broken Seal

SIDNEY GRICE WAS especially irascible when he returned. 'How did the trial go?' I asked, and he dropped his eye into a cupped palm.

'How trials always go.' He shook out a rolled eye patch. 'According to the whims of twelve ignorant men.' He tied the patch behind his head. 'I spent forty-eight minutes explaining how Mr Cornette could not possibly have been in Barnet on the night in question, with the whole box of them nodding along, only for fifty per centum of the exotically named South Sea Songstress Sisters to oscillate her Bactrian eyelashes and snivel *Oh, but I saw him there* for the full dozen to change the remnants of their troglodytic neural ganglia.'

He tossed four letters, unopened, over his shoulder into the bin.

'Oh dear.' I held up my jug of water. 'You would like a cold drink while you wait for your tea?'

'I never like cold drinks.' He threw two more letters into his wastepaper bin. 'They are usually warm.' And then he ripped open a pale rose-tinted envelope. 'That is the second countess who has proposed marriage to me this month.' He dropped that into his wire basket for filing and opened the flap of another to peruse it suspiciously. 'How do so many algebraists manage to get murdered?'

'I have often lain awake pondering that,' I said. 'Speaking of marriage.'

He tore a blue paper letter in four and then one of the quarters in four again. 'I was talking of algebraistocide.'

'Yes, but before that.'

'That is one of our few areas of common ground.' He reassembled the seven torn pieces on his desk. 'Neither of us will ever enter into that ridiculous contract.'

'Well, I might,' I began tentatively, and he dipped his head.

'Oh, March.' He smiled fleetingly. 'Even you are not that stupid. What man would be worth betraying me for, after all the time I have expended in patiently teaching you and all the confidences I have entrusted to you, in the understanding that you wished to follow – however ineptly – in my footsteps?'

'Yes, but surely I could—'

'Knowing that I could never work with another man's...' He paused to give his final word the magnitude of disgust it deserved. '*Wife.*'

Sidney Grice broke the white wax seal of a huge ivory envelope, glared at the card he had extracted and made that odd quick bark that served him as a laugh. 'A princess this time.' He threw it into the basket. 'Well, she shall have to settle for a lesser man.'

I tried to bring the subject back to what I wanted to tell him. 'But I would still—' I managed as the doorbell sounded, but I was not sure what I would still be to him when I was Mrs Pound. 'There is something we must talk about,' I added quickly, but my guardian was reinserting his eye and running his fingers back through his hair.

'There are many things,' he said, 'beginning with why you have a nail protruding from the heel of your left boot, which is scratching my inadequately polished Hampshire oak floor.'

'I broke the heel.'

'Is this relevant to any of our cases?'

'No.'

'Then stop jibber-jabbering about it.'

Molly entered. 'He told me to read it straight out so I wontn't not forget it.' She held the card at arm's length and squinted. 'His,' she managed before bringing it up to her nose. 'His Illustrated Highness Prince Ul-errrrmmm-rich...' She turned back into the hall. 'Is this an April Fool?' she demanded. 'A-L-B-what?' She screwed her eyes tight. 'That's not how you spell Albert. Oh,' she threw up her hands indignantly. 'Sklu-something.' She waved the card accusingly and called over her shoulder, 'You made that last one up.'

'Prince Ulrich Albrecht Sigismund Schlangezahn,' I told her, and she leaned back disbelievingly. 'This is like what they do in that street game when they get you to say things about sea sells she shells, and all laugh and say I got it wrong when I didntn't not.'

I squeezed past the immovable bulk that was my guardian's maid.

'Good evening, Prince Ulrich,' I said coolly. 'Can I help you?'

The prince looked even more splendid than I had remembered, I was chagrined to note, for I would have preferred him to be a shuffling, weaselly man with a bulbous runny nose, but, standing a few inches before me, immaculately attired in a perfectly tailored charcoal coat and trousers and boots that gleamed like black quartz, was one of the most strikingly handsome men I had come across in years.

'Miss Middleton.' He snapped his heels together and put out his hand, but I did not take it.

New boots. I recalled Lucy's account of the opium den.

The prince's face was precisely and symmetrically carved with a long slightly hooked nose over his immaculately waxed, upturned military moustaches. And he had not followed many of his countrymen's predilection for horridly luxuriant side-whiskers. His chin was square and clean-shaven, and unblemished apart from that scar.

'Can I help you?' I repeated firmly, and was about to ask him to leave when my guardian came out.

'Your Highness.' He held out his hand with more bonhomie than I had known him to exhibit for any living human being before. 'Please excuse them. They are females.'

'Zo I am observing,' the prince said in a doomed attempt at gallantry.

He was still a poor second to George, I decided.

'Come through.' Sidney Grice ushered our visitor towards my chair.

'But I cannot sit while the lady stands,' Prince Ulrich protested.

'Oh, I do,' Mr G assured him, and proceeded to demonstrate. But the prince remained standing, his back as straight as his silver-topped walking stick, for it appeared he shared at least one of Sidney Grice's practices – that of carrying one indoors.

'Tea,' Mr G barked, and Molly made her way back down the hall.

'I come for two reasons,' the prince began. 'First, to know that you haff quite recovered, Miss Middleton.'

'From you threatening to assault me?' I enquired, and his immaculately tended moustaches rose like eyebrows in surprise.

'It cannot be you are still believing that after I explained?' His eyes, deep-set under a prominent brow, flashed topaz as he directed them at me.

'It can be,' I assured him, and Prince Ulrich reddened a fraction in the jowls.

'I am an officer in the Imperial German Army, cousin to Kaiser Wilhelm and a gentleman of the highest standing in my country. You are thinking I would outrage a voman?'

'When somebody pays a procurer and pokes me about like a pig in a cattle market, I cannot help but have my suspicions,' I rejoined.

His brow fell and those eyes were almost jet, but still compelling in their gaze. 'You cannot condemn me for acting my part vell.' His lips had a sensual fullness to them that I might have found attractive, if I had allowed myself to do so.

'You are about to find out that I can.'

'But you and your friend were acting it alzo.'

Sidney Grice lay back in his chair, watching us both with mild amusement. 'I think it might be better if you sat, Prince Ulrich. Miss Middleton is in danger of dislocating her cervical vertebrae from trying to look you in the eye at a nine-inch disadvantage.'

The prince shrugged. 'As you vish.'

Our visitor helped himself to an upright chair from the central table and, with his higher vantage and greater height, I was hardly any better off when I settled into my armchair.

'Perhaps you would like to tell Miss Middleton the second reason that you came,' Mr G suggested.

'Indeed,' the prince acquiesced. 'Though I am having doubts as to whether you will give your assent, Mr Grice.'

This sounded disconcertingly as if Schlangezahn were seeking permission to ask for my hand in marriage, and it flashed through my mind that my refusal might be an opportunity to announce that I was already spoken for. But I dismissed the idea even as it floated into my mind.

'For what?' My guardian pressed his fingertips so hard together that the tips blanched.

'I am seeking your dispensation to invite your vord to dinner.' Our visitor grasped the arms of his chair as if preparing to leave.

'Oh, she's just had that.' Molly trudged in with a tray. 'And even little Miss Greedychops dontn't not need two dinners.'

As it happened I sometimes did, sneaking off for proper food after pushing Cook's swill around the plate.

'I have admonished you before about your unsolicited inter-ruptions,' Molly's employer rumbled and she grinned, though less toothily than she used to.

'He do use long words to say thanks,' she told our visitor, and drew back her elbow as if to give him a chummy nudge but, luckily for her employment prospects, instead chose to puggle in her ear.

'I shall not stand in your way.' Sidney Grice shooed Molly away. 'But I doubt that she will accept.'

I smiled sweetly at the Prussian and tried to flutter my eye-lashes but, unlike Mr G, I was never much good at that.

'You haff something in your eye?'

'Aqueous humour.'

'Miss Middleton.' Prince Ulrich cleared his throat, doubtless regretting his decision now.

'Yes?'

'I know vee haff had an unfortunate start and I should not like to read in one of your excellent accounts vot a monster I voz.'

'Indeed you would not.' I tossed my head, again an unimpressive manoeuvre with my hair so tightly pinned and tied back.

'So I am hoping you vill accept my invitation to dine viv me at my hotel.'

'Very well,' I replied, in what I hoped was a haughty manner.

'What time,' my guardian blinked slowly like a lizard on a warm rock, 'will you expect us?'

'The two of you?' Prince Ulrich's face was impassive but his voice betrayed his surprise.

'You do not want my maid to come too?'

'*Nein nein.*'

'Friday is convenient for me.' I poured three teas.

'At seven?'

'Oh, very well.' Mr G adopted the tone of a browbeaten husband whilst I set to pondering what I should wear.

The prince declined my silent offer of milk. 'In Berlin we drink our tea with lemon.'

'An improvement on the glandular excretions with which Miss Middleton pollutes her beverages.' Mr G stretched his mouth without exposing any teeth.

'I hope you will not be going to Limehouse again, Miss Middleton.' Prince Ulrich stirred a dab of sugar into his drink.

Sidney Grice clamped his teeth together.

'I shall go where I choose.' I realized that I had put four sugars in my tea, though I normally have only one.

'It is a dangerous place for a man.' The prince tilted his head, the scar flashing towards me like white lightning on his skin. 'Much more zo for a lady.'

'Are you afraid I will arrest you again?' I sipped my syrup.

'I would not put it past her.' Sidney Grice paddled his own tea vigorously in a to-and-fro motion from north to south that I had not seen him use before.

'I was thinking more of the safety.' Schlangezahn's finger-plates were nicely cut, I noticed as he lifted his saucer.

'And you are wise to do so.' My godfather changed course, rowing leisurely from east to west. 'Miss Middleton can be a highly dangerous woman. Before you rush off...' he said, though our visitor had given no indication that he intended to do so. Sidney Grice put a hand to his waistcoat. 'I wanted to ask you about this, Your Highness.'

The prince raised his eyebrows in polite interest as my guardian brought a carved box out of his pocket.

'I do not take snuff, Herr Grice,' Prince Ulrich said.

'Neither does Herr Grice,' I told him, mainly because I wanted a chance to refer to my godfather in that way.

Mr G flipped up the lid to reveal the button nestling in white cotton.

'May I see?' The prince held out his hand and Sidney Grice tipped the button into it, watching him closely.

'It bears my family crest,' Prince Ulrich confirmed. 'Where did you find it?'

'Miss Middleton finds things.' Mr G frosted around the edges. 'Most of the time one might more accurately say she stumbles over things. I seek and discover them.'

The German chuckled. 'You are not telling me.'

'Is it yours?' I asked.

'It looks like one of my vaistcoat buttons,' the prince commented.

'Have you noticed any missing?' I asked.

He shrugged. 'I am not thinking zo.'

'Surely a gentleman who takes such care with his appearance as you clearly do would notice immediately,' I reasoned, and he slapped his head theatrically.

'Maybe I did find one gone last veek, maybe not,' he said vaguely. 'But I did not pay so much attention.'

Sidney Grice leaned back.

'Your valet would know,' I pointed out. 'He must check everything.'

Prince Ulrich grinned. 'You are good at this.'

'It is my profession,' I responded and Mr G pursed his lips.

'I shall get him to check,' Prince Ulrich decided. 'And, if he has slipped up, I shall sack us both for incompetence – him for not noticing and myself for employing him.'

He waited for a laugh and I managed the seed of a smile.

'Perhaps you could explain to Miss Middleton why you did not notice.' Sidney Grice pointed his right thumb down like a Roman emperor condemning a gladiator.

'It was the day some stupid street child spilled a bucket of stinking vaste over me. I voz late for a meeting and I had to return to my hotel to change.' He watched that thumb hover horizontally. 'I might even haff pulled it off myself in my rushing.'

The thumb shot up and the Prussian raised the corner of his lips uncertainly.

'Would you like more unsophisticated leaves soaked in water?' I offered, and Schlangezahn snorted at my reference to his words in Marylebone.

'Of course he would not.' Sidney Grice clamped a hand over the pot. 'He is leaving.'

Our visitor shifted in bemusement. 'Then I shall expect you

both,' he emphasized the last word a fraction tetchily, 'on Friday at seven.'

'Assuming that I have not been murdered in the meantime.' Mr G swirled the dregs of his tea, peering in like a fortune-teller.

'Are you expecting to be?' The prince was all at once a concerned parent. 'I can arrange some protection.'

'There is no need,' I assured him. 'It is just that one must always expect the unexpected in our business.'

'If one could expect the unexpected it would become the expected.' Sidney Grice demolished my claim.

The prince drained his tea and rose. Mr G stretched over the back of his chair and gave the bell rope one pull. I never liked the skull joggling on the end of it.

Our visitor bowed and Sidney Grice wiggled his fingers but did not rise.

Prince Ulrich straightened his coat. 'I am happy to see you are none the vorse for your experience, Miss Middleton.'

'So am I.' I went with him into the hall.

I let him kiss my hand. It was not that I was convinced by his account of what had occurred that night in Limehouse, but I rather liked being kissed by men with moustaches now.

46

Scented Wrens and Recrudescent Swans

THE OUTER OFFICE of Spry and Fitt constituted one small dark room, lit by a smoky gas mantle over the head of a clerk perched on a high stool, his back arched over a lower desk on a wide dais. He was so busily scratching away in a large red-backed ledger that he hardly seemed to notice our entry.

'C. S. Derwent Assurance, first floor, but closed today. Any correspondence in the tray. Good day,' he said, without looking up or pausing from his work.

His head was hairless and the skin wrinkled like newspaper that has been dropped in a puddle.

'As recrudescent swans,' Sidney Grice shot back at him.

'What?' Hair sprouted from the clerk's face like badly sown grass seed.

'Or...' Mr G reflected for perhaps half a second. 'Acarus scented wrens.'

The clerk pulled out the nib of his pen, his hand stained India Black by his employment. 'What are you talking about?'

'They are anagrams of C. S. Derwent Assurance,' my guardian told him.

'How did you do that?' I marvelled, as the clerk pushed a fresh nib into the semilunar slot in his pen and slid the brass ring back over it.

'It is quite simple,' he told me. 'One merely rearranges the letters until they are in the sequence of different words.'

'But you did it in your head.'

'Where else should I do it?'

The clerk dipped his nib.

'Well, most people would need paper and pencil and a good dictionary.'

'It is more convenient to do it in my head.' Mr G ran a finger under the ledger and sniffed the dusty smudge. 'For I always have my head with me and there is no such publication as a good dictionary, though the Oxford comes close.'

The clerk was writing busily when Sidney Grice kicked up his right leg with a litheness that would have done credit to a cancan dancer and plunked his foot on the desk.

'What are you doing?' the clerk cried out, and Mr G turned his glass eye towards him.

'Gaining what we should have obtained the moment we achieved ingress to this shabby sham of a premises,' Sidney Grice told him. 'Namely, your exclusive attention.'

'Is Mr Spry here?' I asked.

My guardian removed his foot with less agility, hopping backwards to retain his balance.

'Who wants to know?'

'I do.'

'And who might you be?' He asked so nastily that I did not feel like telling him.

'I might be anyone,' I responded. 'But I am not likely to be you. If I were, I should have learned better manners.'

Mr G began to stroll round him, climbing the one step on to his dais, cane swinging as if on a pleasant country walk.

'Why are you behind me?' The clerk half-swivelled on his stool.

'First, because I am not on any other side of you and, second, my motivation is that I am not tall enough to read your ledger from down there,' my guardian said. 'And it is unkind of you to remind me of that – not that I look to you for benefaction.'

There was a trap occupied by a mouldering mouse on the unswept hearth.

'How dare you?'

'It is not an especially brave act.' Mr G whacked his cane across the book to stop the clerk slamming it shut and the clerk jumped sideways. 'I once entered a subterranean labyrinth populated by nineteen ret-ic-ul-at-ed py-thons.' He separated the syllables until they were almost distinct words. 'That required a great deal more courage, though the aforementioned acrimonious and ill-mannered serpents were better company than you.' He clipped on his pince-nez and leaned over, lifting the clerk's arm out of the way by the sleeve. '*And that is why I strangled Silas Spry*,' he narrated.

'Oh Lord,' the clerk moaned. 'I knew I wouldn't get away with it.'

47

The Quiet of Graves

I CLAMBERED ON TO the low stage as well and peered over the clerk's head, now buried in his hands, elbows on his heavily used blotting pad.

'*He was a tryant and a Scruge,*' I read. 'I think you mean tyrant,' I pointed out. 'And that last word should be spelled with a double O in the middle instead of the U.'

'It is only a rough draft,' he moaned.

'And there are two S's in confession.'

Sidney Grice lifted his cane away, letting it hover as if about to bestow a knighthood. '*S-L-O-R-T-E-R-E-D,*' he spelled out in horror. 'You are no better suited to being a scribe than you are a murderer.'

'Murderer?' The clerk shot up and caught my chin with the back of his head, clacking my teeth together.

'Blim—' I checked the stream of expletives that sprang to my bitten tongue and satisfied myself with slapping his ear, admittedly much harder than I had intended.

'Blimmid 'eck that stung.' The clerk clearly did not share my scruples. 'I haven't murdered no one, though Lord knows I've been tempted.'

'You are writing a story,' I realized and leafed back to the first page. '*There was a message engraved in the locket,*' I read aloud. 'That is not a very exciting beginning.'

'I know.' The clerk rubbed his head as if it could possibly

be hurting as much as my jaw. 'But I have to fill my time somehow.'

'Business is slow?' I surmised.

'Quiet as a grave,' he confirmed. 'You won't tell Mr Spry, will you? It's not much of a job but I'll never get another with my spelling, and I can't add up.'

'Some graves are far from quiet,' Sidney Grice mused. '*Exempli gratia*, the non-resting place of Miss Thythily Thythe of Hythe whilst being dug up by Canis Lupis Dingos.'

'Do you have nothing to do?' I asked, wondering if it would be decent to check that my upper incisors had not been loosened.

'Not very much.'

'And yet...' Sidney Grice put his mouth two inches from the clerk's unstruck ear and raised his voice to one level below a shout. 'You do not respond favourably to the telegramic requests I have sent using a variety of aliases for an appointment.'

The clerk winced. 'Mr Spry has given me strict instructions not to accept any more clients.'

'How many,' Mr G demanded, 'and I will accept an exact number – clients do you have?'

The clerk scratched his pate with his pen, drawing quite a good likeness of an oxbow lake.

'Assuming none of them have died.' He counted off on his fingers as his lips shaped their names. 'Eight, but I cannot recall when any of them last came in.'

'And what about Mr Spry?' I enquired, as the lake sprang a leak.

'Hardly ever,' the clerk said, 'except to pay me and check that I am here.'

'Does he have far to travel?' I mopped his head with a torn sheet of blotting paper.

'He used to.' The clerk sighed contentedly at my attentions, but did not enquire why I was giving them. 'Until he moved to Berkeley Square about four years ago.'

Mr G pulled open the drawer of a cabinet and rifled through the few files ranged in it, all of them propped upright by a plaster bust of General Gordon in a glossy red fez. 'At last a use for you.' He leafed through them. 'Where, to within one nine-teenth of a seven thousand, nine hundred and twentieth of a furlong, are Mr Silas Pother Spry's records apropos of Miss Lucinda Seraphora Bocking?'

The clerk twisted on his stool. 'They are never kept here,' he said.

'Where then?' Sidney Grice patted the clerk's coat, as if expecting to find the records there.

'Well, I can only presume—'

'Never start a sentence with *well* when nothing is,' Mr G advised. 'Never-never *only* do anything when you are not required to do it at all, and never-never-never *presume* anything when I require a fact. The truth is like the fatuously dubbed Cleopatra's Needle in that respect. It towers and you can do a great many things with an Egyptian obelisk but you cannot presume it.'

He took a letter out of an envelope.

The clerk rubbed his eyes like a child waking up. 'I don't know, sir. In fact, I don't even know your name.'

'Then we are on an equal footing in that regard,' my guardian stated. 'For I do not know yours either. Come,' he signalled to me. 'It is never wise to waste more than nineteen minutes with a man whose younger sister will not speak to him.'

'How on earth could you know that?' The clerk gaped and sat back on his stool.

'Goodbye,' I said and he absent-mindedly snapped his pen.

'So you did not think much of my story?' he asked, distracted by my guardian patting him again.

'Instead of making up something about a doctor, you should write about what you know,' I suggested, and he made a noise like a disappointed puppy.

'I only know about being a clerk and not a very good one at that,' he snuffled. 'Who would be interested in the diary of a nobody?'

*

I was halfway down before I realized that Sidney Grice was not following me and, when I craned my neck, I saw that he was heading in the opposite direction.

'Where are you going?' I asked.

'Up.' He sprang away two treads at a time.

'Up where?'

'Up here.'

I sighed and followed, my skirts dragging annoyingly in the dust.

The door on the next landing was closed and, in confirmation of this, a black-lettered sign slid into a board on the wall declared *CLOSED* beneath the words *C. S. DERWENT ASSURANCE CO. LTD.*

'Well, that alters the anagram somewhat,' he said accusingly.

'Colt went to dances.' I struggled but was quite pleased with my effort, until he pointed out, 'You still have seven unused letters.'

'Squidge,' I blustered.

'I shall make enquiries about the lineage.' Mr G brushed his fingertips along and down the words like a blind man reading Braille. 'And marital status of the elusive Spry.'

Underneath the board, affixed by a pair of steel hooks and eyes, another sign read:

IN CASE OF CLOSURE
PLEASE DEPOSIT MAIL
AT GROUND-FLOOR OFFICE

Sidney Grice put his ear to the door and rapped with his knuckles.

'Ahah.' He pulled away with a sharp breath as if he had burned his ear and unscrewed the handle of his cane.

'Which stick is this?'

My guardian tossed his fine head of black hair. 'The Grice Patent-Denied Housebreaking Cane.' And he tipped what looked like an oversized corkscrew out into his hand.

'What is that?'

'A bradawl.' He clipped it into the handle to give himself a grip and put the point to the woodwork, twisting it in deftly.

'But,' I protested, 'this is criminal damage.'

'Exactly one of the nineteen objections the Patent Office made to my invention.' He set to work vigorously, stopping to reverse and pull his drill out. 'One day I shall design a clockwork motor small enough to perform the rotations for me.' He pulled it out again, showering sawdust on to the floor, and put his eye to the hole.

'What is it?' I asked.

'A hole,' he told me.

'Can I look?'

Sidney Grice scratched his chin. 'Very well.' He dismantled his device.

'What's going on up there?' The clerk's voice rose querulously.

'We are looking for the way out,' I called over the bannister as he tramped up.

'The way you came.' His head appeared.

'Thank you.' I went meekly down.

'Our investigations seem to have hit a brick wall,' Sidney Grice grumbled as he refixed the handle.

*

'So how *did* you know about his sister?' I asked, as the eighth occupied hansom trotted by.

Mr G raised his cane to no avail. 'He had a letter from her in his coat pocket.'

'When you patted him? But that was a personal letter,' I protested and blew a shrill blast between my fingers.

'It is just as well that I am a personal detective then.' Sidney Grice growled as another cab ignored us. 'At this rate you shall have to walk home and send a hansom back to me.'

'If I have to carry out the first instruction, I shall not be doing the second,' I warned.

My guardian put out his hand and nearly had it taken off by a speeding empty cab. 'How sharper than a serpent's tooth it is to have a thankless child,' he quoted, readying himself to do battle with a tiny elderly lady in a red dress for the next vehicle to appear.

48

The Message and the Street Fighter

MOLLY WAS OUT on some errands and there was a telegram on the hall table.

'Open it,' Sidney Grice commanded so peremptorily that I was tempted to shred it in front of him, but I complied, not from obedience but nosiness – a useful trait in my future profession, I told myself.

FREDDY OUT PLEASE COME QUICKLY BEFORE SHE RETURNS DO NOT TELL HER ABOUT THIS LUCY

'I like a client who does not waste money on punctuation,' Mr G remarked, and I saw that he was reading it from the hall mirror behind me. 'It leaves them all the better equipped to imburse me.' He slipped his gloves on. 'The flag,' he commanded, and I set to work on the wheel.

*

Lucy sat in the library at a simple birch escritoire. She wore a pretty powder-blue dress, respectably high-collared, and with a thin black belt laced at the front to emphasize her wasp waist. Her hair was tied back, the fringe not entirely hiding the X carved so crudely into her flesh. The lower left arm of it gleamed white with reddened margins.

'Lucy, what has happened?' I hurried to kiss her, and it was obvious that she had been crying. Her eyes were dark and the lids puffy.

'Oh, March, thank you for coming.' Lucy hugged me and returned my kiss. 'And you too, Mr Grice.'

'I trust I am not expected to indulge in such displays of affection.'

'Does he ever?' Lucy asked, though it was clear that her mind was not on what she was saying.

'He is fond of my cat,' I answered automatically. 'Are you all right?'

Lucy laughed hollowly. 'Do I look all right? I look like a street fighter.'

'Which one?' Sidney Grice regarded himself in the mantle mirror.

'The bruising is going down around your eye.'

'And the shattered cheekbone is becoming all the more obvious,' she said bitterly. 'I am sorry. I should not be looking for sympathy.'

'Rest assured that you will get none from me.' Mr G flipped open his empty snuffbox. 'So, rather than await it, you may regale us with a response to Miss Middleton's first and uncharacteristically pertinent enquiry.'

Lucy took a breath.

'You are aware, since I have appraised you of the fact, that I charge by the hour.' Mr G tapped his hunter, still tucked into his waistcoat pocket. 'But, though I hire out my services, my time is worth more than money. Every unused one hundredth of a minute is a wasted tick of my brain.'

'Your brain ticks?' Lucy managed a smile.

'Indeed, though you cannot hear it,' he told her gravely. 'Though, of course, it does not tock. That could drive a man insane.'

'One is tempted to wonder if it has succeeded,' she said mildly.

'Unlike you I rarely submit to temptation.' He slipped his thumbs into the upper pockets of his waistcoat and Lucy's mouth tightened.

'Just when I thought we were beginning to get on.'

'Get on what?' Mr G deposited his satchel on what had been Freddy's chair.

I leaned towards her. 'Why did you telegraph us, Lucy?'

'I teased your guardian,' she conceded, 'but you may wonder if I am the one who is demented.'

'Without my wishing to hurtle precipitously to a definitive and possibly erroneous diagnosis, it may be that what you diagnose as madness is just yet another example of your overly emotional feminine irrationality,' Sidney Grice told her kindly.

I reached out and took her hand. 'What has happened, Lucy?'

'And I think I speak for both of us when I tell you that we would appreciate an answer this time.' Mr G's eye twinkled encouragingly and Lucy chewed her lower lip. 'We have nothing to appreciate yet,' he observed mildly.

'It is Freddy,' Lucy said at last.

'Do you think she has come to some harm?' I squeezed her hand.

Lucy brought out a handkerchief and unfolded it. 'I am not frightened *for* Freddy. I am frightened *of* her,' she said hesitantly.

'Why?' Mr G leaned so far forward that I thought he might topple off his chair.

'Excuse me.' Lucy blew her nose. 'Freddy has changed of late,' she said reluctantly. 'Or perhaps I am seeing her as she has always been.' She took a breath. 'I have always thought of her as my one true friend, the only person who truly... loves me.'

'I have certainly gained that impression,' I agreed.

'Impression,' my guardian snorted.

'Based on my observations of you both together.' I justified my remark more for his benefit. 'And the way she talks about you.'

Lucy crumpled her handkerchief. 'Oh, she always knows the right things to say. *Poor Lucy. You will be better soon. You must rest now.*' Lucy closed her eyes briefly as if about to do so, but when she opened them they were close to tears. 'But I am beginning to think that she hates me.'

'Surely not,' I protested. 'But why would you think that?'

'Little things at first.' Lucy wiped her eyes. 'Silly things like the other night.'

'Which one?' Sidney Grice pressed her. 'All previous nights can faithfully be described as *the other*.'

'Oh, I do not know.' Lucy shook her handkerchief out. 'It does not matter.'

'It docs to mc,' he assured her. 'I cannot vouch for Miss Middleton, but you are talking to a man who cares.'

'A day or two before I met March,' she guessed. 'I know it sounds trivial but Freddy had just come into the pink room.'

My godfather shivered. 'It sounds very trivial indeed.' He crossed his legs. 'Is that all you brought us here for?'

'Miss Bocking has not finished,' I snapped, and Lucy nodded gratefully.

'I was in the low armchair looking out. It was getting dark.'

'So, more evening than night,' he corrected her.

'What? I suppose so.' Lucy waved her left hand in frustration. 'For a man who is in a hurry to get an answer, you are an expert at delaying its arrival.'

'There is nothing to be gained by hurtling towards an incomplete or inaccurate response,' he informed her. 'Pray continue.'

'I was talking – some inconsequentiality about the glorious sunset we had seen over London once when my parents took us to Primrose Hill. Freddy was behind me, but I saw her reflection in the window pane and she was mimicking me, mouthing my words and copying my hand movements in an exaggerated way – you know the way you do as a child when a grown-up annoys you.'

'No, I did not,' Mr G denied hotly.

'I used to,' I remembered. 'There was a Sunday school teacher in our village who I detested.'

'There you are,' Lucy cried. 'You only do it to people you hate. If it was a joke she would have done it in front of me and I would have thrown a cushion at her.'

'Perhaps she knew you could see her,' I suggested, but Lucy demurred.

'When I asked quite amicably what she was doing behind me, she snapped *Nothing* and stormed from the room.'

'Perhaps you had done or said something unintentionally that annoyed her,' I proposed. 'We all annoy each other sometimes.'

'You are fortunate that you do not have to share a house with Miss Middleton,' my godfather agreed wholeheartedly. 'She once threw her soup at me.'

'It was rotting parsnips and I was trying to demonstrate how it stuck to the bowl,' I defended myself, and turned back to our client. 'There must be more than that.'

Lucy folded her handkerchief. 'Lots of little things,' she said, 'but they mount up. Hiding things that I know I put down in one place and then pretending to find them somewhere else. And breaking things – favourite ornaments – on purpose, or pretend-ing she cannot hear me so I have to keep repeating myself.'

'It all sounds very childish and annoying, but why are you frightened?' I asked.

'A few weeks ago I would have trusted Freddy with my life.'

'I have never completely understood that species of claim.' Mr G slumped back in his chair.

'I meant I thought she would have died for me.'

'Oh.' Sidney Grice put a finger to his eye. 'So you could not have trusted her with her own life.' He folded his arms left over right. 'But we shall adjourn briefly whilst you meditate on how best to justify your asseveration that you have been stricken with a species of friend-who-was-like-my-sister-phobia.'

My guardian bowed his head as if it were he who had pro-
vided an explanation.

Lucy drew a breath. 'I tried to pretend that Freddy and I were
equally at fault for what occurred that night.' She shifted uncomfortably. 'Partly because I did not want you to judge her badly.'

She held a frilled handkerchief, dyed to match her dress.

'I never judge anyone or anything badly.' Sidney Grice
refolded his arms with great precision, right over left. 'It is my
job to judge all things well. More than that...' He leaned to his
right as if travelling round a sharp corner. 'It is my self-given
mission, some might describe it as my mania. What was or were
the other part or parts to your motives for withholding or dis-
torting information yet again, Miss Lucinda Scraphora Bocking,
daughter of Mr and Mrs Clorence Bocking, late of New House,
Abbey Road?'

He rocked to his left.

Lucy screwed her handkerchief between both hands. 'I did
not want to believe it. I kept telling myself that I was being
unfair, but...' She braced herself against her own words. 'It
was Freddy who persuaded me to go to Limehouse. I had
heard enough to be frightened of going there, especially at
night, but she kept on and on about what fun it would be and
what a stick-in-the-mud I was. I had never even thought to try
opium before.' Her fingers were blanched with the strength of
her twisting. 'And it was Freddy directed the driver and told
him where to stop, and who suggested that we went into the
Golden Dragon.'

Lucy stopped, her face filled with horror at the accusations
she was levelling. I thought about what they implied and could
not quite believe it, not of the Freddy who I was getting to know.

'So.' Sidney Grice unfolded his arms and crossed them over
his chest. 'Tell us about the lead-crystal posy vase.'

I was about to ask what he meant but Lucy had no doubts.
'It was something Freddy said.' She tugged at her handkerchief.

'*I think Miss Bocking has had enough of your outrageous behaviour, Mr Grice, and so have I*,' my guardian quoted from memory. 'And the reason you dropped the vase was?'

'It brought it back to me and this is why I fear I may be going mad.' Lucy let go of her handkerchief and touched the scar on her forehead. 'But it occurred to me that the voice that said *Had enough?* in that cellar was not my attacker's...' Lucy coughed. 'But Freddy's.'

—◆◆◆—

49

Bedbugs and the Gettysburg Address

S IDNEY GRICE WHISTLED three notes very softly. 'I think this might be an opportune moment.'

'For what?' I asked and he clacked his teeth together.

'For Miss Bocking to show us the evidence.'

'What evidence?' I looked at him and then at her.

Lucy hesitated. 'I know I should not have—'

'Then why did you?' He appeared to be miming the shuffling of a pack of cards.

'I had to be... to be certain.' Lucy stumbled over her words. 'I searched Freddy's room.' She puffed her lips. 'I would never dream of doing such a thing normally.'

'Are you telling us that you dreamed of doing it abnormally?' He dealt us three imaginary cards each on to an invisible table.

'I meant that I would not think of doing it under normal circumstances,' she clarified, lifting a stray lock of hair back behind her ear. 'Why do you keep interrupting me?'

'Because I have yet to hear anything to which it is worth listening.' Mr G turned his cards over expressionlessly.

'You have hardly given me a chance to speak yet,' she complained.

'You have been permitted to manufacture ten sentences.' My guardian dealt himself another card. 'Which is as many as so-called President Lincoln required one score years and one ago for his address at the Soldier's National Cemetery in Gettysburg.'

Lucy had quite pointed ears, I noticed, and they had gone rather pink.

'What did you find, Lucy?' I asked gently, and Lucy leaned backwards to open a drawer of her desk.

'This.' She placed a red-backed book on the flat surface.

'May I?' I picked it up and opened the first page.

The diary was printed in gold lettering on the flyleaf and on a glued-in plate was handprinted *This book belongs to Freda Wilde* and beneath that *If found please return to Steep House, Abbey Road, London.*

All the pages were blackened around the edges. 'Was this rescued from the fire?'

'I assume so.' Lucy locked her fingers. 'This is the first I have known of it.'

'Freddy never mentioned it?'

'If she had done so Miss Bocking would be foolish indeed to have made her most recent assertion.' Mr G collected all the cards from where he had dealt them in mid-air and came close to peer over my shoulder.

I went to the first of January and there was written in violet ink, ageing into brown, *A lovely crisp start to the year.*

'It is the last entry that worries me.' Lucy's voice had a slight tremor. 'I have bookmarked it.'

'For the benefit of idiot detectives,' Sidney Grice mumbled, but she did not react.

Lucy Bocking's eyes were fixed on me as I went to the back of the diary.

The final few pages were blank and crumbling to my touch, and the last entry was badly charred, but I could still make out the words.

I hate Steep House and everybody in it. I shall destroy them all.

'I assume it is Freddy's handwriting,' I said, and Mr G bffffed for he hated anybody, especially me, to assume anything.

'I am positive,' Lucy said. 'As you can see, I have a letter here that she wrote to me a few months before that.' Lucy brought a folded sheet of notepaper from an envelope in a pigeonhole. 'The style is exactly the same – the way she dots her I's with curved lines, for example.'

Lucy unfolded the sheet of paper and held it up for comparison.

My Dearest Friend Lucy,
I trust that you are keeping well.
Things are much the same here but we miss you dreadfully.

'Close the book with exaggerated care,' Sidney Grice instructed and I obeyed, aware that, in his eyes, my extreme caution would just about match his most careless actions. 'Hold it out.'

He took the diary from me as a monk might handle Holy Scripture. 'Where, precisely, did you find it?'

'In the bottom of her linen chest at the foot of her bed.'

'Front? Back? Left? Right? Middle?'

'The front left-hand corner, underneath her petticoats.'

'I should very much like to see those,' my guardian declared.

'I shall not ask why.' Lucy wrinkled her nose. 'Aellen can fetch them for you.'

'That will not do at all.' Mr G placed the book on a nearby table. 'For I absolutely must see Miss Wilde's undergarments without delay. Describe how one might most conveniently gain entry to her room.'

Not for the first time Lucy gaped. 'On the first floor at the front of the house, on the right.'

'What a pity.' Mr G stood, legs akimbo. 'I had a morbid fancy to turn left.' He pointed in the manner of Napoleon urging his army to one final effort.

'You could walk backwards,' I suggested. And then, as he took one step in reverse, 'That was a joke.'

'I am sorry that Miss Middleton finds your predicament hilarious,' my godfather said in all sincerity. 'I have tried to improve her manners but, when all is said and done, she is only a woman.' He raised his stick towards the ceiling. 'Farewell, Miss Bocking. Unless I acquire a compelling motive for tarrying, we shall rendezvous here in five and a half minutes. Come, Miss Middleton. We are already nineteen seconds behind schedule.'

With that he shouldered his cane and marched back into the hall, dipping to his left as if that were his shorter side.

'You will not go into any other rooms?' Lucy called after us.

'Not unless I decide to,' he reassured her.

Sidney Grice had an ability which I have never come across in other men, that of running silently – neither a footfall nor a rustle of his clothes to be heard. The stairs were dog-legged and he had raced to the half-landing before I was even on the first step.

Lucy's voice chased after him. 'But I do not want you to.'

'And your wish is my command,' my guardian yelled, and then more softly, 'though I feel no compulsion to obey it.' He disappeared round the corner only for his head to poke back round it and to whisper, 'Mount the staircase one step at a time and wait on each stair for twenty seconds before proceeding in an orderly fashion to the next.' He shot to the top. 'Sing loudly,' he hissed over the bannister rail, 'but cease to do so when you place your huge foot upon the summit.'

And, before I could protest at yet another insult, Mr G was gone.

With nobody to see, I hitched up my skirts an obscene six inches or so and followed at the leisurely pace instructed. On the first step I cleared my throat and let rip.

'I'm only a cockney sparrer
I live in a chimney pot
My nest is sooty and narrer
But it keeps us nice and 'ot.
My mate said he was nevva leavin'
But now 'e's gorn orf with the flock
Leavin' this poor sparrer grievin'
A hen wivawt no—'

It was only at this point that I remembered what the next word was and concluded, rather unconvincingly, with, 'mate'. The second verse was decidedly risqué, I recalled, and was relieved when Lucy called out, 'Are you all right, March?'

'Yes, thank you. It is just that I am nervous of staircases today and have to sing to keep my courage up.'

'That must be embarrassing.'

'It is for Mr Grice.' I reached the top. 'Especially when we have visitors.'

There was a pretty rose-coloured runner pinned to the white-painted wood by gleaming brass rods and complementing the beautiful, and very expensive, William Morris daisy wallpaper, and I wished my guardian would give me a free rein with his more austere decorations.

The patterns were continued on the landing, lit by a stained-glass skylight at the top of the stairwell and the sun coming from an open door on the right. Sidney Grice was kneeling in a corn-flower bedroom to the side of a white-painted chest, placed, as Lucy had described, at the foot of the bed.

'Just in time.' He stretched out his cane and lifted the hinged lid as if expecting something dangerous to leap out. 'Safe,' he breathed and shuffled on his knees towards it.

The trunk was filled with neatly folded undergarments and he lifted each one aside to lay it carefully on the bed. There was a long ivory chemise on the lowest layer and he took it out to hold up to the light. 'How delicate the needlework is,' he marvelled, though I had never known him to show an interest in such things. He refolded the garment exactly along its creases again. 'Hold out your hands.' He draped it over my arms. 'What can you smell?'

My senses, as my guardian never tired of telling me, were nothing like as highly attuned as his and so I knew that he was testing me rather than seeking my opinion. Feeling more than a little uneasy at this intrusion into Freddy's personal possessions, I lowered my face to within an inch of her undergarment. 'Laundry soap and sandalwood.' The strong resinous aroma of the latter was unmistakeable, the chest having been lined with it as a defence against bedbugs.

'Excellent.' He clapped his hands twice like a sultan summoning one of his harem slaves. 'Comment upon the quality of hygiene of the interior of the chest.'

I kneeled beside him, not wishing to be castigated for missing a speck of dust in a corner or the eye of a flea lodged in a seam. 'It looks clean enough,' I pronounced uncertainly.

'Enough for what.'

'Clean.'

'So your use of the adjective *enough* was superfluous?'

'Yes.'

'I see.' Mr G looked disappointed at that admission as he laid the chemise back and repacked the box, making minuscule adjustments to the line of a crease or frill. He closed the lid with a sigh. 'So what have we learned from this exercise?'

'That Freddy keeps her linen fresh and clean,' I hazarded and my godfather clicked his tongue.

'Sometimes you say some very silly things,' he reproached me. 'That was not one of those times.'

It was always difficult to tell if he was trying to be nice. 'Shall we go down?'

Sidney Grice tugged at his scarred ear. 'I fervently hope so for

I have no wish to languish here for the residue of my corporeal existence.' He got to his feet. 'Come.'

Muriel was on the landing, presumably having been sent to check on us.

Mr G strode to the maid and tipped her chin up with the side of his forefinger, his head bending to hers. 'You have a blemish,' he breathed, as if he were making love to her. 'Which men, myself included, might describe as a freckle.' Oblivious to her blushes he ran his middle finger down the side of her nose. 'And it has increased in diameter by one hundred and twentieth of an imperial inch since fate threw us together.' He turned her head from side to side. 'There are only four things which freckles should do and nine which they should not, and first amongst the latter category is to grow.' He released her with a sigh. 'Tell your mistress to send you at her own expense to Mr Greene, the der-matologist at University College Hospital, on Tuesday ante meridian.'

'Yes, sir.' Muriel looked at him in the same way I imagine young girls must have swooned at Lord Byron.

'Go away now,' Sidney Grice told her sharply and she hurried past us to another room.

————◦•◦◦•◦————

50

The Potency of Envy

WE MADE OUR way down, Sidney Grice placing both feet on every step before continuing to the next one. 'Did you find it?' Lucy looked up, her face lined with worry.

'Find what?' He touched the side of his nose as if checking that the freckle had not leaped on to him.

'The room.'

'I should be a poor detective – which I am not – if I had not,' my guardian said severely. 'I also managed – without recourse to Miss Middleton's assistance – to locate the chest you so sparsely described to us.'

Lucy plucked at her cheek. 'And did you find anything in that?'

Mr G brought a flat calico pouch from his satchel.

'Other than what you had already told me...' He placed the pouch and his cane on the table. 'Nothing.'

Lucy pulled her right sleeve down from the quarter-inch it had risen. 'Then you have wasted your time,' she sympathized.

Sidney Grice twiddled his long slender fingers. 'On the contrary, there are times when finding nothing can tell one a great deal.'

He slipped the diary into the cloth bag.

'What are you doing?' Lucy asked. But she had clearly got the measure of the man for she added hastily, 'Well, I can see what you are doing. Why are you taking Freddy's diary?'

'It is...' I am almost certain that Mr G winked at Lucy Bocking as he put the bulging bag into his satchel. 'Evidence.'

'I did not say that you could take it.' Her eyes darted side to side.

My guardian strapped his satchel shut. 'A truthful and pertinent assertion.' He retrieved his cane. 'I should like to see the vessel in which it was contained.'

'It was not in anything,' Lucy said distractedly. 'What if Freddy should look for it?'

'You need have no fear on that score,' he vowed. 'She will not find it.'

'But what would I say?' Lucy looked around for an escape route.

'I imagine that you would lie and deny all knowledge of it.' Sidney Grice ambled to the door. 'Goodbye, Miss Bocking. I anticipate us renewing our acquaintance in the very near future.'

'When is Freddy due back?' I asked and Lucy looked at the clock. 'In about an hour.'

'Are you really afraid of her?' I asked. 'I can stay, or help you to book into a hotel.'

'No.' Lucy waved a hand wearily. 'I do not think she will try anything whilst you are both protecting me.'

'I most certainly am not,' Sidney Grice retorted as if she had made an improper suggestion and, bidding her a fond farewell, ambled from the room.

'I hope he knows what he is doing,' Lucy said as I kissed her goodbye.

'Of course he does,' I said firmly, but thought, *I hope so too.*

*

My guardian was already boarding a hansom when I caught up with him.

'Do you think Lucy is right to be afraid?' I began breathlessly and Sidney Grice gave my question some thought.

'Miss Bocking may have grounds to be very frightened indeed,' he decided at last. 'Though not, one might hope for her sake, petrified. Being petrified does not benefit one in the slightest.'

'I know you are always telling me not to judge people by my feelings about them…' I tailed my own sentence off.

'Good,' he said so abruptly that I knew there was no point in adding *but*. But I truly believed that Freddy Wilde loved Lucy Bocking and that Lucy had been telling the truth when she said they were like sisters.

'Never underestimate the potency of envy to corrupt the human spirit,' my godfather philosophized.

'But surely Freddy—' I stopped, aware that I was again doing what he was always telling me not to do.

'I have made a study of the way people position their bodies.' Sidney Grice orated now in the same manner as I had once heard the Earl of Kimberly make a speech in parliament. 'It is a minor branch of the forensic sciences which I call *Grice's posturology*. And it seems to me that there is a certain tension between Misses Bocking and Wilde.'

'But do you really think it could be envy?'

'Where there are women, there is always envy.' He brought out his coffin-shaped snuffbox and flipped open the skeleton-engraved lid.

'But surely Freddy is grateful to Lucy for taking her in.'

He took a pinch, although the box was empty, and deposited it into the hollow of his thumb web. 'Are you grateful to me?'

'Sometimes.'

'Gratitude,' he closed his right nostril and inhaled sharply through the left, 'is the second shortest-lived and the most easily poisoned emotion known to man. There are few things which people hate more than being constantly in another's debt.'

'Besides which,' I contributed, 'Lucy is rich and will be pretty again whereas Freddy's looks and fortune have been lost forever.'

'At last.' He sucked through his right nostril. 'You are starting to think like a woman.'

He put a finger under his nose to suppress a sneeze.

'Is that a good thing?'

Mr G snapped the lid shut. 'Disgusting habit.' He blew his nose and I was not sure if he meant thinking like a woman or the taking of non-existent snuff.

51

The Maniac Cathedral

I HAD BEEN PAST St Pancras when I first arrived in London. Molly had come to meet me but I was so taken with all the bustle of traffic and the crowds that I hardly noticed many of the buildings.

Attached to the station stood the Midland Grand Hotel, George Gilbert Scott's gigantic Gothic construction. It was described by some as a *maniac cathedral* and one could easily see why. A hundred arched windows punctuated the massive red-brick frontage or jutted like pulpits from the facade, the honey-coloured pillars already greying in the grime of the city. Wherever I looked a different carving caught my eye, but my vision was drawn ever upwards. On the right-hand side a monolithic clock tower stood, topped by a soaring pinnacle, echoing the spires that rose from its corners and from the lower tower to the other side of the entrance.

Saluted by a lavishly uniformed doorman, we passed through the huge portico and I was about to complain that the man who invented revolving doors had never tried negotiating one in billowing skirts when I emerged into the lobby, my guardian pushing impatiently behind me, to find my breath taken away.

The grand staircase ascended magnificently in richly carpeted white stone with intricate iron balusters and a dark wooden rail. Dizzyingly high above was the bottle-green ceiling, glittering with countless painted stars. Polished green

and pink limestone adorned the vermilion painted walls sten-
cilled with thousands of golden fleurs-de-lis. Everywhere I
looked were carved sunflowers, fruit, peacock tails and myriads
of other designs.

'For goodness' sake, March.' Sidney Grice nudged me. 'You
are gawking like an American.' There were few worse insults in
his exhaustive – and often exhausting – vocabulary.

I tore my eyes away and forced myself to concentrate on our
business, as he ignored the long oak reception desk and marched
straight to the concierge, who had been commandeered by a tall,
podgy, befurred woman accompanied by a pageboy struggling
to control three yapping Pekingese dogs snapping at his legs.

'Inform Prince Ulrich Schlangezahn that Mr Sidney Grice has
arrived,' my guardian commanded, and the concierge, a well-
built middle-aged man with a military bearing, glanced up.

'Certainly sir. I am just...'

'I have not travelled all the way from the exotic occidental
wilds of Gower Street to chitterchat about what you are *just*
doing,' Sidney Grice scolded, as though our journey had been
one to rival Burton and Speke's search for the source of the Nile,
'but to instruct you in your duty to me.'

The concierge was flustered. 'As soon as I have dealt with this
lady, sir.'

'Now,' Mr G insisted. 'I am here on unofficial business.'

The way he said *unofficial* made it sound very important
indeed and the concierge jumped to his feet immediately.

'Certainly, sir. Prince Ulrich, you say.'

'I do not, but I did.' Mr G leaned on the desk like a drinker
at a bar.

'Do you know who I am?' The lady's fur became erect like an
angry cat.

'I know who you are not,' Sidney Grice replied nicely. 'For
your fake pearls, counterfeit perfume, canine pelt coat and inaccurate diction invite me to venture that you are unentitled to the

aristocratic monograms on the luggage being transported this way.'

'How dare—'

'And I suggest that you quit this establishment.' Sidney Grice pinched at something on his Ulster as if she had given him a flea. 'Before I divulge some of my observations to the manager of this garish hostelry.'

We are none of us who we pretend to be, I recalled Jones/ Chang asserting.

In an instant the lady threw her hand into the air. 'Take everything away,' she commanded the porters grandly. 'I shall not stay in an establishment that admits such riffraff as this parvanu.'

My guardian blinked slowly. 'Though it is unmerited, I believe the word you are dredging from your truncated vocabulary is par*ven*u.' He articulated the last word precisely and the alleged-lady expanded.

'You frebbing crup.' Her jaw chewed in an elliptical motion like that of a grazing goat. Her head went back and she threw it forward.

Mr G stepped smartly aside.

'*Mein Gott*,' a voice murmured. 'You keep delightful company.'

And I turned to see Prince Ulrich Albrecht Sigismund Schlangezahn, resplendent in his uniform of Prussian blue, adorned with black looped cords and braids, a magnificent golden epaulette on his right shoulder and a pool of spittle at his feet.

52

The Black Prince

PRINCE ULRICH BOWED in a quick formal manner.

'Herr Grice.' He snapped his heels together, his extraordinarily burnished knee-high boots so tightly fitting around his jodhpurs that they might have been painted on to his legs. 'And Miss Middleton.'

I wondered, in a brief moment of frivolity, if I was supposed to curtsy, but he took my hand in his and pressed it to his beautifully trimmed and waxed imperial moustaches, and I decided that I would train George to adopt that habit as soon as possible.

'You look enchanting.'

His voice was so deep and resonant that I resisted the urge to tell him that he did too, or to advise him to consult an oculist. Sometimes I like to be lied to, and this was one of those times. In his civilian clothes the prince had cut an impressive figure. In uniform he was spectacular.

'How do you do?' was all I could manage and I hoped to heaven that I was not simpering.

'A client?' the prince asked.

His eyes flashed the many colours of our surroundings as he surveyed us both.

'We have had worse,' I assured him.

'You must be very proud of your guardian.' The prince released my hand. 'Herr Grice is a hero of the German Confederation. He is probably too modest to tell you that he saved the life of our Crown Prince Wilhelm at great risk to his own.'

Modesty was not one of my guardian's most outstanding virtues but I replied demurely, 'I believe that is how he lost his eye.'

'And gained a Grand Cross.' Prince Ulrich jutted his jaw.

'Not much use for seeing with,' I observed and the prince smiled uncertainly.

'I am always apologizing for Miss Middleton,' Mr G explained. 'She has a sense of humour.'

'But that is delightful,' the prince assured him.

'You like a woman with spirit,' I reminded him and Prince Ulrich inclined his head.

'Tonight, Miss Middleton, with your permission, we make a fresh start.'

'We shall see,' I said non-committally.

The prince offered me his arm and led me across the multicoloured Minton tiles and round a Moorish screen. He was slightly stiff in his right leg, I thought. We passed into an antechamber – a small room by this hotel's standards – mahogany-lined, with long rose drapes matching the carpet and the starred ceiling.

'Are you in England for long, Prince Ulrich?' I asked as he settled me on a sofa.

'Three or four months,' he replied.

'Have you visited before?'

'Many times.' The prince carefully arranged his coat to avoid creasing it as he sat in an upright armchair. 'It is almost a second home for me.'

'I hear you have come from the Berlin conference,' I remarked.

Mr G leaned back in his chair, but Prince Ulrich's back was straight and I could not imagine him ever slouching.

'You might say I am an informal delegate.'

'The scramble for Africa,' I murmured, and the prince turned to me quizzically.

'You are not approving?'

'Miss Middleton has unusual views and never knows when to keep them occult,' Mr G broke in.

The prince laughed. 'I like a voman viv her own mind.'

'She certainly has that, Your Highness,' my guardian assured him.

'Please call me Ulrich, and that applies alzo to you, Miss Middleton.'

'Then you must call me March.'

'I cannot fully reciprocate,' Mr G informed him, 'for though I am immensely pleased with my Christian name, I dislike hearing it spoken almost as much as the squawking of Jenny Lind or the braying of donkeys.'

'I am not sure Mr Grice can tell the difference,' I said, as our host straightened his back again.

'Of course I can,' my guardian retorted indignantly. 'Donkeys have longer ears and rarely wear dresses. Why are you both laughing?'

'Forgive me.' The prince snapped to attention. 'I voz thinking you are making the joke.'

'But why?' Mr G looked uncharacteristically baffled.

The prince and I coughed.

'May I call you *Grice* in that case?'

'You may,' Sidney Grice conceded. 'And I shall throw formality to the winds and address you as *Sir*.'

'Very vell.' The prince showed us each to our own sofas and settled in a third – his cane propped against the side – and, at a click of his fingers, a waiter appeared from the adjacent room, bearing a tray with two deep saucer glasses and one tall tumbler.

'I hope you like vine,' Prince Ulrich said.

I would have preferred a Bombay but I took a sip. 'This is very good.'

'Sekt made with the Riesling grape,' he told me. 'It is similar as champagne but better because it is from the Rhine.'

'Take mine away and evacuate the contents,' Mr G instructed the waiter.

'My apologies,' the prince said. 'I understoot that you always drink vater.'

'Clearly I cannot always drink water,' my godfather told him, in much the same tone as he adopted to lecture me, 'or I should not have time to do anything else. But this water has ice in it and I do not trust ice.'

'It is perfectly clean, sir,' the waiter assured him. He was an elderly man, with a stooped back and a few strands of hair swept sideways on his pate.

The prince sought to reassure his guest. 'I have had ice here vit no problems.'

'I do not trust ice not to clink against the side of the glass,' Mr G explained. 'It unsettles me and I do not like to be unsettled.'

'I shall fetch a fresh glass immediately, sir.' The waiter went away.

'I am interested in how you think vee should solve the African problem, Miss Middleton.' Our host was holding his wine untasted whilst I was halfway through mine.

'But why is it a problem?' I asked, and Mr G shot me a warning glance.

'Vee must to divide the dark continent fairly,' Prince Ulrich explained and raised his glass.

The waiter reappeared with a more satisfactory drink for my guardian.

'Shall we prepare the first course, Your Highness?'

'Do so.' The prince flipped a hand and the waiter drifted away.

'But what right have we to take any of Africa in the first place?' I saw no reason to leave him with the closing remark.

'I should think the same right as the British have in India,' Prince Ulrich replied, unperturbed by my question.

'Having lived in India for three years, I am not sure that we have any right to be there either.' I finished my glass of wine.

Sidney Grice clipped on his pince-nez and inspected his fingerplates.

'Then you have seen how the lot of the ignorant natives is improved by civilization,' Schlangezahn told me.

'They are not ignorant.' I rounded on him with ill-concealed fury. 'The Indians have a culture of literature, art, architecture and music stretching back to when our nations were living in mud huts.'

'The Gascony Le Grices still are,' my godfather contributed.

'There you haff it.' Prince Ulrich clapped his hands together. 'The Indians are half-civilized already and some of them are having quite light skins, but the Africans are a different breed altogether. They cannot read, they eat each other and they haff not even heard of Gott. Most of them are hardly human. Vee cannot leave a whole continent in the hand of vild savages.'

The prince explained that so reasonably that I was tempted to grab his stick and crown him with it, but Mr G was already reaching over.

'Did you ascertain from whence that button came, sir?' He picked the cane up and our host watched uneasily.

'Indeed.' The prince clicked his fingers and called, 'Hans.' And a dignified man in a black frock coat appeared with a bow and carrying a grey silk waistcoat over his arm. 'Hans is my valet,' Schlangezahn introduced him.

'May I see?' I asked.

'*Die fraulein wünscht es zu prüfen,*' Sidney Grice translated and the valet brought it to me.

The lowest button was missing and the threads still hanging, but other than that I could see nothing unusual.

'Oh yes.' Sidney Grice gave it a cursory look. '*Das ist alles.*'

The prince said something else; Hans bowed again and left.

'How long do you expect the conference to last?' I enquired, unwilling to let his remarks on the subject go.

'True craftsmanship,' Mr G commented and banged the cane on the floor like the staff of a town crier.

'Take a care, Grice,' Prince Ulrich warned. 'It is loaded and at full pressure.'

Sidney Grice rested the cane across his knees. 'Is this the safety catch?' He twisted a projection.

'Yes.' The prince put out a hand. 'And you haff just released it.'

'And this the trigger?'

'*Ja* and very—' He searched for the word.

'Sensitive,' I supplied, and saw an index finger poise over a silver button set into the underside of the handle.

'Watch out,' I cried. 'It is pointing straight at me.'

'A straight cane cannot point any way other than straight,' my guardian informed me, and his finger crooked.

There was a sharp snap – I had heard that sound before – and a whacking noise close by. I leaped back and saw that my handbag, on the sofa beside me, had jumped at the same time and that the sage green material, chosen with such care to match my dress, was torn open and trickling clear liquid on to the cushion. You have shot my father's hip flask.' I ripped open the clasp. 'And his cigarette case.'

'Good gracious,' Sidney Grice breathed. 'I had better return your weapon within one hundred and nineteen seconds.'

The waiter reappeared.

'Dinner is served, Your Highness, sir and miss,' he announced, with a wary glance at my guardian peering down the muzzle of the gun.

'Good.' Sidney Grice passed the cane back to our bemused but unruffled host. 'I dislike dining with anybody who has the means to shoot me.'

'And I viv anybody who is careless with firearms.' Prince Ulrich smiled as he offered me his arm.

'Have no fear on that score.' Sidney Grice limped ahead of

both of us. 'I shall not permit Miss Middleton to lay an anthrop-
oidal dactyl upon it.'

I had always thought that my fingers were no worse than
anyone else's. They are moderately, though not overly, long and
fairly slim, and George Pound had kissed every one of them. I
only hoped that my knuckles did not drag too noisily along the
carpet.

53

The Black Forest

WE SAT AT a circular table covered with a white tablecloth and set with crystalware that glittered in the light of a gas chandelier suspended over it. Three waiters stood to attention, their backs to the walls, facing the centre, and each came forward to pull out a chair.

'Did you bring your own cutlery?' I picked up a heavy rattail pudding spoon and looked at the intertwined MR design stamped on the spoon. 'Obviously not, but I have never seen anything this good in a railway hotel before.'

'You would not expect a member of the Hohenzollern dynasty to eat off the same quality of implement as a travelling salesman.' Sidney Grice rotated a salt cellar a quarter of a revolution counterclockwise and a few degrees back again.

'I am not so interested in such luxuries as you might think.' The prince signalled for a waiter to pour more champagne, though I noticed he had not touched his own drink. 'I have eaten vild boars off a hunting knife in the Scwarzwald.'

'The—' my godfather began.

'Black Forest,' I butted in before he could belittle me with a translation.

'Penultimate train from Burton-on-Trent is eight minutes late,' he continued over me.

'But how do you know that?' Prince Ulrich raised his glass in a toast and put it down untasted.

I took a good swig of mine and a bottle instantly came over my right shoulder to top me up. I could get used to Sekt, I decided, and being waited upon so attentively.

'Because I heard it pull in at platform six almost nine minutes ago and it is the only service still using that particular combination of locomotive and rolling stock on this line.' Mr G sampled his water and closed his eyes in appreciation of it on his palate. 'I shall meditate upon the advisability of lending you a copy of Radleigh Raddisons's *Railways of the Landlocked Counties*.'

The prince shook his head. 'I can hardly hear the trains at all, let alone distinguish between them.'

I waited for Sidney Grice to explain that the German's senses were in every way inferior to his own but he only said, 'When I was five my father trained my auditory faculties by blindfolding me and tying me to a post. If I could not guess which wood a switch was made from by listening to him tap his way along the stable floor, he would slash me with all his might across the face.'

'How brutal,' I cried, as a waiter ladled soup into my bowl – tomato, not my favourite.

'Not really.' Mr G replaced his glass in precisely the same spot. 'For I never got it wrong.'

'But if you had?' our host asked, in the closest thing to concern I had seen from him yet.

'If I have one cognitive blind spot – and I admit to three – the first is my inability to see the point of getting things wrong.' My guardian sampled his soup. 'Oh, what a shame. It has its own flavour.'

I tried mine and he was right. It was not the usual watery gruel that Cook served up and sometimes poured over our boiled cabbage, under the impression that it was also a sauce.

Schlangezahn dipped in his spoon. 'I believe you haff some experience of military life, Miss Middleton.'

'How did you know that?'

I haff read your excellent book about your father, *Colonel Geoffrey Middleton, His Life and Times*.'

'That places you in a very select group,' Sidney Grice commented drily.

Prince Ulrich dabbed his mouth. 'I voz sorry to learn of his accident, especially as you vere an only child viv no mother.'

I did not tell him that my father had been murdered but said, 'I hope you found it interesting.'

The prince swallowed his soup. 'The descriptions of the battle were excellent. One can almost be imagining that you ver there.'

'My father was a good raconteur and my fiancé had been in a few skirmishes so he was able to give me some idea of what it was like.'

The soup was the colour and consistency of blood. Mr G had unscrewed the cap of a cellar and was trickling salt into his.

'But you are not married?'

'He was killed in an ambush in India.'

I had another secret so dark that I hardly dared tell it even to myself. I had left Edward to die and his life had sprayed into my face as he gasped my name with his last breath. I pushed the soup away, slopping it on to, but not quite over, the rim.

'I am sorry.' Prince Ulrich put his spoon down. 'How long haff you been knowing Mr Grice?'

'Since the nineteenth of May eighty-two, the day I moved in,' I told him.

'Nineteen thousand, seven hundred and fifty-eight hours ago.' Mr G groaned, as if he had suffered torment every minute of every one of them.

'Might I ask if you married?' For some reason I did not feel comfortable using the prince's first name.

He wiped his mouth. 'I am thinking I am married to the Imperial Army.'

'Do you have any siblings?' I picked at a soft white roll.

The prince tore his bread in half. 'I haff four brothers, all younger, and we vere haffing one sister.' For the first time I saw real emotion in the Prussian's face, the mask pierced with pain, but almost immediately he had repaired it.

'Gerda,' he said reverently. 'She died in London four years ago of – I am not knowing what you call it in English. In Germany we call it cholera.'

'We call it that here too.' I had seen countless victims of the disease in an epidemic in Bombay – the profuse rice-water diarrhoea, the clear vomiting, the dehydration, the sunken eyes and the laboured breathing. So few sufferers survived it. 'Can I ask how old she was?'

'Seventeen,' he said, not quite believing his own words.

'So young.'

Prince Ulrich clicked his fingers. 'Take this soup away,' he commanded. 'Miss Middleton does not like it.'

*

The rest of the meal passed quietly. There was turbot and lobster and saddle of mutton and pheasant and ices and cheeses, though Sidney Grice ate next to nothing, explaining politely that he had anticipated the food being muck and eaten before he came. But I did more than justice to whatever was put before me.

Sidney Grice and Prince Ulrich found a mutual interest in philately; the prince sent for his album and the two men spent the rest of the evening poring over it.

There were many excellent wines, though neither man touched them, but I felt I had a duty to try and was so successful in my efforts that I fell asleep and, the next thing I knew, the prince was laughing and assuring me he had lost count of the number of meetings, plays and concerts in which he had dozed off.

'I generally try to pack her off to bed by about ten o'clock,' my guardian declared.

'But he has never yet succeeded,' I vowed, as the prince kissed my hand in farewell.

54

The Lion's Share

A COMMISSIONAIRE PACKED US into a hansom, looking at my shilling as if it were a dog dropping.

'I cannot imagine why Prince Ulrich would need to force himself on women.' I wondered if it was just the motion of our cab making me feel a bit queasy.

'Ours is to reason why.' My guardian sounded uncharacteristically philosophical. 'Explain the grounds for your incomprehension.'

The streets of our capital city were never quiet, but the amount of traffic at night was a fraction of that in the daytime.

'He is rich, titled, handsome and charming,' I reeled off. 'All very desirable attributes.'

Mr G pondered my remarks. 'You might be wise not to set your sights on him as a husband,' he advised, as we swerved round an oyster stall set up illegally on the road.

This was my chance and, emboldened by alcohol and his mellow mood, I decided to take it. 'Speaking of—'

'Motives.' He completed my phrase by substituting his own word. 'Some men do not want women to acquiesce but get a distorted pleasure from the distress that they cause.'

'And you think Prince Ulrich may be one of those men?'

'I have not said so.'

I had almost forgotten my grievance until I reached out to stop my handbag sliding off the seat and felt it still damp. 'You fired that air gun deliberately,' I accused.

'I have never activated a firearm accidentally,' he admitted, elbowing me into giving him his usual lion's share of space.

'To stop me starting another argument with the prince about Africa,' I surmised.

'If that had been my purpose I could have aimed at you,' he reasoned, uncorking his flask, which the concierge had arranged to have replenished for our long journey along two streets. 'But it was a collateral bonus.' Mr G waited until we had passed the new pet shop, where he knew the road would be less potholed, before he poured half a cup of hot tea. 'And how else was I to obtain and retain the missile?'

I opened the clasp and rooted through. Apart from my father's cigarette case and flask and, of course, the bag itself, I could find no other damage as we whisked along through the intermittent pools of gaslight. A misshapen ball of lead had come to a halt after bruising but not piercing my travelling journal.

I reached in.

'Do not scratch it,' my guardian urged anxiously and I was sorely tempted to throw the useless lump out into the gutter.

'There.' I tipped it into his gloved hand and he regarded it fondly. 'Now all I have to do is find a way of restoring it and its fellow to their original shapes.'

'That should be easy,' I remarked, and he glanced at me.

'Was that—'

'Sarcasm,' I said, before he had the chance to ask.

Sidney Grice leaned hard against me. With any other man I might have thought he was making advances, but we were swinging left into Gower Street and he was more interested in preserving his beverage than in my comfort.

'One twenny-fize,' our driver announced.

'It is a different breed,' Mr G muttered, flicking the last of his tea on to the floor and my dress.

'Wottiz?' The cabby hauled open his hatch.

'I am so sorry.' My guardian passed up three coins. 'I only understand eight languages plus a smattering of American. I never troubled to learn Inarticulacy.'

And Sidney Grice was rapping on his own front door before I had pushed my way out though the flaps.

55

The Cat, the Rats and the Clown

SIDNEY GRICE LOOKED almost as tired as Molly, who dragged herself in, having climbed two steep flights of stairs from the kitchen to serve his breakfast from the dumb waiter behind him. His newspapers – usually ripped and strewn by the time I came down – lay untouched in two neat stacks on the floor, but he had compensated for that with dozens of balls of scrawled-on paper, scattered like giant hailstones over every surface.

'What is fifty-five thousand, six hundred and ninety-three and four-sevenths divided by twelve thousand, six hundred and twenty-one and thirty-one thirty-thirds?' he rapped.

I sat at my end of the table and got out my journal.

Molly pushed her hat sideways, spilling a ravel of red hair, whilst she considered the problem. 'Even I aintn't not got not quite enough fingers for that one,' she decided.

'I was not asking you.'

Molly's brow became a badly ploughed field. 'But I dontn't not think Splirit can do addings, sir.' And Spirit, curled up on a chair next to him, opened one eye.

'I think he was asking me, Molly,' I said.

Something moved under Molly's tight uniform like a pack of rats, and I was reminded horribly of when I had been drugged and thought my cell wall was made of them, but I forced myself to concentrate. The thing wobbled up and down and squeaked and I – restraining my own squeak – realized that the writhing mass was Molly.

'Why, Lord bless you, miss, Mr Grice wouldn't not expect you to know something like that.' She slapped her own thigh like she had seen a clown do every time he hilariously soaked his audience of terrified children with buckets of water.

'About four,' I reckoned.

Molly checked her left hand carefully. 'Oh, I've got more than that,' she declared because, of course, she could have done the sum all along.

'Be precise,' my godfather demanded.

'Four and a thumb,' his maid told him, though nobody, other than my cat, was interested.

Spirit plucked Molly's sleeve while I considered the leftover numbers. 'Approximately four and two fifths,' I declared, and Mr G put his pen down like a particularly irascible schoolmaster who has reached the end of his tether.

'My knowledge of history is not much better than that of an above-average Cambridge professor,' he said, with unusual modesty. 'But I cannot recall the date when it was decided that *precise* and *approximate* were interchangeable synonyms.'

'Christmas Day is always a Thursday,' Molly contributed helpfully.

Spirit dabbed the apron string dangling over her head, while I scribbled furiously. 'Four and thirteen thirty-thirds,' I decided.

'But the other is four and seventeen thirty-fifths.' The headmaster glared accusingly.

'I do not even know what the other is,' I told him. 'So that is hardly my fault.'

'Oh, this is futile.' He splotted ink over the tablecloth.

'No, it aintn't not,' Molly whispered to my cat. 'It's a founting pen.'

'If *he* were here with his mighty brains...' Sidney Grice intoned, and I at once knew who was meant. 'He could have solved all these equations in nineteen seconds,' Mr G continued sadly, perhaps regretting that he had blown those brains all over a cage with his revolver. 'Though I fear the calculation is of no use to me.' He raised his face pathetically.

'I assume you are trying to match the two bullets.' I took a slice of something that was closer to bread than toast.

My guardian retied his black eye patch. 'I have made one hundred and fourteen measurements of each projectile.' He whirred through the pages of a thick notebook. 'But the trouble is – as even you might have anticipated – not only have they distorted, but they have distorted in different ways.'

Spirit tugged and Molly's apron came undone.

'Oh, for heaven's sake.' Sidney Grice covered his eyes from the expanse of black dress that greeted them. 'Go away, woman, and get dressed.'

He could not have been more shocked if Molly were dancing naked and singing the Vegetable Song.

Molly cupped her hands on her cheeks. 'Oh, sir,' she said coyly, as if he had just proposed marriage.

'Get out.'

Molly grinned, revealing a recently acquired gap between her upper right central incisor and canine. 'He called me *woman*,' she exalted and skipped from the room, rattling the plates on the sideboard even from the staircase every time she landed.

—◦◦◦◦◦◦—

56

Harriet and the Huntress

I WENT TO Huntley Street and rang the bell three times in
quick succession, the code for all members of the Artemis
Club, as it had come to be known. It was named after the
Greek goddess, huntress and protectress of women. The door
was opened not by Violet, the proprietress, but by a tall slender
woman aged about thirty. Her hair was long and black and
hung freely – something that would have disgusted my guardian,
for loose hair was indicative of loose morals as far as he was
concerned. Despite prurient speculation, though, the society
was run on lines more respectable than some clubs I had heard
about for so-called gentlemen.

'Violet is unwell,' she told me. 'And you are…?'

'March,' I said. When I first joined the club we all used false
names, a practice that began when the police took an interest in
the Artemis, but they had not troubled us for years now. Some
wives still stuck to their aliases, though, terrified that their husbands might find out they were relaxing and even enjoying
themselves. 'I am a friend of Harriet's.'

The lady smiled brightly. 'Oh yes, she has told us all about
you – the famous lady detective. I hope you have not come to
arrest us.'

'The only crime that you have committed is allowing the gin to
run out, Rosie.' Harriet came out of the sitting room. 'March! I
thought I heard your voice.' Harriet hugged me, kissed me on both

cheeks and held me out at arm's length. 'You look lovely.' She was the only person apart from George who told me that. 'Amongst March's investigations,' she told Rosie, 'she has come upon the elixir of youth. I swear she looks younger every time I see her. If this carries on, March, they will be sending you back to school.'

'I wish you would sell me some,' Rosie said plaintively.

'Oh, you do not need it, Rosie.' Harriet put a loose tress up behind my ear. 'But I could do with a few gallons. When I see myself in the mirror these days my face looks like a washboard.' She mimicked a scowl at our reaction. 'It is not funny. My husband sharpens his pencils on it.'

Rosie chuckled. 'I will restock the cabinet.'

Harriet and I went to the sitting room. It had seemed quite glamorous when I first arrived in London, but the chintz sofa was getting threadbare on the arms and the cushions were splitting now.

'I hear that Vi has been dipping into our funds,' Harriet whispered. 'Apparently the accounts made no sense at all at the AGM, and she has absconded with this year's membership fees.'

'Then I am glad I have not paid mine yet,' I said.

'Do not tell Rosie, but Vi was so busy fiddling the books she did not notice that I have not coughed up for the last three years.' Harriet sat close to me. 'It is difficult enough getting money for train fares when Mr F makes me keep household accounts and goes through them every month.'

I did not ask Harriet how life with her husband was, for I knew that he was hardly aware of her existence. Rosie returned with a fresh bottle of Bombay, put it on the table in front of us with two glasses, and left us alone.

Harriet poured.

'You are distracted,' she observed as we clinked glasses.

'I am sorry.' I brought out my old cigarette case and we lit two Turkish. Harriet put on a white glove to protect her hand from staining but I never bothered.

'When most girls are distracted it is love. I assume you are still estranged from your gorgeous policeman.' Harriet puckered her lips to puff out a train of miniature clouds.

'Well,' I began cagily and Harriet sat up.

'Oh, March.' She grabbed my arm. 'He has not? You have not?'

'He has.' I laughed. 'And I have accepted.'

'Oh, March.' Harriet flung her arms round me. 'Oh, March.' She burst into tears. 'But that is wonderful. When? How? Why? Well, I know why, but what made him change his mind? What did your guardian say? I bet he was livid.'

'I have not told him yet.' I pulled back to look my friend in the eye. 'And this is our secret until then.'

Harriet blew her nose and dabbed her cheeks and kissed me. 'Is that why you are perturbed?'

I shook my head and we drank for a while without speaking. Harriet was one of the few people I have ever met who knew how to use silence to draw me out. 'I am worried about a case,' I admitted at last.

Harriet put her glass down and topped mine up. 'A murder?' No matter how she tried, Harriet lit up in anticipation of some gruesome details.

'He has not killed anyone directly yet.' I inhaled nervily. 'But it may only be a matter of time. A man is attacking women – forcing himself upon them and beating them brutally.' It sounded very clinical when I put it into words. 'We think we know who he is but we have no proof. His victims never see him clearly enough to identify him.'

'What did you mean by *directly*?' Harriet took up her glass again. I sometimes wondered why she ever put it down.

'One that we know of was driven to suicide and she was only seventeen.'

'Have you no clues?' Harriet asked. 'Not even part of an insect?'

I had told her once how the leg of a woodlouse had helped to solve a murder in Highgate.

'Mr Grice has two lead balls that he wants to prove came from the same gun.' I smiled wryly. 'He got the first from a man's head and the second by shooting my handbag. It passed straight through my cigarette case and hip flask.'

'I noticed that you had a different case.' Harriet clutched her own bag protectively. 'But how can they help him?'

I took a swig of gin. 'The rifling and scratches in a barrel mark bullets when they are fired,' I explained, 'and he believes that the marks for every gun are unique. But the balls are too flattened to be able to match them.'

'A pity they are not footballs,' Harriet remarked. 'Then he could pump them up like I have to do for the boys. Their father is much too busy for such a mundane task. Cricket may be his second religion but, when his sons want to play, yours truly is the one who gets roped in to keep wicket.' She pulled a face. 'And I am absolutely hopeless at it. I am just thinking what I wouldn't do for a smoke when a lump of leather comes smashing into my head. It's a blessing I have not lost any teeth – yet.'

I laughed. 'Oh, Harriet, I wish you could be here all the time.'

'So do I, March. But we must think of a plan.'

'We?'

Harriet pulled at her fingers one at a time, quite hard, as she did sometimes when she was concentrating. 'If you cannot find any clues, then we must find a way to trap him,' she decided at last.

'We?' I stubbed out my cigarette in a blue glass ashtray, though I had not finished it.

'We caught your father's murderer,' Harriet remarked, though I needed no reminding of that night. She dabbed her cigarette out and her shadow on the wall swayed.

'And we made good partners in Scarfield Manor,' I reminisced with a shudder. 'But I tried entrapment with one of the victim's brothers in an opium den.'

'Opium?' For once I thought I might have shocked my friend, but Harriet's expression was dreamy. 'I have not had that since I sneaked out of a Mothers for the Empire meeting in Hull.' She poured us both another gin. 'What happened?'

'The police did not like our methods and now her brother is missing.'

'Killed?' There was no twinkle in Harriet's eye now.

'We do not know but I fear so.'

Harriet paused. 'We shall have to think about this very carefully.'

'If we were to set another trap,' I said cautiously, 'the man who commits these crimes always chooses a young pretty woman.' I paused. 'And neither of us fits into both those categories.'

My friend pouted but knew better than to protest. She would have fitted the bill once, but I never could.

'Come upstairs.' Harriet jumped up so suddenly that I clunked the glass into my teeth. 'It is about time that you met some of the other members.'

57

Dulcie and the Swine

'L ADY DULCET BROCKWOOD,' Harriet explained as we went back into the hall. 'Young and very pretty indeed.'
'How young?' I asked warily.

'Eighteen, I think.' Harriet mounted the stairs. 'Unmarried, unengaged and very rich.'

I followed as closely as our dresses allowed.

'Then why has she not been snapped up?' I wondered, for we both knew how the marriage market worked.

'I believe Lady Brockwood refuses to be snapped,' Harriet said. 'She is determined to marry whom and when she pleases.'

'I like the sound of her.' We reached the top. 'But would she be willing to help?'

'When she was fourteen she disguised herself as a cabin boy and boarded a ship to see the world,' Harriet told me. 'They got as far as Trinidad before she was discovered and sent home.'

'I am not sure,' I said, 'that we should be putting someone so young at such risk.'

'Why not let her decide?' my friend suggested. 'She should still be here.'

We went along the corridor to the boardroom at the end. Lady Dulcet Brockwood was playing stud poker and, to judge by the pile of coins at her side and the few that her three companions possessed, doing rather well.

She rose from the table, tall and slim with long golden-blonde hair tied back in a simple chignon, her coral-pink dress pinched in for a waist I could have almost put my hands round, and I should have hated her but she had such a lovely welcoming smile and held out her hand and said, 'March, I have been dying to meet you ever since Harriet told me of your adventures.' Her fingers were long and held on to mine long after Harriet had introduced us.

'I cannot equal your escapades at sea, Lady Brockwood,' I said and she frowned.

'Please call me Dulcie.' And she leaned forward to whisper in my ear. 'I made all that up but don't tell them.' She pulled back and winked. 'I was about to have a G and T. Will you join me?'

'I shall forego the T,' I said as she linked her arm through mine. 'I had more than enough quinine in India.'

'I think I have read all your accounts of your escapades with Mr Grice.' Dulcie poured the four of us a drink.

'He would not be happy to hear them called that,' I told her.

'From what you write, I wonder if he is ever happy at all.'

'I could make him happy,' Harriet said wistfully, never having met him.

'You would eat him alive,' Dulcie prophesied.

I laughed. 'I think you would find him indigestible, Harriet.'

'Cheerio.' Dulcie clinked my glass.

'March and I are planning a little adventure,' Harriet said and I listened warily, for this newcomer was not lacking in confidence but looked very young indeed.

'I think I will call it a day while I still have enough for a cab home,' one of the women at the table called out.

And her companion stood up. 'I have to get back to the swine.'

And only when she had shut the door behind her did I ask, 'Does she mean her husband or does she keep pigs?'

'Both,' Dulcie told me and we laughed.

58

The Eye of the Dragon

THERE WERE TWO other women at that poker game.
Marjorie Kitchener was a sturdy, striking twenty-
five-year-old who had been widowed six years ago when
her husband committed suicide on their honeymoon. Despite –
or, as Harriet whispered later, because of – this she was a jolly,
outgoing woman with an athletic physique.

And there was another girl I had not met before, called Sally
– fresh-faced and petite, and looking even younger than Dulcie.

'How old are you, Sally?' I asked and she blushed. 'I am
twenty-two.'

And before I could make a judgement, Dulcie said, 'Do not
be taken in by Sally's diffident manner. I met her at fencing
classes. She can out-parry any man and is as brave as a lion.'

'And I can box,' Sally assured me shyly.

I laughed. 'Where did you learn that?'

'Three older brothers,' she told me, 'and a father who taught
it at Harrow.' She was so pink-faced and mouse-like that I found
it difficult to believe Sally was not joking.

'She can too,' Marjorie vouched. 'Tell them about that Covent
Garden porter, Sally.'

'Oh dear me,' Sally began timidly. 'He insulted Marjorie and
the beast would not apologize so I had to teach him a lesson.'

'Hulking great brute and she knocked him out cold.' Marjorie
laughed.

'Well, you would seem to be a very useful person to have in a fight,' I conceded, 'though I hope it does not come to fisticuffs.'

'Oh, so do I,' Sally assured me nervously. 'If you do not think it showing off, I have one other skill.' She unclipped her handbag. 'Which picture did you say you did not like, Harry?'

I had never heard my friend called that before.

'The one of Baroness Worford.' Harriet pointed to a portrait of a former lady president. 'She was the dragon Saint George was lucky not to meet – terrified all the members into voting for her.'

'And she tried to ban smoking,' Marjorie recalled. 'Luckily for us she died. Unluckily, her husband bequeathed that to the club, so we put it in here out of the way.'

Sally's hand went up and back and flicked forward. 'Right eye,' she said quietly as something flashed from her.

There was a thud and Baroness Worford was impaled through the pupil by a dagger, the horn handle flittering with the quivering blade.

'Bloody hell,' I said. 'Welcome aboard, Sally.'

*

We sat at the table, poring over maps, drinking and planning, but the more concrete our plans became, the more I knew I could never enact them.

'Goodness.' Harriet jumped as the clock struck the hour. 'I am supposed to be helping serve tea for the staff against the old boys' football match, and Mr F thinks I have only popped out to get potted beef.'

'Perhaps we should all call it a day,' I said.

'We must meet again to fix a date,' Dulcie said, so firmly that I decided to argue about it another time. With any luck they would all cool on the idea after they had slept on it.

'Football,' I pondered. 'Harriet, you are a genius.'

59

The Rubber Solution

MOLLY OPENED THE door warily.

'Oh, miss, he's as cross as a pancake,' she whispered. Molly's whispers could have been heard in the gallery of any music hall on a bawdy Saturday night.

'But why?' I whispered back.

'Misssss,' she hissed like *The Flying Scotsman*. 'He'll hear you.'

'Why is he angry?' I asked quietly and Molly flapped her arms.

'I dontn't not know.' She looked over her shoulder nervously. 'But he showed me his teeth and threatened to increase my wages,' she struggled to remember the word, 'frorth-width.'

'But that means you are getting more money,' I explained.

'Oh.' Molly's mouth drooped even further. 'But then I'll have to go out and spend it and be married by wicked Sir Gasper.'

'Sir Jasper is a made-up person, Molly.'

'I could see he was made-up,' she rejoined. 'I was right on the front row at the front and I could see his red cheeks running down his neck in the heat of the slimelights, but he was still wicked and ohhhhhh, poor sweet Miss Clara was—'

'What did you do?' I broke in before I heard the entire plot of *The Farmer's Daughter* for the eighth time.

'Well, what could I do?' she reasoned. 'I just sat there and sissed every time he came on.'

I tried again. 'What did you do to make Mr Grice raise your pay?'

Molly screwed up her apron and chewed the hem. 'I just only told him that those things with what he was playing with looked like those toads what had been squashed and couldn't be unsquashed again after I stood on them, and then he got all different and told me I was a stute, and I said I didntn't not know what a stute was and he laughed. Heavens below it was terror-ifying, miss. He laughed like a person and then he said he was going to do that thing to my wages what I never get anyway, with breaking things and swearing. I ran out of the room and didntn't not come back until he rang his bell for tea immediantly after, and now I have to go to the fishmongerers.'

'But why?' We both knew that her master would not allow fish in the house.

'On an errant.' Molly watched me hang up my own bonnet and roll my parasol and put it in the stand.

'Then you had better do it.'

'Yes,' she agreed.

Molly stood like a monument. I went round her and into the study, which might have survived an invasion by the Goths, but only just.

Sidney Grice had his coat off and his sleeves rolled up and his cravat pulled open. His face was splattered with something resembling cement and there was something pink clinging in plaques to his waistcoat.

'I have had an idea,' I told him, my excitement deflated like one of Molly's unfortunate toads.

'Good, good,' he replied distractedly. 'In the meantime—' he indicated the carnage on his desk, mixing bowls half-full, some tipped over, clogged-up test tubes, spatulas caked in assorted crusts—'I have had a better one. I have made alginate impres-sions of both pieces of shot and used those to make precise gymsum replicas of them.' He pointed to two large watch-glasses, each bearing the now-familiar lumps, one whiter than, but appar-ently identical to, the original grey version, apart from each being attached by a blob of yellow wax to a wide-bored glass pipe with an L-turn at that end. 'So as to avoid abrading or scratching the actual specimens. I have been obliged to deface these models, but I intend to make nineteen copies of each specimen and insert my glass pipe into a different position every time.' He paused and looked at me as if expecting a ripple of applause. 'And now—'

'You are going to coat them with rubber solution,' I chipped in, as he paused again for the ovation that was never to come.

'You guessed.'

'It was also my idea.'

'It was mine first.' He had a beaker of water simmering on a tripod over a spirit burner.

'What time did you have your idea?'

'At fourteen minutes after the hour of two post meridiem.'

'That was before mine,' I admitted. 'But then I did not have the benefit of Molly's technical advice.'

My guardian bridled. 'If you are to laud that calamitous dolt of a skivvy for unwittingly triggering my genius, you might as well credit an apple for the discovery of gravity, though the fruit probably has a greater intellect than the maid.'

'Shall we do one each?' I suggested, and he brought his sense of effrontery under control.

'Very well.' He swept aside an assortment of his equipment with no concern for what was shattering or spilling or crashing to the floor.

Mr G brought out a large brown bottle and removed the cork bung and, like a genie, the smell uncoiled, an invisible cloud filling the room with its fumes.

I coughed. 'Shall I pull up the sash?' The only time I had ever done so in the study before was to clear the air of cyanide coming from the corpse at my feet.

'Certainly not.' Mr G handed me a new stiff-bristled paint-brush. 'An open window is far too much temptation to a mischievous ragamuffin with a ready supply of sunbaked horse droppings at his feet. Besides which,' Mr G inhaled as if it were sea air and he were taking a cure, 'I find it rather invigorating.'

He started to paint his plaster model – the thick black liquid dripping over his already filthy blotter – and I joined in.

'How thick do you want it?'

'One sixteenth of an inch.' He waved his brush, showering his bookcase like a priest with holy water but, fortunately, failing to bless me.

We painted steadily and soon had two glistening blobs like shrivelled toffee apples on the sticks. I rotated mine. 'How long does it take to dry?' I was pleased to see that there were no air holes while Mr G was dabbing some more on one spot.

'According to my earlier experiments, approximately fifteen minutes. Keep turning or it will sag.'

'So I have to stand for all that time just waiting for it to dry?' I was getting bored already.

'Of course not.' He held his up like a lollipop but did not lick it. 'You must wait for the latex to coagulate at the same time.'

I shifted my weight. 'That makes the process so much more interesting.'

'Indeed.' My guardian clipped on his pince-nez with his left hand and watched the process avidly. 'Did we finish our light chat about the differential identification of rodential earwax?'

'We did not,' I confessed.

'Shall I resume my diatribe?'

'Not unless you wish to induce rigor mortis.'

My godfather considered my proposal. 'I do not,' he decided regretfully. 'What would you like to talk about?'

'Something that doesn't involve murder.'

'Everything involves murder.'

'Music does not.'

'Leaving aside the hundreds of operas which depict violent deaths and the number of composers who have killed or been killed illegally, music *is* murder.'

I considered and rejected poetry, art and flower pressing. No doubt he would know of a homicidal collector of omnibus tickets or all about the massacre of a conference of beekeepers.

'Keep turning it,' he said.

'I never stopped.'

'I did not say you had.'

'That is like me telling you to keep breathing.'

'Useful advice if I were in a room which I believed to be full of toxic gases but you knew not to be.'

I dabbed a puddle on the leather top, peeled it off and turned it over. It was dry. My guardian prodded it with a silver toothpick.

'So what do we do now?' I asked.

'We exhale.' He put the pipe to his lips and blew. With his cheeks puffed out, he was all at once a child blowing bubbles.

I tried mine. The rubber was much less stretchy than I had expected. Perhaps my latex was too thick, for I could feel my eardrums bulge as I struggled to expand it, but at last I had something resembling a ball. 'That was more difficult than I expected,' I puffed.

'And now you must do it again.'

Whilst mine had deflated to a large prune, Mr G had a finger over the end of his glass pipe to stop the same happening.

'But it will happen to yours the moment you let go,' I prophesied.

Sidney Grice pfffed. He had five different pfffs and this was his least dismissive one. 'But I shall not let go.' He sidled along his side of the desk and lowered his ball into the beaker of bubbling water. 'Until it has hardened.'

The water splashed over a stack of calculations but that did not seem to perturb my godfather, so intent was he on his task.

I reinflated mine and slipped a finger into my mouth this time. Mr G removed the ball, letting it drip over an open Latin dictionary where I could just make out *Decollavi* – which even

I knew meant *beheaded* – underlined in red ink. He pricked at the rubber.

'Huzzah.' He spoke quietly, an uncharacteristically military ejaculation from a man who had never been in uniform. 'What now?' he challenged, and I realized that I had not thought beyond this stage and that all the information we needed was inside our creations.

'Well.' I immersed my balloon before it had a chance to lose any air. 'We cut them in half, turn them inside out and glue them back together.'

'What an ingeniously stupid idea.'

I tried but failed to hide my indignation. 'What then?'

'We pour melted wax inside.'

'Well, that goes without saying.'

'Clearly,' he murmured, slotting a funnel over the end of the tube. 'Whilst the pipe is still warm.' He took a stick of white modelling wax, held the end of it above the flame, and removed it to drip into the funnel and trickle down into the ball. 'Take yours out and hold this in the water.'

I did as I was bid, so that only the funnel projected above the surface. Mr G repeated the process.

'Another eighty or ninety applications should suffice,' he calculated.

My hand was already uncomfortably warm and my sleeve damp with steam. 'I have a quicker way,' I said, inspired by my own discomfort. 'If you put the wax into a syringe and heat that, then you should be able to inject the wax straight in. It would be quicker and you are less likely to trap any air bubbles.'

'Why, March,' Sidney Grice bobbed behind his desk, 'your technical advice is almost as good as Molly's.'

'I have never met a man more adept at turning a compliment into an insult,' I complained as he yanked open a lower drawer.

'I am not convinced,' he rose as if on a lift, 'that such a man exists.' My guardian waved a syringe – probably the same one he had used to inject me once – pulled the plunger out and forced two sticks of wax into the chamber. Two or three minutes later he had the ball filled. 'And here comes that bootless lumpen wench.'

The front door crashed open and closed, and then the one into the study, and Molly lumbered in, laden with an iron bucket. 'Sorry, sir, but he wouldntn't not let me have any ice without buying an eel so I had to stop on the way back and eat it.'

'You ate raw fish?' I questioned and Molly guffawed.

'Oh, bless you, miss, they aintn't not fishes. Eels are snakes and snakes are always raw. I've seen them at the zoo.' She looked down. 'And now most of the ice has vanished like the invisual elepant I saw in Hyde Park last year.'

'Put it on my desk.'

Molly hauled her load up. 'Oh, sorry, miss, a teeny big lot of it jumped on to your old dress.'

It was a new dress and I was about to tell her so and that I was soaked to the skin, but her master smiled magnanimously.

'Oh, do not worry about that.' He dipped his rubber ball into the icy water. 'Just run along and make some tea.'

Molly curtsied like a puppet whose strings have become tangled, before she departed, while Mr G swirled the ball around, untroubled by the clinking of ice against the sides of the bucket. 'That should do it.'

Sidney Grice whipped a cut-throat razor out of the air and ran the blade rapidly round the ball. 'The time of truth.' He peeled the rubber apart to reveal a perfect white sphere. 'And now for the other one.'

I went upstairs to change into something dry and, whilst I was there, I smoked a cigarette out of the window, overlooking the courtyard garden. By the time I returned, Sidney Grice had two wax balls on a bed of cotton wool beneath two magnifying glasses on brass stands on the round central table, the only uncluttered surface in the room now.

'Take a look at this, March,' he invited me eagerly, and I stood over them.

'They look very similar to me. Which is which?'

Sidney Grice pointed. 'This is my replica of the ball, which – if we are to believe that grotesquery of a medical student – came from Wallace's cranium, and this, your inferior attempt, from your handbag.'

'Why inferior?' I bristled

'Because it is over-inflated.'

'How do you know that yours is not under-inflated?' I asked, knowing full well he would have an answer.

'Because mine is a point four five two calibre, the same bore as Schlangezahn's weapon, which I ascertained by the simple means of inserting my index finger into the barrel – and a man who does not know the exact dimensions of all his digits might as well fritter away his life performing charitable deeds – whereas yours is point six three, not a bore which has been used since bores have been calibrated.'

'And I bet you were one of the first,' I muttered, adding more loudly, 'So do they match up?'

'Judge for yourself.' Mr G traced the course of a long scratch on the first ball with his silver toothpick, a fraction of an inch above it. The line curved one way and then the other, then split and rejoined before breaking up into a delta. I looked at the second ball and it had been scored in exactly the same way.

'There are nine other abrasions which match, or will, when I devise a method of making these replicas exactly the same diameter,' Sidney Grice forecast.

I rotated the balls on their glass pipes. 'There is a large gouge in my one which I cannot see in the other,' I observed.

'I would be desolate if there were not many marks which did not match,' he told me. 'For one ball passed through hair, skin, skull, meninges and brain tissues, whereas the other penetrated the tanned and dyed hide of a cow—'

I completed the list for him. 'My handbag, cigarette case and hip flask.'

'Which is bound to create other blemishes,' he said, oblivious to my sense of outrage.

'So you can prove that Johnny Wallace was killed by Prince Ulrich's air gun,' I concluded.

'Indeed.' He viewed the mess of materials on his shirtsleeve with a wounded sigh. 'It might be slightly more difficult to prove that the prince himself fired the rifle but, bearing in mind the way he tries to avoid putting his weight on to his left toes, I would like to be granted a viewing of his naked foot.'

'When he was running across the ceiling.' I had noticed the way the prince walked but was not about to admit that I had thought nothing of it.

'Possibly.' Sidney Grice placed his hands together in a Namaste – Hindu greeting – pose. 'But no jury would convict on such esoteric evidence.' He scraped some plaster off his cufflink. 'Incidentally, you have a speck of rubber on your collar.'

'Then why go to all this trouble?' I demanded. 'At least I do not have any in my hair.'

'And I hope that is of consolation to you.' He tilted his head back to look at the ceiling. 'Because we have come into possession of something more precious than money or tea itself – the truth, March. I know it, you know it, and I shall make sure that His Illustrious Highness, Prince Ulrich Albrecht Sigismund Schlangezahn, knows it.' He glanced in the mirror. 'Oh,' he said. 'I see what you mean.'

60

❖·❀·❖

The Bridge of Sighs

T HERE WAS A long queue for the toll.

'The Bridge of Sighs,' I quoted.

'Is in Venice,' my godfather corrected me. 'This is Waterloo.'

'I was referring to a poem by Thomas Hood about a girl who committed suicide here,' I explained. 'It reminded me of Albertoria Wright.'

'That was Westminster Bridge.' He drained the dregs of tea into his tin cup.

'We are on the move,' I leaned out for a better view.

'I did not think the scenery was slipping backwards,' he remarked acidly, but then perked up. 'When we reach it, I shall indicate the spot where Samuel Gilbert Scott died.'

'How?'

'Probably with a languid droop of my left hand.'

'How did he die?' I clarified, for it was obvious that he was itching to tell me though I was more fascinated, as always, by the great ships arriving from and departing to every corner of the world, and the bustle of boats ferrying goods and passengers across the water.

'He hanged himself.'

'Why?'

'Scott was a foolish American.'

'Is there any other kind?'

292

Sidney Grice had scant respect for our lost colonies, but he continued to speak over me. 'Who described himself as *The American Daredevil*. He specialized in flinging himself from great heights – masts of ships and, or so he claimed, that silly waste of water, the Niagara Falls. At noon on the eleventh day of January 1841 he leapt from a scaffolding stage at this point.' He indicated as promised. 'And got his neck entangled in a carelessly arranged noose. The crowd, assuming it was part of the act, watched him strangle to death before anybody realized. Bedlam stands to our left.'

Tiring of his role as excursion guide, my guardian spent the rest of the journey entertaining us both by calculating the occupation of anyone I chose to challenge him on.

'Vitreous souvenir paperweight seller,' he diagnosed of a man dragging a large suitcase, as we reached our destination.

I had never been to Clapham Common. Although only five or six miles away from Bloomsbury, the inconveniences of travel on the surface of London and the refusal of my guardian to travel – or allow me to travel – beneath it on the Underground railways meant that I would have needed a good reason to journey there.

Rose Cottage had no roses but plenty of thistles in its untended front garden, yet was a sweet-looking house with trellised windows and pink rendered walls. We went up the short brick path and Mr G rapped on the front door with the handle of his cane.

'One moment,' came from within, and Mr G sniffed. 'How revoltingly fresh the air is here.'

'I think it makes a pleasant change.'

'I like to smell the engines of industry turning,' he said. 'How long can it take a man to button up his shirt?'

'I am not even going to think about it,' I decided. 'How can you possibly know he is doing that?'

'Because,' my guardian crouched to roll an upturned beetle

back on to its legs, 'if you used your ears instead of bombarding mine with mindless wittering, you would have heard him saying *Dash these fiddly shirt buttons*.'

The beetle staggered an inch and toppled back over, waving feebly.

The door opened and an elderly man appeared, still struggling with the stud in his left cuff. He had a chalk-striped long coat on and a beautifully pinned grey cravat.

'Alfred Fairbank?' Sidney Grice demanded, in the tone of an arresting officer.

'Yes?' The man's voice was weak but steady.

Mr G thrust a card at him. 'Mr Sidney Grice, personal detective.'

The old man wired his spectacles around his ears and studied it. 'Order of the Grand Cross,' he read. 'Are you some kind of a Catholic?'

'I am not any *kind* of anything,' my godfather said stiffly.

Alfred Fairbank turned the card over and Mr G whipped it away.

'I have been expecting you,' Mr Fairbank said.

'It would have been a waste of one sheet of notepaper, one hundred and nineteen inches of Dr James Stark's iron gall ink, one envelope, a dab of gum and an outrageously overpriced postage stamp, plus my time and that of my irritating though loyal maid, and all the energies of Her Majesty's General Post Office and the lackeys employed therein, if you had not.'

The old man scratched his high-domed head. 'Had not what, sir?'

'Good afternoon, Mr Fairbank,' I said. 'I am Mr Grice's assistant, Miss March Middleton. May we come in?'

Alfred Fairbank admitted us to a cosy sitting room with two threadbare chintz chairs by the hearth, and settled me into one.

'Mr Grice does not mind standing,' I lied, before the old man was forced to surrender his own seat.

The floor was herringbone brick and the walls distempered.

'We shall not take tea,' Mr G avowed, though none had been offered. 'And – to save my invaluable and your worthless time – I shall break a habit which I have adhered to for nineteen years and commence my interrogation with a leading question.' He cleared his throat. 'You, Alfred Fairbank, were employed by Mr Frederick Wilde at Steep House, Abbey Road, were you not? And you may answer yes or no.'

'For nineteen years, sir,' Alfred Fairbank confirmed.

'A more polysyllabic response than I beseeched you to grant me,' my guardian said pleasantly, 'though nineteen is an excellent number.'

'Were you happy there?' I asked. My seat cushion had virtually no stuffing on the right-hand side, pitching me at an awkward angle.

'Very, miss,' the old man said. 'It was my first position as butler, though. Of course I had been in service for many years before that – and it was a bigger leap in responsibilities than I had anticipated. But Mr and Mrs Wilde were very patient with my early failings and Miss Freda was a delightful child.'

'Did you know the Bockings?' I shifted my weight in an attempt to sit up straight.

'They were frequent visitors, miss,' Alfred Fairbank recalled. His lips were pale and his skin blotched with colourless patches, like a watercolour that had been stored in the damp. 'A more flamboyant couple than the Wildes, but always very pleasant. Miss Freda and Miss Lucy were great friends.'

'What about Eric?' I slid forward in the hope that the front edge might be more level, but it was not.

'A charming young man.' Alfred Fairbank smiled faintly. His lower eyelids sagged redly. 'Devoted to his mother and sister, and I dare say he took a bit of a shine to Miss Freda, not that she paid any attention to that sort of thing. It was all very innocent.'

'Are there degrees of innocence?' Sidney Grice picked up a

toby jug from the mantlepiece – a fat man in a red waistcoat and green tricolour hat.

'Do you remember Jocinda Green, the maid who was sacked?' I asked, and the reminiscent smile died instantly.

'How could I forget?' The old butler fumbled with his cuff. 'Such a lovely girl and such a silly waste to kill herself like that. What on earth did she want all those things for anyway? She never even tried to sell them.' The memory of it all clearly disturbed him still. 'Mr Wilde said some girls are like magpies. They can't stop themselves collecting things, but that dress would not even have fitted her.'

'Did she often help with the laundry?' I asked, and he scratched his jaw where he had missed a tuft when he shaved. 'Every week, as I recall, and Muggy, one of our maids, would regularly help at New House. Neither family entertained on a grand scale as a rule, but if Mr and Mrs Bocking had a large reception I would go with our footman to assist.'

'So the two households got on well?' I twisted round and jammed my bustle against the arm of the chair to steady myself.

'We even had a joint staff party the day after Boxing Day at New House to make it more lively, and because they had a ballroom built on at the back with space for a band.'

'It is just as well I am standing or I might be nodding off.' Mr G replaced the jug. 'Tell me about the fire.'

Alfred Fairbank drew a shuddering breath. 'A terrible night.' He wiped his hand down the side of his face. 'Terrible.'

'As you have already remarked one sixth of a second previously.' Mr G measured out the length of the floor – three long paces and one short. 'Who discovered the fire?'

'I did, sir.'

'How?' he called from the back of the room.

'I smelled smoke.'

'For the sake of brevity I shall amalgamate my next three questions. At what time? Where were you? And what did you do?'

'It was shortly after midnight, sir. The Wildes kept regular hours and were usually in bed by ten thirty. I had just polished my boots – I have always liked to do my own – and was about to undress in my bedroom. I thought perhaps a log had reignited in the main siting room and rolled on to a hearthrug. It had happened once before when a maid swept the hearth and did not put the guard back properly. And so I went to look.'

'And found?'

'The hall filled with smoke and the Christmas tree alight.'

'And your actions were?' The detective went down on to his hands and knees.

'I shouted *Fire! Fire!* And I banged on the dinner gong. Then I ran out of the back door.'

'May I ask why?' I ventured.

'You have just done so.' Sidney Grice scratched at a stain on the floor with his middle fingerplate.

Fairbank's left arm was twitching now like a frog's leg being galvanized. 'There was a pump out there and a bucket.' He dug his fingertips into his cheek. The plates were gnawed. 'I filled it and threw two loads on the tree but it was hopeless. I never knew a tree could burn so fiercely.'

'So what did you do next?' I enquired, as Mr G crawled towards the old butler in full view from the side.

'I banged the gong again and shouted as loudly as I could, but the smoke was choking me. I covered my mouth and nose with my cravat.' Alfred Fairbank touched the one he was wearing. 'And ran upstairs to Miss Freda's room.'

'Oh.' Sidney Grice reached the butler's chair. 'Why hers?'

Alfred Fairbank rubbed both his eyes. 'I suppose—'

'I *hate* suppositions. I bear the very word a grudge and wish it nothing but ill. It tastes of sour earth and smells like a donkey.' My godfather rested his chin on the arm of the butler's chair, like a dog hoping for a treat.

'I suppose,' Alfred Fairbank repeated in confusion, 'that I

thought she was the most vulnerable, being the youngest and a girl and the furthest from the others.' He rubbed his mouth with the back of his hand. 'But I banged on Mr and Mrs Wilde's door and threw it open and shouted, on my way there.'

'How strange you did not mention that before.' The detective began to crawl backwards. 'Especially as they were at opposite ends of the house.'

'It was all very confusing.' The old man trembled. 'There was so much smoke and the flames were rising. You cannot imagine what it is like being in a burning house.'

'I do not need to.' Sidney Grice stood up jerkily. 'For I have escaped eleven conflagrations.'

That made my two experiences seem meagre, I thought.

'And what greeted your nebulous eyes when you reached Miss Wilde's room?' My guardian dusted his knees.

'It was ablaze, sir.' Alfred Fairbank shook. 'Miss Wilde must have woken and tried to get to the landing but been overcome by the smoke. She was lying on the floor by her bed and that was already in flames. Her hair was on fire.' The breath shuddered out of him. 'I carried her out. The fumes were so thick by then that I could not even call out any more. I tried to hold my breath and when I reached the hallway again I saw young Eric climbing in through a broken window. I tried to stop him but he rushed past me. I got to the window and half climbed, half fell out on to the front terrace and passed out. When I came round I had been dragged clear by Miss Lucy. Mr Bocking was tending to Miss Freda. She had been dreadfully burned but, thank God, she was unconscious.'

'And the others?' I hardly dared ask.

'Nobody else got out.' The old butler buried his face in his hands and sobbed.

I half rose but Sidney Grice held out his arm to halt me. He walked backwards to the front door and called to the profile of the bent old man. 'Oh, Alfred, Alfred, Alfred Fairbank, prematurely aged and comfortably superannuated butler, pre-tender to the title of Miss Freda Wilde's rescuer, why…' Without glancing down, he found the big iron key and turned it in the lock. 'Why – and you shall not leave this quaint sitting room alive until you answer me truthfully – why,' he slipped the key into his trouser pocket, 'are you lying?'

The Tangled Earth

LFRED FAIRBANK SAT up and his hands fell away, and there was no doubt that he had been crying.

'I do not know what you mean, sir.' He found a white handkerchief, dabbed his eyes and blew his nose.

'The last time I collated my figures which, you might be inspired to learn, was Saturday the fifteenth day of April in the year of our Lord eighteen hundred and eighty-two, I calculated that the proportion of people who have told me that they do not know what I mean when it transpires that they do – excluding, of course, waitresses and bank clerks who rarely know what anybody means – it was ninety-two point seven per centum. This is not an encouraging statistic for you, Alfred Maurice Fairbank, especially as it is patently clear that you know *exactly* what I mean.' Sidney Grice was leaning in the doorway like a skirt-scanner assessing a parade of women on The Strand but his voice was fast and compelling.

'Identify the injuries that you bear from your adventure.'

'They have all long healed,' Alfred Fairbank managed.

'After you fought your way into, through and out of a con-flagration which, if your account is to be believed – and who am I to doubt it? – tore through a one-hundred-and-twelve-foot-fronted mansion in a matter of minutes?'

'I had many burns and blisters at the time,' the old man said, 'but, as I explained, I covered my face.'

'The average house burns in the region of one thousand of Daniel Gabriel Fahrenheit's elegantly though eccentrically calibrated degrees of temperature,' Sidney Grice took on the drone of a bored professor lecturing equally bored undergraduates on the most boring part of their curriculum. 'And yet you survived your ordeal without so much as one lonely scar?'

'Mr Fairbank was mainly troubled by smoke,' I argued, but Sidney Grice was not to be deflected from his course.

'Unswayed by my assistant's sapless logic, I shall put aside your breathtakingly absurd claims of incombustibility for the present and proceed to your pretence that Miss Wilde's slumberous chamber was conflagrant. I shall not weary you with the fact that the inner surface of the outer wall of her room which now lies supine upon the tangled earth showed none of the twelve signs of scorching known to man, nor of the five additional signs with which I have acquainted myself.'

'If you mean soot, sir, it would have been washed away years ago,' Fairbank protested.

'You are sharp, Alfred Maurice Job Fairbank,' Mr G said with more admiration than he had greeted anything I had ever said. 'Which is also not a point in your favour, for I might have put some errors in your statement as the result of stupidity or senescence, whereas any attempt to feign forgetfulness from henceforth will be met with a degree of scepticism you may find alien to the genial persona with which I have presented you thus far. Putting that evidence also towards the rear of my colossal brain, just starboard of but below my subparietal sulcus, I shall permit Miss Middleton to change the direction of this investigation.'

'Invest...' Fairbank's voice collapsed in alarm.

'Miss Wilde used to sleep with a doll on her window ledge, did she not, Mr Fairbank?' I asked.

'At an age when other children are more usefully employed in coalmines and factories,' Sidney Grice observed.

'Though you did neither,' I remarked.

'I was never *other children*,' he said stiffly.

'Cynthia.' The old butler smiled in remembrance. 'A pretty little thing, made in Germany, I think.'

Sidney Grice chewed his cheek. 'You may wish to remember that morsel of truth, Miss Middleton, but I doubt you will find it brings you comfort in the cold twilight years of your spinster-hood.'

'I found that doll, Mr Fairbank,' I told him, not sure why it mattered.

'Concussed by a conjugation of events – its descent being abruptly interrupted by the cold earth.' Sidney Grice brought his right hand out of his pocket, held up the key and enclosed it in his fist. 'And the section of wall that landed upon it had, in the succeeding years, offered Cynthia some protection from the elements.'

'And what does that prove?' Alfred Fairbank asked, with none of his former deference now.

'The doll's head was made from porcelain.' Mr G opened his hand to show that it was empty. 'And, as anyone will attest, who has accidentally – and who has not? – put their Ming or Tang vase into a furnace, porcelain at high temperatures chars or even melts. More to the point—' My guardian nodded to me to continue.

'She had real hair and a pretty dress on,' I continued. 'None of which showed any signs of damage by fire.'

Fairbank puffed. 'Whatever Mr Grice may say about his numbers, I still have no idea what you are talking about.'

'Miss Freda's room was not destroyed by fire.' I calculated as I spoke. 'It fell into the garden when the lower floors collapsed.'

'Then how do you explain her burns?' the old butler demanded, slapping his chair to drive home his point.

'It is not for me to explain them,' I replied rather lamely, I thought.

But my guardian let out a triumphant '*Ha*' and opened his left fist to reveal the key.

'Nor, apparently, is it for Alfred Maurice Job Cyril Fairbank to reveal.' He threw the key up and it disappeared.

'Why do you keep giving me extra names?' Alfred Fairbank asked peevishly.

'To peeve you.' Sidney Grice smiled thinly. 'Tell me how Miss Freda Wilde achieved her partial cremation, Alfred Maurice Job Cyril Henry Fairbank.' He ambled back towards us, but stopped halfway and stuck out his cane at the old servant. 'Tell me the truth, Fairbank, or does Miss Middleton have to wring it out of you like soapy water from a poorly rinsed grubby brown dishcloth?'

I tried to look menacing, but I was not sure what wringing the truth out of an old man might entail.

'I do not—'

'I am not listening.' Mr G clapped his hands over his ears and started humming loudly with no tune or rhythm.

'What are you hiding from us, Mr Fairbank?' I asked and he bowed his head. A terrible thought struck me. 'Did you start that fire?'

'No.' The old butler recoiled in shock. 'No, of course not. I loved that house and everyone in it.'

'Then tell us what really happened,' I urged, and Mr G flung his hands from his head.

'I am listening now,' he proclaimed.

'I cannot.' Alfred Fairbank pushed down his twitching arm.

'At last we are getting somewhere,' Sidney Grice said, though I was thinking the opposite.

'You must,' I pressed the old man.

'No.' Alfred Fairbank curled himself up. 'You don't understand, miss. I cannot because I do not know.'

62

The Burning

SIDNEY GRICE SAUNTERED round the old servant, whistling softly between his teeth.

'Why do you not know, Mr Fairbank?' I asked. But he had buried himself into himself, folding his arms in a tight embrace.

'Let me assist you in formulating a reply,' Mr G suggested cheerfully. 'Is it, perchance – and you may remediate my suggestion, should it be fallacious – because you were not there?'

Fairbank said nothing but eventually dipped his head.

'Where were you?' I enquired.

'There was a fellow butler, Crofter Tamley, next door, on the other side to New House – Elderberry House, it was called.' Fairbank's voice rustled so softly that I had to strain my ears. 'His master had a well-stocked wine cellar and left care of it to Tamley. If Crofter said a wine was corked he was never questioned. I fell into the habit of going there – after Steep House was put to bed – and sampling some rare and expensive vintages, almost every night towards the end.'

'Did anybody else see you?' I tried to imagine him doing anything so deceitful.

'Never, and Tamley is dead now, about five years ago, I think.'

'How convenient,' Mr G muttered, stopping behind Fairbank's chair, 'though not necessarily for him.'

'So what happened?' I urged Fairbank on.

'We had drunk about half a bottle of a good claret in his pantry when we saw a light flickering. Tamley went to look out of the window. He couldn't see much from where we were below stairs, but then he said, *Bit late to be having a bonfire, isn't it?* And I was just getting up to see for myself when he said *Hello, that isn't a bonfire. It's Steep House.* I jumped up and he was right. *Send for the fire brigade,* I shouted and ran out.

'There was no doubt about it. The flames were coming through the roof and out of the windows in the south wing where all the Wildes slept. There was a gap in the hedge I used to use. I ran through it and saw that all the front of Steep House was ablaze. Masonry was already crashing down. The heat was so intense I couldn't get to within thirty feet. There could be no hope of getting inside.

'I could see the flames through the below-stairs windows and somebody in the light-well from the cellar – hands reached out through the bars and a face pressed between them. I could not think who it might be for none of the servants lived below stairs, and then I realized it was Eric Bocking. It was just like Master Eric to risk his life for others and I can only suppose that he got lost in the smoke. My first thought was to thank God that he had reached safety. But then I remembered that the grating was padlocked and I saw that his clothes and hair were on fire, and he was begging and screaming... There was nothing I could do. I watched him burn and, when he fell, I staggered backwards, just getting away, and nearly tripped over Miss Freda. She was lying on the lawn.'

'Prone or supine?' Mr G broke in.

'On her back,' the old man said. 'Lying on her back.' It was as though, now that he was telling us the truth, he did not believe it himself. 'I could see straight away she was badly burned and at first I thought she was dead, she was so... charred. But then she made a noise, a whimper, I suppose, and I knelt down beside her and said *Help is on its way, miss.* And she said,

Daddy, Mummy. And I realized they must still be in there with Bethany and Lisa, the maids, dead or dying – dead, I hoped, after what I had seen.' He coughed violently.

'Would you like a glass of water?' I offered, but he flopped his dappled hand weakly to decline.

'Miss Bocking was the first to arrive. She said *You have saved Freddy, Fairbank*. And, when she came back, she said, *I will see you rewarded for this*.' He coughed again, drily. 'What could I do – deny it and admit that I had neglected my duty when I might have been able to help them? Or take my reward?'

'Which was?' I asked.

'The rent of this house for life and thirty pounds a year through a trust fund that Miss Lucy asked her father to set up.' Alfred Fairbank hugged himself miserably. 'And now, I suppose, I shall lose everything.'

'Back from where?' Mr G pounced.

'I'm sure I don't know, sir. Changing her dress, I suppose. It got covered in ash and singed.'

'Oh, Alfred.' Sidney Grice flung out his arms like a pantomime damsel in distress. 'Rarely was a man less fitted to bear the name of our wise Wessex monarch. I can only recall the names and dates of birth and death of a great many men and women who have been so unfittingly rewarded. But, as far as I am concerned – Al, Alfy, Fred, Alfredo – you may keep your thirty pieces of silver.'

Alfred Fairbank struggled to his feet. He held out his hand and Sidney Grice viewed it in disgust.

'I should like to thank you, sir.'

'When I survey the uncountable things I want in this squalid world,' he said, 'your gratitude is not amongst their number. But do not become too cheerful, Alfred Maurice Job Cyril Henry William Fairbank, for you may be sure that, before the moon has repeated its repertoire, your grievous sins will find you out.'

Sidney Grice spun balletically on his heel and strode back to the door where the key was already in the lock, magically, it seemed.

A tabby cat lay curled in the sunshine. 'Not a cloud in the sky,' I commented.

'There is little hope of finding one elsewhere.' Sidney Grice batted an acorn off the path and came to attention on the kerb. And so he remained, immobile and staring straight ahead, for another forty minutes until a hansom came by.

63

The Bees and the Box

THE TELEGRAM CAME just as Molly was trying to hang her master's coat upside down.

MARCH COME NOW GERALDINE

'Tea.' Sidney Grice headed for his study, knocking on the door before entering.

'I had better go then,' I said wearily, for I had been looking forward to a beverage myself and I had no good news to give her.

'Indeed.' He shut me out and within two minutes I had rejoined the affray optimistically known as traffic.

'I took it orf 'm for stayin' awt,' Mrs Freval said in response to my enquiry about Turndap's hat. 'Lawd she aint 'appy.' She rolled her eyes up. 'Been squalkin' like a cod she 'as. Got muggins to send that message. Missed my callin' as a slavey, I did. At least I'd get paid.'

'Not if you worked for Mr Grice,' I told her.

And she was still complaining as I trudged upstairs. I knocked and heard a yelp.

'Geraldine, it is me, March.'

I heard shuffling and a chair being dragged away, and two bolts being withdrawn and a lock turning. 'Oh, March,' she sobbed.

Geraldine Hockaday's face was more pinched than I had ever seen it and streaked in long red lines like a child who had been playing with greasepaint.

'Are you going to let me in?'

Geraldine unhooked the chain to admit me, slamming and barring the door quickly in my wake.

'What is it?' I asked, but Geraldine was making choking sounds and flapping her hands as if fighting off a swarm of bees.

'What has happened, Geraldine?' I moved towards her, but knew better than to touch her.

Geraldine did not reply. She doubled over, retching, and fluttered her right hand out, and I realized that she was indicating a small cardboard box resting on creased wrapping paper. I went over and lifted off the lid. Inside was a severed ear and I knew at once that I seen it before. There was an unmistakeable old laceration across the lobe.

64

⬦

The Destruction of Hope

I CAUGHT MY BREATH. 'When did this arrive?' I asked, as steadily as I could.

'This-this-this morning,' she managed.

'By post?'

'P-pushed through the letterbox... Mrs Freval brought—'

There was a sheet of waxed paper on the table too, the sort you might get your fish or cheese in. It did not smell of anything.

'It is Peter's,' Geraldine cried out.

'Yes.' I unfolded the paper and saw pencilled inside:

IF YOU WANT THE REST OF HIM
PUT £50 THROUGH THE LETTERBOX OF
97 HOPE STREET BEFORE NOON TOMORROW.
NO TRICKS.

I brought out my new hip flask and found two glasses.

'What is it?'

'Gin,' I said.

'I... don't.' Every syllable was a battle for her.

'You do today.' I poured her a tot and put it in her shaking grasp.

'I do not have fifty pounds,' she said and sipped at it like a baby bird dipping in a fountain. 'I cannot even pay the rent since Peter went away.'

'I can get the money.' I swallowed mine in two quick swigs and poured myself another. 'But, Geraldine...' I drew a breath. 'You must realize that these people might not give you Peter back.'

Geraldine Hockaday threw up her hands and sloshed her drink. 'But of course they will, March. They must know that he is not a criminal by now. Peter is no use to them and they will not want to house and feed him forever.'

'I will post the money in the morning,' I decided with a heavy heart.

Geraldine nodded avidly. 'And Mr Grice will not try to follow them and risk frightening them off?'

'He will not,' I vowed and finished my drink. 'Shall I take this?' I put the lid back on the box and made to refold the brown paper.

'No,' Geraldine said urgently. 'Don't. It is all I have of him.'

'I will come back tomorrow,' I said. 'You will keep your door locked, won't you?'

I knew I had no need to ask that last question for she was up immediately and ready to wedge the chair back as soon as I was gone.

*

'What is the nineteenth clause of Grice's nineteenth law?' Sidney Grice demanded when I had told him what had happened.

'Never admonish your goddaughter,' I mumbled wearily, for I was not in a mood to be harangued.

'Never allow the client to retain evidence,' he quoted, without looking up from his latest invention, 'unless the retention is likely to stimulate fresh evidence.'

'Do *you* think he is dead?'

'Kidnapping for ransom is not Hanratty's style.' My guardian turned his latest gadget upside down. I had no idea what it was – a steam engine with no funnel or wheels? 'And most criminals stick more rigidly to their modus operandi than an orthodox

Jew to the Shabbat. He might want some compensation for the trouble of returning a body, though.'

'So you're convinced that his disappearance is Hanratty's doing?'

'If anybody else had committed such a crime in his fiefdom the hounds of Hagop would be baying for blood all over London.' Sidney Grice loosened four screws and levered a panel open.

'So I will be paying fifty pounds for a corpse?'

He fiddled about inside and something whirred. 'From what you tell me...' He replaced the screws. 'I should say that is probably the case.'

I had thought as much the first time that I saw it. A cow's blood may clot but a joint cut from it does not have the necessary chemicals and does not coagulate. The blood in the ear was definitely clotted and so it had been cut from a dead man.

'I shall spend tomorrow with Geraldine,' I decided.

'As you wish.' He turned his invention back up and depressed a lever. Nothing happened. 'Excellent,' he murmured with great satisfaction.

*

Hope Street ran parallel to Oxford Street, but there was no hope for it at present. The houses were being demolished to create space for a new department store and work was well under way. I climbed over piles of rubble and tipped a workman for dragging out the old door so that I could cross a trench, though I knew full well he had probably hidden the door in the first place.

Number 97 consisted of a one-storey facade, but it still had a door with a letter slot in it.

'Ain't none livin' there but rats,' another workman yelled over the smashing of sledgehammers into a wall opposite, as he spotted me about to make a delivery.

'Even rats get hungry,' I called back, wondering if he would be straight over the moment my back was turned, but there was a tug on the envelope as I slipped it through and it was whipped out of my hand so hard that I barked my knuckles on the flap.

I crouched and tried to peer through but saw nothing except more rubble and dust, and a few half-bricks rolling down a mound as the taker of my money scrambled away.

*

George came to see me – a very quick call on his way to Liverpool Street Station. They wanted him back in Ely for a case with which he had been dealing before he left. It should take a week at most.

We kissed surreptitiously for my guardian was upstairs.

'You will take care of yourself.'

'I won't forget to clean my teeth,' he promised.

'I mean it.' I held his face. 'You must come back to me.'

George touched my chin. 'I love you with all my heart.'

And, when he had gone, I burst into tears for I had a horrible premonition that something dreadful was going to happen to him.

65

The Washing of Words

I LET MYSELF IN. Molly was clomping downstairs with Spirit under one arm.

'Been a very naughty puppy, she has.' Molly shook a finger at Spirit. 'Got dust all over your room, she did. So if you think I lied on your bed and had forty blinks instead of dusting, you'd be very much mistakened indeed.'

'So I will not find my pillow flattened?' I asked, as Spirit jumped on to the bottom step.

Molly mimed puffing on a clay pipe. 'Well,' she began uncertainly before gaining speed, 'I know you like it flattered 'cause you flatter it yourself every night, so I flattered it for you.'

I smiled. 'That was thoughtful.'.

Spirit cantered back up the stairs.

'And dontn't you not go making a ring round the bath what I cleaned when I wasntn't not sleeping,' Molly called up and Spirit snaked her tail.

Mr G stood behind his desk like a shop assistant hoping to sell me Freddy Wilde's diary, which lay closed on a clean sheet of foolscap paper. 'I have been considering the pattern of incineration of this tome,' he announced. 'Perhaps you could rouse yourself to do the same.'

I picked the journal up. 'Both covers have been burned.'

'On Grice's Scale of Carbonization, how badly?'

'Four and a quarter,' I guessed.

'And a quarter?' Sidney Grice clipped on his pince-nez and took a closer look. 'I will grant you one eighth,' he conceded.

'And I shall treasure it always,' I promised. 'The edges of all the pages are charred too, and I shall not bore you by putting a figure to that.'

'I should be fascinated,' he told me, 'since I invented the system not three minutes ago.'

'Then that was hardly a fair question.'

'On the contrary.' He tossed his head indignantly. 'It was not fair at all.'

I held Freddy's diary to the light. 'The page looks a bit oily.'

'That is one way of describing it.' He hugged himself. 'So perhaps you would like to tell me whether the book was open or closed whilst being oxidized?'

I leafed carefully through it until I came to the last entry. Mr G had removed the bookmark.

'It must have been at least partly open here for the flames to get in.'

'And lick the recto, or right-hand page – but not the verso, or left?'

'What then?'

'What indeed?' he responded unhelpfully. 'Ink acts in two ways. First it mechanically sticks to a surface – rather as graphite does – but, more importantly, as even you must know, it stains the material one is writing upon, most commonly paper. Hence, and you may have observed this, one can rub away a pencil mark, leaving only a pressure indentation, whilst you cannot erase an inked manuscript without abrading the actual fibres. Why – and you probably know the answer to this if you think very hard about it – do we use blotting paper?'

'To remove excess wet ink before it smudges,' I tried.

He had a way of making me doubt that even the most patiently correct answer would be foolish, but this response

315

seemed to satisfy him for he continued with, 'And for how long does ink stay wet?'

I knew full well that whatever figure I gave would be greeted with scorn and was not going to be entrapped so easily this time.

'That depends,' I said, 'on various factors.' I put my fingers behind my back to count hastily. 'Six of which I shall presently enumerate. They include the type of ink, the type of paper, the amount of ink dispensed by the nib, the temperature of the room and the presence or absence of a breeze.'

'You seem to have ground to a halt at five, thank goodness.' Mr G yawned. 'Excuse me.' He covered his mouth. 'But you have a gift for making even such an attention-transfixing subject almost unbearably tedious.'

'What would your answer be then?' I challenged, and braced myself for a stream of figures and mathematical formulae.

'If I wish – as I always do – to be precise, I should say some-where in the region of a few minutes.' Sidney Grice picked up his patent self-filling pen and wrote on a piece of fresh notepaper. *This fine work of calligraphy is intended solely as a sample of pigment.* He blotted and blew on the word. 'Is that dry now?'

'I should say so.'

'Then do so.'

'Yes, it is.'

'Give me your hand.'

'In marriage?'

Mr G fought something down and took hold of me, pressing my palm over the word.

'And what do you see?'

'*Ample* in mirror image on the ball of my thumb.' I knew better than to ask why he had not used his own hand for the demonstration.

'And quite clearly too,' he remarked with some satisfaction.

I rubbed it with my handkerchief. 'So ink takes longer to

dry than you might think.' I licked the handkerchief and rubbed harder.

'It takes exactly as long as I anticipated.' My guardian huffed at the very idea of him misjudging anything. 'Oh, and you need not worry about washing that off. It is indelible.'

'Then you must find a solvent.'

'I am not compelled to do so.'

'I wonder if it is dry now.' I grasped his wrist and pushed his hand on to the ink, surprised by his lack of resistance.

'Of course it is.' Mr G shrugged at my childish prank, but I was only disapointed to see that the *pig*, though printed quite clearly on his palm, was written backwards. 'Perhaps I shall search for a solvent after all,' he conceded and handed me his third-best magnifying glass. 'Scrutinize the verso.'

I looked at the left-hand page. About half an inch of the top edge was burned away and the page beneath discoloured. The last entry was still clearly visible:

I hate Steep House and everybody in it. I shall destroy them all.

And below that nothing.

'The surface has not been abraded,' I observed. 'So nothing has been erased.'

'I provisionally accept that interpretation. Regard, if you can, the recto.'

I held the glass over the top of the page. 'It is only singed along the rim.' I screwed up my eyes. 'There are some very faint smudges on the first four lines, the lower two of which...' I viewed both pages at once, 'are exactly in line with the previous entry. You don't think—'

'Do I not?' He pouted. 'I thought I did.'

'So, if the book were closed too soon, the top two lines could be a blotting of the missing words.' I hurried to the window and held the book up, but there was nothing other than the faintest of meaningless marks. 'If it were pencil we could do a rubbing,' I said disconsolately.

Sidney Grice titivated his eyebrows. 'In what colour was this otherwise tiresome juvenile chronicle inscribed?'

'I would think it was violet originally.' I gave him back his magnifying glass and he polished it vigorously on his elbow. 'Though it is turning brown now.'

'Would you violently disagree with me and storm out of our home never to return if I suggested that originally it might have been purple-brown?' he asked meekly.

'You said *our* not *my*, and *home* not *house*.'

Mr G blinked. 'I heard myself.'

'You said *our home*.'

'I am glad to find you paying such close attention to my words.' He retied his patch. 'Though your repetition of them might irritate a man not blessed with my saintly patience, and I think it only fair to inform you that the deeds of this property are in my name.'

'I know that.' I wanted to lean across the desk and kiss the tip of his elegant nose, but I only said, 'Purple-brown sounds about right to me.'

'Thank heavens we navigated that emotional crisis without being cautioned for affray,' he said.

'But why would I have argued about it?'

'You argued about the colour of the drapes in the sitting room.'

I remembered cuddling up to George Pound on the sofa up there and resolved to tackle my guardian on the subject later. For now I satisfied myself with, 'Only because you wanted to change them for black ones.'

'Charcoal,' he insisted before resuming his tutorial. 'Purple-brown inks are sold under the description of Iron gall. They contain – amongst other ingredients – ferrous sulphate, not to be confused with ferric sulphate which is used as a mordent to fix dyes rather than a dye in its own right. A pertinent property of ferrous sulphate is its reaction with sodium carbonate – vulgarly known as washing soda or soda ash – of which I have a bottle here.' He withdrew an unlabelled green bottle which he had lodged in the mummified claw of Ekriel Coy, the Aspic Killer of Merthyr Tydfil. 'The resultant exchange of molecules results in the creation of sodium sulphate and, more relevantly, ferrous carbonate, a precipitate and a serviceable sepia pigment.' He unscrewed the cap and inhaled, though even I know it has no aroma. 'So if I apply this over these marks I may be able to darken them enough to be legible.'

'But, if the ink should be made of another chemical, what will the soda do?'

'There is a chance that it will do what it is purchased in vast quantities to do and remove the stains,' Mr G told me lightly and, before I could object that he might try to think of another means, commanded me: 'Seek and find 19 January, then seek and find the inscription *skating*.'

I did as I was bade and the word sprang immediately, darker and clearer than the preceding *we went* and the succeeding *on the pond*.

'You tested it,' I realized.

'I am not quite the simpleton you portray in your published accounts,' he declared with a toss of his thick, black, backswept hair.

'But I have always emphasized your cleverness,' I protested.

'A performing flea may be described as *clever*.'

He took the book back from me and I sniffed. 'I shall try to do you justice in future.'

'You will fail,' he predicted. 'Pay close attention for there is a chance that it will be washed away and there are occasions when three eyes are better than one.'

Sidney Grice dipped a flat brush into the soda solution, wiping the excess liquid off on the neck of the bottle, and painted it sparingly over the top third of the last page. Nothing much happened. He re-wet the bristles and tried again and, this time, the effect was instant.

'Your head is in the way,' I complained.

'My head is where it always is,' he snapped. 'Firmly, though not rigidly, attached to my first cervical vertebra.' Nonetheless he edged to the side.

And, reading right to left, we narrated in unison: '*he told me, "I hate Steep House and everybody in it. I shall destroy them all."*'

'So that was why Eric was in the cellar,' I realized.

The pigment was watery and starting to trickle down the page.

'I find myself ill-equipped to refute your premise.' Sidney Grice tried to blot the words, but they had already floated away.

66

Footfalls on the Stairs

GERALDINE HOCKADAY LET me in.

'I thought it might be Peter.' She secured the door.

'Geraldine—'

'Do you like my costume?' She had a pretty new dress on, dark pink with a lace trim on the cuffs and around the collar. 'This is the first time I have ever worn it. Papa bought it for me before... all this.'

'It is very pretty and you are looking brighter too.'

Geraldine's face was almost as pink as her clothes and there was renewed life in her eyes. 'I wanted to look nice for Peter. And see – I have set his pipe and tobacco by his chair.'

'Geraldine,' I tried again, 'there is something I have to say. You must prepare yourself for the possibility—'

'What is that?'

There was a scuffling noise. I went over to listen and heard growls and bumping. It came from downstairs.

'Peter.' Geraldine jumped up.

'I do not think so,' I said and opened the door a crack.

'You can't leave it 'ere,' Mrs Freval was saying, 'blocking the entry. Come back 'ere you crebbed-up bleedin' bleeders.'

'Wait here and lock the door,' I told Geraldine and hurried down.

'I told them they can't just leave it 'ere,' Mrs Freval yelled up at me. 'Bleedin' cruck-faced Prikes – not that I could see their poxy faces – silly scrabs with their mufflers on in this wevver. It aint 'xactly snowin'.' She held out her hand to demonstrate the absence of flakes. 'Is it?'

There was a big laundry basket half-filling the hall when I made my way down and I did not like the way Turndap was sniffing it excitedly. 'Perhaps you had better take your dog inside,' I said.

'Your dog?' she parotted in disgust. '*Your dog?* 'E's gotta name as you well know.'

'Please,' I said nervily. 'Please take Turndap away.'

Mrs Freval made several gargling noises and picked her pet up. 'It was a rubbish 'at anyway,' she muttered, though she was the one who had chosen it.

I pushed on the basket but could not shift it. There were two pegs through loops and I pulled them out.

'Is it Peter?' Geraldine was coming down the stairs. 'He might not be able to breathe in there.'

'Stay there, Geraldine,' I warned. But she was hurtling down the last steps and flying into me, flattening me against the wall.

'Peter.' She had hold of the lid.

'Don't,' I cried, but she had flung the lid up and back.

Geraldine Hockaday was all at once frozen, bending down, her face still mixed in concern and joyous expectation. I just managed to catch her as she fell and dragged her on to the one bit of clear floor at the foot of the stairs. She was as light as a child.

I had known in my heart that Peter Hockaday, the brave, tall, fresh-faced young man I had left under that shelter in Limehouse, would be dead. I had feared but did not know that he would be squatting in that basket, his face beaten out of shape. I looked in his open mouth and wished I had not. And never, for one moment, had I imagined that he would be cradling his intestines, long shimmering tubes and folds of white membranes, in his lap.

67

The Ice Houses

I PUT THE back of my fingers to Peter's bruised brow. It was
still warm.

'Oh, Peter,' I breathed uselessly.

I shut the lid and told Mrs Freval as little as I could. She took
Geraldine in, sat her on the one pine chair and wrapped her in
a moth-eaten and very smelly blanket. Turndap got up on his
hind legs and pawed her for it back, but I do not think Geraldine
knew that either of them was with her. I do not think she even
saw them or anything beyond what was in that basket.

I found a policeman just about to finish his shift, but his
weariness vanished at the prospect of a good murder.

There was an undertaker's round the corner. I had noticed
it before but not paid much attention. I hoped it was not like
the last undertaker with whom I had dealings, and was pleasantly surprised at their professional manner and reasonable
rates. They would pick up Peter from the morgue as soon as
the coroner released his body and they would make sure he
had a good coffin at a good price. I gave them my card for
the bill.

The basket was already being dragged on to the back of a
wagon when I returned. It left a long brown streak on the
pavement.

Geraldine rejected my offers to stay with me in Gower Street
or for me to stay with her. She had no friends whom she wanted

me to contact. She hardly spoke except to say that she needed to be alone.

'I'll check on 'er,' Mrs Freval promised as Turndap licked the floor. She touched my arm. 'Oh and that 'at – it's a dandy one really.'

*

'Cadavers warm up as decomposition sets in,' Sidney Grice told me. 'I hesitate to ask since I know that you are incapable of keeping your feminine emotions in check and it is an unpleasant question.' He put down his book – *The Life Cycle and Mating Rituals of Cornishmen* – open but upside down on his lap. 'Did he—'

'No,' I broke in. 'He did not smell decayed.'

'Hagop Hanratty,' Sidney Grice pronounced the name with great precision, 'has the use of a number of ice-houses. They enable him to provide fresh eels and oysters at a premium price long after the seasons have finished.' He closed the book. 'It is possible that he kept Lieutenant Hockaday's cadaver preserved in one of those until he decided what best to do with it.' He stretched up.

'But what was there to think about?' I queried.

'Hanratty is in the habit of displaying his victims' remains in public as a caveat to others who might be considering infringing upon his territory.' He reached back and dropped the book over the back of his chair, letting it thud to the floor and startle Spirit, who was curled up on his desk. 'In this case he may have decided that the gruesome condition of the cadaver would attract too much attention and frighten his customers away.'

I slumped in my chair. 'You do not think...?'

Sidney Grice looked at me with something approaching feelings. 'Hanratty is a pragmatic man. What would be the point in disembowelling a corpse?'

I held my head. 'I cannot hope to stop a gang the size of his,'

I said eventually. 'But I can try to stop the man for whom we entered such a world.'

Sidney Grice took off his pince-nez and watched me. 'You will not do anything foolish?'

'When?' I demanded. 'When have you ever known me not to?'

And Sidney Grice's lips moved. I knew it would not be, because he did not believe in God, but it was almost like he was praying.

———◆———

68

The Windows of the Soul

THE STREET WAS almost deserted except for a gawky young man in a brown cotton coat, rolling tar-saturated strands of tobacco into a spill of newspaper.

'We don't want no more deliveries today.' Mrs Freval viewed me suspiciously. 'Turndap was in a right old state after the last one. 'Ad nightmares all night, 'e did, and now 'e's gottanedache.'

'I am sorry,' I said, 'but I did not bring the body here. In fact I arranged to have it removed.'

Mrs Freval prodded a bristle on her neck, apparently trying to push it back in. 'Bring? Remove? It's all to do wiv draggin' bodies round my 'ouse.'

'I shall just leave it here next time, shall I?'

I could hear Turndap snoring inside.

'Oh!' His mistress squalled. 'It's coming back, is it? Well, let me tell you—'

But I never found out what I was going to let Mrs Freval tell me for there was a racket outside of two women fighting, and she hurried away to watch through her net curtain.

I headed upstairs, but there was no reply at Geraldine's door. I knocked again and listened. No doubt Sidney Grice would have heard something significant, but I could only hear the cat-erwauling outside and Turndap yapping excitedly. There was a dead rat in the middle of the floor, I noticed, and wondered if Mrs Freval would blame me for that too. I rapped harder.

'Geraldine.'

No reply.

I raised my voice and hammered on the bare pine panel with the side of my fist, and rattled the handle, and, to my surprise, the door came ajar.

'Geraldine?'

I pushed it in and stood back. If there was one thing my guardian had taught me – though I did not always remember – it was not to rush blindly into rooms. I could hear a clicking.

'Are you all right?'

Geraldine Hockaday sat in her usual chair knitting frantically. She did not glance at me.

'Your door was not locked,' I told her but she did not respond.

I tried again. 'What are you making?'

The needles whirred against and around each other. 'I am finishing the scarf that I promised to Peter.'

I crouched to try to look into her eyes but they were not focused on me. 'You do understand what happened?'

Geraldine wriggled her nose like the child she often seemed to be. 'I understand what,' she said quite calmly – too calmly, it seemed – 'but I do not understand why.'

'We will catch the people who did it,' I vowed and touched her knee.

Geraldine started another row. 'Just as you caught the man who did this to me?' she asked with chilling politeness. Then her voice sharpened. 'Have you forgotten already that my brother died trying to do your job for you?'

'I cannot tell you how sorry I am,' I said uselessly, and could not bring myself to add that I had been trying to stop Peter committing murder.

Geraldine carried on knitting. It was then I noticed that there was a dried brown crust on the lace sleeve of her pale blue dress.

'Have you tried to sleep?' I asked.

'And what would I dream of?'

'I can get you some laudanum,' I suggested.

'Opium?' Geraldine spat out the word. 'You think that will help?' She jabbed a needle so close to my cheek that I twisted my head away and edged backwards. 'It was opium that got us into this mess.'

Mess seemed a very tame way to describe any of what had happened. I paused. 'Did you go to a den, Geraldine?'

'The Golden Dragon.' Her needles clacked again. 'I was on my way back from it,' she admitted. 'That is why I made such a poor witness. I did not really know what was happening.'

'But nothing happened to you while you were there?'

'The owner would not have let it.' Geraldine puckered her lips. 'He was very worried for me being alone and advised me the safest route to walk back.'

We would have another chat with Jones/Chang, I decided.

'Why did you not tell Mr Grice?' I went down on my haunches, just clear of her boot swinging up and down.

'Do you think he did not disapprove of me enough already?'

'It might have helped his investigations,' I steadied myself on the arm of Peter's chair, 'if you had told him what you saw.'

'Do you want to know what I have seen?' Geraldine put down her knitting but picked it straight up again. 'I have seen my beautiful brave brother, my only support and comfort, made into something disgusting.' She wrenched the knitting off and threw it on the floor. 'And that is all I see now. I see him more clearly than I see you. He is trapped inside my eyes, March.'

'I shall send my doctor to give you something,' I resolved. 'He is a very kind—'

But I never finished my sentence for Geraldine turned those needles to peer closely at the tips. I rose. 'I cannot bear to see him like that,' she cried. 'I would be better blind.' And she plunged the needles in.

The left needle went about an inch and stopped, juddering against the bony back of the socket. Geraldine screamed. I ran towards her, ready to grab her hands but the right needle slid deep. It must have passed through the sphenoidal fissure to penetrate her brain.

Geraldine's mouth gaped and she screamed again. 'Christ God it hurts!'

She pulled.

'No!' I yelled. But Geraldine was beyond hearing. The left needle came out to leave a burst eyeball oozing gel, but the right was clearly jammed. She grasped it with both hands, not noticing that she had pierced her cheek with the freed needle. I got to her and grabbed her wrists, but she had a strength born of agony now and clung to the needle still embedded in her skull.

'Geraldine! Let go.'

Her left hand came away but only to claw at my throat. I choked and pulled her hand away but she was still wrenching at the needle in her eye and wiggling it now, her skewered eye revolving in her frantic attempts to pull the needle free.

'Oh God! Oh God! Oh God!' In one desperate effort she drew that needle out. I heard the bone crack and I saw the eyelids part and stretch and bulge and there was a tearing sound and the needle came free but on it was skewered a horrible bloody white ball haloed in a fringe of meat, the torn cord of the optic nerve dangling at the back.

'Oh dear God, Geraldine. Dear God!'

The door flew open behind me. 'What in heaven's name is all that commotion?' Mrs Freval said, Turndap dancing round her feet. 'Oh cruck.'

She covered her mouth and staggered back against the wall, sliding down it with a bump. And when I turned back I saw that Geraldine Hockaday, mercifully, had fainted also.

*

I dashed next door and, as luck would have it, just caught Dr Goddard coming down his front steps. He fetched his leather bag immediately and followed me in. Geraldine had come round in a frenzy of pain. She could not catch her breath even to scream. I rolled up her sleeve and held her left arm as still as I could, and Dr Altman put her back to sleep with a massive injection.

She looked so peaceful, but, watching Geraldine slumber, it was obvious that we had only postponed her suffering. Too soon she would awaken in dark agony to a world which had savagely mutilated and killed the one man she had loved. And it was then that I made my decision. This could not continue. It was time to go back to Huntley Street.

69

The Unity of Four

WE MET AT the club at ten o'clock sharp. Marjorie was already there with Sally, who was looking abashed as always, when Harriet and I went upstairs and, before we could speak, Dulcie came in. She had a simple yellow dress on, tied around her slender waist, a long saffron cloak and a thin-brimmed velvet hat, jauntily held in place by a ribbon under her chin.

'Dulcie, you look stunning,' I told her to general agreement.

'Wait until you see my accessory.' Dulcie's eyes twinkled as she brought a neat yellow-handled pistol out of her matching handbag.

'Do you know how to use it?' I asked.

'I had a French army instructor,' she told me. 'And I managed to wing my governess from fifty yards with this revolver.'

'Oh, Dulcie, you are worse than Harriet.' I laughed despite, or because of, my misgivings, and she leaned towards me. 'That one is true,' she murmured in my ear.

'I've been in contact with Mr Chang at the Golden Dragon,' Harriet announced, 'and paid a retainer to keep his room free for a group of women, and told him we will be exploring the area first. If March's hunch is correct about that poor girl, Geraldine, the owner will have informed the attacker we are coming.'

'I need to speak to you all,' Marjorie boomed unexpectedly. 'I have been giving this a lot of thought and it seems to me we are being reckless. Anything could happen out there.'

'I think we can all look after ourselves,' Harriet said, with some justification, for she had saved my life once at great risk to her own.

'Well, I think we should leave this man to the police.'

'He has been left to the police for heaven knows how long now,' Sally told her with unexpected spirit. 'How many other girls can he destroy before we stand up to him?'

Marjorie tightened her mouth. 'I am sorry but I cannot be a part of such a foolhardy enterprise.' She tried but failed to stare me out. 'You may toy with danger, Miss Middleton, but we are ladies and unused to such things. I am going to my home now and I hope you all will have the sense to go to yours.'

And with that she brushed roughly past me and down the corridor, slamming the door after her.

'I knew she was unsound,' Harriet said. 'Where did she find that bonnet?'

I tried to smile. 'Well, that has ruined our scheme,' I said ruefully but also half-relieved, for I had a nagging feeling that Marjorie was right.

'Why?' Dulcie demanded. 'I know the plan was for me to be the bait with two at each end of the alley but you and Harriet can still work as a pair and I have every faith in Sally if she does not mind working alone.'

'I cannot allow that,' I protested.

'I would prefer it,' Sally insisted. 'I was never happy being teamed with her – much too jumpy. She would only have got in the way.'

'We are better off without her,' Harriet agreed. 'She would have swooned the moment a man appeared on the horizon.'

'If any of the rest of you would like to pull out now, I shall not blame you,' I said, and we all looked at each other. 'I have no right to ask anyone to endanger her life.'

'You have no right to forbid us,' Dulcie argued, 'not while

there is a chance of putting a stop to this monster before he hurts another girl.'

'I warned them that this might happen,' Harriet told me, for she knew me better than anyone. 'And we have talked about it.' She took my shoulders and held me in her gaze. 'We are going to do this with or without you, March – though, obviously, we would feel much safer if you came.'

'Getting cold feet?' Sally asked, and I glanced at Baroness Worford glowering on the wall, Gricean with her missing eye.

'Not I,' I said.

'Good.' Dulcie breezed over to the sideboard. 'Then that is settled.' And she poured five stiff brandies – not my tipple, but I was never more glad to have one.

70

The Silver Fox

ULCIE'S BROUGHAM WAS waiting on Huntley Street, a maroon four-wheeler, with the Brockwood crest of a silver fox crossed by two swords on the door.

It was a clear, dry night, though a light wind was getting up.

'This is Geoffrey.' Dulcie introduced her coachman with a familiarity towards her servant that would have shocked my guardian.

'You can always rely on a Geoffrey,' I said, for it was also my father's name.

On the back were two burly footmen, both professional pugilists in their day, Dulcie assured us, and the older man, Lenny, grinned almost toothlessly to lend weight to her story.

I sat facing forwards with Harriet at my side, Dulcie and Sally opposite us, holding hands.

'Shall we do that?' Harriet asked and our fingers intertwined.

It was a long, slow journey. Geoffrey was highly skilled at pushing into gaps that looked narrower than our carriage to me, and the footmen had no compunction about lashing out at beggars or urchins who tried to slow us down. But a brougham takes up a lot of road and the streets were increasingly narrow and crowded with pedestrians, and it seemed forever before we pulled up in the square.

Harriet slid towards me. 'Whatever happens, I love you.' I felt her tremble.

'Tell me that when we get back to Huntley Street,' I said softly, and raised my voice. 'Last chance to change your minds.'

'Tosh,' Dulcie said, as the younger footman lowered the steps and opened the door.

'I love you too,' I whispered to Harriet and she kissed me.

The square was deserted. Geoffrey was down from his seat and prowling the peripheries, his whip at the ready. He bestrode the whole area before rejoining us.

'It is not my place, milady,' he towered over his mistress, 'but I would be much happier if me and the men could follow at a discreet distance.'

'And who will look after the horses?' she enquired.

Geoffrey flapped a leather-gloved hand. 'Oh, they can look after themselves. Black Bess would break the skull of any man who came too close.' He scanned the unglazed windows all around us. 'But if you're really worried, Dick can stay. They trust him.'

Dulcie touched his sleeve. 'I appreciate your concern, Geoffrey, and I am truly grateful for the offer, but we are all armed and alert and we have a plan.'

'Your father—'

'Will never know,' she assured him.

'The trouble is, two or three big men like you might frighten our quarry away,' I explained.

'Very well,' Geoffrey agreed reluctantly. 'But at least take this.' He reached behind his head and lifted a cord over his hat to hand her a huge antique silver whistle. 'Any trouble and you give that a blast. Hear it halfway across London on a quiet night like this.'

'Thank you, Geoffrey.' Dulcie hung it around her neck. She craned up and for a moment I thought she was going to kiss her coachman, but she only told him conspiratorially, 'I spotted a nice old pub three streets back.'

Geoffrey broke into a broad grin. 'So did I, milady – the Ship Inn – but we will stay here and wait for your signal.'

'I could go an' fetch a jug,' Dick, the younger footman, offered hopefully.

'We will *all* stay here,' Geoffrey said firmly, ignoring their disgruntled moans.

'Did you remember the lamps?' I asked, and Lenny clambered back up to open the postilion box, handing down four lanterns one at a time for his colleague to light. I had learned one thing from my experiences at Scarfield Manor – the stupidity of stumbling about in the dark. But we might just have managed without them that night, for the moon was full and the sky was the clearest I had ever seen in London. The wind was coming in gusts now, as it often did near the river. It made Dick's task more difficult but it had blown the fumes away.

'We should all keep our handbags undone,' I advised. 'You do not want to be fiddling with clasps in an emergency.'

I had toyed with the idea of taking my father's old service revolver. It was far more cumbersome than Harriet's dainty weapon – the only present her husband had ever given her, she had joked once – but mine was capable, my father had boasted, of bringing down a rhinoceros.

'Not too many of those grazing in Limehouse,' Harriet had told me. She knew I would not carry a gun but pressed a black-handled one on me. 'A starting pistol,' she had explained. 'But it looks like the real thing and makes enough of a bang to get the little devils running on sports day.'

I unclipped my bag and put the gun on top. It was quite light but looked real enough to me.

We went as a group down the road, turning right then left, then through a maze of passageways, some occupied by sleepers, one by a sprawling drunk who clung to Sally's skirt until she twisted his finger back.

We stood at the top of Card Street, really no more than a gap between the long rows of back yards, and chosen as our main route because it was long and straight and we had studied our map at the club until we knew exactly where the all the other alleys crossed or came off it and where they led to. There was no danger of getting lost if we stuck to the main route. A woman lay at the top of the street, curled on the stones with two skinny children in her arms. I put a coin into her outstretched hand and she took it weakly without opening her eyes. Her children were breathing rapidly and I resolved to get them to a doctor upon our return.

Sally turned her wick down. 'I do not want to frighten him off,' she said, 'before he sees our bait.'

'Probably the first time I have been called that.' Dulcie squeezed her friend's shoulder.

'If he is around, the chances are he will try something on our way home when he will expect us to be befuddled with opium,' I forecast. 'But we cannot be sure of that, so take care, stick together and no heroics.'

We all hugged and Sally went ahead, tentative at first but soon getting into a confident stride. A baby cried somewhere and a cat shot out, making Sally jump, but she kept going. There was an unnamed very narrow alley on the left after about thirty yards. She stopped, turned her wick up a fraction and peered down it, stepping just inside before reaching out to wave the lamp in signal that the way was clear. Dulcie stepped round the woman. Sally emerged and started down again and Dulcie blew us a kiss before setting off after her.

'Lord, if I were a man, I would be sniffing round her,' Harriet whispered as Dulcie strolled as elegantly as any woman could along a narrow, cobbled alley with a rubbish-strewn central gulley, and I could see what she meant. Dulcie was not only a beautiful woman but she oozed her beauty in a way that most of us could only dream of.

Sally was going faster now, a dark shape in the darkness, but it did not really matter for she would wait at the next crossroads for Dulcie to get past the first side street. Dulcie paused as she reached it until she saw Sally's lamp flare up, perhaps another thirty yards ahead, and wave to urge her on.

Dulcie carried on. Harriet and I set off after her, with a quick glance over our shoulders. Geoffrey stood watching us uneasily. The surface was more uneven than I had imagined and slippery, probably from a sewage overflow, but we made the first alley without incident, just as Dulcie made the second and Sally stopped to check the third. We all passed on our way. The fourth break was another, very narrow alley, and we had to wait a while before Sally was satisfied it was safe. We turned right at the end towards where we had calculated the Golden Dragon to be, and then left. I had never seen the streets so quiet.

Sally reached another junction and stopped to check it. The lantern swung to signal the way was safe and then went out.

'Damn.' I strained to see. 'I hope she has a Lucifer. Oh, it is all right.'

The lamp reappeared, turned very low, and we could only see it rise and fall like a firefly, so far from us now. Dulcie set off after it, turning her light up to negotiate a pile of filth and to make herself more visible.

'Perhaps we should try a busier street.' Harriet hitched her dress to step over a greasy puddle.

'Yes,' I agreed. 'Nobody is likely to be looking for a victim in such a place. Why is it so deserted?'

Dulcie reached the narrow turn-off and was about to saunter past when she stopped.

'What?' She stepped towards the alley and Harriet touched my arm. We hesitated. 'Sally!' Dulcie put her lamp down.

'What is it?' we called in unison.

'Oh my God, Sally!' Dulcie stepped into the gap and her lamp went out.

'Stay there!' I shouted. 'Wait for us.'

Harriet and I hurtled along the street, slithering and nearly falling over each other in our rush.

'If something is wrong, blow your whistle.' I pushed ahead. It was then I heard a sob and the sound of drumming boots and a scuffle. 'Shoot into the air, Harriet,' I called, skidding so badly that I crashed into the wall as I swung round to the left.

Harriet's gun shattered the silence, the explosion ricocheting in every direction.

Sally lay crumpled. I held up my lamp and saw a darkness frothing from her breast. I kneeled in the pool and Sally wheezed.

'Oh, Sally, darling,' I whispered, and cried out, 'Dulcie. Dulcie, can you hear me?'

There were more scufflings and then from behind me a rush, and the figure of a man hurtling towards me, flinging me face down on top of Sally, her breath grunting bloodily into my mouth.

71

The Scabbard in the Hand

I ROLLED.

'Get out of my way,' the man yelled, and it was a moment before I recognized the voice as belonging to Sidney Grice, but he was gone, racing jerkily round a bend, his safety lantern swinging wildly.

I struggled to my knees, barely aware that they were scraped raw. Harriet was behind me. 'Stay with Sally,' I told her. 'Try to staunch it.'

But I knew there was no hope. I saw Sally's eye flicker, and the empty scabbard in her grip. 'I am so sorry.'

Sally's lips moved and her fingers crushed the scabbard. She sighed and I could not see any fresh frothing.

There was a distant cry and a thudding. 'Look after her.' I got to my feet. 'And use your gun if he comes back.'

I snatched up my lamp and gave chase.

This alley was so narrow that my skirts dragged along the rough bricks on both sides as it curved this way and that, unbroken even by a doorway or window, the body of a large dog sprawled across my path. I tried to jump it, but mistimed and heard the ribs crack and felt my foot sink in. I shook myself free and carried on.

There was a pink handbag in the gutter, its contents strewn. I could not see the gun. Did I hear a muffled wail? My neck prickled but I drove myself on.

The alley bent at a right angle to the left now and opened into a small deserted court, completely enclosed by a wall some ten or twelve feet high. There were three plank doors leading off, one to either side and one straight ahead. I tried them all but they were locked solid.

'Can anyone hear me?' I banged on the right-hand door. Nothing. Was that a rustle?

'Mr G?' The words came hoarsely but were unanswered.

A definite rustle this time. The sound of stiff bolts being pulled back. I brought out my revolver. 'I am armed,' I warned, backing against the wall and ready to jump either way. Banging noises preceded another bolt being forced back, and the middle door opened. 'I shall shoot.'

'No, you shall not.' Mr G came into the yellow sea of my lamp. His hat was off, his coat crumpled and his trousers torn at the knee.

'Dulcie,' I said. 'She was—'

'She was,' he agreed wearily and stepped aside. 'I should warn you—'

But I was not listening. I rushed through the gateway into a back yard – ten feet square and backed by a tall, dark building. Sidney Grice's lamp was on the floor and in its glow lay a woman on her back, her legs splayed out and the skirts pulled up above her head, and I did not need to pull them down to know that it was Lady Dulcet Brockwood. But when I did I saw, by the dancing flame, the terrible nothingness that filled her now.

An ornate horn-handled knife had been driven into Dulcie's neck up to the hilt and on her forehead was a hastily carved X.

I kneeled and took her hand, still warm but without a spark of the life that had radiated from her – could it really have been only a few minutes ago?

'Move away,' Sidney Grice said.

'What?' I heard his words clearly but they meant nothing to me.

'Away.' He pushed my shoulder roughly and I staggered to my feet.

Sidney Grice was crouching between hers, his lamp held over her torn undergarments. He pulled a test tube out of his satchel.

'What are you doing?' I hardly understood my own words.

'Something that the police surgeon will not do and is best done while it is still fresh.'

'It?' I asked numbly.

'The corpse.'

His words buffeted into me and I watched in horror as he took a lint ball in his locking tweezers and inserted it into her.

'Has she not been desecrated enough?'

Sidney Grice glanced up from his task. 'Do that in the corner.'

And it was only then that I realized I was vomiting down myself. I turned sideways, and when I had finished he was putting his test tube away.

'And what did you find?' I asked bitterly.

'Blood,' he said flatly. 'Just blood.'

'What on earth did you expect?'

Sidney Grice sprang up, his body twisted in rage. 'Whose work was this? Was it mine or yours?' He screwed himself up, fists clenched, his eye flying, bouncing over the stones, his right socket empty, as he stared at me in horror. 'By God, girl, if there were any justice in this cruel, savage, repulsive world, this would be you instead of Lady Brockwood.' There was a fury in his voice I had never heard before and a new disgust on his face. 'You stupid stupid girl.' He made as if to slap my face with the back of his hand, and I wished to God, and I have wished it ever since, that he had knocked me cold. 'I cannot speak to you,' he said. 'Who is there?'

That last remark was not addressed to me.

'Show yourself.' He had his ivory-handled revolver in his right hand.

I had still heard nothing.

Sidney Grice stood straight, feet apart, his head tipped back, scanning the building behind me.

And then there was a piercing shrillness and a quick, low laugh.

'I have you, you filth.' Sidney Grice raised his gun and fired, and the shutters on the fifth floor shattered. He threw himself backwards against the wall and, gun in both hands now, let off three more shots. The shutters exploded into a cloud of splinters, showering over us.

Silence.

'Did you get him?'

Sidney Grice put a finger to his lips. He was walking forward, intent upon that window, gun aimed straight at it.

Another laugh – a longer one this time – and something flew down, clattering at my feet. I bent and saw that it was the coachman's whistle.

'Go and look after your friend,' my guardian said quietly. 'She must be terrified.'

I had almost forgotten about poor Harriet. I turned dumbly, numbly, to leave. I could not look at Dulcie again but I would see her for the rest of my days.

'And, March,' he said softly, 'I am sorry.'

In all the time I knew Sidney Grice, he never said a kinder or a crueller thing.

72

The Dead and the Damned

I COULD NOT speak when I found Harriet. She had covered Sally's face with a bloodsoaked handkerchief.

'Oh, March.' She shrank back. 'What have we done?'

There were heavy footsteps and a man's voice calling, 'Here they are.'

Geoffrey, the coachman, and his two companions appeared breathlessly. 'Milady?' Geoffrey asked, and I found I could not look at him. 'Stay with the women,' he told his companions and squeezed past me up the alley.

His heavy footsteps faded and stopped and I heard a gasp as a man might make if he is punched in the stomach, and then a strange noise, a cry gathered and growing into the howl of a man who has lost the mistress he adored.

There was a severed finger in the dirt.

*

The woman and her children were dead by the time we returned to the square, from slum fever, no doubt, and Dick, the young footman, had laid a blanket over them. She still had my piece of silver wedged in her fist.

*

I cannot remember when I found out that Marjorie Kitchener was Hagop Hanratty's sister-in-law – she did not advertise the fact – and she had told him of our plans in the hope of getting us stopped.

But Hagop had other plans. If we caught the attacker so much the better. The streets were so quiet because he had ordered people inside. But he did not want us taking any unnecessary risks and, just to make sure, he had sent a message to Sidney Grice.

*

I do not know how I got through the next few days and nights. I only know that the gin did not help.

After three days, Geoffrey the coachman came to see me. He was whey-faced and his eyes bloodshot. He was very quiet and respectful. Lady Brockwood would not have wanted him to be otherwise, he told me.

I tried to say how sorry I was but he brushed that aside. I told him I was quitting as a detective and was about to tell Mr Grice.

'Oh no, miss.' An odd smile came over Geoffrey's lips and he shook his grizzled hair. 'The way I see it is, you got my mistress killed and you will get her killer or die in the process – begging your pardon, miss – but after that you can drown in your own piss-pity for all I care.' He made a deep bow and spoke confidentially in my ear, though nobody else was in the room. 'God damn you and keep you rotten writhing in your box, you self-righteous bitch.' He straightened up. 'Good day, Miss Middleton. I will see myself out.'

There was no point in telling him that I had damned myself a long time ago.

*

I put away my gin and had a long hot bath.

Sidney Grice was mashing a boiled onion, though it did not take much effort. I helped myself from the domed dish in the middle of the table and sat opposite him.

'You have a choice.' He did not look up from dusting his mush in white pepper. 'You can destroy yourself and, if you do, you will never recover.'

'How can I ever forgive myself for what I have done?' I picked up my fork for lack of anything else to hold on to.

'And I am the one you portray as arrogant.' He sowed his dinner with salt.

'I do not understand.' I put my fork down.

'Who are you to forgive yourself for what has happened?' He banged the cellar on the tabletop. 'It is for the injured and, perhaps, the God you believe in to forgive.' He slipped his napkin out of its bone ring. 'I shall continue my proposal with the alternative.' He tucked the napkin into the top of his waistcoat. 'You can destroy the man who murdered them.'

'Can I?'

Sidney Grice formed his food into an exact square before he replied. 'With my help, you can do it or die in the attempt.' He rotated his plate forty-five degrees. 'Either way should atone for your mistakes.'

'Is that all they were?' I asked wretchedly.

'Your plan was defective.' He filled his tumbler. 'But your motives were immaculate.' He raised his glass and looked at me through it. 'And our net is ever tightening.'

'Is it?' I asked hopelessly. 'Is it really?'

'We have hold of one rope each, March.' He closed his fist. 'Will you be the one to let go and set him free?'

I did not reply for we both knew the answer to that.

73

The Secret and the Shame

SIDNEY GRICE HAD gone to see Mr Jones/Chang, who wished to speak to him alone, and so I went to the Empress Cafe. I needed the small comfort of their chocolate cake, and the waitress was just showing me to a table when I spotted a familiar shape with her back to me, her green veil pulled up.

'Good morning, Freddy. I thought it was you.'

Freddy had clearly had the same idea as me, for her plate was scattered with dark crumbs. She had also beaten me to another of my plans and was sucking on a cigarette, her third, to judge from the ashtray at her side.

'March.' She smiled. 'Do join me. Has Mr Grice given you leave or are you playing truant?'

'The latter.' I sat to face her.

I gave my order just in time to get the last slice, and Freddy asked for another pot of coffee.

'Is Lucy not with you?'

'It would have been Eric's birthday today,' Freddy told me. 'She is visiting his grave.' Her left eye was dry and more inflamed than usual from her not being able to close it fully.

'You do not go with her?'

Freddy stubbed out her cigarette. 'She prefers to be alone. They were very close.'

I looked at Freddy, her expression so open and giving every appearance of being pleased to see me. Could she really be such an accomplished actress to have so deluded me? The Freddy that I knew loved her friend. And I found it almost impossible to believe that she would have maliciously burned her own house down with her parents and servants still inside. We all write things in our diaries that we regret as we get older. I decided not to bring the topic up.

'How is Lucy?' I did not mention that we had seen her for ourselves.

'She is well.'

There was a hesitancy in her reply that I could not ignore. 'Is something wrong?' I gave her one of my Turkish and struck a safety match.

'She seems very low in spirits lately. I do not know why.' Freddy blew smoke across the table over my head. 'But she has hardly spoken to me since Monday.'

'Does she get such moods often?'

Freddy shook her head sadly. 'Not even after the attack.'

There was a crash and I looked up, and Freddy turned round.

'Oh, Mummy,' a little boy cried. 'A monster.'

The mother shushed him but it was clear that she too was shaken.

'I shall never get used to that,' Freddy said softly.

'Is there no kind of cosmetic paint you could try?' I asked.

'To mask my ugliness?' Freddy hissed, but instantly reached out to touch my arm. 'I am sorry. I know you mean well.' She breathed in. 'Mrs Bocking took me to the New Royalty Theatre once and got Ellen Terry herself to show me how to apply greasepaint. But what looks natural under the glare of the limes looks garish in the daylight, besides which, it irritated my raw skin.'

'How strange,' I said. 'When we were in the library I glimpsed your profile and thought it very like hers.'

'People used to say I could be her daughter.' Freddy bowed her head. 'What a stupid woman I am to dwell on that.'

The waitress returned with our order and hesitated.

'Yes?' I asked.

She cleared her throat. 'The manager sends his compliments,' she began sheepishly. 'But he wonders if madam would mind...' she coughed again, 'lowering her veil.'

Freddy put a hand up, clearly used to such requests, but I half-rose and touched her wrist.

'Kindly send my regards to the manager,' I instructed, 'and tell him he had better start pretending to be a man and ask madam himself.'

'Yes, miss.' The waitress blushed and bent to take Freddy's used crockery. 'He made me say it.'

'I know.' Freddy lifted her veil back again and, when the waitress had gone to relay my message, added, 'It is easier to comply.'

'You do not strike me as a woman who does things the easy way.' I sat back.

'That much is true.' Freddy smiled lopsidedly.

'Is it very sore?' I asked.

'Very,' she said, 'but I could live with that.' She delved in her handbag. 'Do you know what is really painful, March?' And she brought out a green handkerchief to dab her eyes. 'It is knowing I am so hideous that I once terrified three hardened criminals on their own street at night.' Freddy blew her nose. 'It is seeing you kiss Lucy every time you see her but being too repulsed to kiss me.'

'Oh, Freddy.' I put a hand to my mouth. 'It is not that at all. I am always frightened of hurting you.'

Freddy threw her handkerchief back into her bag. 'Can you think of a better way to do so?'

I was so overcome with shame I hardly knew what to say. I said, 'Can I kiss you now?'

'No,' she said. 'It would have been forced from you.'

'I swear that was the only reason,' I vowed, and Freddy nodded.

'I believe you are different from the others. I see the way you look at me and how Mr Grice does too.' She clipped her bag shut. 'He is a horrible man but he meets my gaze without a shudder.'

'Perhaps one day you will meet a man who will love you for who you are.'

'And what a great catch he would be,' Freddy said mockingly. 'To settle for a woman who is ugly and poor.'

'Do not say that,' I said urgently. 'The more I know you, the more I see you for what you are – a fine, brave, loyal woman.'

'Men do not seek to marry *brave* women,' she told me.

Behind her, near the door, I could see the manager gesticulating angrily at the waitress.

Freddy said, 'Can I tell you a great secret?'

'If you are going to confess to a crime,' I warned, 'I cannot promise to keep it a secret.'

Freddy sucked her lower lip. 'I believe that this would only be a crime if I failed.'

'Go on.' I leaned towards her.

'Attempted suicide is an offence,' she told me. 'To succeed is not. I have on me the means to do it here and now.'

It flashed through my mind that Freddy might produce a knife or razor or a gun, but then I saw her touch the amulet that hung around her neck. I had taken it for a perfume bottle.

'Poison?' I mouthed, and Freddy's lips said, 'Cyanide.'

'Why?'

'How happy do you think my life is?'

I leaned back. 'Why are you telling me?' I asked. 'To make me feel guilty if you do it?'

'Because I wanted to know how it sounded,' she said.

'To me or you?'

'To me mainly.' Freddy looked lost. 'When I was in that den, I knew more than anything that I wanted Lucy to live, but I was not so sure about myself.' She plucked at her collar. 'Sometimes when I go to bed I pray that I shall not wake up.'

'I said that same prayer for years,' I admitted for the first time. 'My fiancé died in great pain because of me. And then, when I thought I never could, I fell in love with a man who would not have me. Do you think scars are easier to bear because nobody sees them?'

It seemed hypocritical, but I could not rub salt in her wounds by telling her how George had come back to me.

'And now?' Freddy touched my hand.

'There is a man out there performing monstrous deeds and I believe I can help to stop him.'

'Then you have a reason to live.' Freddy dabbed the outer corner of her eye.

'Do you think Lucy has not suffered enough?' I asked. 'Should she also lose her one true friend?' I saw Freddy waver. 'I watched a man die from cyanide poisoning,' I pressed on, 'and it was horrible. He had seizures and a heart attack and his lungs filled with fluid and he choked to death.'

'Really?' Freddy looked shocked. 'I thought you just fell asleep.'

'You drown inside yourself,' I said, 'in agony.'

'Honestly?' Freddy looked at me long and hard. 'I shall throw it away,' she decided.

'It is too dangerous,' I said. 'Give it to me and I will take it to the chemistry department at the university.'

Freddy unclipped the chain. 'I have sometimes worried what would happen if the glass broke.'

I wrapped it in my handkerchief and put it in a side pocket in my handbag and stood up. 'Now you will never have to find out.'

'You have not eaten your cake.'

'I have lost my appetite.'

I left payment on the table and marched straight up to the manager. He viewed me edgily. 'I trust everything was to madam's satisfaction.'

'No, everything was not to my satisfaction,' I said, much too loudly, and was gratified by the hush my words produced. 'There is a cockroach in this cafe.' And several squeaks of dismay from my audience served to reward me.

I am not very good at swishing out of places as a rule. I catch my heel or snag my dress or trip over my feet. But I did a swish that day which would have done credit to Sarah Bernhardt. My only regret is that nobody noticed. They were too fascinated by Freddy pushing my chocolate cake into the manager's face.

*

Back on the street Freddy grinned and said, 'I rather enjoyed that.'

'And you would have missed it if you were dead.'

She looked down. 'When this is all over—' She broke off and tried again. 'Have you ever stayed friends with a client?'

'Never,' I assured her and her face fell. 'But it is about time I did.' I took both her hands. 'But you have to stay alive for that.'

She forced a smile. 'I will try.'

'Succeed,' I said in my best Gricean manner, and Freddy laughed.

Then almost as quickly her eyes filled with tears and she pulled her hands free, but only to fling her arms round me. 'It is hard, March.' She trembled. 'So hard.'

And I knew that there was nothing I could say to make it easier. 'Too many women have died for nothing.' I leaned forward and kissed her. 'Do not become one of them, Freddy.'

And I turned and ran until I could not catch my breath. Detectives do not sob their hearts out in front of their clients.

74

The Painted Suns

SIDNEY GRICE WAS unusually cheery over dinner that evening, humming what might have ben a tune once as he browsed a crisp new copy of Stringwater's *Illustrated History of Clog Fighting*.

'How was your trip to Limehouse?' I asked.

Cook had roasted some vegetables for a change and, with great quantities of salt and pepper, they were almost worth eating.

My guardian dusted his carrots with mustard powder. 'I managed to persuade Mr Jones/Chang Foo that talking to me was preferable to a visit from Inspector Pound, who has gained an unfortunate reputation for being incorruptible.'

Spirit sprang into the chair next to his.

'Unfortunate?'

'Nobody believes in reputations any more,' he said, in what sounded like the start of a witty aphorism but never became one.

'And did Mr Jones tell you anything useful?'

'Indeed,' he agreed readily. 'He told me there is a clipper with a consignment of high-quality Assam tea waiting to dock in the morning.'

'And did he happen to mention anything relevant about Lucy Bocking?'

'He told me one thing.' He poked a toothpick in the hole of his salt cellar and blew. 'That while she was being assaulted she cried out, *Stop it, you fool.*'

'Was he in the room then?' I asked, and my guardian exchanged patient glances with Spirit.

'I thought it was so obvious that I did not trouble to mention it,' he explained. 'The inkwell Jones peered into is a periscope. When I dropped so elegantly to the floor during our first visit, I saw that there was a pipe leading from it through the ceiling. It also acts as a hearing tube.'

'Into one of those painted suns,' I guessed.

'You are guessing,' he complained.

'No, I am not.'

'Nonetheless you are correct.' He trickled vinegar on to his potatoes.

'So Mr Jones not only permits women to be attacked on his premises,' I deduced. 'He likes to watch.'

'We all like to watch.' Mr G folded the bottom corner of a page down and, before I could express my distaste at his remark, continued, 'It is what we like to watch that differentiates some of us from beasts or stockbrokers.'

'Why, when you insist that food should be tasteless, do you always use so many condiments?' I poured myself some water.

'Food should not have flavour.' He dipped a spoon into the horseradish. 'But flavourings, by definition, should. I have received,' he slipped an envelope out from under the tablecloth, 'a very civil letter from St Philomena's Convent, outlining all the holy works they perform. If you would care to peruse it, I can place it upon my Tableware Transference Device and convey it to you in twenty-three seconds.'

'No, thank you.'

Mr G pouted at this lost opportunity to play with his new toy – a continuous belt of thin wooden slats running the length of the table and powered by a foot pedal.

'The Mother Superior leaves me with no reasonable doubt that they would appreciate a donation and the larger the better.'

Molly was tramping up the stairs.

'Then they must be happy that you offered one.'

Sidney Grice greeted my statement blankly. 'You appear to have mistaken my enquiry as to whether they would welcome a donation for an intent to give them one.' He turned the page over. 'And so apparently has the Reverend Mother Mary Peter, who has offered to say prayers for my soul, though I am not sure—' he refolded the letter and placed it tantalizingly upon the transference belt—'what gave her the impression that I had one.'

'The fact that you are human?' I remained untantalized.

'Am I?'

Molly burst in and Spirit jumped.

'Why are you here?' Sidney Grice snapped.

'I've come to clear,' Molly announced.

'But we have not finished eating,' I told her, before her employer could give her the same information more aggressively.

'What?' She pulled her neck back incredulously. 'Cook didntn't not never think you'd eat any of that.'

And two storeys below us the doorbell rang.

75

Blood in the Brandy

T HE BELL RANG three times before Molly got to the front door and I followed at her heels for its summons sounded urgent. George Pound stood on the steps.

'Yes?' Molly demanded.

'I am on my way to the Midland,' he announced over her head, 'and I thought you and Mr Grice might want to be there.'

'Oh, I aintn't not got no time for that.' Molly sighed. 'Take Miss Middleton instead.'

I wished he could – I wished he would take me in his arms there and then, and I could tell him how happy I was to see him and all about my silly premonition, but I took my bonnet calmly off the table while Mr G donned his soft felt hat.

'Prince Ulrich?' I asked. 'Are you arresting him?'

The inspector rushed back to his waiting Black Maria. 'Bit late for that,' he called as we hastened to join him. 'We've just had a report that Schlangezahn has been murdered.'

'Oh, what a pity.' Mr G pushed past me into the back of the van, where five uniformed policemen were already seated. 'I have selected the wrong cane.'

And I barely had time to squeeze on to the bench beside three men who were cursed by an inability to sit with their knees less than two feet apart, before George Pound slammed the door shut and went to join the driver up at the front.

'What's that whistling?' A sergeant twitched his nose to sniff out the source of the noise, which I would have described as more of a high-pitched whine.

'If you are referring to the musical tone, it emanates from my Grice Patent Canine Sonar Repellent Device,' Mr G divulged haughtily.

The constable opposite me gawked. 'You what?'

'It should be playing a note undetectable by the human ear, which dogs find distressing.'

'I'm not enjoying it much myself,' I confessed.

'The pitch is supposed to be one and three-quarter octaves higher.' Mr G twiddled the handle and the volume increased.

'Can't you turn it off?' The sergeant wiggled a finger in his ear.

'I am endeavouring to do so.' He twisted it three half-revolutions clockwise. 'But the valve appears to have jammed.'

'Oh good.' A constable clamped his hands to the sides of his head.

The noise grew louder and began to warble.

'Dash it.' Sidney Grice banged the handle on the floor and I looked ahead innocently. I did not like to tell my guardian that Molly had taken it upon herself to use some of his sticks to fish laundry out of the copper, and I had helped her to dry them and put them back in the rack before he came home.

Ten jostling, bruising minutes later we were there, Mr G waving his stick so vigorously to discourage two collies that came prancing over to greet him that he caught a young lady under the chin. 'Both our evenings would be much improved if you would take more care and make less noise,' he advised above her howls.

The cane clicked and she and it fell mercifully silent.

Shooting from the Hip

THE ENTRANCE TO the Midland Grand Hotel was guarded by two doormen, supplemented by a constable. A man in a frock coat hurried across the strangely deserted lobby to greet us.

'Cecil Simms, the under-manager,' he introduced himself. 'I am afraid the manager is away this evening.'

'Did he elope with a smoking gun?' Mr G asked hopefully, and Simms flapped.

'Indeed not, sir.'

'Why a gun?' Pound asked.

'If you quit your habit of setting fire to tobacco, you might be able to detect it too.' Sidney Grice swept past. 'Plus the aroma of burning wool and singed flesh.'

I inhaled and thought I smelled something.

Two Prussian soldiers stepped aside at the sight of Inspector Pound's warrant card to let us pass into the anteroom where not so very long ago I had sampled a sparkling Riesling. The smell of cordite was strong now and as Pound turned to his left I saw the body.

The prince was on the same sofa from which he had toasted me a few nights ago, but he did not look so magnificent now. Ulrich Schlangezahn was slumped back, mouth agape. There were three bloodstains on his Prussian blue coat and the golden epaulette on his right shoulder had been torn apart – by a fourth bullet, I decided.

Sidney Grice strolled to the back of the sofa. 'Two of the bullets went completely through.' He indicated with his stick the splintered holes in the mahogany wainscoting.

'Whoever it was must have taken him by surprise.' Pound slid a partly smoked cigar out of the dead man's right hand. Ulrich's trousers were starting to smoulder and the skin of his thigh to char. His air gun was propped untouched against the seat cushion. Pound sniffed and asked me, 'Can you smell perfume?'

'He wore an eau de Cologne.' I looked into those blind, staring eyes.

The sergeant tutted. 'Not very manly.'

'But preferable to the stink of stale sweat,' I muttered, having had a throat-full of that in the confines of the van.

'There is a second, more feminine perfume,' Mr G announced before a fight broke out.

George Pound walked behind the sofa, poked his finger into the holes in the panelling, paced back again and crouched before the body. He dabbed at the coat and sniffed his finger.

'A woman,' the sergeant deduced cleverly.

'A small one, I'll wager,' George pronounced. 'His coat is covered in gunpowder so the gun was fired at very close range. There is not room between sofa and this coffee table to kneel, or space on the table to sit on it.' A tumbler of brandy sat untouched apart from the gore splattered over the cut glass and into the spirit. There was still a soda syphon waiting to be used. 'So somebody stood directly in front of him. The entrance and exit wounds are almost in a line parallel to the floor, so she did not tower over the deceased, even though he was seated, and,' he pointed to the pool of blood on the floor, 'you can see five small footprints leading away.' He looked about. 'So a short woman who will be covered in burnt cordite and blood.'

'The presence of a lady's perfume in a room does not mean

that she was here when the shots were fired, or even that she has ever been in here at all.' Sidney Grice opened the double doors a fraction, peeped into the private dining room and inhaled.

'Somebody could have sprayed the scent, I suppose,' I conceded, reluctant to see George Pound's diagnosis so easily dismissed.

'Also, some people shoot from hip level.' Mr G kept his back to us all. 'Especially those fortunate enough to have escaped the occidental regions of the temporarily United States of America. But,' he slid his palms upwards from the handles, 'I would think it prudent to ask what information the short lady, who wears that perfume and is liberally adorned in gore and cordite, possesses about Prince Ulrich's death.'

George Pound and I glanced at each other. Sidney Grice bunched his arms and flung the doors apart.

Wisporia Wright sat facing us across the table, in deepest mourning, her black veil up and her face, as the inspector had predicted, splattered in fresh blood.

77

The Executioner

I WAS SO taken aback by this revelation that I hardly noticed the man standing behind Mrs Wright, gripping her shoulder. I recognized him at once, though, as the red-headed man in the long maroon cloak who I had seen at the Golden Dragon the night that Peter and I entrapped Prince Ulrich. The man was struggling hard to keep his expression blank, but the muscles of his face were bunching and unbunching continuously.

'Rittmeister Heidrick Hildebrand.' He introduced himself with a stiff bow of the head. 'I am Prince Ulrich's aide.'

'*Was*,' Sidney Grice corrected him.

Wisporia Wright had both hands resting open on the stained white cloth. 'Mr Grice.' She spoke steadily and clearly. 'And Miss Middleton. As you can see, I have done your job for you.'

I stared at her in shock. 'You killed him?'

'With that.' She waved the back of her hand towards a little double-barrelled handgun, a Remington Derringer, lying like a visiting card on a silver tray in the middle of the table.

Hildebrand tightened his grip and, from a contraction in his mouth, he would have preferred it to be round her neck.

George made a calming motion with his hand. 'I am Inspector Pound of the Metropolitan Police.' He showed his card.

'We bought it for Albertoria,' she continued, as if he had rudely interrupted her anecdote at a soirée. 'But she refused to carry it. If she had,' Mrs Wright reflected, 'she might have done the job herself, and saved her father and myself a great deal of upset.' From the way she carped, Albertoria might have been refusing to practise the piano.

'Let us be quite clear about this.' Inspector Pound walked round to her side. 'Are you confessing to murdering Prince Ulrich?'

Wisporia Wright tinkled with polite amusement. 'Oh no, Inspector. I have not murdered anybody. I executed him.'

I saw the aide's free hand go back, but George Pound put out his arm to guard his prisoner's face.

'Come with me,' the inspector said and took her by the arm.

'I always imagined that he would look evil until the inquest,' she chattered as she let him guide her away. 'But he was a handsome devil and tonight he was so charming, you would not have thought he needed to stoop so low.'

'Give me ein minute mit her,' Hildebrand snarled, but the door closed behind them. He grasped the back of his chair and brought himself back under control. 'The finest man I ever met,' he said.

'Quite possibly.' Sidney Grice went to the sideboard and poured a large brandy. 'Drink that, Rittmeister Hildebrand, and then we can talk.'

78

The Hunter of Men

THE PRUSSIAN DID as he was bid, taking his drink in quick gulps as I had seen some Cossacks do with vodka once.

'Prince Ulrich Schlangezahn never raped a voman in his life,' he began without prompting. 'As even *she*,' he almost vomited the last word, 'said, he never needed to. Zu prince voz being vott you vould call a vomanizer. He made a sport of seducing them and daring zer husbands, brothers, fathers to challenge him to duels. Most knew his reputation too vell but some took up zu challenge. The prince voz one of zu best swordsmen and shooters in zu Imperial Army. He never lost but he never killed a man, just vounded them.'

'Well, that is all right then,' I muttered acidly, but the aide hardly noticed.

'He voz not alone in this behaviour. A lot of his fellows did zu same and vorse. Zen Gerda, his younger sister, voz attacked or seduced – it is not for sure vich – in London. She killed herself. The authorities let it be said zat it voz... I do not know the English vord.'

'Cholera,' I told him.

'Zo.' He nodded. 'You are knowing zis much.' He toyed with his glass.

'Would you like another?' I asked.

'Vy not?'

I got up. There were low voices and heavy noises coming from the antechamber.

'Prince Ulrich changed. You have an expression about stealers of rabbits changing sides.'

'Poacher turned gamekeeper,' I proffered.

'Just zo,' he agreed. 'He hunted zees men down. Every night he is going round the East End and Limehouse looking for zem, sometimes viv us but mostly alone. It becomes his obsession.'

'Did he kill Johnny Wallace?' I asked.

'Viv his Vindbusche,' Hildebrand confirmed. 'And zer was a man he drowned in a rain barrel last year. The police thought zat was a drunken accident.'

'Camford Berrick?' My guardian clipped on his pince-nez to examine nothing, as far as I could see.

'I am thinking that voz his name.'

This was all a bit too cosy for me. 'What about Albertoria Wright?' I demanded. 'Your fine prince was seen trying to drag her away.'

'To save her from zat place,' Hildebrand told me. 'He could see she voz young and... vulnerable.'

'Then why did he not say that at her inquest?' I banged the table.

'He vould not lie.' The rittmeister looked up at me. 'Voz he to tell the parents zer daughter voz behavink as a whore? Alzo,' he took another drink, 'he vanted his reputation to be bad so ze real procurers vould trust him.'

I had one last go. 'He tried to rape me.'

Hildebrand closed his eyes wearily. 'Prince Ulrich thought your man waz vot he postured to be and voz trying to entrap him.' His voice shook. 'Even his murderess. She voz coming asking for help and he voz trying to give it.' The aide finished his drink. 'And now you vill excuse me. Zer is much to arrange.' He stood up. 'Prince Ulrich held you in high esteem, Mr Grice.'

He clicked his heels.

'And I he,' Sidney Grice said. 'It is because of men like him that – in the next war – our two countries will unite, as they did at Waterloo, and crush those foppish rascals the French once and for all.'

Heidrick Hildebrand saluted my godfather and made a clipped bow to me, and went back into the antechamber to tend to his master.

The Death of Hope and the Deepest Cut

GERALDINE HOCKADAY HAD been taken to the Royal London Ophthalmic Hospital in Lower Moorfields, but, other than removing the infected remains of her left eye and dressing the wounds, there was nothing they could do for her. She was taken to University College Hospital to be closer to her family home, but her parents did not avail themselves of that convenience.

I paid her a visit.

Geraldine's eyes were bandaged but, more surprisingly, so was her left arm and both wrists were tied to the sides of the bedframe. She had slashed herself with a broken glass, the matron – a tall woman with a severe face but a kindly manner – had explained.

Geraldine jumped when I approached.

'It is me, March.' I sat beside her.

'Oh, March. I had a dreadful visitor today, an Inspector Quigley.'

'He is a horrible man,' I agreed. 'But what did he want?'

Geraldine twisted her head in a sweeping circle.

'Would you like some more medicine?' the matron asked, but I do not know if her patient even heard her.

'He told me that attempted suicide was a criminal offence punishable by prison and that I should not survive long in there.'

'I am sure any judge, when he knows what you have been through, would not want to punish you any further.'

Something metallic clattered to the floor and she let out a cry.

'But he said it would be different if I cooperated and told him the name of Peter's customers.' She threw her head back so hard I thought she would rick her neck. 'I told and told and told him that Peter was not like that, but he would not believe me. And then he said not to worry about prison because he had got two doctors to certify that I was insane, and that I should be put in a madhouse and kept in a straitjacket for the rest of my life.'

'He does have a certificate,' Matron confirmed quietly, 'and they are coming back this afternoon.'

She went to settle a girl who was weeping noisily.

'I shall see what we can do to fight it,' I promised, but without much hope, for even Sidney Grice with all his ingenuity and powerful contacts had not been able to keep me out of an asylum.

'I should have cut deeper,' she whispered.

'Do you think Peter would want that?'

'He is the only person who will be pleased to see me.'

'He wanted you to live again,' I argued.

'For what?'

'I have a friend who was a beautiful child,' I said, 'but her parents were killed and she was badly disfigured in a fire.'

'Is that supposed to make me feel better?'

I remembered her fears just in time to stop myself touching her hand. 'For many years she thought she had nothing to live for and kept the means to kill herself.'

'Was she violated?' Geraldine squirmed.

'No, but she was forced to witness her friend being attacked and she is in constant pain.'

'Is this one of these stories children are told about other people being worse off?' She squirmed. 'Oh hell, March, I cannot even cry.'

I forgot Geraldine's fear and took her hand, and she must have forgotten too for she curled her tiny fingers around mine.

'How did your friend plan to do it?'

'She carried an amulet filled with cyanide,' I replied.

'Oh.' Geraldine made a sour face. 'That is a horrible way to die. I read about it in your story.'

'She gave it to me to get rid of,' I told her. 'Because she realized that she wanted to live.'

Geraldine writhed and arched and let out a sob. 'It comes in stabs,' she cried and banged her head up and down on the pillow. 'Oh, Daddy, it hurts so much.'

A nurse hurried over and gave her an injection and, almost immediately, Geraldine settled down.

'When I was a child and my daddy loved me – no, do not tell me that he still does – he used to tell me stories every night. "The Firefly" was my favourite.'

'I do not know that one,' I said, but she was already asleep.

*

'We cannot keep her like this forever,' the matron confided. 'The effects of the opium are wearing off quicker and she needs bigger doses – too big. Much more will kill her.'

'Would that be such a bad thing?'

The matron crossed her arms tightly. 'I entered this profession to save lives, not to take them.'

'I am sorry.'

She relaxed her arms. 'The Lord will take her when he is ready.'

'I hope he does not wait too long then,' I said, and I do not think she had it in her heart to disagree.

*

For perhaps half an hour Geraldine slept peacefully, but all too soon she awoke with a jolt, already whimpering in pain. Matron was attending to a young woman who was vomiting blood across the aisle.

'You remember what you told me about your friend with her amulet and how it brought her good luck?' Geraldine asked. 'Do you still have it?'

'Yes,' I answered warily.

'I could do with some luck,' she said blandly.

'Are you sure?'

'It is my only hope.' She put her free hand on top of mine. 'Don't let them do it to me, March.'

'We can fight it,' I tried again.

'And if we fail?' Geraldine asked simply. 'And, even if we win, what is there for me now?'

I reached into my bag. 'There is a screw cap on top.' I put it into her upturned palm.

'Like a watch crown? I feel it.'

'Geraldine...' I tried one last time, but I was too tired.

'God bless you, March,' she said. 'You can leave me now.'

I kissed her goodbye, and knew God would not bless me for that day's work. I doubted that he would ever bless me again.

80

The Head of the Hound

THERE WAS A flat parcel at the bottom of the pile and Mr G opened it first, cutting the string with his cord-knife, carved from the femur of Marchioness Froughsborough, recovered from the gibbet by one of her acolytes. He peeled back the thick brown paper and lifted out a white letter bearing a gold and red crest of a shield topped by the head of a greyhound and subtitled with a blue scroll bearing the words *DEO DANTE DEDI*.

'Charterhouse School,' he informed me, letting the letter skim through the air to alight face-up on the green leather seat of his swivel chair.

There was a second parcel inside the main one and my god-father unwrapped it, smoothing the creases from each of the five layers of paper as he went along, eventually uncovering a photograph in a frame. 'They cannot think I would want to hang it on my wall,' he grumbled, lifting it out and laying it under his desk lamp.

I peered over. It was the image of a youth in a dark blazer and light, baggy trousers and a white shirt, the collar so wide that it overlapped his lapels. A peaked cap cast a flimsy veil of shadow over his eyes.

'Eric C. Bocking,' I read from the tiny brass plaque on the mahogany frame. 'Charterhouse School Middleweight Boxing Champion 1876.' Eric had his chin up and was holding a trophy, about the size of a silver eggcup, in both hands at chest level. 'Oh,' I said.

'There is more eloquence in that syllable than in half an hour of your usual babble,' my guardian told me. 'For once I would like your silly female opinion.'

'I am only sorry that I do not have one with which to oblige you,' I sniped. 'But, if you would like a reasoned feminine judgement, he is not at all what I expected. Lucy said he was beautiful. It may be a bad photograph and I do not like to be unkind, but this boy is distinctly ugly.'

I picked up his second favourite magnifying glass and took a longer look, but could find no reason to revise my opinion. Though he was sturdily built, Eric Bocking's face was not attractive. His nose, arising from between small round eyes, curved sigmoidally towards a snubbed tip with upturned nostrils over thin lips, parted in an arrogant smirk to reveal two upper central incisors severely splayed and twisted.

'Not plain then?' my godfather checked.

'Not even in a bad light,' I said guiltily, for I had endured enough barbs about my own looks not to wish to insult another's. 'No wonder Freddy did not encourage him.'

'Age him,' Sidney Grice suggested, taking the glass off me and substituting his third choice. 'Give him a hard life and a poor diet. Take off his cap and dress him in shabby clothes.'

I screwed up my eyes and tried to imagine a greying of the pallid complexion, a drooping of the mouth, some bagging below those haughty piglet eyes.

'Who have you now?' Mr G urged.

'It cannot be.' I lowered the lens and the image jumped out at me, leering horribly from under that cap. 'Johnny "the Walrus" Wallace.'

'Indeed.' And Sidney Grice prised the handle of his magnifying glass from my fingers as if I were a corpse. His fingers, I noticed, were as cold as if he were one himself.

81

The Death of Captain Bligh

I WAS RUNNING short of cigarettes and W. Twiggs, the tobacconist's shop, was having a half-day, so I rushed up Gower Street and just managed to catch Mr T before he turned the *Open* sign round in the front window.

Sidney Grice was coming down the stairs as I unclipped my cloak and hung it up.

'You have been running.' He aimed an accusatory finger. It did not take a detective to observe that I was still out of breath. 'Ladies never run.'

'Not even if they are being chased?' I unpinned my bonnet.

'Ladies are *never* chased.'

'Perhaps you should tell the gentlemen that,' I suggested.

Molly came, dragging a bucket and smearing the floor with a string mop. 'Oh, miss.' She slopped dirty water over my boots. 'I could have helped you with that.'

Molly grasped my hat with soapsuddy hands, crushing the silk marigolds on the side, and rammed it back on my head.

'No,' I started to explain, but Molly was saying, 'There you are, sir.' And she handed her employer a stick. 'Is that the one that turns into a stepping ladderer?'

'Leave my things alone.' Mr G snatched it from her.

'What, all your things, sir?' Molly grinned dreamily. 'What, not touch your cups and sorcerers, your food plates, your dusty furniture and screwned-up newspapers? Oh...' She clasped her

hands ecstatically. 'What a life of bridled pleasure I shall have.'
Her face fell. 'Only I dontn't not much like pleasure... much.'

'I do not think you will be overburdened with it in the near
future,' I forecast, as Sidney Grice's expression changed from
grumpy to very grumpy.

I gave up trying to uncrease the orange petals.

'Oh.' Molly flung my cloak into my arms. 'I dontn't not
know if you rememberer, miss.' She selected another walking
stick but her employer whipped it away. ''Cause your remem-
bory aintn't not much good,' Molly went on. 'But when I said I'd
had swallowed a live mouse...' She slapped her bosom so hard
that I winced. 'I couldntn't not have, could I?' She cackled, grabbing Mr G's hat off the stand so violently that she dented the
crown. 'Silly me.'

'Well, it is not very likely.' I checked my hair in the mirror
and decided it did not look too bad by my standards today. I had
pinned it up a bit higher and thought it suited me.

'No,' she cackled. ''Cause Cook explainered it. A mouse is
much too small to swallow. It must have been a rat.'

'At last, a brain inside you.' Sidney Grice inspected his cane
suspiciously.

'What brain, sir?' Molly put a hand up to try to hide the
damage.

He sighed. 'The rat.'

'Oh no, sir,' Molly explained patiently. 'It was me who swallowed it, not Miss Middleton.'

She made a grab for another stick and he slapped her hand
away.

'Tea, please, Molly,' I said, before it occurred to her to slap
him back. Molly scowled because she had been enjoying the
game and my guardian scowled because I had said *please*.

'Somebody has been polishing my canes,' he announced icily.

'That was Miss Middleton, sir,' Molly put in quickly. 'I tried
to stopper her. I begged on blended knees.'

'Humph.' Mr G grumbled. And I took the blame because she would have been in much bigger trouble than I, though I could not help but conjecture that Molly had not just swallowed a rat, she had become one.

*

I had my first cup of tea wordlessly, while Sidney Grice made some urgent notes at his desk then sorted through the rest of his mail, ripping and screwing up and hurling almost all of it away until, with a loud *rhyrrhh*, he threw himself into his chair.

I poured his drink and topped up mine. 'I was just thinking.'

'Nobody *just* thinks.' He stirred his tea vigorously. 'They do at least forty-three other significant things simultaneously. Shall I enumerate?'

'No.' I tickled Spirit's ear as she promenaded past me. 'I was thinking how fortunate it is – and I am not sure that it can just be good luck – that none of the women who were violated is with child.'

Mr G stopped stirring. 'Not one,' he agreed carefully.

'I would not have thought he would be considerate enough to use French—'

'Indeed,' my guardian interrupted, still capable of being shocked at the things I knew. He leaned back, untouched tea swirling around the handle of his spoon, while he braced himself for what he was about to articulate. 'Come now, March,' he chivvied. 'Finish your sentence. You cannot afford to be priggish in cases like these.'

'Letters,' I said, and he hurrumphed.

'Quite so.'

And I had a strange feeling that in one field at least I might be less squeamish than he.

'Expound twelve major causes of women not conceiving during congress.' He took an avid interest in his watch.

'The woman may be too young or too old,' I began. 'She may

be infertile. It is believed that women are more fecund at certain times of the month.'

My guardian looked as if the milk he never consumed were sour, but I continued. 'She may already be with child or only just have had one. She may be congenitally barren or have had an infection.'

'We do not need to dwell on the nature of that,' he assured me hastily.

'How many is that?' I asked.

'Eight.'

'Is that all?' I racked my brains and remembered that, despite what men like to believe, it was not always the woman's fault. 'The man may have had an infection such as mumps or be congenitally barren. He may be incapable of,' I struggled to find the right words, 'spilling his seed.'

'One more.' Sidney Grice looked distinctly green.

'He may have no seed to spill,' I ended, to his undisguised relief.

'Let us consider that last proposal first.' He stretched forward to paddle his tea again – six times in each direction. 'Since you are invariably slow to say something relevant. Why would a man have no seed?'

'He could be a eunuch in a harem,' I suggested weakly, 'or a castrato in the Sistine Chapel, or have had an accident. Or sometimes men are castrated for medical reasons.'

Sidney Grice rose like a man in a dream and sleepwalked round his desk to his cabinets. He pulled open a top drawer and plunged his hand in, apparently randomly like a child at a lucky dip, but withdrawing the file he sought in his first attempt.

'We simply must,' he declared, raising the brown envelope high above his head, 'and we must do it now.' He waved the envelope triumphantly. 'Pay a visit to Captain Bligh.'

'I have some bad news for you.' I put down my cup. 'Captain Bligh is dead.'

'What?' Sidney Grice slapped the file down on to his desk. 'Dead? Do not tell me he is dead – although you have already done so. Dead when, where and how and why, and why was I not informed?'

'I think about seventy years ago,' I hazarded. 'I do not know what he died of, but I thought everybody knew.'

Sidney Grice clapped a hand to his head. 'You must have been mixing with Molly too long to have become so obtuse,' he said kindly, 'to imagine, even for one dull-witted moment that I was referring to Captain, later Vice Admiral of the Blue, William Bligh FRS RN, who died, incidentally, on Sunday 7 December 1817, sorely missed – though not, I suspect, by the naughty crew members of His Majesty's armed vessel *Bounty*.' He threw himself back in his chair. 'I am of course – and you will feel almost as stupid as you are when I rectify your misunderstanding – referring to Mr Captain Bligh, the retired General Surgeon of Great Russell Street.'

'Why was he called that?'

'It is his patronym.'

'You know full well what I mean.'

'His father was Mr Bligh and a great admirer of his namesake.'

'I see.' I got up, hoping that George would not want to call our firstborn *Ounces*, though I could just about live with *Sterling*.

Sidney Grice clinked his cup with the spoon as if about to make a speech. 'I cannot possibly drink that now,' he complained. 'It is grossly over-stirred.'

And, while he rang three times for his flask, I got up and glanced at his urgent notes. He had sketched a pole with alternating bars hingeing out of the sides. *The Grice Ladder Cane* was printed underneath.

The Mystery of the Missing Bells

T HE BRITISH MUSEUM has been described as the biggest
building site in Europe and they had only finished its
new White Wing a year or so ago, but even then, I had
read, it struggled to house the vast quantities of antiquities
flooding in from every corner of the empire. I am ashamed to
say that I had never troubled to visit it and we had only a
glimpse of the roof today, for Mr Captain Bligh lived in a neat
terraced house at the Bloomsbury Street end of Great Russell
Street, furthest away from Tottenham Court Road.

'I shall answer it,' we heard being called, and the householder
himself responded to my knocks.

Despite being, as my guardian had informed me on the way,
nearly eighty years old, Mr B seemed in robust health, straight-
spined and solidly built, with a florid complexion and a
handshake too strong for my, until recently, pain-free fingers.

'You will take tea?' he offered after the introductions.

'What sort?' Sidney Grice asked suspiciously while wiping
his hand.

'Nepal.' He had a good head of wild peppery hair and whiskers to rival those of an unsheared ram.

'That is acceptable.'

Mr Bligh ushered us into a cosy sitting room with deep armchairs of crumpled leather, and books stacked in multiple
columns and pyramids on the floor.

'I see time has not mellowed you, Mr Grice.'

I smiled. 'Not that I have noticed.'

'Little girls very rarely notice anything beyond the fashion plates.' Mr Bligh rummaged about in his beard.

'I would not know.' I picked up a leather-bound book with gold lettering on the cover. 'Not having socialized with many little girls since I was one myself.'

'When the criminals of this world bask in gentleness and benignity, I might follow suit.' Mr G snatched the book from me.

'I doubt it,' I said, stung by his failure to defend me.

Mr Bligh strode into the hall and boomed out, 'Tea.'

'Is your bell not working?' I asked.

'I do not like bells.' Our host delved back into his whiskers. 'I cannot have one in the house.'

'Why is that?' I asked.

'Because I do not like them,' he said, slowly and indulgently.

Mr G rolled his eye. 'Miss Middleton does not listen.'

'I wondered why you do not like them,' I tried to explain.

'Because I cannot have one in the house.' Mr Bligh was markedly less patient this time. He jumped on to a hefty brown tome to increase his height advantage over us both.

'You will recall, unless you have subsided into senility...' My guardian clipped on his pince-nez and opened the tome. 'The outbreak of scrotal carcinoma at University College Hospital in—'

'Seventy-eight,' Mr Captain Bligh broke in. 'I am not likely to forget that.'

'Unless you have subsided into senility.' Mr G immersed himself in the book.

'Can one of you enlighten me?' I enquired.

'I am not sure,' Mr Bligh replied, 'given your inability to grasp the idea that I do not like bells and cannot have them in the house.'

'Please try.' I resisted the urge to stand on a book myself, as I felt sure I should be scolded if I did.

There were six carriage clocks on the mantle shelf, all ticking, but each set five minutes earlier than the one to its left, the one furthest to the left being about three hours fast.

'They are clocks,' Sidney Grice responded to my puzzled gaze.

'It is a short and simple story and not worth sitting down for.' Mr Bligh jumped off his dais. 'Is that the only reason you have come here?'

'Yes,' Sidney Grice said, before I could concoct an account of having long been anxious to meet the famous surgeon.

'In that case...' Captain Bligh marched back to the hall and bellowed, 'No tea and hurry,' before taking centre-stage again on the hearthrug. 'There was an outbreak of inflamed crusty growths of the scrotums of all our patients in St Agatha Ward. Mr Lamb was in charge and he diagnosed it as carcinoma. An ex-sweep's boy suffered – as they are prone to do – from the affliction and Lamb subscribed to the unpopular theory that certain types of cancers are transmittable and that the only cure was surgical excision before the whole body was affected.'

'Castration,' I clarified.

'Castration,' Mr Bligh clarified for my benefit. 'If you know what that means.'

'I used to help at a farm,' I said and he looked at me pity-ingly.

'And I am sure that you were very good at planting potatoes.'

'It was sheep,' I corrected him, and he sniggered.

'Have some sense, child.' Bligh took his fingers for a walk through his side-whiskers. 'You cannot plant sheep.'

I would not have minded planting him at that moment.

'Whilst we are on the subject of things ovine,' Mr G said urgently, 'would this even more than usually incompetent surgeon Lamb be Mr David Anthony Lamb?'

He pencilled a footnote and turned the page.

'I am not sure about the Anthony.' Mr Bligh wandered to the hearth to rattle the fire irons.

'One can never be sure about Anthonys,' Sidney Grice pronounced sadly.

'Were all the patients emasculated?' I asked, not sure if the conversation was leading anywhere.

'What on earth does she mean?' Bligh grasped the poker like a storybook illustration of a householder confronting a burglar, and I winced for I had been attacked with one of those before and still suffered occasional headaches.

'Perhaps I should rephrase that.' My guardian eyed me reprovingly. 'Miss Middleton was wondering if all the patients were emasculated.'

'All bar the sweep.' Mr Bligh drove the poker into the unlit coals. 'He escaped by climbing out of a window.'

'And what happened to him?' I asked, and Mr Bligh made an *ufff* noise.

'He escaped by climbing out of a window.'

'After that?' I tried again.

'Yes.' He made no attempt to hide his irritation this time. 'After that he escaped by climbing out of a window.'

'Do you know what happened to him subsequent to his escape?' Sidney Grice tore the bottom paragraph off a page and held it up like a manifesto.

Mr Captain Bligh extracted the poker in a decidedly Arthurian manner. 'I would have told you if your idiot girl hadn't kept pestering me to repeat myself. Is she deaf?' He raised his voice. 'Are you deaf?'

'As a dog,' I replied.

'Many dogs have excellent hearing,' he told me.

'Unless they are deaf,' I quipped, uncertain how I had got into this squabble.

'What was the ultimate fate of the sweep?' Mr G asked, and Captain Bligh resheathed his weapon in the stand.

'How in the name of Cosmas, Luke and Damian should I know that?'

'I think you mean *names*,' I muttered.

'But,' Mr Bligh condescended to tell us, 'he was re-diagnosed when he was put into Lister Ward with a fractured pelvis from falling out of the window, as having a bad case of crusted scabies, which – as you, but not your mentally retarded ward, will know – is highly contagious. It transpired that a trainee nurse – who was Irish and a Roman Catholic and therefore afraid of dirty bits – had given all the patients a wash down there.' He pointed as if she had carried out the task in his cellar. 'With the same flannel.'

'And was he cured?' I was almost flattered that he felt no need to explain to me what a flannel was.

'You cannot cure a broken pelvis, which is—'

'The hip bone,' I chipped in.

'The hip bone,' he informed me. 'You just have to hope it heals itself.'

'Did the other patients ever find out about Lamb's mistake?' Mr G replaced the torn-out paper upside down.

'Many did,' Mr Bligh told him. 'It was supposed to be hushed up, but the nurse confessed to anyone who would listen and many who would not. Lord above knows why but she blamed herself.'

'Catholics are trained to feel guilty,' Sidney Grice remarked, 'especially the Hibernians.'

'It is in their blood,' Bligh corrected him.

'You are probably thinking of poteen,' I chipped in to blankness. 'Could you enquire of your friend if any of the patients took legal action?' I asked my guardian, and he did.

'Some of them threatened to sue but they would have got nowhere.' The surgeon grasped his own lapels. 'Goodness me, if a doctor is not allowed to make mistakes, who is?'

'Nobody,' I guessed, and picked up a slender blue volume.

'We are not talking about nobody.' Mr Bligh stamped his foot. 'It is only through making mistakes that medicine makes advances.'

'Not through research and careful observation?' I glanced at the title – *Cheeky Maids Love to be Spanked* – and wondered if Molly would agree, and, seeing that the old surgeon had no intention of responding, asked, 'Where would the records of those cases be kept now?'

Mr G was wiping his hands on a green handkerchief decorated with images of leaping red ponies.

'They would be kept in the hospital records.' Mr Bligh put on a pair of smoked spectacles.

'And are they?' Mr G shook out his handkerchief, making the ponies prance playfully round their field.

'No.'

I glimpsed myself in the surgeon's blanked-out eyes.

'Perhaps, for Miss Middleton's benefit, you could elucidate.' Mr G mopped his forehead, though the room was on the chilly side.

'Very well.' Bligh felt his way forward in a manner similar to my godfather's crossing of the beam in Steep House. 'I shall explain in the simplest possible terms and, in order to hold her fleeting attention, in the style of a brief anecdote.' He bumped into a low, square table, upsetting a pillar of journals. 'After the possibility of a misdiagnosis came to light Mr Lamb took all the patients' medical notes to check through them, but had them stolen on the way home, and so the hospital lost all records of the names and addresses of all of the patients.'

'How unfortunate,' I said.

'How should I know how unfortunate it was?' Mr Bligh rubbed a barked shin. 'I only know that the hospital authorities were not very happy and that Mr Lamb retired, probably worn out by all the other complaints against him.'

'Do you know what they were about?' I asked.

Mr Bligh glowered at me. 'You have not understood a single word I said, have you?'

I tried one more tack. 'If the sweep was in Lister Ward, surely they must have made their own records?'

'Oh, for heaven's sake.' Bligh grabbed hold of his own hair. 'It goes without saying that he was deaf and dumb, which – I had better explain – means he could neither hear nor speak. We only knew him as *Sweep* and we called him that because he used to be one, otherwise we would have called him something else.'

'Like *Baker*,' I suggested, and Mr Bligh threw back his head like a wolf at the moon, but, I was disappointed to find, did not howl.

'No, not Baker. He was a sweep – a sweep-a sweep-a sweep. How many more ways can I say it.'

'You have only said it one way but four times,' I argued.

'It is time to go.' Mr G spun on his heel.

'Can you explain about the bells again?' I asked meekly as my godfather headed for the door.

The surgeon stumbled on to his knees over a footstool. 'Bother.' He picked himself up. 'I sometimes wonder why I wear these things.'

'Goodbye, Mr Captain Bligh.' Sidney Grice waved like a signalman trying to flag down a train in an emergency and, when we were outside, he explained, 'Mr Captain Bligh does not like bells and, incidentally, when I talked about the criminals of this world basking in gentleness and benignity, I have no serious expectations of that happening.'

Lies, Lucifer and the Leper Colony

I N THE CAB I asked, 'Why do you never stand up for me
when people insult me?'

Sidney Grice took a swig from his flask, something I was
never allowed to do with mine. 'Why do you not for me?' He
tapped the cork back in. 'In fact you twice made remarks about
my lack of mellowness.'

And I realized that he was right. 'I did not think you cared.'
I shaded my eyes against the sun and wished I could have borrowed Mr Bligh's spectacles.

'You were not wrong to adopt that belief.' He nibbled the
collar of his Ulster overcoat with his lips.

We sat in silence, jostling over a rough surface that had been
temporarily repaired before I came to London.

'Would you like me to be nicer to you in future?' I asked after
some thought.

'Good Lord, no,' he protested. 'You are kind to street urchins,
beggars and stray animals. Am I to be included in their numbers?'

'Perhaps not.'

'What causes scabies?' He rattled his halfpennies.

'Lice,' I said, though he must have known the answer.

He cupped his ear.

'Lice,' I repeated.

'Louder.'

'Lice,' I shouted.

'Three times in rapid succession and as loud as you can, if you please.'

'Lice-lice-lice,' I yelled at the top of my voice.

A young man carrying a pyramid of brown paper parcels nearly spilled them; a miniature poodle hid in its mistress's skirts, and the hatch slid open.

'Tell 'er the truff for gawdsake, squire, before the 'orse 'as annart attack.'

'I knew I could rely on you to make a scene,' my guardian said with evident satisfaction, as we turned left into Gower Street.

*

Sidney Grice popped his eye out as he habitually did in the evenings. They fitted much better since he had permitted me to make a gutta-percha impression of his socket and they looked better, after I had the idea of getting a young painter by the name of Sickert to match the colours and tones of his left eye on a piece of card.

'I know we agreed that the attacker may be unable to father children.' I perched on my armchair. 'But there must be plenty of other men in such a condition apart from those unfortunate patients.'

'Twenty-seven thousand, four hundred and eighteen hours and nineteen minutes ago, Mr Anthony Lamb was battered to death in Brompton Cemetery.' Mr G tied on a violet patch.

'I remember reading about it. They never caught his murderer, did they?' I went to the window. A boy was doing cartwheels across the road and springing up with his hat held out, in the vain hope of a donation, and I wished that I had seen him earlier. 'But how can you prove that the killer was one of his patients?'

'If my unparalleled powers of reminiscence have not failed me, which they never have yet, I believe that the witnesses reported hearing shouts of *Lies, they were lies*, as the crime was being committed.'

I clicked my fingers. 'And when I shouted *lice*, our cabby thought I was saying *lies*,' I realized, 'which shows that the murderer may well have been one of those patients. But we do not even know their names, and how does it demonstrate any connection between him and Lucy's attacker?'

'Pertinent questions,' my godfather conceded, striding behind his desk. 'But there is something itching inside the parietal lobe of my right cerebral cortex and I cannot scratch it.'

'A mental louse,' I suggested helpfully.

'Something very like that,' he agreed. 'There is a link and I know it, but I cannot quite join the pieces together.' He wrenched open a drawer of his filing cabinet and leafed through the files. 'Now, where are we? Lacey, G. – Lacey, R. – Ladd, P. –' His fingers raced through the rows. 'Ah, here we are – Lamb, D. A.' He paused. 'Lamb, D. A.,' he murmured in puzzlement. 'Lamb, D. A.' Sidney Grice froze. 'Oh, how stupid you have been.'

I was not sure if he was talking to me or himself, for his eyes were transfixed by the title at the top of his brown envelope.

'What does Lamb, D. A. spell, March?'

'Lamb, D. A.,' I repeated stupidly.

'Say it all as one word,' he commanded.

'Lam-day.'

'Harden your *ay*.'

'Lamb-da,' I tried. 'Lambda, the...' I counted on my fingers. 'Eleventh letter of the Greek alphabet.'

'Write it.' He thrust the envelope at me. 'Write it on the back.'

I placed the envelope on his desk. 'Can I use your pencil?'

'Certainly not.'

'Or your pen?'

'Are you mad?

'That was not the most tactful of questions,' I complained.

'I am not the most tactful of questioners,' he assured me,

which, of course, made everything all right. 'But, if I had to worry about people's feelings, I should have to start worrying about people instead of the important things in life.'

I folded my arms and hoped I did not look too much like our maid. 'I suppose I am not important then.'

'When?' He slid the envelope back towards me.

'Now.' I glared at him. 'Well? What is your answer to that?'

He listened blankly. 'The last question you posed concerned permission to use my pen and I believe that I was insultingly dismissive of that request.'

I threw up my hands and got my bag from beside my chair, and found my own pencil with the notebook I kept but rarely used.

'It is like an upside down V,' I said, and wrote Λ.

'By Lucifer.' Sidney Grice almost danced on the spot in his frustration. 'Must I spend every waking hour with a stubborn idiot girl?'

'I was not aware that you knew any.'

'For goodness' sake.' He threw back his head. 'This is no time for one of your puerile sulks. Draw it in lower case, woman.'

I supposed that *woman* was an improvement on *girl*, but it did not sound much like one. I gritted my teeth and wrote λ.

'At last.' He stabbed at my inscription with his left thumb. 'And what – if I can persuade you to activate that minuscule part of your so-called mind that is not completely occupied with fashion and frippery and buttons and silly-silly frills – does that remind you of?'

I traced the symbols with my finger. 'A badly drawn X,' I said.

Sidney Grice let out a deep breath. 'At last,' he said

The Sultan's Slave and a Greek Goddess

S IDNEY GRICE BROUGHT out his Mordan mechanical pencil, which it was perfectly in order for him to use, and demonstrated his point.

'I thought it odd when I asked Miss Bocking how the attacker had carved his symbol and she told me—' He swung the pencil towards me as my cue.

'*In the same way as he beat me*,' I quoted, to finish his sentence, '*slowly and deliberately.*'

'And yet,' my guardian lowered his pencil, 'in every case we have seen –Mistresses Hockaday and Bocking and Lady Brockwood – the X was wanting its upper-right arm.'

'And Lucy said that he had cut both lines downwards,' I recalled. 'If you were drawing an X carelessly, it would be the end of your stroke that would be missing, not the start.'

'Precisely.'

I paced back to the window and looked out. The boy was still performing and still being ignored.

'But, if Lucy's attacker had been castrated,' I reasoned, 'surely – and, I am sorry, I cannot think of a more delicate way of phrasing this – he would not have been capable of... having congress.'

Sidney Grice blanched at my mouthing such an obscenity but steeled himself to continue. 'Are you familiar with that fascinating novel, *I was a Sultan's Slave*, by Lydia Lovely?'

This was not a conversation I had expected to be having with any adult male when I had read the book surreptitiously with Maudy Glass in the old barn at the end of Wood Lane in Parbold.

'Yes, I have read it,' I confessed, half-expecting to be scolded.

'Good.' He put his pencil away. 'Then you will be familiar with page seventy-six where one of the three hundred and fourteen unsavoury incidents is described in lurid detail – namely, the seduction of the sultan's nineteenth wife, the voluptuous nineteen-year-old Fatima by—' He jerked his right elbow towards me.

'Abdul, the eunuch,' I remembered. Maudy and I had been appalled and thrilled by that episode. 'But surely it is a work of fiction and rather overheated at that? In fact I am surprised that you are familiar with it.'

Sidney Grice blinked rapidly. 'It is what our filthy Gallic neighbours call a *roman-à-clef*.' Two halfpennies appeared in his left hand. 'A true story in which the names of the characters have been changed. Miss Lydia Lovely is now the wife of a prominent banker and Grand Master of the Ancient Order of Shrivers.'

'I do not suppose such a revelation would do his reputation much good.'

'Not in quarters with whom his business is likely to prosper,' he agreed.

'I do not want to belabour this,' I began hesitantly, 'but surely a castrated man cannot achieve—'

'Clearly he cannot produce seed,' Mr G completed my thought hastily. 'But the seminal vesicles, prostate glands and bulbourethral glands can and do produce quantities of fluid. Lord...' He fiddled with his cravat. 'I have not had such an awkward conversation since I had to explain to my mother how she came to be gravid with child, *id est* me.'

I gaped. 'Did she really not know?'

'She thought she had swallowed me in a rock pool.'

I went back to my chair to recover from a coughing fit. 'If only we had the names of those patients,' I managed to say at last.

'Hospital records are scant and their filing muddled at the best of times,' Sidney Grice told me. 'But let us consider – apart from his mutilation – what kind of man we are looking for.'

'His voice would not be high if he had already reached maturity,' I observed, 'though I do not suppose he would have much facial hair.'

I did not add *like you*, for my guardian regarded his smooth skin as an evolutionary advance.

"Do make an effort to say something less obvious.' Mr G rattled his coins impatiently.

'You are always telling me not to ignore the obvious,' I retorted.

'Not to the exclusion of all other thought,' he huffed.

'Well, he must be well-educated to make such a pun on the doctor's name.'

'But not wealthy enough to be in a private room,' my guardian pointed out, quite obviously, I thought. 'And...' His expression became even more sour than usual. 'Why do you persist in wearing that same pair of boots? You will have ploughed through my floor within nineteen years at this rate.'

'They are very comfortable.' I excused myself with a guilty glance at the scratched boards. 'And, the next time we see the cobbler, I can get him to hammer it in properly.'

'He cannot be much good at his craft,' my guardian remarked. 'That gentleman in the green paisley waistcoat, the two-tone cravat, the pinstriped grey trousers and black, side-buttoned boots was complaining about a repair he had done.'

'He even dropped—' I stopped and Sidney Grice looked at quizzically.

'Go on,' he urged.

'His hammer.' My words were hardly audible to my own ears

as I tried to reconstruct in my mind what had seemed to be a trivial conversation. 'He charged me fivepence,' I remembered.

'And you paid him that for banging in a nail?' Mr G was incredulous.

'Even worse,' I said. 'I had nothing smaller than a sixpence.'

Mr G pfffed. 'And, needless to say, he had no change.'

'No,' I agreed automatically. 'And he said, *Oh fanks, miss, you're an oops-a-daisy.*'

He watched me keenly. 'At what point in the proceedings?'

'After I had handed him the money but – and this is the odd bit – he said *oops* before he dropped the hammer.'

'You are sure of that?'

'Positive. I thought the act seemed contrived at the time, but then the flower girl who stands on the corner said he was always doing silly things for a laugh and I thought no more about it.'

'Until?' Mr G asked eagerly.

'I do not think he said *oops-a-daisy* at all,' I pondered.

'Then why did you waste your breath and my time telling me that he did?' Sidney Grice hurled the coins away, but I did not hear them strike anything.

'It was his pronunciation.' I could almost hear the boot-maker's voice. 'I think he said *Ops* and then tried to cover it up.'

'For once my ignorance is more profound than yours. What does *ops* mean other than a sickening abbreviation for operations or an acronym for the Obliteration of Penguins Society, of which I am a member.'

'What have you got against penguins?'

'Nothing very much except for their nasty jauntiness,' he assured me. 'It is just that I am of the opinion that the fewer species with which we have to share this ludicrously cluttered planet, the better.'

'Ops was the wife of Saturn and the Greek goddess of plenty.' I struggled to get back to the subject. 'And munificence. He was saying that I was generous.'

'A smooth-faced man with a knowledge of Greek mythology,' Mr G said grimly. 'And you told me that your shoddy and over-priced boot repair was not relevant to any of our cases.'

'I did not think it was,' I protested.

'What is the point of not thinking that?' he demanded angrily.

'What are you writing?' I asked, as he printed something on a blank sheet of paper.

'A telegram.' My guardian brought his temper back under control just as quickly as he had lost it. 'To Chief Inspector Pound. He should be settling into his new office by now.'

'Oh,' I said. 'You know about his promotion?' And I said a silent prayer that he had not pulled strings to help get it, for I wanted George to ascend on his own merit.

'Of course,' he said. 'In fact I recommended,' he shot me a glance, 'that he should not be given it.'

'But why?' I demanded indignantly.

'Because he will spend more time in meetings and writing memoranda than doing what he is occasionally not too bad at – for a policeman.' Mr G cupped his left palm and his two half-pennies fell one at a time into it. 'Investigating crimes.'

This seemed as good an opportunity as ever. 'Now that he is a Chief Inspector—'

'In the morning,' my godfather ploughed on, 'we shall take breakfast, bicker about something irrelevant, and seek out this irritating tradesman to see if he can explain himself.'

'We can try,' I mumbled, and he turned sharply.

'What now? Why are you looking like a bloodhound caught ingesting his master's slipper of tobacco?'

'Nobody keeps their tobacco in their slippers.'

'Silly people do. Explain your discomfort.'

'I am not sure,' I said, 'but I think he might have realized he had given himself away.' I hung my head. 'He has probably gone into hiding by now.'

'I hope you are right, March.' He rested Charley Peace's

patella on a diagram of the internal workings of his ladder stick. 'For you can be sure of one thing. He has not been loitering in Grosvenor Square for the fresh air.'

'Lucy,' I cried.

'Ring for tea,' he said nonchalantly.

'Is that all you care about?'

Sidney Grice took out a fresh sheet of paper. 'He will not make an appearance at night. That would attract too much attention, especially as his face is known in the square. In the meantime...' His new gunmetal pen was on his desk but he picked up his patent self-filler. 'I shall send her a telegram.'

And, as Sidney Grice began to print: *BEWARE THE BOOTMAKER*, Molly trundled in.

'Listen carefully,' her employer instructed, and she cocked an ear rather as Spirit did when he was confiding in her. 'You will take these telegrams immediately. Do not even change into your outdoor boots. Your mission is urgent. Do you understand?'

Molly crossed her fingers and her eyes. 'Telegramps immedi- antly – which means urgent – indoor boots, urgent – which means immediantly,' she recited with such concentration that I wanted to give her a ripple of applause.

'Money.' Mr G rammed a cotton pouch into her hand. 'Go.'

And Molly was off. I had seen racehorses make slower starts but they were the ones I had money on.

———•━━•———

85

This, That and the Uvva

T HE HANSOM CAME while I was still raising the flag and
Sidney Grice groaned when he spotted the driver.

'Grosvenor Square,' Mr G bellowed, with enough
volume to rouse an army.

'Grow what where?' Old Peter cupped his ear and I repeated
the name.

'Grosvenor Square, it is, miss.' Old Peter pulled his string to
release the flap.

'I said it more clearly than you,' my godfather grumbled as I
tugged on a wisp of loose stuffing that was sticking through a
rip in the upholstery

'Yes.' The wisp was longer than I expected and getting thicker.
'But your lips move differently from those of other men.'

And that seemed to satisfy my guardian for Sidney Grice
hated to be thought the same as others. It reeked of equality
to him and, when I sneaked a sideways look, I caught him
mouthing the words proudly. I had about half of a horse's
hair now.

'If this man is the one we are looking for...' I tried to push
the stuffing back in but it had expanded. 'Why would he go out
of his way to draw attention to himself?'

Sidney Grice pushed harder, though it was him, not me, who
was taking two thirds of the seat. 'Perhaps you would care to
attempt to answer that question yourself.'

'To taunt you.' I poked the stuffing with my finger. It did not seem possible that so much had come through such a little slit.

'Try again.'

'I *am* trying.' I got out my pencil to ram the thick wad down and the leather bowed under the pressure, but none of the stuffing went back in.

'I was referring to your answering your own question.'

'Inspector Pound told me that some habitual criminals are so sick of their own acts that they are relieved when they are apprehended, even if they face the severest penalties. Perhaps he wants to get caught.' I had a nasty feeling that the rip was getting bigger.

'Some do,' Mr G agreed, 'But not this one. Try harder.'

I racked my brains. 'I cannot.'

My godfather pulled the cork out of his flask. 'It would be odd indeed if he had not drawn attention to himself. A street tradesman who hides in the shadows would have aroused suspicions immediately. Local residents would probably have reported him for loitering.'

'But why is he hanging around outside Lucy's house?'

Sidney Grice grimaced. 'Let us hope that we get an opportunity to ask him.' He banged on the roof and, when the hatch opened, shouted, 'Faster.' And mimed holding the reins of a galloping steed.

'Oh sorry, guv. Goin' too fast for you?'

The hatch closed and we slowed to a gentle walk. In the end it made no difference for a hot-air balloon had come down in Maddox Street, blocking the road, attracting a curious crowd and frightening the horses. And, when we finally arrived in Cavendish Square, the bootmaker was nowhere to be seen.

'No sign of him,' I commented.

'Apart from those splashes of dubbin and blacking on the pavement.' Sidney Grice swept his cane over a wide area. 'Or the scratch on the railing where he sometimes hung his placard.'

'Apart from those,' I conceded.

'Or the snapped twig where he pushed his trolley into the rhododendron bushes,' Mr G continued.

'I meant there is no sign that he is here,' I snapped, and Mr G grunted.

'Why would there be when he is not?' My guardian appeared to be checking his chin for a beard.

A hansom pulled up, the horse shying at something I could not see or hear, and Inspector Pound leaped down.

'Good afternoon, Mr Grice. Your telegram sounded urgent.'

'A telegram has no sound other than the rustle of paper or a swish if it is dropped and perhaps a light pat as it lands, depending upon the surface which interrupts its trajectory or—'

'Excuse me interrupting your trajectory,' the inspector said. 'Good afternoon, Miss Middleton.'

'Inspector.' I shook his hand and felt him give mine a squeeze. 'I trust you are well.'

'Of course, if it alighted upon water, ranging from a puddle to an ocean,' my guardian spoke over him, 'the sounds would be very different but never urgent.'

'I am very well, thank you, Miss Middleton.' George winked at me. 'I hope you are too.'

He had a new suit on and looked very smart.

'Miss Middleton made a semblance of that ignorant blunder regarding my doorbell when I made the uncharacteristic mistake of admitting her into my invigorating household,' Mr G droned on.

'We think we may have identified the murderer,' I said.

'We?' my guardian queried. 'Oh, I suppose Miss Middleton does serve one purpose. She proposes so many ridiculous explanations that the only one left must be correct. Unless you are going to arrest my ward, Inspector, I suggest you release her at your earliest convenience.'

We let go of each other's hands.

'So who and where is your suspect, Mr Grice?' George Pound asked.

'Two obvious though pertinent questions,' my godfather almost complimented him, 'to which I have, as yet, no veracious response.'

'There is a bootmaker who usually stands on that corner around this time,' I explained, 'and we think he may be the culprit but it is possible I have frightened him away.'

I stood on tiptoe and whispered in his ear.

'If only the other women had possessed your ability to terrify him,' Mr G commented drily.

'Well, apart from the polish, branch and scratch and the smell of trimmed leather, there is no sign of him now,' Pound declared.

'What smell?' Mr G snuffled about like a bloodhound.

'Oh, it is quite distinctive,' Pound said airily. 'Is that flower seller usually here?'

The girl stood on the opposite corner, short and slight, in a patched dress much too big for her, a forlorn sight with her tray of unsold forget-me-nots.

'Yes,' I said.

'Which is one of my six motives for engaging her in friendly banter,' Sidney Grice set off towards her at a brisk pace. 'You there, juvenile female floral purveyor.'

The girl looked over in alarm.

'Be no more afraid than you ought to be,' my godfather sought but failed to reassure her, 'for I intend you no harm, though my intentions may transmogrify as our intercourse pro-gresses.'

The girl let out a squeak, but it would have been more than her life was worth to put down her tray and run.

'It's all right,' Inspector Pound's voice rang out reassuringly. 'We just want to talk to you.'

The flower girl hopped from one foot to the other.

'We were just wondering,' I told her as we drew close, 'where the bootmaker is today.'

'Blimey,' the girl gasped. 'I fought you was gonna ask where I stealed these flowers from.'

Pound picked up a wilting nosegay. 'Do you know where he is now?" he asked gently.

'That last word was tautologous,' my godfather informed him pleasantly. 'If somebody *is* somewhere they must be there at the present time.'

'What, old Bootsy?' The girl grinned. 'Oh, 'es a larf.'

'That does not even meander vaguely in the direction of a reply,' Sidney Grice scolded.

'In what way?' I asked.

'Well, like the way 'e frew that 'ammer down,' she guffawed. 'And one time 'e got me to spill rubbish over some posh foreign geezer's boots, just so 'e could clean 'em up and not even charge 'im. Mind you...' She spluttered in mirth. ''E cut orf one of the gent's waistycoat buttons. Don't fink 'e knew I saw that.'

'I do not *fink* you would be here if he did,' Mr G mumbled.

'I could do with a good laugh,' Inspector Pound mused. 'Do you know where he is now?'

The girl looked about and her voice dropped. ''E ain't in no trouble, is 'e?'

'Of course not,' I lied, before my guardian broke in with the truth. 'It's just that I have a loose heel and I can't walk very far.'

'Didn't know gentry like yourselfs walked thery far anyways,' she bantered.

George Pound put the nosegay back and selected a pink carnation. 'How much is this?'

The girl assessed her customer, and no doubt his clothes at least doubled the price.

'Them's a penny each,' she declared.

'Outrageous.' He sniffed the petals. 'It must be worth at least thruppence.' And he slipped her a silver coin.

'You can 'ave six for that,' she told him.

'I only need one but I'll take a pin.' He smiled and presented the flower to me with a slight bow. 'Have you seen him today?'

I fastened it to my dress

'Who? Oh yeah.' The flower girl sniggered. 'Comes wiv-art 'is cart this morning. Lor' but 'e's gotta nerve. *Gotta fearful drought in me, I 'ave*, he says. *See if I can't p'suade a friendly skivvy t'give me a bit of a cuppa and bit more of the uvva.*' She cackled and nudged the chief inspector. 'Bold as brass straight to the front door, 'e was. And 'e must be gettin' plenty of the uvva the lengf of time 'e's been in there.'

'Did you notice which house he went in?' Pound asked casually.

'Vat one,' she pointed.

'Amber House,' I said in alarm.

86

The Shattering

CHIEF INSPECTOR POUND was off, coat flapping behind him. He was a tall man but not particularly fast – especially since his injury – and I soon caught up. But Sidney Grice, dipping wildly, was ahead of us both. He was slightly built and no taller than I, but I never knew a man with faster reactions and acceleration. By the time we reached the opposite pavement he was already at the front door, but instead of ringing the bell, my godfather stopped and brought out his gold cigarette case.

'Three lever,' he scoffed. 'You might as well use a ribbon in a bow.'

He flipped his case open and selected half a dozen slender steel picks, inserting them one at a time into the keyhole and giving each a tiny twist.

'Ever thought of ringing the bell?' Pound asked a little breathlessly.

'Certainly.' Mr G slipped what looked like a blank key between the picks. 'But I dismissed the idea as reckless. We only have four advantages – our numbers, your brutish bulk, my ingenuity and, I hope, the element of surprise.'

Even in our hurry I reflected that the only merit of my presence seemed to be in making up numbers.

The inspector watched uneasily – fully aware that he was witnessing a criminal act – as Sidney Grice made a few tiny adjustments and twisted the key anticlockwise. There was a click, and he bfffed in satisfaction before extracting his instruments and replacing them in the same order.

'Hurry, man,' Pound urged quietly.

'Hurry is a bent fork,' Mr G told him cryptically.

'Then unbend it,' I suggested, not at all sure what either of us meant now.

'Stop shouting.' He turned the handle and, standing to one side, pushed the door open with his cane.

The hallway was deserted as we stepped inside. I closed the door carefully.

'Slide your feet,' my guardian instructed, and we shuffled along, me lifting my heel to stop the nail scraping along the floor. 'If only you had taken such care in *my* house.'

'I thought you said it was *our* house.'

'Our home. My house.'

Sidney Grice held up his hand and we stopped to listen. Nothing. He shook his head and we edged down the corridor alongside the stairs. The doors to either side were shut, but the sun came through the fanlight and a stained-glass window at the far end. And, as my eyes accustomed themselves to the relative shade, I noticed a brighter patch running across the floor behind the back of the stairs and bending up on to the bamboo-patterned wall. We stopped just before it and Mr G opened his satchel, taking a four-inch circular mirror and slipping it over the ferule of his cane, stretching it outwards to view round the corner.

'Well, he has certainly been here.' He pulled the cane back, dipped into his bag again and, when his hand emerged, it was holding his ivory-handled revolver. He pulled back the hammer with great care but the click, as it locked, shattered the silence. 'Bother,' he breathed and stepped out.

The door facing him now was ajar. He took two swift paces and flung himself through.

'Oh, dear God.' I clamped a hand over my mouth.

Aellen and Muriel were sprawled on the kitchen floor, the shimmering pools of deep red oozing from their stomachs merging into a thickening pool under the table that separated them. Aellen's face was turned away but Muriel had a large lambda gouged into her forehead.

'Examine them, Chief Inspector,' my guardian commanded.

Sidney Grice was skirting that pool and using his mirror to check the room off to the left, before he revealed it as the pantry – unoccupied, with a back door bolted. He hurried through to what I judged at a glimpse to be the bootroom.

Chief Inspector Pound was bent over the bodies, his face as grey as when he had lain on the brink of death in the London Hospital. Was that really only just over a year ago?

'Hardly more than girls.' George Pound crossed himself. 'God rest you both.' He straightened up and touched an empty cake tin on the table, and then all the pots and pans on the range, as if it were some kind of ritual.

'And God damn the man who did this,' I added.

Pound doubled over the sink so low that I thought he was going to be sick, but he turned back with a puzzled expression and ran a finger under the tap.

'I have hopes that we shall damn him ourselves before this day is out.' My guardian took in the room.

'The strange thing is—' Pound began.

'There are many strange things. Tell me later,' Mr G rapped.

'Oh, poor Lucy and Freddy,' I said fearfully.

'Indeed.' My guardian looked lost. 'Good servants are difficult to replace.'

Sidney Grice went back along the hall and was at the foot of the stairs when he stopped again. I listened too and heard something – a stifled cry, I thought.

'Through there.' The chief inspector pointed.

'The pink room,' Mr G said, with more loathing than he had

greeted the murdered maids. 'I think I can safely say that we have lost the element of surprise.'

He went over and struck three times with the handle of his cane before opening the door.

87

Blood on the Steel

FREDDY SAT SIDE-ON, twisting towards us.

'Good afternoon,' Sidney Grice called out cheerily, as George Pound followed him in with me close on their heels. 'I do not suppose that you ever thought you would be pleased to see me, Miss Wilde.'

'Oh, thank God.' Her wrists had been tied with blue wool to the arms of her cherry-wood chair.

'God must be at the very pinnacle of fashion from the number of times he has been invoked this day,' Sidney Grice chatted as he turned his back on her.

'Freddy.' I hurried over.

'Leave her.'

I spun round to see that the voice came from the bootmaker. He was standing behind Lucy who was also in her chair, manacled to it with red wool, a knife held under her chin.

'I have been looking for you,' I told him. 'That repair you did was hopeless.' I went towards him. 'Listen. You can hear the nail scratching the floor.'

'It has done reparable damage to my Hampshire oak floor,' my godfather confirmed.

'Stop right there,' the bootmaker commanded. 'Now go and stand by the ugly sow.'

'There is only one pig in this room,' I told him.

'Not so close,' he said, and I moved a couple of feet away.

'You – the famous Mr Grice – point that gun towards your friend in the flashy suit... lower the hammer gently... Now put it on the floor.'

'Don't do it,' Pound urged. 'You can put a bullet in his brain before he can move a muscle.'

'Had your eyes checked recently?' the bootmaker asked mockingly, and put the tip of his knife to a silver line on Lucy's throat.

'Cheesewire,' I realized.

There was a loop of it round Lucy's neck and the bootmaker held up a length behind her.

'The other end is tied through my belt,' he explained with great satisfaction. 'So, if I should fall over, it will slice her head off like a ball of cheddar. Put the gun down.'

'Please do as he asks.' Lucy trembled and Sidney Grice obeyed.

'Now...' The bootmaker smirked with milky-coffee lips. 'Kick it towards me.'

'This is most embarrassing.' Mr G took off his Ulster overcoat and put it folded on to the occasional table beside him. 'For I am forced to admit that I am hopeless at kicking and I always have been. I was never selected to play in any games at school.'

'Just do it.'

'Very well.' My guardian placed his soft-brimmed hat on top, rubbed his hands, leaned heavily on his cane, swung his right foot back and let fly. The revolver rose a few inches, clattered down and shot across the floor to stop at the side of Lucy's chair.

'Actually, that was not bad, was it?' Mr G tossed his head proudly.

'Well done you,' Pound said tersely. 'I suppose you couldn't have *accidentally* put it out of reach?'

'I do not have accidents, Inspector.' Mr G expanded his chest and flexed his shoulders like a weightlifter warming up for a new challenge. 'You should have known that by now.'

'And now that silly satchel.' The bootmaker stroked Lucy's cheek with his free hand and she shrank back.

'This is chrome-tanned Highland doeskin,' Mr G retorted indignantly but skimmed it over to stop just by the bootmaker's feet.

'Help me,' Lucy beseeched, and her captor grinned. He had good teeth, I noticed, regular and clean.

'I am the only one worth begging, darling.' He combed his fingers through her hair, lifting it back to show her scarred brow.

'What do you want?' George asked.

'That is for me to know.'

'If you were going to kill them, you could have done it well before now.'

'And spoil the fun.' The bootmaker grinned. 'Who are you anyway?'

'I am Chief Inspector Pound of the Metropolitan Police and I must warn you—'

'No, you must not,' the bootmaker shouted. 'The only thing you must do, Officer, is to keep quiet and do as I say.'

'Those are two things,' Sidney Grice pointed out.

'And you can shut your soapy mouth too.' He pulled the knife back, forcing Lucy's chin up, and she gasped.

It was a terrible-looking instrument, a good eight inches long, similar to those that the knacker's men used to dispatch horses in the street, and there was blood already on the steel.

'You speak very well,' I commented.

'When I choose to,' he agreed.

'For a man who has spent some time in Uckfield,' Mr G observed.

'I told you to shut your mouth,' the bootmaker snapped.

'You told me that I could, not that I should,' Sidney Grice differed.

'Well, shut it then.' But curiosity was already getting the better of the man. 'How did you know that?'

'I made many studies of accents.' Sidney Grice smiled

modestly. 'And the dialect in the south-western quadrant of High Weald is unpleasant but quite distinct. However, you were not raised there. You did not, *exempli gratia*, pronounce *only* as *oany*, which those indigenous to that area of Sussex never quite manage to mask. I must confess, however, that I am struggling to isolate all the ingredients of your speech.'

'You are too damned clever for my liking,' the bootmaker snarled.

'I cannot deny it.' Mr G raised his cane. 'Would you like me to transmit this to you too?'

'Well now.' The bootmaker allowed Lucy's head to drop a fraction. 'Why would you be offering that?' He toyed absently with a bow at the front of Lucy's dress. 'I have read about your trick canes.' He tugged the button open. 'How do I know it is not one of those dynamite walking sticks you had in *The Red-Handed League?*'

That adventure was a Fleet Street fantasy by one of the many journalists who Sidney Grice was taking to court.

'You may also have read that I never tell a lie,' Sidney Grice told him, 'and you have my word that it is not.'

'He is infuriatingly truthful,' George affirmed. He had edged perhaps six inches along the wall but was standing bolt upright.

'Hold it up.'

Mr G did so with the flourish of a drum major. Most of his sticks had globe tops, but this had a handle at a right angle to the shaft.

'What does that catch on the side do?' The bootmaker squinted. 'Show me.'

Sidney Grice pressed it and the top of the handle sprang open to reveal a brass lever with each end rounded into a disc.

'What the hell did you bring that for?' Pound demanded furiously. 'Honestly, Grice, I know you have a reputation for eccentricity to live up to, but a Morse code key! When exactly were you planning on using it?"

'Mr Grice to you, Pound.'

'Chief Inspector Pound to you, *Mr* Grice.'

'Stop it, both of you,' I scolded. 'Mr Grice often has trouble finding a telegram office,' I explained. 'He can connect this to any convenient telegraph wire and send his own message.'

'Which is a criminal offence,' Pound pointed out in disgust. 'And that's on top of illegal entry.'

'I shall not press charges,' Lucy promised.

'Would you rather I had brought my musical cane or the one with the built-in periscope?' Mr G queried.

'As this gentleman implied, a weapon might have been a good idea.' Pound groaned despairingly. 'A swordstick, for example.'

'It's a long time since a policeman called me that.' The boot-maker looked slightly mollified.

'I had my revolver,' my guardian protested, 'and I saw no reason to bring a bomb.'

'Point it towards your girl and let me see your thumb.' The bootmaker screwed up his eyes. 'Now push the lever.'

My guardian was expressionless as he complied. Nothing happened.

'I still don't trust you.' The man pondered. 'It could be on a timer.'

'Shall I take it outside?' I offered.

'Place it on the table pointing at your girl,' the bootmaker decided. 'But if I hear so much as a click...' He brandished the knife and Lucy cried, 'No, please.'

'I like it when they beg.' He smiled grimly. 'So what have you got in your sack, girl?'

'Shall I show you?' I went to the table, unclipped my handbag and brought out the wad of seat stuffing.

'What's that? Your spare wig?' The bootmaker guffawed.

'No, that is at the laundry.' I put it down beside Sidney Grice's cane. 'My gin flask and cigarette case followed – handkerchief, notebook and pencil, bottle of sal volatile, parma violets, perfumes, my purse. When I had constructed a small mountain, I held my bag upside down and gave it a shake. 'Happy?'

The bootmaker laughed. 'You are worse than my—'

'Mother?' I suggested, and his face stiffened.

'Just put it all away.'

'In the Golden Dragon you called your captor a fool, Miss Bocking,' Sidney Grice declared. 'Perhaps you would like to explain why.'

The bootmaker laughed – not the jolly chuckle he had used in the square, but two sharp yips like an excited puppy.

'That is an excellent idea, Miss snout-in-the-air Bocking,' he sneered. 'Tell them.'

Lucy's head went back and she exhaled through her mouth.

'Tell them.' The bootmaker raised his right elbow.

'All right.' Lucy gasped and I could hardly hear her words, much less believe them. 'Because I arranged to have Freddy assaulted.'

The Order of Death

FREDDY DOUBLED UP, winded by shock. 'Lucy!' She breathed fast. 'That cannot be true. Why are you making her say it?'

'The man I hired was just supposed to kiss and cuddle you,' Lucy protested. 'I thought you might enjoy it, but he sent this man instead.'

'Naughty.' The bootmaker tweaked the wire and Lucy sobbed as he continued. 'That's not what Johnny the Walrus told me.'

'All right.' Lucy choked and he ran his forefinger under the wire to loosen it, exposing a vivid red mark. 'I paid him to violate her.'

The noose might have been round Freddy from the noise that escaped her.

'And tell her why you chose to approach Wallace,' I challenged.

'I went to the trial because I thought it might be fun.' Lucy forced an odd air of lightness. 'It didn't last very long because the case collapsed, but it was obvious that he did those things.'

'Why him especially?' I insisted.

'I do not know what you mean.' Lucy adopted as haughty a manner as she could muster.

'We have a photograph of Eric,' I said flatly, and Lucy tapped her chair with a flapping hand.

'All right, he was older than my brother would be if he were still alive, but he looked a bit like Eric,' she admitted sulkily. 'But that was just a bit of silliness.'

'Oh, Lucy, you cannot mean that.' Freddy was aghast.

'I did not think he would use violence.' Lucy looked blankly ahead. 'I thought you might want to know what it was like – to have a man – and that way there would be no guilt on your part.'

The bootmaker cocked his head. 'That might be true,' he conceded pleasantly. 'All I know is Wallace boasted he was to be paid to have a woman. I got him blind drunk and took his place.'

'Animal,' Pound breathed. He had moved another few inches towards the man.

'We are all animals,' the bootmaker retorted. 'Only some of us have the sense to know it.' He wrapped a rag around his left hand to give a better grip on the wire.

'How quickly and smoothly the conversation moves from molestation to philosophy.' My guardian leaned on the table. 'And, since we are seeking the deeper truths, and Miss Bocking has failed to demonstrate any affection for them, perhaps I could be of assistance in our quest.'

'Go on,' the bootmaker said.

'Don't worry,' Inspector Pound assured him. 'He will.'

Mr G ignored him. 'I wrote a letter of complaint to each of thirty-one insurance companies about the unconscionable delay in settling the claim for the destruction of Steep House.'

Freddy spoke wearily. 'My solicitor has been doing so for years, but I do not have the means to take them to court.'

Sidney Grice did not even glance at her. 'Two lies in one sentence.'

'I beg your pardon,' she began indignantly.

Mr G sniffed. 'Provide me with the name of your aforementioned but, thus far, anonymous and seemingly ineffectual legal representative.'

'Mr Spry of Spry and Fitt,' Freddy said.

'Lucy's solicitor,' I pointed out.

'It is easier to have the same man look after our interests.' Freddy reacted defensively, though I had not accused her of anything. 'Especially as I cannot afford my own. But is this really the time to worry about such things?'

'Bearing in mind it may be our last opportunity to do so, yes.' Sidney Grice gave her what might otherwise have been a reassuring smile.

'Oh, for pity's sake, Mr Grice,' George Pound admonished him.

'You shall find precious little pity,' my guardian told him, 'from this odious churl.'

'You want to watch your tongue.' The bootmaker bristled.

'I am often told that, though I suspect that people mean *they* want me to do so.' Sidney Grice touched his glass eye. 'But it has had no effect on my manners thus far.'

'Not for the better, at any rate,' I testified.

'Let me make a prediction,' Mr G continued, as casually as he would when holding forth to me in the comfort and security of our study. 'You may be consoled or appalled to know, Miss Wilde, that – if your captor has his way – you will be the last to die.'

'No.' Freddy went white.

'You are a bright fellow, Mr Grice.' The bootmaker relaxed the pressure on Lucy's throat. 'Maybe you could tell them why.'

'If I were in your position,' Mr G brought out his two halfpennies, 'which I do not expect to be, I would assess my intended victims. The policeman is big and strong and most likely, you might think, to put up a fight. Then there is me. I am a handsome fellow but short in stature and, fools might imagine, handicapped by my unequal lower limbs and glass eye. You are not a fool, however, and know that I have done battle with many a criminal, though few as loathsome as yourself. Two of the women, being restrained, could do little to resist, so Miss Middleton would be the next in line.'

'Go on.' The bootmaker waved the knife.

'I imagine you will want to have your way with Miss Bocking and, since you strike me as a man who rejoices in cruelty, you would probably like to make Miss Wilde witness your act and the sight of her friend being slaughtered before you dispatch her at your leisure.'

He rattled the coins like dice.

'Very good.' The bootmaker made a mock bow. 'Only, with the other two tied up, what is to stop me having my way – as you so delicately put it – with Miss Middleton?'

George bunched his fists and crouched a fraction at the knees, but he caught my eye and stayed where he was.

My guardian winced. 'I was hoping that would not occur to you.'

'I'll bet you were.'

'For it puts me under an obligation to grant you something precious,' Mr G continued.

'Think you can buy me off?' The bootmaker snorted.

'It is knowledge.' Mr G made a flourish with his left hand, reminiscent of an organ grinder turning his handle. 'The consciousness that you only have one card to play and that, once you have played it, your game is over.'

89

The Keeper of Secrets

T HE BOOTMAKER DID not even blink. 'If you mean that, once I have decapitated this bitch, you can all rush me, you cannot have forgotten that you gave me another card.' He bent and picked up the revolver. 'Six, to be precise.' He took aim at my godfather. 'How do you fancy your chances now, cripple?'

'I shall take a personal pleasure in watching you hang,' Sidney Grice forecast.

'The gun is not loaded,' I bluffed, and the bootmaker broke the breech.

'It looks fully loaded to me.' He clicked it back together.

'They are blanks.'

'Are they, Mr Grice?'

'No,' my godfather admitted.

'Thought not.' The bootmaker tucked the barrel into his waistband.

'Why in the name of all that is holy could you not have stepped off your pulpit and told a lie for once?' Inspector Pound exploded.

My guardian regarded him coolly. 'Did you want him to put the lie to the test on my ward?'

'I suppose not,' George conceded.

'Only *suppose*?' Mr G raised an eyebrow. 'I thought you held my goddaughter in higher regard than that.'

'That is not what I meant.' George Pound threw his head back. 'And you know it.'

'Whilst we are having such a nice chat,' the bootmaker said, 'what was all that carp about chewed-face's insurance?'

Accustomed though she must have been to such insults, Freddy's raw cheek still ticked.

'I was wondering when somebody would take an interest in that.' Mr G wound his hand the other way. 'Steep House, Miss Wilde's family home, was razed to the ground, and she gave me to believe that the insurance company was refusing to pay for it.'

'I gave you to believe the truth,' Freddy insisted. 'But I cannot see why it matters at this time.'

'What is the name of that company?'

'C. S. Derwent Assurance.'

'Acarus Scented Wrens,' mused my guardian and, for once, at least I knew what he meant.

'They have an office above Spry and Fitt, your solicitors,' I remembered.

'I know they share an address,' Freddy said distractedly. 'But I have never been there.'

'Nor shall you.' Mr G stopped winding, but his lower arm still jutted out at a right angle to his side. 'Even if you survive this tiresome ordeal – and, rest assured, I have almost every intention of delivering you from it intact, regardless of Miss Middleton's indifference to your fate.'

I did not trouble to dispute his allegation, for I had an inkling by now what his tactics were.

'You are quite mad,' Lucy raged. 'We are all facing death here.'

'And possibly none so imminently as you,' Mr G agreed amiably. 'For I do not believe that this creature feels under any obligation to adhere to my schedule.'

'Is all this actually leading anywhere?' The bootmaker rested the hand holding the knife on Lucy's shoulder, the blade dangling over her breast. 'If you are playing for time, it will serve no purpose.'

'I shall cut to the quick.' Sidney Grice tidied out a kink in his watch chain.

'So shall I,' the bootmaker quipped.

'After we visited the offices of Spry and Fitt, Miss Middleton and I made a brief excursion to the first floor. The dust on the stairs and landing suggested that my ward and I were the first to explore that area for many months.'

'The hem of my dress got dirty,' I remembered.

'And yet you made nothing of it.' Sidney Grice shook his head despairingly. 'Once there we came across two intriguing plaques. One was inscribed *CLOSED* and the other *IN CASE OF CLOSURE PLEASE DEPOSIT MAIL AT GROUND-FLOOR OFFICE*, and their obvious permanence inspired me to penetrate the woodwork with the aid of a bradawl in my Grice Patent Denied Housebreaking Cane. Upon doing so, I found myself presented almost immediately with a London Stock building block. In short, C. S. Derwent Assurance does not, nor ever has, existed.'

'You kept that a secret from me,' I huffed.

'No, I did not,' Sidney Grice retorted. 'I told you we had hit a brick wall.' He appeared to be checking his upper jaw now.

'Yes, but I thought you meant figuratively.'

'Most companies denied having issued any policies for Steep House.' Mr G gave his temples a cautious examination. 'But one trading under the name of Appleyard Alliance was insistent that they had settled this matter as soon as the police and the Metropolitan Fire Brigade confirmed that there were no suspicious circumstances.'

'They are lying,' Freddy insisted. 'I have never seen a penny.'

'I have formed the opinion that they and you are both telling the truth,' Mr G said, to everyone's apparent confusion, 'for Mr Appleyard himself assured me that he has a receipt for a considerable sum paid to the customer's solicitor, one—' He indicated Freddy.

'Silas Spry!' she exclaimed, her fear pushed briefly aside by her sense of injustice. 'He stole my money.'

'Naughty boy.' The bootmaker grinned.

'I think it unlikely that Miss Bocking would have permitted him to do that?'

'What, in the name of sanity, are you raving about now?' Lucy flared.

'Silas Spry has very few clients and yet he does not accept any more,' I recalled. 'And he lives in Berkeley Square.'

'My enquiries reveal that Spry does not come from a wealthy background, nor did he marry money.' Sidney Grice palpated his Adam's apple.

'What, just from a share of the insurance payment?' George objected.

'Even Miss Middleton remembered that Mr Clorence Bocking, Lucy's father, was embroiled in an expensive court case with his sister for purloining the design of her invention.' Mr G stood on tiptoe and craned his neck, as if the lady in question were to be discovered hiding behind the sofa. 'Eventually he settled out of court. Clorence Bocking lost everything, including New House, which, for the sake of kinship, his sister had granted him the use of for his life.'

'So when he died Lucy had nothing,' I concluded.

'This is nonsense,' Lucy exploded. 'Utter fantasy from start to finish.'

'Whereas,' my guardian added, 'Mr Tormead Wilde bequeathed a sizeable range of profitable concerns to his only remaining heir.'

'But I have nothing,' Freddy gasped.

'You have a considerable fortune,' Sidney Grice told her, 'though, inconveniently for you, it is in the hands of Mr Spry, who acts at the behest of the lovely though imperilled Miss Bocking.'

'That is not possible.' Freddy shook her head violently to cast the thoughts away.

'Who read your father's last will and testament to you? Who informed you of his dire financial straits?' Sidney Grice fired his words like bullets from a Gatling. 'Was it perchance the subject of so much of our intercourse today, the elusive Mr Silas Spry? Is it mere coincidence that he dramatically improved his domestic accommodation a matter of months after the death of your parents? I shall break one of my strictest rules by answering both of those conundrums myself: it was and it is not.'

'And has it ever occurred to you that I had also been fed lies by Silas Spry?' Lucy demanded.

'Numberless possibilities occurred to me long before I even accepted you as a client.' Sidney Grice turned his palm down. 'However, I rejected that one as it fails to explain how you obtained this house and all its expensive, if repellent, fixtures and fittings.'

'Oh, I quite like it.' The bootmaker amused himself by twisting Lucy's ear. She gritted her teeth but eventually he laughed to hear her cry out.

'But why is Steep House still in ruins?' Freddy asked. 'If they had control of my estate, why have they not sold it?'

'The money was probably in a trust fund which Spry can administer,' I conjectured, 'but a house cannot be transferred without the owner assigning the deeds, which are probably in a bank vault somewhere.' I measured my words. 'And how could Spry have asked you to access or sign those over without arousing suspicion?'

The bootmaker snorted. 'So this bitch—' he waved the blade in front of Lucy's eyes—'stole all that bitch's money. Is that it?'

'Not if you want to know how you came to be selected.'

The bootmaker gripped his knife so furiously I thought he

would use it there and then. 'What in the name of Zeus are you drivelling about now? Nobody *selected* me.'

Sidney Grice windmilled his arms carelessly. 'If you are not more cautious with that knife, you will never know.'

90

The Lampless Alleys

THE BOOTMAKER'S EYES travelled from person to person. 'This had better be good,' he threatened, but his grip relaxed.

'Miss Bocking approaches Johnny Wallace with an offer to do what she thought he did for his own amusement.' Mr G took to patting an imaginary large dog. '*Id est* violate another woman. However…' He tickled behind the imaginary dog's ears. 'Wallace was not a rapist. He did not mind assisting others to perform the acts for a fee, but it seems that all but the vilest criminals – such as this forensic specimen behind Miss Bocking – have their scruples.' He shooed the dog away. 'In fact, in some ways, Johnny was an exemplary figure. He did not smoke and he did not drink.'

'Well, he did when I met him,' the bootmaker remarked. 'Like a camel. That's how I was able to get him drunk and take his place.'

'Barmaid's gin,' my guardian told him.

'Water?' The bootmaker spluttered. 'So he was faking it?'

'Do you know why Johnny Walrus was so keen to hand the job over?' Mr G fluttered his long curled lashes.

'Suppose you tell me.'

'A wise supposition. You have heard, I take it, of Hagop Hanratty?'

'Who hasn't?' The bootmaker screwed up his face. 'Even the Chinamen pay him dues.'

'Hanratty has dedicated a substantial amount of his life to bringing the wealthy and gullible into his establishments.' Mr G half-crouched. Even his chair was fanciful now. 'And he was having considerable success until a series of attacks on women frightened them off the area. And he was so infuriated by the bad publicity generated by the attack on a Miss Hockaday that he withdrew his protection from Johnny Wallace. The trouble is, as we know, he could frighten Wallace off, but not only did the attacks not end, they increased in frequency and viciousness. When Albertoria Wright was found, Hanratty put a bounty on the capture of any man guilty of attacking women in his territory, and was determined to make an example of him. Unfortunately, Geraldine's brother, Peter, made too convincing an impression when he pretended to be a procurer and paid for his act with his life.'

'But surely, once he had explained he was her brother—' Pound began. He had edged a good foot or more further.

'I do not think they gave him much of a chance to talk,' I said. 'His tongue was cut out.'

'Like Princess Philomena.' The bootmaker chortled.

'You have a good knowledge of the Classics,' I remarked, and his face darkened.

'That prying tongue of yours could get you into trouble,' he warned. 'And you have quite a tongue too, Mr Grice.'

'And it has a great deal more to tell you yet,' Mr G replied, with no evident concern. 'Including a revelation which you might find distressing. Mr Hanratty has vowed to crucify – and he means that quite literally – the murderer of those two fine though reckless ladies in the lampless alleyways of Limehouse.'

'You can't blame me for that.' The bootmaker waved his knife like an angry schoolmaster with a rule. 'They tried to trap me. In fact the second one—'

'Dulcie,' I breathed, sickened at the memory.

'That damned vixen pulled a gun on me,' he told us in wounded tones. 'And if her friend had not distracted her by begging for help, she could have done for me. But I saw my chance and took it. One chop with this knife and I had half her hand off and the gun with it.' He paused in memory of the event. 'She was a game one, though – not a glimmer of fear as she tried to fight me off. Gave me a good old knee in the crotch, tore at my hair and cracked my skull on the wall – made my head ring like a Sanctus bell. I would have liked a lot more time with her.'

'You disgusting—'

'Don't, March,' Pound cautioned. 'It's exactly what he wants. But he's no man when he can only frighten women and girls.'

I wondered briefly if George knew the true significance of what he had just said, but realized that he could not have.

The bootmaker's face blazed, but it was then that I saw his powers of self-control. In a moment his expression turned to a sneer. 'Still on first-name terms?' He grinned. 'Which of you wants to watch the other die?'

It was then also that I saw George Pound's self-possession. 'If I rush you now,' he said calmly, 'you won't have time to aim for my head and it will take at least three shots in my belly to bring me down before I get there. Think Mr Grice will stand calmly back while you fire them off?'

'Think Miss Middleton will?' I added.

'Please don't,' Lucy implored.

The bootmaker narrowed his eyes as he weighed us up. 'Let us try it out, shall we?' He tried to outstare George, but Pound met his eyes coolly. 'Only, if I disable you and this pipsqueak first, I can promise you one thing, Inspector, your lady friend will have a very messy end indeed.'

'And, as I have already hinted to my unusual ward,' Sidney Grice chattered blithely, 'jealousy may well be the root of the malice that ignited – then smouldered – in the ruins of Steep House.'

'How in the name of Hades did we get on to the subject of that infernal house again?' the bootmaker expostulated.

'Because that unworthy emotion,' Sidney Grice plucked floating petals from the air over his head so convincingly that I could almost see them myself, 'was not germinated, nor did it take root or flourish within the noble heart of Miss Freda Tulsima Wilde, for she loves her friend who, it transpires, hates and envies her.'

'Envy Freddy?' Lucy scorned. 'For what?'

'It was Miss Wilde whose parents were rich whilst yours, though she did not know it, were facing penury. It was Miss Wilde who was clever and witty and turned all the boys' heads. Most pertinently, it was Miss Wilde who stole the heart of your beloved brother, Eric.'

Sidney Grice watched his petals float away with an almost-beatific expression.

'That is a lie!' The chair rocked violently and if Lucy Bocking could have broken her bonds, I would have feared for my guardian's safety. 'Eric may have had a crush on Freddy but I was the one he really loved.'

91

The Heart of the Fire

SIDNEY GRICE STARTED humming, scaling hitherto unexplored continents of tunelessness, whilst tapping both feet in different rhythms.

'Before,' he broke off, his feet still drumming frenetically, 'we venture down that thorny path, I should like to consider the condition of Steep House.'

He stood still.

'Well, maybe I wouldn't.' The bootmaker amused himself by wrapping a tress of Lucy's hair tightly round his fingers, pulling up hard and sawing it off with his knife.

My guardian put his hands on his hips. 'Let us consider the origins of the fire,' he persisted. 'We were expected to believe that it started in a Christmas tree, the candles having been left unattended.' His hands cupped into a megaphone. 'Were your parents moronic, Miss Wilde, or, perchance, in the habit of retiring in such states of intoxication that they were unaware of what they were doing? Were they such democratic employers that they sent their servants to bed before they followed suit? If not, did not one of those minions observe that the waxen illuminations had not been extinguished?'

'The fire brigade and police thought that one of the wicks must have been left smouldering and reignited,' Freddy explained. 'And, no, my parents were neither stupid nor drunk.'

His megaphone fell apart. 'I did not say that they were.'

'I did not say that you did,' Freddy whipped back, and Mr G inclined his head.

'*Sehr gut.*' He paused admiringly. 'I have, however, another undisclosed number of difficulties in subscribing even luke-warmly to that scenario. First,' he held up one finger for the benefit of anyone who was uncertain which number he referred to. 'The worst fire damage was to the south-east of that, to wit, the right-hand side as one faces the architectural corpse.'

'There was paraffin stored in the cellar against my father's instructions by one of the maids – who wanted to save herself having to go outside for it at night,' Freddy explained. 'But she paid for that with her life.'

'And three others.' Mr G's right foot thrust out like a big game hunter posing with his first lion. 'Quite a steep price, some might argue. However, you have yet to convert me to your cause for, when I examined the generously proportioned entrance hall, I was filled with wonder, as Miss Middleton can bear witness, to come upon a varnished floor.'

'Many places have those,' Pound objected, 'including this one and the house I live in.'

'Oh, Chief Inspector.' My godfather mimed tossing a weighty object into the air. 'Must you dominate proceedings with your embarrassing domestic anecdotes? The varnish,' he continued, before George could reply, 'was blistered.'

'Of course it was,' Lucy rejoined. 'There was a fire.'

'*Coniferophyta* burn with a vigour which may be gratifying or alarming, depending upon one's aspirations,' Mr G pondered, lowering his foot cautiously. 'If I were to set one on fire here and now – though you may rest assured that I have no intention of doing so – I would be overweeningly confident that the intense heat would melt the varnish and set it alight in very short order.'

'So why didn't it?' Pound had slid another inch.

'The question I asked myself,' Mr G inclined his head like an adult listening to a shy child, 'is how did the conflagration travel from the tree to the cellar?'

'Fire moves in funny ways.' The bootmaker unfastened another button of Lucy's dress very gently, and she shivered.

'No, it does not,' Sidney Grice argued. 'Heat and flames move upwards most readily, laterally less readily, and downwards least readily. If you want to burn something quickly you place it above, not at the side of your heat source, and certainly not below it. If the blaze had started in the tree, it would have spread to the staircase and ceiling. Fragments of the staircase still stand.'

'The ceiling collapsed, though,' Freddy pointed out.

'And landed on the non-ignited varnish, the thick plaster-work protecting it from the full effects of the heat.' Mr G prodded the floor with his boot, as he had when testing the floor of the ruins. 'Indicating that the fire was on the upper floor first. The logical conclusion, therefore, would be that the fire did not start at the tree.'

'Does any of this actually matter?' The bootmaker yawned.

'I am sorry if we are keeping you awake,' I murmured.

'Let us pretend,' Mr G invited us, 'that the primary source was in the most readily flammable part of the house, which was where, exactly, Miss Wilde?'

'Where the paraffin was stored,' Freddy said, 'under the front of the house to the right.'

'Where poor Eric was found.' Lucy sighed.

'But why would Eric have gone into the heart of the fire?' I asked.

'To try to put it out,' she replied, as if I were stupid.

'Or to try to escape,' Freddy volunteered. 'There was a window leading into a light-well there. He managed to smash his way into the well but there was a locked grating over it.'

'And the flames would have been sucked up into the air over him,' the bootmaker imagined with relish. 'Roasted like a suckling pig.'

'Shut up.' Lucy strained her arms and lowered her head in a hopeless attempt to block the words out.

'I do not think you are in much of a position to give me orders.' The bootmaker snatched another fistful of Lucy's pale blonde hair and yanked her upright. His mouth went to her cheek and I thought he was going to kiss her, but he brushed it against her ear and murmured, 'Must have made a nice lot of crackling.'

Lucy wrenched her head away and strained at her bonds, a muffled howl escaping from her clenched teeth but failing to drown him out.

'For pity's sake, man,' Pound railed. 'Have you no humanity?'

'Some.' The bootmaker licked his lips showily. 'But none to spare.'

'Go on,' my guardian urged, and mouthed something about *control*.

'The flames would go up through the floors until they reached the roof.' I pictured the wreckage with its still-standing bay, 'And along each floor and the roof, every layer would have been collapsing onto the one below as it became too weak to support itself. So,' I tried to superimpose one image on another. 'New House had a large central skylight. If that collapsed, the top of the stairs could have been blocked quite early on. The flames would have shot through the roof and gone the only way they could – sideways.'

'Everyone was trapped by the bars on the windows,' Freddy said miserably. 'Daddy had them put on after a spate of burglaries in the area. But, because my bedroom was at the side of the house, Fairbank managed to get to me from the servants' staircase at the back – where the fire was less intense – and carried me out. But I was unconscious, overcome by smoke and pinned down by a burning beam. By then the flames were too intense for him to get back in.'

'What a touching tale.' Mr G put his hand to his heart. 'If only it were true.'

'But he told me so, and Lucy saw him carrying me out,' Freddy said.

'Good old Lucy.' Sidney Grice waved his handkerchief in celebration. 'Except that she did not.'

Both women opened their mouths but neither spoke.

'We went to see Mr Fairbank,' I explained. 'And he told us he was in Elderberry House, next door, when the fire started, and Freddy was already lying on the ground.'

'This is outrageous,' Lucy blustered. 'He has been claiming a pension from the estate. He was even given a house as a reward for his bravery.'

'And he saw you nearby,' I continued, 'as soon as he arrived.'

'The man was a drunk,' she stormed.

'And freely admits as much,' Mr G said. 'I did not only search through Miss Wilde's undergarments.'

'For your diary,' I explained hastily, and her indignation was transformed into perplexity.

'I do not keep a diary.'

'The one you kept in Steep House,' I said guiltily, for I hated my guardian's habit of finding and reading mine.

Freddy greeted that news with overt confusion. 'But it was lost in the fire.'

'Or possibly stolen,' Sidney Grice said, and shushed any objections by saying loudly and clearly, 'Whatever its provenance, it was certainly not stored in your chest. It was charred and yet there was no ash, nor the lingering aroma of combustion in your immaculately laundered and stored petticoats.'

'But where was it?' Freddy searched our faces.

'Well, don't look at me,' the bootmaker told her jocularly.

'I found it and kept it,' Lucy announced.

'And partially incinerated it,' Sidney Grice chipped in. 'Miss Middleton, occupier but not owner of 125 Gower Street, commented privately to me that the surface was shiny. But she failed – as is her wont – to notice that the lower two thirds of the page were not, and the facing page had only a light sheen. If only – and my life is festooned with such regrets – she had touched it with one of her indifferently manicured fingerplates.'

'You told me not to,' I railed.

'I told you to be careful but, if you had performed that unchallenging action, you would have realized that this glossy area was oily from the drip-dripping of candle wax, the page having been deliberately burned to conceal Miss Wilde's report of a conversation.'

I quoted from memory: '*he told me, "I hate Steep House and everybody in it. I shall destroy them all."*'

Freddy's lips parted, but my godfather's arm shot out towards her in a Roman salute. 'Oh why, oh why – and you may answer this at my earliest convenience, Miss Freda Tulsima Darovena Wilde – did you start your sentence with a lower-case h?'

'It said *She*.' Freddy tried but failed to wipe her inflamed left eye on her shoulder. 'Lucy made that threat, but my diary went on to say that it was just because she was angry at not being invited with me to the New Year's ball, and I knew she did not mean it. After all,' she continued less certainly, 'it was Lucy who saved my life.'

'At the risk of my own,' Lucy pointed out.

'I also took stock of the contents of your trunk, Miss Bocking,' Mr G, closely watched by the bootmaker, slipped a hand gingerly in and out of his breast pocket, 'whilst my inelegant and sometimes mendacious godchild was regaling you with a bawdy ballad.'

'I think not.' Lucy smiled uneasily. 'The padlocks were not broken and only I have the key.'

'Grice knows no locksmith.' He flicked his cigarette case open to display the picks. 'Though that is not literally true. I know of seven hundred and three, and have met one hundred and eighty-six. It is just that I was trying to coin a neat turn of phrase.'

'You did very well,' I assured him.

'Was that sarcasm?'

'It was not.'

'Thank you.' He made a slight bow before raising his voice. 'You could not bring yourself to throw it away, could you, Miss Bocking – the notorious yellow dress that meant so much to you.'

Lucy flushed. 'I rescued it from the fire,' she said.

'But where did you find it?' Freddy asked.

'In the garden. It must have fallen out,' Lucy blustered. 'I saved it for you, Freddy, and then I thought it might upset you too much, so I locked it away – along with your diary.'

'The hem was badly scorched,' Mr G told her.

'Of course it was,' she responded incredulously. 'It had been in a fire.'

'But why only the hem?' I pressed. 'Oh, Lucy, Mr Fairbank saw you wearing it.' I did not know if that was true but Lucy soon confirmed my hunch.

'He is a liar,' she spat. 'He always has been. My father nearly sacked him several times but always felt sorry for him. That man has been trying to blackmail me with false allegations for years.'

'Then why not cut off his allowance?' I asked. 'Or is it paid to keep him quiet?'

'My father set up a fund that I cannot touch. I should have...' Lucy began, and I could only guess what she thought she should have done to her father's old butler.

'Shall I tell you what I think happened?' I said.

'I wish somebody bleeding would,' the bootmaker complained. 'I'm itching for my fun.'

'Fun?' Sidney Grice mused. The word held a special meaning for him.

'That's right.' The bootmaker took a breath and drew his knife across Lucy's throat.

Below the Blade

LUCY SCREAMED AND Freddy sobbed out, 'No!'
'It is all right,' George Pound held up his palms and pushed them down in a calming motion. 'He is using the blunt edge.'

'What?' Lucy looked at him wildly, gasping, and trying to bury her head in herself before she absorbed what he was telling her.

'Got you going, though, didn't I.' The bootmaker smirked.

'If by that you mean Misses Bocking and Wilde, you may be correct,' Sidney Grice said amiably.

'Shall I tell you what I think?' I began, but had a better idea. I unclipped my handbag.

'What's she doing?' The bootmaker gestured angrily.

'I just want to show you something.'

The stuffing was first out again. I rammed it back in and delved deeper. 'Oh, for goodness' sake.' I rooted through all my paraphernalia until I found the cold metal handle. 'Oh, here it is.'

I brought out the starting pistol.

'What's the idea?' The bootmaker looked rattled for the first time.

'Let us call it my insurance policy,' I suggested, levelling the barrel in his direction. 'I shall not make the first move but, if you should decide to use the other edge, I will kill you.'

'But you shook your bag out.'

'I pinched the leather to hold the gun inside.'

'You did it very well.' The bootmaker threw me a morsel of praise and I forced myself to reward him with a wink.

'Do you want to give that to me, March?' George suggested, for he knew how unintentionally dangerous I could be with firearms.

'No, thank you, Chief Inspector,' I said stiffly, for it might look too obviously light in his strong grip. 'I should not like you to get into trouble for bearing arms whilst on duty.'

'Well, we seems to have reached an impasse,' the bootmaker conceded. 'Let us see who blinks first, shall we?'

Mr G made as if to sweep dust off his left lapel and shot me an anxious glance. 'Then the metaphorical floor, Miss Middleton, is yours.'

'Is it?'

'You were about to tell us what you think,' George prompted.

'Oh yes,' I remembered. My throat was dry. 'I think Lucy went in and dragged Freddy out, which is how she burned the hem of her dress.'

Lucy puffed out her cheeks. 'You are right, March, I did. But, when Fairbank turned up and begged me not to tell anybody he had been absent, I felt sorry for him and let him take the credit.'

'What an exemplary client you could be.' Mr G made a clapping motion with his left hand. 'Brave and generous – if only you were not such a liar.'

'How dare you?' she exploded. 'Nobody speaks to me like that.'

'I do.' Sidney Grice treated us to a rare, though not jolly, smile. 'Would you like me to leave?'

'Why were you wearing the dress, Lucy?' I asked.

'I liked it,' Lucy faltered. 'I should not have taken it, I know, but I was young and girls do silly things.'

'They certainly do,' my guardian concurred wholeheartedly, and the bootmaker snuffled in amusement.

'Why did you change the dress before anybody else turned up, Lucy?' I asked, keeping my gun trained on him.

'So that I did not get into trouble,' she said simply. 'And that is why I let Fairbank take the credit. We did each other a favour, really, keeping each other's secrets.'

'But, Lucy,' Freddy said in bewilderment, 'the dress was in my wardrobe that night. How could you possibly have got to it?'

'Unless you were in the house before the fire,' I concluded.

And Lucy hung her head. 'I went in earlier and took it. I was going to put it back. But I had nothing to do with the fire, I swear.'

'That's funny,' George Pound mused. 'Nobody said you had.'

Lucy slapped the arm of her chair as much as her restricted movements allowed. 'Well, that was the implication of their questions.'

'Sounded to me like they were asking about some stupid dress,' the bootmaker chipped in. 'But now it sounds like you started that fire and I know how to prove it.' The bootmaker rotated his knife so that the point rested under the angle of Lucy's jaw. She winced. 'Here's the deal,' he said. 'You tell me the truth and I don't dig this in any deeper. Tell me one lie and I do, and it'll be too late for your plank-faced pal to do anything about it.'

'I am not bluffing,' I bluffed.

'Ditto.' The bootmaker winked back.

'But how can you know if Lucy is telling the truth or not?' Freddy asked nervously.

The bootmaker shrugged. 'Well, everything she's said so far that they've caught her out on, I've known in advance. So let's play.' He applied a little pressure and I saw Lucy's skin indent. 'Did you set fire to the house?'

'N—' was all Lucy managed before she jumped in pain. 'Yes, yes, I did.'

A drop of blood sprang up just below the blade.

'No court will ever take this as evidence,' Pound warned, and the bootmaker tossed his head.

'Let me put it this way. I'm not coming forward as a witness for the prosecution.' The bootmaker gave his attention back to Lucy, who was squirming in pain as her blood broke through, hanging like a teardrop. 'How and why? And no more porkies, girl, or the next one might be your last.'

'Take the knife away,' Lucy begged, 'and I'll tell you everything.'

'See?' The bootmaker grinned. 'There isn't anything to being a detective after all.'

'I shall deny it all afterwards,' Lucy muttered, and the bootmaker wiped his knife on her dress in a slow cross over her left breast.

'What makes you thinks there'll be an afterwards?' he asked.

A look of shock shot across Lucy's face, and it took me a while to realize that there was anything strange about that.

'But we have—' She stopped herself and George Pound clicked his fingers.

'Of course,' he said, to my and Sidney Grice's puzzlement. 'Now I get it. You were going to say you had an agreement.'

'Nonsense,' Lucy blustered. 'No wonder we need private detectives with such stupid policemen.'

'And personal detectives,' Mr G added sotto voce.

I took my eyes off the bootmaker for a moment. 'What sort of an agreement?'

'To let him in.' George stepped forward.

'Get back against the wall,' the bootmaker snapped, and then, 'How did you work that out?'

'Because the maids didn't,' Pound replied. 'By the way, where is your cook?'

'Why on earth are you mithering about that?' Lucy demanded.

But Freddy explained. 'She has gone to a funeral. All five of her nieces died of scarlet fever in Edinburgh.'

'Edinburgh.' For once Sidney Grice was visibly moved. 'Oh, what a terrible waste.' He rubbed the back of his neck. 'Of granite.' He pulled himself together. 'But why have you not employed an agency woman?'

'We were going to,' Freddy replied.

'Going to where?' he snapped.

'Going to hire one,' she clarified. 'But the last one was so awful that the girls said they would have a go. They both liked to help Cook.' Freddy lowered her head. 'They were lovely girls,' she sobbed.

'Certainly were.' The bootmaker licked his lips ostentatiously.

'You filthy—' Pound caught his words before any more escaped. 'They were in the middle of making scones and both of their hands were covered in the mix. If one of them had gone to the door, she would have wiped her hands or washed them. All the cloths were clean and the sink was dry. I had a close look at it.'

That must have been when I thought he was going to vomit, but he was checking the tap.

'Perhaps she let him in before she started to help.' I prayed that he would be able to gainsay my suggestion.

George was sceptical. 'When I was a handsome young pup of a constable,' his eyes sparkled as in days of old, 'I wasn't averse to sweet-talking my way into a few sculleries on a wet winter's night. First of all, I would never have gone through the front way. The householders would have wanted to know what I was up to. The maid wouldn't go on helping Cook and ignoring me. Otherwise why would she have let me in? She'd cut me a thick slice of bread – with jam, if I was lucky – and give me a mug of tea. The kettle was cold.'

'*Gut gemacht.*' Sidney Grice was undisguisedly impressed.

And George Pound grinned. 'I've waited ten years to hear him say that,' he told me. 'Whatever it means.'

And it was all I could do not to run over and kiss him.

'At last.' The bootmaker saluted. 'A peeler with brains. You're wasted as a copper, Chief Inspector.'

'The day I see you in the dock, I shall count my time well spent,' Pound said, with a power that made me shiver.

'But why?' I asked Lucy, unable to bring myself to use her name.

'To lure me in.' Sidney Grice put a hand to his brow in an odd salute. 'With a view to curtailing my life.'

'Not just you,' the bootmaker said. 'Your girl has been causing no end of trouble.'

'She is very good at that,' my guardian assured him, his hand still in place as though he were squinting into the sun.

'If I have made your life a bit difficult, I humbly apologize.' I performed the tiniest of curtsies. 'For that was never my intention. I meant to make your life very difficult indeed.' I paused. 'But why did you hire us in the first place, Lucy?'

'I wanted you to find the man who attacked me,' she replied simply. 'I was not to know you would go delving into Steep House and Silas Spry.'

'And you really thought he would let you go?'

'I gave him a non-cancellable bankers' order for one thousand pounds, but it is post-dated by a week and my accounts will be frozen if I die.'

'I am not sure that he cares about the money,' I warned, and Lucy met my gaze beseechingly as the bootman smirked.

'Think you can hold that gun up forever, do you?' he asked solicitously. 'Arm not getting tired?'

'I am quite comfortable, thank you.' Though, in truth, it was starting to ache.

He laughed sarcastically. 'I'm going to enjoy hurting you.'

'I am not sorry to disabuse you,' Sidney Grice said. 'But I could not possibly permit that.'

'How you going to stop me?'

'He won't need to,' George vowed. 'I will.'

'Excuse me, Chief Inspector.' My guardian puffed indignantly. 'But I am quite capable of looking after my own goddaughter.'

'Well, you ain't making too good a job of it at the moment,' the bootmaker sneered.

'Oh, she always looks like that,' Sidney Grice assured him, and the bootmaker cackled.

'You.' He gave Lucy a couple of light slaps as one might try to rouse an inebriate. 'Tell us about that brother.'

'And, for the benefit of your erstwhile partner in felony,' Sidney Grice chipped in, 'you might like to explain why you killed him.'

'What on earth are you talking about?' Lucy's pique fragmented into a yelp as the wire dug in. 'All right.' Tears of pain and frustration sprang up in her eyes. 'I'll tell you everything.'

'Before you do, Lucy...' Freddy paled. She fought to continue. 'I think you should know something. When you were in my dressing room I saw you.'

'What are you talking about?'

'I thought it was a burglar and that he might go away if I pretended to be asleep, and then I saw you – in my new dress with Eric.' Freddy almost choked on her own words. 'He was... pawing at you... slobbering... You—'

'Slobbering?' Lucy raged. 'It was not his fault his lips did not meet.'

'That is not what I meant.'

'You spurned him,' Lucy accused. 'My poor Eric was not pretty enough for you, was he? But do not trouble yourself on that account. He had a dutiful sister to make up for that.' Lucy looked at the assembled company defiantly. 'Oh, what is the point?' she spat. 'Whether or not you try to escape, the result will be the same.' For a fraction of a moment Lucy looked almost serene. 'Whatever happens, I am not getting out of this alive.'

93

The Light and the Dark

I RESTED MY RIGHT elbow on my hip for support.

'I told you that Eric had a soft spot for Freddy,' she began hesitantly. 'But it was much more than that. She obsessed him. He could hardly talk of anyone or anything else – the way she looked and moved, the way she laughed, things she said and did. It was endless. But he was not good enough for dear sweet high-and-mighty Freddy. She hardly even noticed him.'

'I could not help but notice Eric,' Freddy objected. 'But I tried not to. He made me feel uncomfortable, the way he stared.'

'Of course he stared.' Lucy kicked the leg of her chair with her heel. 'How could he not, with you flaunting yourself, smiling and flirting.'

'I did not,' Freddy cried. 'I never encouraged him.'

'Just get on with it,' the bootmaker said.

'Eric was desolate. He wanted Freddy so much but he was too shy to approach her. I offered to speak to her, but when I broached the subject of my brother, Freddy laughed and said he was a funny one. Funny!'

'I was a child,' Freddy objected.

'You were twelve. Girls used to get married younger than that.' Lucy chewed her cheek. 'Eric changed. The happy prankster with whom I had grown up became moody and irritable. On more than one occasion he snapped at me and made me cry and, when I complained to my mother, she told me that it was my own fault. I should be doing more to make Eric happy. I did not understand what she meant, but she told me not to ask so many questions. If I were a good sister I would have more understanding of Eric's needs.'

'Can I ask,' I began carefully, for I still hoped her account was not leading where I feared, 'if Eric was your real brother – and your mother was too?'

'Her mother cannot have been her brother,' my godfather objected.

'Miss Bocking knows what I mean.'

'Of course they were.' Lucy bridled, as if anything else would have been indecent. 'To start with it was awkward. I was shy and felt too embarrassed to ask, but once Eric realized how much I wanted to please him, I soon discovered what was expected of me.

'At first he was easy to satisfy. I did things for him and he was happy with that. And then I let him do things to me— No, that is not quite true – I encouraged him. His needs became greater but I was more than willing to fulfil them. I was just so happy that my darling brother had me instead of Freddy. But he kept talking about her and how much he wanted her, and so I let him call me Freddy.

'Freddy and I had always kept our drapes open since we were children. No one could see us, but we could see into each other's rooms and wave to each other. Freddy always had a night lamp. She was afraid of the dark. And so we would turn my light off and Eric would do things and get me to do things, while he watched her lying in her bed, and called me Freddy, Freddy, sweet darling Freddy, over and over. But still it wasn't enough.'

Lucy seemed unaware that her captor was undoing another button.

'I saw how Eric had looked at Freddy that summer in her yellow dress. She was so stunningly beautiful that he couldn't keep his eyes off her, and so I stole the dress – it was easy. We were always in and out of each other's houses. And I put it on for him and that helped a lot. He wanted me all the time then. It was heaven. I made up my hair like hers and even tried to speak like her, in her pretty-prissy way, and Eric was beside himself with want. Once he saw Freddy getting disrobed and he was in ecstasy.'

Lucy's face lit up with something close to the same emotion.

'When it was discovered that the dress was missing I hid it in the attic beside the maid's room, but then her ceiling came down after a leak and she moved rooms, and when I went to get it, she saw me, and so I had to put other things in her room. It was her word against mine.' She swallowed and cleared her throat.

'And you let her go to prison?' I remembered.

'Well, you could hardly expect me to go.' Lucy's voice rose self-righteously.

'So what happened to...' I combed my mind for the name, 'Jocinda?'

'When she came out – after far too short a sentence – she tried to blackmail me. I knew she had no proof, but she could have besmirched my reputation with her filthy insinuations.' Her tone fell. 'I told her I had money in a box tied under my window sill, but I was not tall enough to reach it. She was so stupid. I could not believe anyone would be that gullible, but she leaned out to get it. I said I would hold her legs to stop her falling, and I tipped her out.'

Lucy's face dropped and drained, and she could hardly get out the next words. 'And then the disgusting creature that spawned her killed my father and my darling, darling mother.' Her voice broke.

'Boo-hoo.' The bootmaker pulled a faux sad face. 'So what about dear Eric?'

'I was no use to Eric after the dress was found.' Lucy's eyes overbrimmed. 'I offered to get an identical one made but he said it was no good, it would not be hers, and there was no point in me taking another dress. He wanted one that she had worn.' She arched her back stiffly. 'So the next time I went to Steep House I sneaked down and left the back door unlocked. I knew that Fairbank, the butler, would not check it because it was never used. And I took Eric into the house that night, and we crept into Freddy's dressing room and I put the dress on. It was a terrible risk but that was part of the thrill, and I played Freddy for him in that room next to hers, and just before the end I opened the door a crack so he could see her lying in bed facing him. I was terrified she would wake up, but so excited I could hardly breathe.'

Lucy took a few sharp breaths in memory. 'But in the cold light of day I realized how dangerous my acts had been and I refused to do it again. Eric was so upset he wouldn't speak to me for weeks.' She pouted. 'And, when I burst into tears over dinner, Mummy dragged me away and said that I had obviously upset my brother. She did not want to know why. She only knew that I should at least try to be an obedient and loving sister.'

She spoke very carefully now. 'And so I found a new way to please him and at first it was enough, but he would sit all night in my window afterwards, watching and wanting.' Lucy laboured to catch her breath. 'Freddy – always that damned Freddy-Freddy-Freddy.'

94

The Burning of Flesh

S IDNEY GRICE FOLDED his arms and surveyed her bowed head. 'You spent six months in a convent, did you not, Miss Bocking?'

'St Philomena's.' She scowled. 'What of it?'

'Even now defiant.' Mr G reached into his jacket.

'Not so fast,' the bootmaker snapped, and Sidney Grice withdrew his hand a fraction at a time to reveal a folded letter.

'I wrote to that institution, asking if they would like a contribution to their funds, and had a very civil response from Mother Superior Sister Mary-James, outlining all the holy works they perform. Miss Middleton was too idle to read it but I imagine the contents will be of greater interest to some members of this assembly. The particular calling of the Sisters of Misfortune is suggested by the name of their community, for Philomena is the patron saint of infants and their duty is to tend to foundlings and the children of fallen women.'

'I did not think one could with one's own brother,' Lucy admitted in wonder. 'But I had a child – a monster, they said, who could not even be christened for it was the devil's spawn. I never saw him and, for all I know or care, they drowned him in the font.'

'You had a boy,' Freddy said wonderingly.

'They wanted to lock me away,' Lucy said flatly, 'for I had committed unspeakable sins. But my parents could not countenance the disgrace and so they forgave and took me back.'

'Did they punish Eric?' I asked

'Of course not.' Lucy's eyes flared. 'I had led poor Eric astray, they said, but the strange thing is—' she became a lost girl—'I did not really understand what we had done.'

'Did he stop making demands of you?' I tried, and the boot-maker snorted. He had four buttons undone now and I could see the top of Lucy's chemise.

'He told me Freddy had smiled at him on a few occasions and that she had asked about me, but he knew that it was really just a pretext to get close to him.'

'Oh, for heaven's sake,' Freddy broke in despairingly.

'He did not want me now that I was despoiled.' Lucy's eyes took on a strange lifelessness. 'And I suppose you could not blame him for that.'

'I think I could,' I muttered furiously.

'But I could speak to Freddy for him,' she said in a monotone. 'It was then that I made my mind up. The day after Boxing Day, I told Eric that I had done as he asked and that Freddy had sworn that she loved him too and wanted him to come to the house and spend the night with her, but he must say nothing in the mean-time to her or anyone, just to tell our parents that he was staying with a friend. I took him into the cellar and told him Freddy had set up a feather bed in the back room. He was so eager that he never even stopped to think and, when he went to look, I slammed and bolted the door. It was next to the paraffin store. There was a barred aperture between the room and Eric was shouting and cursing. He thought it was just a silly practical joke until he saw me open the taps and smelled the fuel, and then he started begging – Eric begging from me.' Lucy shook her head in disbelief. 'It only took one Lucifer and a soaked rag. Eric was hammering and screaming before the flames even reached him and I stood and listened, but then I worried that he would wake somebody up. So I called *Goodbye, my darling brother* and went upstairs, and you could not hear a thing when I shut the door into the hallway.

443

'The Christmas tree was very pretty.' Lucy smiled in remembrance. 'I lit the candles and watched from the terrace until I was sure that the flames had taken. I smashed a window to make it look like a burglary and hurried back to my room.'

'You must have waited a long time then.' Sidney Grice held up a crooked finger.

'How can you know that?'

'Because the flat window glass lay on top of the curved from the dome,' he said. 'But pray continue with your narrative, Miss Bocking.'

Lucy huffed, as she used to when he first irritated her. 'I could not go to bed. I sat in my window in my beautiful dress – I had taken it that afternoon – and stroked myself as Eric had liked to, and watched Steep House become a bonfire.'

The bootmaker had slipped his hand inside her dress and Lucy closed her eyes. 'Eric.' She stretched as if from a lovely dream. 'And then, when I saw figures on the lawn, I had to go and see what was happening.'

Her smile became distant as the bootmaker's hand moved slowly round.

'Do you feel no remorse?' I asked.

Lucy grimaced. 'The only reason I encouraged my parents to take Freddy in was so that I could watch her getting uglier every day. And that was my one regret, knowing that Eric had not lived to be repelled by her.'

The bootman withdrew his hand, but only to rip open the rest of her dress to the waist. Lucy hardly glanced to see what he was up to.

'Over the years, though, I started to realize that I had had no choice. He would have abandoned me and I could not have let him go to Freddy or any other woman. This way was perfect. He had been mine and nobody else's. And the more I thought about it, the more I realized that it was all Freddy's fault. If she hadn't been so beautiful and funny and clever and had that lovely yellow dress, he would have been happy with me forever. And the worst of it was, she did not even want him. *She* should have had the child and been cast aside. But there she was – so happy and more beautiful than ever, and taking an interest in some earl's son who had invited her to a New Year's ball. Surely she had to be punished for that?'

Sidney Grice had the same expression as he wore when sorting out a difficult mathematical problem.

'Punished?' Freddy cried, with such passion that Lucy jumped. 'I have certainly been *punished* – all these years of pain and disfigurement that will never get anything but worse. And for what? For being naive? For not wanting to be leered at by your disgusting brother?' Freddy saw her fellow captive about to protest, but she would not be silenced. 'If I had faults,' she wept, 'my God, they have been expiated.' She strained every sinew of her body. 'But know this, Lucy Bocking. When I saw you and Eric...' Freddy gasped and fought to control her emotions. 'And in all these years afterwards... I never condemned you – not once – because I thought that he had made you.' Freddy almost choked. 'I felt sorry for you.'

'*You* felt sorry for *me*?' Lucy tore uselessly at her bonds.

The bootmaker clapped Lucy's shoulder in mirth. 'Oh, this is rich.' The man chuckled. 'What a pair we have here.'

'Shut your mouth,' Lucy shrieked, but he roared with laughter, wrenching the dress aside to bare her shoulder.

I would have expected my guardian to be shocked, for I had known him to be nauseous at the sight of an ankle – especially one of mine – but he only said, 'I can see one of your contusions now.' He had the face of a poker player. 'I told you I might.'

'Well, I hope you are satisfied,' she flared back.

'I shall never be that.'

'This has gone far enough.' Pound clenched his fists impotently.

'Oh, we have much further to go yet,' the man vowed, and bared the other shoulder.

But Lucy paid no attention. She had the look of a beast now, her head rolling so violently that I thought she would dislocate her neck. 'Want to know why I saved you, Freddy?' The words sprayed messily from her mouth. 'Because I wanted you to see how grotesque you had become.'

'And how did Miss Wilde become so badly burned almost exclusively on the face?' Sidney Grice pounced, and Lucy banged her head back on the chair with a great cracking sound.

'The shovel,' I realized.

'I told you that you would work it out,' my guardian said, with a tilt of his chin.

But Lucy looked at me venomously. 'What the damn does it matter now?' She was all at once still. 'I found her on her back. She must have been overcome by the smoke, but she had staggered almost to the door before she collapsed. Her hair was singed but she did not look too badly hurt. My mother was there. She handed me the garden spade and told me to do what I had to. I think she meant for me to finish Freddy off, this prissy bitch who had caused all this trouble, and I had every intention of doing so. But, looking at that perfect button nose and beautiful bow lips, I had a better idea. There were some red-hot ashes nearby.'

Freddy howled but she could not shut the next words out.

'I shovelled them on. By Satan, she sizzled.' Lucy's words were rapturous. 'Even in all that smoke, I smelled the burning meat that was her flesh.'

'Oh, how priceless.' The bootmaker hooted and swapped hands with his knife. 'What an excellent note to end on.'

And with that, he grasped the ivory handle of Sidney Grice's revolver.

95

──◦•◦──

The Human Stain

I RAISED MY STARTING pistol a fraction.

'But we have not talked about you yet,' I pointed out, for I knew no man could resist that topic. And, seeing him tip his head in semi-assent, I continued, 'You do not do it for gratification. You could get that in many places for the price of a drink. You do it because you hate women.'

'Why, Miss Middleton, you should be an alienist.' The bootmaker's smile was forced this time, I thought, but he took his hand off the gun

'You are beyond medical help,' I told him, and the smile congealed.

'Do not talk to me about doctors.' His fingers blanched on the knife handle.

'There is one that we really ought to mention.' I waved the gun in an attempt to relieve the cramp in my arm. 'You see, we know that you murdered Mr Lamb.'

'Oh yeah?'

'The surgeon?' Pound's question went unanswered. He had edged another couple of inches.

'And we know why.' I looked the bootmaker in the eyes and saw them smoulder, his lips still fixed mirthlessly. 'For the same reason,' I said carefully, 'that Lady Brockwood did not disable you with her knee. There was nothing for her to damage.'

The smile shrivelled into scorn. 'It took you a long time to work that out.'

'But those women never did you any harm,' I burst out.

'You think not?' The embers burst into flame. 'Have you any idea what it is to be despised for an injury that wasn't your fault?'

'Shall I answer that one?' Freddy asked quietly, and the flames dipped briefly.

'I take your point,' the bootmaker conceded. 'But it is different for men.'

'Really?' she demanded. 'The only man I ever kissed screamed.'

The bootmaker wiped his nose on the inner bend of his elbow. 'It is being laughed at that I cannot bear.' He leaned towards her confidentially. 'The first woman I went with was a widow. She knew what to expect and she mocked me. I ran away that time but never again.' His mouth worked like a man building up spit. 'The girls I go with now have no idea what to expect and half of them do not even understand what has happened. But there's one thing for sure – they never laugh.' He chewed at nothing. 'You complain about screaming, but I like that part best and – once I get going – by Beelzebub, you should hear them squeal.'

'But you are punishing innocent girls for what the medical profession did to you?' I tried to reason with him.

'One incompetent surgeon did for me,' the bootmaker said matter-of-factly. 'And I dealt with him. But there's not a woman of the world who would not despise me if she knew, and so I take them before they have the chance.' His tone became conversational. 'When I was whole I was engaged to an heiress.' He rested his elbow on Lucy's left shoulder. 'Very rich and not bad-looking. But I had a rupture lifting a crate that fell off a wagon on to my foot. I was worried I wouldn't be able to consummate the marriage with that and it could be annulled, so I went to see Lamb. He said he could put me right, and then I caught cancer – or so he said. He was just supposed to clean me up.' He looked at my guardian bitterly. 'But when I came round from the ether, he said it was more advanced than he thought and he'd had to be more radical to save my life. I didn't know what he meant until they changed the dressing.'

Sidney Grice jerked upright like a sentry caught almost asleep on duty. 'And that is why you were so angry with Miss Bocking,' he surmised, 'and called her – to quote – a *dirty dirty girl.*'

'I assumed she was a virgin,' the bootmaker agreed. 'But, when I found out she wasn't, I realized that she would know what was wrong with me.'

'I did not notice,' Lucy reassured him. 'I was in a drugged stupor and did not really believe it was happening.'

'Did not?' The bootmaker was incredulous. 'Then I have hung around the square all these weeks, shouting rubbish and trying to sew leather, for nothing.'

'But what,' I asked, though I feared I knew the answer, 'were you waiting for?'

'Take a guess,' he challenged.

'You thought about it later and were worried that she would be able to tell the police about you, and they could check all hospital records,' I surmised. 'But how did you know where Lucy lived?'

'I knew she and her friend were well-to-do by their accents and attire. So I toured all the good roads and squares until I saw a woman with a bruised face and another in a green veil coming out of this house.' He looked at the calluses on the fingers of his left hand. 'There's not too many of them. I thought I would catch her alone to make it easier, but in the end I decided it would be safer to do it in the privacy of her own home.'

'So why did you turn from rape to murder?' Pound enquired, as casually as one might ask for directions in the park. 'It's a very different crime.'

'Not very,' I argued. 'Both of them are about crushing women.'

'What God did not give you in looks he compensated for in brains.' The bootmaker had a greater facility for backhanded compliments than my guardian, I mused. 'But it was you who put me on the road to killing.' He flapped his hands innocently. 'Those two bitches in Limehouse – that was self-defence.'

'And this?' Pound asked calmly.

'The same,' the bootmaker reasoned. 'You and your two friends and this filthy vixen.' He tore at Lucy's hair and she choked back a cry. 'You're all a threat to me, and now this mash-faced one too – you're all witnesses. Besides,' he smirked, 'I rather enjoy it.' He scratched the side of his nose and remembered something. 'So what was that you were saying about me being selected to do this cow?' And, as he spoke, the bootmaker cut a line down Lucy's cheek reminiscent of Prince Ulrich's duelling scar, and she groaned but gritted her teeth.

Sidney Grice curled his fingers and examined the plates. 'I thought I had explained that already,' he said testily. 'Wallace pretended to be drunk so that you would take his place. If you were wondering why he chose you particularly from all the flotsam he could sift through, I would remind you that he was very nearly imprisoned for his role in the attack upon the person of Miss Hockaday at your behest.'

'But he couldn't have known who I was,' the bootmaker objected. 'I kept my face well covered – told him I had a tooth-ache.'

'Jonathon Richard *the Walrus* Wallace liked to know who he was dealing with.' My guardian rotated his hand to peer at his knuckles. 'He had a trick which he adapted from an annoy-ing practice of mine. The first time you met – when he contracted to help you entrap Miss Hockaday – Johnny slipped *Lawsonia Inermis*, better known to the hoi polloi as henna, into your drink. It was a simple thing thereafter to offer the local guttersnipes a meagre reward for spotting a man with orange-stained lips.'

'It had turned brown by the time we first saw you,' I recalled.

'Sneaky crup.' The bootmaker pulled his mouth down in grudging respect. 'I wondered where I had got that. Thought it might be something I caught off a girl.'

'The ladies might like to hum loudly whilst I make my next revelation.' Sidney Grice hurumphed, but none of us took up his suggestion. 'Not only can this detestable degenerate not spill seed, he cannot spill anything.'

The bootmaker turned puce. 'What the hell are you talking about?'

'I took a swab from Lady Dulcet Brockwood and there was blood aplenty and nothing but blood.'

'What? You?' The bootmaker actually looked queasy. 'And they think I am disgusting.'

'Oh, you are,' Mr G assured him. 'I dredge the drains. It is vermin like you that fill them.'

The bootmaker's fist blanched on the handle of his knife.

'What about Prince Ulrich?' I asked, desperate for any delay that would give us a chance to do something, though I had no idea what it could be. 'Why did you try to implicate him?'

The bootmaker spat on the floor. 'That high-and-mighty for-eigner strutting the streets like he owned them – so rich and handsome and titled. I bet he had no problems getting girls. But he wasn't happy with all that.' He wiped his mouth on his sleeve. 'He had to set himself up as guardian-crudding-angel, stalking the East End and escorting girls home. He lost me a good few chances and he nearly had me cornered with that Hockaday bitch, and I bet you anything you like he did for Wallace. I thought about getting rid of him myself, but I was in enough trouble with Hanratty, and killing a member of the royal family is asking for trouble, to put it mildly. So then I thought why not make *him* suffer for *my* sins. I pointed the finger with that button and the accent. I put on some good clothes and I even sprayed some scent, but you were either too in awe of his rank or you saw through it.'

'The latter,' Mr G told him. 'Amongst other factors, if you rip off a button sewn as thoroughly as the prince's was, I would expect to find a few strands of cotton and possibly a piece of torn silk. The threads had been cleanly cut and the waistcoat was unscathed.'

'Also you wore new boots that creaked,' I contributed. 'Prince Ulrich's were oiled and softened.'

'Didn't do him any good, though, did it?' the bootmaker jibed. 'I read about that in the papers. Seems the mother of that silly girl they fished out of the river had more guts and initiative than the rest of you put together.'

'But she killed an innocent man.' I protested uselessly, I knew, but I was running out of things to hold his attention, and George Pound, ever edging forwards, was still a long way from being able to surprise him.

'That's what made it so delicious.' The bootmaker smirked. 'Anyway, I have enjoyed our chinwag.' He wrenched Lucy's head back to bare her throat. 'Think I'm stupid?' He sniggered at me. 'That's not a real gun, is it?'

The question caught me off balance. 'Of course it is.'

But he shook his head. 'Not from the way you've held it steady all this time. It's too light.'

'I am stronger than I look,' I bluffed frantically, levelling it at his head. 'Shall I pull the trigger?'

'Go on then.'

'Only if I have to.'

'I can still make you a deal.' Lucy stalled in desperation. 'I have lots more money and I can help you. I can lure girls here or wherever you want. Who would ever suspect me? And you would not even have to leave the house.' She writhed about and strained her bonds but the bootmaker hardly gave her a glance.

'Shall I go first?' He challenged me.

His eyes had a frightening chill in them now.

'No,' Freddy and I cried as one.

Lucy screamed.

'No-no, I can—' But she was beyond even knowing what she could do now, and tossing her head wildly.

The bootmaker smiled quite beautifully. 'Farewell, my pretty one,' he said softly, and the tip of the blade pressed just into the side of her neck.

96

The Gates of Hell

L UCY SQUEALED, BLOOD trickling down her neck.
'Enough.' In one smooth movement Sidney Grice leaped, swept his cane off the table and raised it to head height. He put a thumb on the lever in the handle and the cane exploded in a ball of flame. Sidney Grice cried out and clutched his face, and in that moment the gates of hell sprang open and sucked all of us in.

'What in God's name?' Pound shouted, and, even in the chaos, I realized it must have been one of the sticks that Molly had put in the wash.

My guardian dropped to his knees, clawing his eyes, and I would have run to him but Lucy was thrashing, stricken with terror and pain, whimpering, the blood a steady flow now. And, behind her, the bootmaker grinned and pulled the knife free.

'I'd say that was a misfire.' And he looked down lovingly, as he stroked her chin and drew that long thin sliver of steel slowly and as deliberately as a surgeon making his incision.

Lucy wailed and her white skin broke and was flooded bright flowing red, and she arched back in a hopeless attempt to draw away and escape the steel which was parting her throat. And her feet flew out, running nowhere, and her wail became a gurgle and her arms strained and wrenched, and the chair rocked and the flood became a torrent, then a pulse, splattering from under her right jaw far out on to the rug where once we had sat drinking tea. It may have only taken a second, but terror stretched that time into an endless agony and snapped it back into an instant too quickly to do anything about.

'Lucy!' Freddy screamed.

I raced towards him and swung the barrel of my gun into his face. I aimed for his eye but he pulled back and I caught his cheek.

'Bitch!' He swiped the knife out of Lucy's neck.

She was still alive. I saw her eyes turn to look into mine, pleading for something I could not give.

The bootmaker pulled back his arm to strike, but a large shape hurtled between us and George Pound threw me backwards, almost upsetting me on to the floor.

'Run, darling, run.'

There was a crash and I spun to see Freddy had rocked her chair over sideways and was yanking her left arm free of the broken chair and scrabbling, dragging the chair with her, towards her friend.

Sidney Grice was wiping his eye desperately with his sleeve and struggling up. 'What is happening? March, are you all right?'

'Yes.'

'It is a pity you are blind.' The bootmaker strolled over, the cheesewire dangling from his belt, a tight knot at either end. 'I should have liked you to see me kill you.' He pointed the gun.

I leaped at his hand but his left fist lashed out and cracked me in the mouth. My jaw jolted back against my skull. I staggered and toppled to my knees, groggy but conscious enough to see the bootmaker grin and, slowly and deliberately, pull back the hammer.

'Who are you?' Sidney Grice whispered huskily.

'Who indeed?' The bootman shrugged. 'We are none of us who we pretend to be.' He slipped off the safety catch, savouring every instant. 'You want my name, Mr Grice? Well, I'm not so formal as you. Just call me Jack.'

'Jack?' Sidney Grice croaked.

'Say goodbye, Mr Grice.' The bootmaker pulled the trigger. And there was nothing. 'What?' He shook the revolver and tried again.

Sidney Grice had his gunmetal pen in his hand. He pressed the clip and a stiletto shot out, as long as one of Geraldine Hockaday's knitting needles but flattened to a razor edge. He lurched up and thrust towards the voice. I saw the tip enter the bootmaker's nose and emerge on the other side.

The bootmaker howled. 'Jesus.'

Sidney Grice twisted the blade and ripped it out, tearing the nostrils wide open.

'By the Christ, that hurts.' The bootmaker's left hand cupped his lower face, his blood instantly spilling over. He hurled the revolver into Sidney Grice's gaping socket and my guardian's head reeled back.

The bootmaker reached behind himself.

'Knife,' I yelled, as he slashed in a wide arc, but Sidney Grice dropped under it, lashing unseeingly with his blade like a sabre into the side of his assailant's arm.

'Stop it.'

Sidney Grice jabbed.

I dived at the bootmaker and his elbow struck my temple, stunning me again. My bonnet came loose and, as my hand went to it, I came away with a hatpin. And, clutching it by the glass bead handle, I grabbed his trouser leg and drove the point into the side of his knee.

'Damn-shit-damn.' The bootmaker grabbed at my wrist and the pin snapped off inside him at the haft. 'Shit-shit-shit.' He raised his knife high to hack it down on me and I tried to roll away, but he had stamped on my dress. 'Die, you stinking bitch.'

Quick as a rapier, Sidney Grice's stiletto plunged into my attacker's thigh. The bootmaker howled, wrenching himself free and away, hurling his knife to clatter uselessly into a sideboard as he half ran, half toppled from the room.

I heard irregular footfalls and the front door slam, and got up blearily and dizzily to see Freddy trailing the broken chair and trying to hold Lucy's head in place. It had, as her murderer predicted, been sliced clean off.

Inspector Pound was on the floor, curled on his side.

'George.' I threw myself over to him and looked. The knife was in his chest, jammed hard, I saw, between his ribs.

'Oh, thank God, it is the right side.' He was leaning on the handle so I turned him on to his back, and he groaned. 'We shall get you straight to hospital. I shall give you my blood like I did before and you will complain about having to recuperate in the countryside. We shall bore our children and our grandchildren with the story of this as we sit holding hands by the fire.'

George smiled distantly and his hand rose to touch my cheek.

'Oh dear God, how I love...' But those fingers never found me. His arm fell and he shivered; his breath fled. Those beautiful eyes faded and the man I loved above all others, above my very self, gave up his soul and became a body.

97

The Cold Earth

I SENT A message to Lucinda. Did she want me to stay away? After all I had almost got her brother killed once, and succeeded the second time, but she replied that I must come.

There was much pomp – a Metropolitan Police guard of honour and a brass band. I think George would have been quietly amused by all the fuss.

The vicar had known the deceased man well, for George had been a regular churchgoer. He was clearly distressed and gave a lovely eulogy. George would have been embarrassed by that.

I sat at the back with Sidney Grice but we were ushered to the front. His eye, normally so alert and taking in every detail, was fixed on that oak coffin in front of the altar.

The last time I had stood by a grave I had begged George to marry me. It was an awful time but I would have given anything to be able to live it again, to have him take off his glove and touch my cheek and tell me that he did not know.

The mourners scattered until there were three of us. My guardian took the vicar away and then there was just Lucinda and me. She came round that terrible hole in the earth and put out her hand.

'I believe you loved George.' Her voice was clear and steady. 'And I know that he loved you. If I hate you he will have died for nothing. I know we will never be friends, but I hope we have learned to forgive each other.'

I took the hand she proffered and held on to it, but I could not speak.

And when I was alone, I took the wilted carnation and let it fall on to his name, cut in brass. 'No shrine,' I vowed, 'my darling.'

My guardian came back for me. He took off his glove and wrapped his long slender fingers around mine, and we watched the first clod crush my flower. 'It is too hard.' My voice flew, thin and unanswered, through the yew trees to the steeple pointing ever upwards, I had been told, to heaven.

And Sidney Grice turned his face away for fear that I would see something.

98

The Heart of Sidney Grice

W E DID NOT speak over dinner. We hardly spoke at all now except in monosyllables. Sidney Grice made no attempt to converse but browsed lackadaisically through some scientific tome.

I chewed and swallowed automatically, hardly noticing what was on my plate and not even bothering with a book.

Molly cleared, having failed to lure Spirit with a dripping frond of cabbage for a ride in the dumb waiter. And we adjourned downstairs.

'I cannot work at this again,' I said.

'As you wish.' He selected some reading matter from the pile beside his chair.

'Tell me about that locket,' I said, unintentionally loudly, and Mr G closed his journal.

'It was before your parents had even met.' He squeezed his right eyelids together.

I reached for the pot and caught my cup with my sleeve, knocking it on to the hearth. 'Uncle Tolly told me that my mother had an understanding with an Oxford undergraduate,' I prompted, and he shrank back in his chair. 'But you studied at Cambridge.'

'I went to Oxford first, but there were too many memories and I detested the architecture.' He took on a hunted expression. 'Spires should point and nothing more. They have no business to be dreaming.'

'Memories of what?' I pressed, and Sidney Grice's right eyelids crept apart again.

'You must promise that you will not tell a soul, nor make a written record of what I am about to tell you, for at least sixty years.' He rested his hands on his knees.

'You have my word,' I promised, and, though I knew he had no high opinion of that, he took it.

Sidney Grice interlocked his fingers in his lap. 'Your mother and I were in love,' he admitted at last. 'I was not in a position to marry her, but I had asked her father's permission to make my intentions clear and he readily agreed. It was hinted that I should take over the running of his clog-making factory, for I had a particular and violent aversion to bootlaces at the time. I took your mother boating on the Cherwell, having meticulously planned a picnic in our third favourite meadow.'

'Why not one of the other two?'

'The second had been given over to a particularly cantanker-ous Hereford bull,' he explained impatiently. 'And the first was, of course, in Bavaria – a little far by punt, as even you might imagine.'

Sidney Grice fell silent. Did he believe his tale to be complete?

'What happened?'

He lowered his head. 'We had rounded a bend and the meadow was in sight. The champagne was chilling over the side.'

I did not want to interrupt his account by pointing out that he abhorred alcohol, but he broke off into another reverie.

'And?'

'A pack of jackdaws swooped down, doubtless attracted to the parti-coloured buttons on my red and blue striped waist-coat.' He ran both hands through his hair to the back of his neck. 'They alarmed me, March.'

'Were you already frightened of birds by that time?' I asked gently.

'Since I was seven years and one day old,' he concurred. 'I stepped back and the boat rocked. Your mother jumped up to save me and the punt capsized.' His hands worked round to take him in a stranglehold. 'I could not swim for I was always too embarrassed...'

He could not quite bring himself to say that it was because of his short right leg.

'And my mother was tipped in too?'

He exhaled. 'I was thrown into the branches of a *Salix Babylonica* – a weeping willow with an effulgent crop of golden catkins – but your mother fell into the water and she could not swim either. I looked about me for a pole or some flotation device, but the boat had drifted away and your mother was being dragged under by the weight of water on her lovely dress.' His thumbs rotated round each other. 'I readied myself to go in after her.'

'Even though...'

'Even though,' he agreed. 'But, as I was disentangling myself, another man jumped in. Connie – your mother – had gone under, only her beautiful golden hair on the surface to mark where she was. Then even that became submerged. I dived in and her hand broke through the surface. Somehow I managed to clutch it and sank with her. At least we would die together, I thought, but then I was aware of the other man grabbing my coat and being hauled up, and both of us being towed to the bank and dragged out on to it.'

'*Foolish pup*,' our saviour upbraided me. '*You might have drowned the most beautiful girl on whom I have ever clapped eyes*. I lay prone, coughing up river water, and saw a tall, sturdily constructed man with military moustaches.'

'My father,' I guessed.

Mr G's thumbs revolved furiously. 'He scooped Connie up as easily as you might lift Spirit. *Follow me*, he said, and carried her off across our once third favourite meadow to a hostelry, but I slunk away. It was three miles to where I was living, but I could not face walking through the streets of Oxford. I marched for the rest of the day and all night, until a van of chickens stopped and took me to London. I never returned to Oxford. I did not even get my very special things sent on.' His thumbs were stilled. 'One month later I got a letter from your mother, expressing her disgust that I had not even troubled to go with them to the inn to be sure that she was safe and comfortable – I could not tell her that I was too ashamed – and with the news that she was to marry our rescuer.'

He closed his left eye and forced the right to follow suit, his fingers jabbing, plucking at the glass eye whose original was buried in Charlottenburg Cemetery.

'And yet you became my godfather,' I observed.

Sidney Grice covered his face. 'It was your father's idea. I suspect he felt guilty, not having realized my situation when he proposed to your mother, and I imagine that she had come to appreciate how humiliating the episode had been for me and wished to make amends. But of course…' He blew noisily into his hands. 'Your mother did not live to see you christened. Your father and I became allies, united in part by our joint loss.' He clutched his cheeks and leaned his head back. 'She was the most staggeringly beautiful person I shall ever meet.' His voice slowed. 'And I do not mean just her appearance.'

'Is that why you went missing in the sixties?'

'I was never missing.'

'Nobody knew where you were.'

'I did.'

And that was it. I picked up my cup unbroken and meditated. Perhaps it was true: we are none of us who we pretend to be. 'Why did your revolver not fire?' I held the cup handle back, but it would never glue. 'I saw him slip the safety catch.'

Sidney Grice rubbed his left eye, which was still inflamed, though the sight was restored. 'It has three safety devices, or I should not have surrendered it so readily.' My guardian slipped his third finger through the jackal ring on his watch chain.

'He was a good man,' he said hesitantly, and I did not need to ask who he meant. 'That was a fine piece of detective work, deducing that the maids had not answered the door.' I waited for my guardian to add that he could have done so himself, but he continued, 'And it was quick thinking on his part to pretend to know that my cane was a Morse key.' This was the first time he had mentioned George since the funeral. My guardian worked his lips against each other. His head was still back. 'I know that I vexed you about not getting married but I would not have stood in your way.'

I gazed at him in wonder, this mean-hearted, big-hearted man. 'Look at me,' I said at last, and his eye opened reluctantly, seemingly surprised to find me still there. And, when I had his full attention, I said shakily, 'I love you.'

My guardian chewed his upper lip and then his lower. 'And, since the moment we met, I have always loved,' he told me hesitantly, 'a good cup of tea.'

And Sidney Grice did not attempt to duck as my cushion hurtled towards him.

99

The Outcast

I MET FREDDY at the Empress Cafe. It was the first time I had been out in weeks and I felt anxious to be amongst people. The decor was unchanged with its green floral tiles and paintings of Paris, but Freddy and I had not been the only ones to fall out with the manager and he had been replaced by a smart and welcoming middle-aged lady, who had brought smiles to the faces of her staff and customers alike.

'I went to the convent,' Freddy told me. 'To find out what had happened to Lucy's son.' She pulled back her veil but the waitress was used to her by now. 'They have called him Ishmael.'

'*The outcast*,' I remembered grimly from my Bible.

'I shall change it to Samuel.' Freddy poured our coffees from a tall silver pot, 'Meaning *God has heard* my prayers for a child.'

'You are going to look after him?'

'Mr Grice is coming with me to collect him tomorrow.' Freddy opened her cigarette case and tutted. It was empty.

'How did he get involved?' I took out two Turkish and handed her one.

My guardian had had my case and flask repaired expertly, though not quite invisibly.

'It was he who suggested it,' Freddy leaned over the flame of my Lucifer. 'He came to see if I was all right after... everything.' She sucked in the smoke and her face lit up, and the pretty girl in her came to the surface. 'Samuel is such a lovely boy, March.'

She smiled. 'So affectionate and full of life, and the image of his mother. They had him slaving in the kitchen but they could not beat him down. I hope you will visit us.'

'I would love to.' I burned my fingers and hastily shook out the match. 'Have you seen much of Mr Grice?'

'Quite a lot.' I could have sworn Freddy flushed. 'He takes me for lunch sometimes to his club.'

'The Diogenes?' I said incredulously. 'Where one cannot speak? That must be fun.'

'Oh no.' Freddy blew out with studied casualness. 'A lovely place in St James's Street. Quite cosy.' There was no doubt about her blushing now. 'Can I tell you something, March?'

'Please do.' I tried to hide my envy, for he had never taken me to dine anywhere.

Freddy spooned in a sugar and slid the bowl to me. 'When we got back from St Philomena's last night.' Her eyes flicked to mine and then away. 'He asked if he might kiss me.' She fiddled with her veil, though it was perfectly straight. 'I asked if you had put him up to it.'

'I did not even know he was meeting you.'

'That is what he told me.' Freddy smiled coyly. 'And, when I said he might, I thought it would be a peck on the cheek.' She inhaled from her cigarette. 'But it was not.'

'Perhaps it was mistimed,' I suggested, for I knew that my guardian was not a lady's man.

'I do not think so.' Freddy laughed lightly. 'For it was quite a long kiss.'

*

'Freddy told me that you kissed her,' I said, as casually as I could, over another boiled-to-death dinner.

Sidney Grice turned the page of his *Art and Science of Mummification* book. 'Her truthfulness is something you would do well to emulate.' He closed his book. 'And if I am also to follow her example, I am obliged to confess that I rather enjoyed it.'

'I think Freddy did too,' I told him faintly.

'In that case, I cannot help but wonder,' Sidney Grice reopened his reading matter by slicing a clean butter knife into it, 'if she might let me do it again.'

A worthier woman might have felt some happiness and I certainly wished it for them both, but I was like a sleepwalker then, making the right movements and saying the right words, drifting through my existence and hoping never to awake.

100

The Handysome Prince and the Client

I SAT ON THE roof watching the nameless people bustle by
– the children playing leapfrog or begging or scavenging the
gutters; the mothers laden with babies in sackcloth slings;
two old men, arms round each other's shoulders for support, in
a hobbling parody of a three-legged race; lumbering goods
vehicles and speeding private carriages, laden omnibuses and
the hansoms ever swooping like crows towards an outstretched
arm. So much life tumbling blindly to where?

I had found the ivory box with my three cubes of opium
placed on my dressing table the night before the funeral but I did
not use them. Some pains are too sacred to numb. The gin flask
lay untouched by my feet, surrounded by stubbed-out cigarettes.
My case was empty. It was time to go down.

'Oh, thank heathens.' Molly bawled so unexpectedly that I
nearly lost my footing on the fire escape. 'I thought I might have
to descend that ladderer to come and get you.'

'Did you want something?'

Molly sucked her thumb. 'Well—'

'Have you come to tell me something?' I added before she
gave me a list of her heart's desires, including a handysome
prince and a glittersome sash.

Molly extracted her thumb and wiped it on her apron. 'Mr
Grice requests your present in the study,' she recited, adding in
a conspiratorial whisper which was louder than her normal

voice, which was more than loud enough already, 'He has a customer.'

'Client,' I corrected, for her employer hates her calling them that.

'Cly ain't what?' She reinserted her thumb. 'And anyway that aintn't not her name.'

'Why?' I sighed. 'Does he not think that I have done enough harm already?"

Molly sucked thoughtfully. 'I dontn't not think he does,' she decided. 'Because he said you'd say *no* but to tell you to say *yes*. And please stop crying, miss, I dontn't not like to see you looking so...' she struggled for the bon mot, 'ugly.'

'Tell Mr Grice I shall be down in five minutes,' I decided.

'Why cantn't I not tell him now?' Molly was enjoying her thumb enormously. 'Before I forget.'

I tried again. 'Tell him now that I shall be down in five minutes.'

'That dontn't not make sense,' she decided. 'I shall go and see if he understands.' And she trudged down the stairs, telling herself, 'No wondrous he's always muttoning on about lumpy wrenches.'

I went to the bathroom and washed my face and hands, then back in my room pinned my hair whilst sucking on two parma violets at once. The least I could do would be to explain in person that I was not going to see any more clients. The very thought of dealing with another death tore at my shredded heart.

Sidney Grice was pacing restlessly when I went down. A young woman sat in my armchair and half rose when I came in, but I ushered her down.

'Mrs Peters, this is Miss Middleton,' my guardian introduced us. He turned to me. 'I should like very much to take on her case. It is intriguing and – better yet – she is extremely wealthy. But I must go to Madrid, of all places.'

'Another sighting?' I hardly dared ask, for he had made six wasted journeys throughout Great Britain so far.

'A man with a scarred nose,' my guardian confirmed, and squeezed my hand before he addressed his visitor again. 'I am obliged to leave in—' He flipped open his hunter and checked it against the mantle clock, poking his head into the hall to double-check against the grandmother clock. 'Ten and nineteen minutes.'

He declaimed that last number with great relish and propelled me towards his client.

'I am so sorry,' I began and held out my hand.

The visitor grasped it, as if to save herself falling down a cliff, and rose. She was a tiny lady and quite plain with mousy hair, and I liked her instantly for that.

'Oh, Miss Middleton,' she wept, and I saw that she must have been crying as much as I had. 'Please make him change his mind. It is my little girl. She has gone missing and the police can find no trace of her. I have been to twelve private detectives, including that charlatan Cochran.' I saw my godfather beam approvingly at this description of his rival. 'I have thirty men combing London,' Mrs Peters continued, 'and put up posters for a thousand pounds reward. And now I am besieged by blackmailers and idiots, but there has been no trace of her.'

'I am truly sorry,' Sidney Grice stole the words from my mouth. 'But I have given my word and lives may depend upon it.' He put his watch away and slipped his third finger through the jackal ring hanging on the chain. 'But Miss Middleton will be able to help you.'

'Miss Middleton,' Mrs Peters looked at me uncertainly and I shook my head.

'I—'

'But of course,' Sidney Grice assured her breezily. 'After all, she is London's premier female personal detective.'

I pulled up a wooden chair and sat beside but facing the lady, and took her hands in mine. 'What is your daughter's name?' I asked.

'I have much to do,' Sidney Grice said and left the room, but not before he had tugged the bell cord twice for fresh tea.

Epilogue

———◦━◦◦◦✦◦◦◦━◦———

I WENT EARLY TO the grave for I had no wish to see anyone or to be seen. The headstone had been erected, simple white marble with the words in black – a rank, a name and two dates – and the space for two more entries.

I had always believed what I read in Deuteronomy, *Vengeance is mine, saith the Lord*. But I wrested that right from God's fingers when I swore my oath. If it took my life, if I lost my soul, George Pound would be avenged.

It was four years, however, 1888, before I was to come across 'Jack' again.

The sun was only just showing over the rooftops as I came away, and it would be a bright crisp winter morning. But that light would never penetrate to the death and depravity buried beneath those burned ruins on Abbey Road. There would forever be a dark dawn over Steep House.

*

I was young again last night. I climbed up to look at the stars and saw George on the roof of the Anatomy Building across the street, so strong and handsome and kind. He held out his arms to me and I started to run but, of course, I fell and, as I hit the ground, I awoke with a jolt, knowing that I was dead. And I would have given anything for it to be true.

There are so many things that I should say, but I am sorry; it hurts too much. I cannot write any more.

M.M.
On George Pound's birthday, 1944